NEW YORK TIMES BESTSELLING AUTHOR

KAREN CHANCE

FORTUNE'S
BLADE

A DORINA BASARAB NOVEL

Copyright © 2024
Karen Chance
Fortune's Blade
All rights reserved.

No part of this publication may be reproduced, distributed, or transmitted in any form or by any means, including photocopying, recording, or other electronic or mechanical methods, without the prior written permission of the publisher, except in the case of brief quotations embodied in critical reviews and certain other non-commercial uses permitted by copyright law.

Karen Chance

Printed in the United States of America
First Printing 2024
First Edition 2024

10 9 8 7 6 5 4 3 2 1

FORTUNE'S
BLADE

A DORINA BASARAB NOVEL

Chapter One
Dory

"Dory," someone was shaking me lightly. "Dory, wake up. We're nearly there!"

I sat up, groggy and disoriented, and wondered why everything hurt. And then the cart I was traveling in jounced over a rock, causing my butt to slam down hard onto the bench-type seat. Oh, yeah.

Now I remembered.

It was a testament to how exhausted I was that I could sleep like this at all. But camping in another world, which was what I'd been doing for three weeks, was nerve racking. I'd tried to rest whenever we stopped at night, but jumping at every sound made that difficult, particularly when I didn't know what most of those sounds were.

Like that one, I thought, as something between a rusty trumpet and a bullhorn went off, seemingly right in my ear. I jerked and stared around, but saw only the same vista that had met my eyes for the last two days: jagged mountains topped with snow, scraggly trees twisted into wild shapes by the wind, and expansive, pale blue skies. And a castle of golden stone erupting from a snowcapped peak in the distance, high enough to part the clouds.

Okay, that was new.

I found myself staring at it as we jounced along, trying to make it seem real to my groggy brain, which stubbornly insisted that it was an illusion. It was too tall, too precarious, and too close to the summit of the mountain, which could have been touched from some of the higher tower rooms. It couldn't be real.

There wasn't even any way up there. No bridge from this mountain, the only one with a road, no trail winding upward, which would have had to be cut at a ridiculous angle anyway. No gates to welcome friends or ramparts to keep out foes.

Just a golden castle perched improbably high and looking like it might fall off at any moment.

It *wasn't* real.

Only it was, and I didn't know how to deal with that.

And then a shadow fell over us, like a low-lying cloud. It made me look around in confusion some more, wondering what was wrong. And, like somebody being stalked in a slasher movie, to slowly look up.

Where my eyes encountered an acre's worth of gleaming scales—almost literally, as they were inches above my nose.

I froze.

The creature that the mass of scaley hide belonged to slid by in a sinuous ripple, despite the fact that nothing that big should even be able to get off the ground. It was a brilliant, fire engine red, with the polish on the interlocking plates that covered it so perfect that a manicurist would have wept. They served as a mirror, allowing me to see myself as a tiny, insignificant thing gazing up in awe as the massive belly slowly pulled ahead of us.

As intimidation moves went, it was God-tier. And it was meant to be, since I hadn't even heard the thing until it was right on top of us. Of course, I'd been in an exhausted sleep, drooling onto my husband's shoulder, but neither of my companions had heard it, either.

And since they were a half dragon and a master vampire, that was . . . impressive.

It could have sent us tumbling down the mountainside before we knew what was happening, since we'd almost managed to do that for ourselves a couple of dozen times now. The goat trail we'd been traversing was rocky and overgrown and the width of *goats*. We'd had dirt and rocks frequently cascade into our ride from hugging the cliff too tightly, along with waterfalls spitting at us and animals pausing to peer curiously out of their burrows at us as if wondering what we were doing up here.

I was starting to wonder that myself.

I also was wondering which kind of dragon this was, as these mountains were home to two very different varieties. The way it had been explained to me was that it was similar to the Were situation on Earth. Some wolves were merely wolves, just animals and nothing more. And some were Weres, shapeshifters of the human type who could change in an instant.

Dragons had the same situation, with the animal type carnivorous, wildly destructive, and casually vicious, and the human-type all of that plus intelligent, calculating, and cruel. I wondered which this one was, and if it mattered. Because the animal-type might well decide to eat us, but the human-type might do worse.

Make that probably would do worse, I thought, noticing the set of my roommate's shoulders in the seat in front of me.

Claire was actually my ex-roommate, since I'd recently gotten married and moved out. But I'd lived with her long enough to know that she didn't scare easily. In fact, she rarely scared at all, facing down things that would make me blanch, and I'd been hunting monsters for five hundred years.

Yet here we were, with her looking as brittle as I'd ever seen her, with her narrow shoulders clenched and her abundant mop of red curls vibrating with some kind of emotion I couldn't read. But it wasn't happy, so neither was I.

I didn't want to be dragon food.

Louis-Cesare, the aforementioned husband, obviously didn't either, as he had his hand on his rapier. That was usually pretty intimidating, considering what he could do with it. As a four-hundred-year-old master vamp, he'd had plenty of time to practice.

Yet I didn't think it was going to help us much right now.

But that might, I thought, when Claire suddenly had enough and erupted from her skin, changing in the blink of an eye into a pewter colored dragon with twisted crystal horns and a riotous lavender mane down her back.

She'd changed while leaping off of our small wagon, leaving us rocking precariously in her wake, and immediately plowed into the giant red creature who'd been buzzing us.

They went boiling off into the sky, wings flapping, throats screeching and giant maws agape, and I stood up reflexively, as if I was going to do something. And then just stayed there, feeling like a fool and completely outclassed. And unsure who to be more terrified for—her or us.

"She'll be all right," Louis-Cesare said, and strangely, he sounded sure.

I looked over at my hubby, to see the wind blowing strands of his auburn hair around as he watched the battling duo. "How do you know?"

The blue eyes narrowed on the latest impossible scene. "Look closer. There is no blood spurting, and both sets of claws are sheathed."

I squinted, but the sun was behind the battling duo. "They're *playing*?"

"Perhaps. Or perhaps it is some strange, ritualistic greeting." He looked as frustrated as I felt. "I am out of my depth here."

I sat back down. That made two of us. And while the sight on the horizon would be one that I'd carry for years, just from the sheer breathtaking awe of it, right now I had other concerns. Namely my sister Dorina, who had been missing for weeks.

That was why we were here, trying to get her back. But so far, we'd only gotten maybe fifty miles from the portal where we'd come in and half of that uphill. And the rest through a less than forgiving countryside where the trees got grabby and the fey got nasty and even a spring of water where we'd stopped to fill our canteens had had it out for us.

The water hadn't been poisonous, but it had made the posse we'd assembled, most of whom were master level vampires, drunk off their asses. Probably courtesy of the herbs that grew by the water source and seemed to have leeched something into it, but the delay had cost us days. As a result, we were almost two weeks into this supposed rescue attempt and no closer to finding Dorina than when we'd started.

Only for Claire to finally locate a few of her scaley relatives and be informed that the posse wasn't wanted. We could proceed alone, we were told, just her, Louis-Cesare and I, on foot or as good as considering the state of our nag. Or we could stay the hell out of their territory. Or stay for dinner as the main course, only that part hadn't been vocalized. But by the way one of them had been looking at Louis-Cesare, as if he'd make a fine Sunday roast, it might as well have been. The rapier had hardly left my husband's hand for two days, and I didn't blame him one bit.

But the fact that we were being let into their territory at all was apparently a minor miracle, and nobody ever gets anywhere arguing with a dragon. So, we'd parked the posse at a village, bought the cart and nag to carry supplies, and headed uphill. I assumed the delay was to give the dragons time to decide what to do with us, but it had heaped bruises onto my bruises, since finding a comfortable spot on the damned bench seat had proven impossible.

And now what was Claire doing?

I couldn't tell, other than getting entirely too far away. Damn it, we'd talked about this! If I ended up as something's lunch, I was never going to—

Our horse stopped.

It frequently did, being geriatric, overweight, and more interested in nibbling the weeds along the roadside than actually getting us anywhere. But this time, it had cause. This time, there was an absolutely massive dragon sitting in the middle of the road, picking its teeth with a sword-sized claw and regarding us narrowly.

Only, no, it was not sitting in the road, as that would have implied that it could fit. It was actually clinging to the side of the mountain, with great claws gouging huge fissures into the already crumbly stone, and part of one massive thigh and tail blocking the path. Whether that was deliberate or not, I had no idea.

I had never felt so out of place in all my life.

After hundreds of years fighting pretty much everything there is to fight, you get cocky. You may not realize it, but you do. Not to the degree of being careless or failing to keep the weapons' stash up to date, but in an I-can-handle-anything-because-I've-seen-it-all kind of way.

I had not seen this.

I could not handle this.

And based on how still Louis-Cesare had suddenly gone, neither could he.

Claire, this would be a damned good time to get your purple ass back here, I thought fervently.

In the meantime, I grabbed my backpack off the floorboard and started rooting around in my supposedly well-stocked arsenal for something that might help. And rooted and rooted, while the dragon patiently waited and waited. It didn't look like it thought it had much to worry about.

Frankly, that was a compelling argument.

I knew a lot of war mages, some of whom made weapons for sale to desperate types like me on the side, but dragon fighting wasn't on their list of offerings. And even the fearsome Vampire Senate, whose stocks I had been known to raid since becoming a senator, fell short. Magical snare? Sure; that'd hold him for about a second. Potion bomb? Uh huh. Like it was getting through that damned hide. Personal shield? Probably just make me extra crunchy—

"Excuse me," someone said.

"Hang on a sec," I replied, and pulled out a nifty little portable portal, only where was I going to send him? New York? Assuming the damned thing even worked in Faerie, which I'd been told was highly . . . problematic . . .

I paused, belatedly realizing who had spoken, and slowly lifted my eyes.

"You are Claire's friends?" the dragon asked politely.

Only it didn't sound polite, but not because he was being rude. But because dragon-kind were just extra about everything, and that included their transformed voices. Werewolves on Earth got hoarse and somewhat guttural when they deigned to speak to you in wolf form, but dragon voices made all my skin want to shudder off my bones and lie there in a little heap at my feet, quivering.

In fact, I wasn't sure that it wasn't doing that, right now.

Louis-Cesare was doing a little better. That auburn mane of his was more red than brown in the dazzling sunlight, and he had the temper to match. Not to mention that master vamps weren't used to being intimidated. He didn't like it, but he also wasn't stupid despite the male model good looks, and knew he'd have to take it.

But he was damned if he was going to sit there with a lump in his throat.

"Yes," he said, his voice a little high. "My wife was Claire's roommate until recently. We have been guaranteed safe passage—"

"There are few things guaranteed in Faerie these days," the dragon said, which managed to make my sore ass clench a bit more.

Any further and my sphincter was going to swallow my body like a human ouroboros, and I'd pop out of existence all together. Which didn't sound so bad right now. Really didn't, I thought, as a neck longer than that of three giraffes suddenly shot out so that the massive head could get in my face.

And breathe on me.

Louis-Cesare looked like his butt was doing some clenching, too, but he stayed seated. And managed to keep his hand off his rapier. All of a millimeter off, but still.

Had to give him credit, I thought, staring up into an eyeball bigger than my head.

This dragon was solid gold, like a great statue carved out of the purest ore. But the eyes were completely black, without even any white around the rims. Or maybe that was me.

My vision was starting to get hazy at the edges, so who the hell knew?

And then, out of nowhere, I laughed. And laughed and laughed and laughed some more, as if I'd never stop. It was probably hysterical, but there was also a note of genuine humor in it, because this wasn't real. It couldn't be. This kind of thing *didn't happen*.

And when it did, it was damned funny.

I guessed the dragon agreed, since after a moment, it huffed out what might have been a laugh, too.

The force of it blew my hair all over the place because I usually kept it short but hadn't had time to get a trim before we left. But I laughed anyway, and then we both laughed together, and then the beast draped the tip of a wing around my shoulders, which had a thick looking barb at the end like a pterodactyl's. If a pterodactyl's wings were tipped with six-inch shivs, that is.

"Claire said you were fearless. Seems she was right," the creature announced. "I'm her father, and your host for the next little while. Rathen-Den of House Eddred. Rathen in this form, Den in the other, you see?"

"*Enchanté*," Louis-Cesare said, because he has flawless manners. "I am Louis-Cesare de Bourbon, and this is my wife, the Lady Dorina Basarab."

"Dory," I managed to gasp out, and the great head bowed slightly.

"Yes, I understand that it's necessary to make a distinction these days," he said, which would have been cryptic, only I guessed he'd talked to Claire about my 'sister' and other half at some point. "Get on."

"Get . . . on?" I repeated, confused.

"Yes, and hurry up. We'll be late for dinner as it is."

Louis-Cesare and I exchanged a look, which thankfully, our host misinterpreted. "Someone will be back for your, er, horse," he said charitably. And then hunkered down as much as that enormous body could, crouching like a cat and looking at us expectantly.

I looked back, trying to come up with words that weren't "Oh, hell, no," but conveyed the same message. And then Louis-Cesare stood up and started searching around for a hand hold. Because of course he did.

"What are you doing?" I asked, my voice calm.

"I don't know whether you noticed," he said, while surveying the unbroken, armored surface in front of us. "But there is no bridge to the castle. No road or path other than the one we're on, which ends just ahead. No way up except by flight."

"We don't get many visitors," Lord Rathen agreed.

"And this is a once in a lifetime opportunity," Louis-Cesare added, and actually looked somewhat enthusiastic about the whole thing.

I just sat there.

It was a terrible truth that my father had approved our marriage partly because he thought I would be a steadying influence on my new hubby. A *dhampir*, the often insane cross between a vamp and a human, was going to be the rational one. And the problem was, he'd been mostly right.

But I didn't know what else to do, and insulting your host isn't a great plan when he could crush you like a gnat and probably never even notice.

I got on. It wasn't easy, even with the cart giving me a lift and Louis-Cesare, who had given up trying to climb the great hide and used vampire strength to just leap up there, pulling from on top. I'm not normally clumsy, but my body really wasn't helping me.

My body was smarter than I was.

And things did not get better when I finally topped Mount Scaley, and discovered that the back in question was warm and alive, but also huge and broad and slick, with no hand holds except for a great mane of black hair.

We grabbed hold of that because the alternative was plummeting to our deaths, hoping it was allowed. And I guessed so, since the huge body got up and went loping up the mountainside like it was no big thing, with the massive talons further shredding the narrow road but easily clinging to the rocky slope. Until it abruptly cast itself off of the cliffside, heading straight for the valley floor, where it swerved just before hitting down and skimmed along the tops of the trees, the knife-edged scales sending some severed leaves flying into our faces as we rode what looked like a green wave.

And then we started back up again.

"*This doesn't happen!*" I screamed for no reason that I could name, while the great wings strained up a hurricane, and the wind clawed at us like we were barebacking a 747, and the sun shone in our faces so brightly that I could barely see.

"It does today," Louis-Cesare said, laughter and disbelief and terror all mingled in his voice, as they were in mine. And then he said it, the absolute bastard, as I should have known he would. "Can we go any faster?"

And we did.

Chapter Two

The castle was even more impressive from the inside, with towering ceilings, huge windows, and walls comprised of massive slabs of honey colored stone. At least, our room was. And it was all I saw because we were dropped off onto our balcony, which was as big as a house and, judging by the claw marks in the floor, regularly used as a landing pad.

But only after we'd taken the scenic route first.

Despite his worries about dinner, our host had had no problem buzzing panicked flocks of sheep, soaring with oversized eagles, and looping wildly around the frozen peaks of nearby mountains, all while adhering to Louis-Cesare's request for speed.

I was cold and wet, because we'd skimmed over a half-frozen river that cut through a towering ice cave. One of the great wings had dipped into the water and thrown up a glittering wave as we exited back into the sunlight, which had cascaded with rainbows and sparkled like diamonds. And soaked me with freezing water until my teeth chattered.

I was quickly tiring, because the mane, while huge and warm and securely attached, had been no substitute for a seat belt. My thighs might never recover, despite the fact that there had been nothing for them to clench around, the back being far too broad. But they'd tried anyway, and now my legs felt like rubber.

But most of all, I was starting to seriously wonder what had possessed me to come here in the first place. Apparently, I'd been playing on easy mode my whole life and hadn't realized it, with my so-called skills, both natural and hard-won, useless here. It had been all I could do to hold on while I was given a gracious ride to the summit!

After staggering inside to the oversized bed and face planting, I still felt like I was flying. Or maybe floating, as I could swear that my body didn't touch the sheets. It was vaguely like being high, with the tingly feeling of blood racing through wide-open veins, as if it was spooked, too.

I used to wonder what people got out of roller coasters.

I thought I understood now.

After a while, I opened my eyes to discover that Louis-Cesare hadn't joined me. He was still on the balcony, leaning over the squat, bulbous columns of the railing and staring downward. Which, yeah, probably had a great view, but how he could bear to do that now was a mystery.

I felt like I never wanted to leave solid Earth again. Or solid Faerie. Or whatever.

I had a bona fide new fear of heights and it had been *earned*.

But my partner clearly didn't feel the same.

"Do we dress for dinner?" I rasped but didn't get a response. Probably because several more impossible things had just flown by, and they seemed to be as interested in us as Louis-Cesare was in them. At least, I assumed that was why a leathery wing brushed the balcony railings as it passed.

It made a *fwip, fwip, fwip* sound, like someone holding a leafy branch against the spokes of a bicycle. Only it was more like FWIP, FWIP, FWIP, because the creature was huge, and the railing was some type of light-colored granite. And yet was still showing signs of wear.

But Louis-Cesare never budged. He was clearly enthralled, and I left him to it. I needed to sort out something to wear for dinner before I embarrassed Claire and the choices were limited.

Although not nearly as much as they once would have been.

I tossed my duffle bag onto the bed, opened the zip and poked my head into another world.

Technically it wasn't a world so much as a closet filled with weapons. But it was kind of appropriate at present, since it was the fey who had taught us how to fold portals back onto themselves, forming a somewhat stable room in metaphysical space. One that you could access from anywhere, simply by carrying around the entrance.

My duffle was the entrance, and was just big enough for me to squeeze through and then to take a short flight of stairs into the portable arsenal I'd designed for myself.

It wasn't much to look at, just a concrete block room with some shelving and some recently installed fluorescents overhead. The fey often had multi-room, semi-palaces in theirs that they could carry around on their backs. Or that their servants could, ready to pitch far more than a tent for their masters at the end of a long day's ride.

But I assumed that those took a lot more power than my little baby, and sleeping rough wasn't something that bothered me. Being in a fight without weapons bothered me, or enough ammo, or first aid gear. So, there were no chaise lounges or four posters in here.

Instead, it was the armory of my dreams, one that I'd have never even imagined was possible in the bad old days.

For most of my five hundred and something years, my biggest problem supporting myself as a mercenary had been coming up with the money needed for the tools of my trade. The mages who did piece work did not do it cheap, which was fair. They were selling their magic, a product of their own bodies, and the fact that they made more of it than they needed wasn't the point.

They knew their worth, and it was high.

But now I was a senator, a member of the feared Vampire Senate itself. And the fact that my senator father had arranged that mostly to give his faction an extra vote didn't matter. I still had the same privileges as everyone else, and that included access to the Senate's armory.

And, boy, had I exploited the hell out of that access!

I looked around in pride at my room full of goodies, and felt their low-grade hum fill me with a sense of genuine peace and serenity. There was nothing like knowing you had the firepower to take out a convoy, and then to blast the hell out of the army that followed it. Hmmm.

I basked for a moment.

Of course, how much any of this was going to help in Faerie was debatable, and took the edge off of my buzz a little. This place felt like being in a video game where, whenever you levelled up, the bad guys did, too. I'd gotten myself one hell of a new advantage, just in time to go into a world where nobody cared.

It was infuriating, but I had come loaded for bear anyway. Including purloining some of the Senate's new, next level stuff that wasn't even on the market yet. And might never be, since they were trying to keep parity with the Silver Circle, the magical organization of which the War Mage Corps was only a part.

The Circle had people constantly working on new magic, so we had to as well. There'd been peace between the two groups for centuries, but the Senate was a strong believer in the old saying: *Si vis pacem, para bellum*—if you want peace, prepare for war. And damn, if they hadn't prepared.

I just hoped that some of this was going to help.

I also hoped that the clothes rack I'd shoved into a corner, behind a couple of grenade launchers, was going to contain something suitable. I unstrapped the weapons, pushed them out of the way, and set about finding us appropriate attire for dining in a castle full of dragons. But like with my arsenal, my wardrobe really wasn't up to the task.

Still, we didn't have all day, so I went with a tux for Louis-Cesare, which would probably work even if nobody knew what it was, since he looked good in anything. And a floor-length, bias cut, amethyst colored evening gown for me. It was a slip type, with spaghetti straps and a plunging neckline, and was mostly unadorned. But I had glittery sandals to match and the straps on the gown, which crisscrossed in back, were set with diamond-like crystals.

I thought it would work.

I carried my best guesses back up the stairs and crawled out of the entrance. And for the first time, took a moment to really look around our room. It was frankly gorgeous.

It was a large semicircle facing the expansive balcony, which completed the circle. It couldn't really compete with the view, but it tried, with brightly colored cushions and gorgeous tapestries and an inset mosaic of tiny glass tiles above the bed, which must have taken someone years to complete. It showed a bucolic scene, with hills and forests and a crashing waterfall, which I had been in no fit state to appreciate before.

There was also a mirror, which . . . yeah. Gonna need more than a decent dress to avoid embarrassing Claire. A lot more.

Thankfully, we hadn't had to walk through the castle itself, saving me from leaving a first impression with my hair looking like a startled cartoon character's, my face wind chapped, and my eyes set on boggle. I combed fingers through my startled locks, which helped not at all, as they just sprang back up again. Then grabbed a comb from a pocket of my duffle and forced them into compliance.

"I found us something to wear," I called out to Louis-Cesare, who was still sightseeing.

There was no answer.

"You want to come get dressed, or what?" I asked.

"I think . . . you might want to come out here," he said, sounding a little strangled.

I went out there, comb still in hand.

And all right, if I hadn't known that we were curiosities before, I did now.

"Where did they all come from?" I asked, surveying a sky studded with dragons, despite the fact that it had been clear when we flew in.

"They're unbelievable, aren't they?" Louis-Cesare said softly.

"They're something," I said, somewhat at a loss for words.

Okay, that was a lie. I actually had a lot of words, all of which I swallowed back down because I didn't know how good their hearing was. I didn't know a lot of things here, which was a problem when facing down creatures who were that powerful. Magical energy peppered my skin like stinging rain, making me have to work not to flinch even through denim and leather, and they weren't even trying.

Guess I should have known, I thought.

It would take a crap ton of magic just to get those butts into the air.

But not all of the flying fortresses were scary. There were a couple of gamboling babies above us, which I assumed were the animal kind, because a woman had them on a leash. She was staring at us from an upper balcony that was set back a bit from ours so as not to block the sun, I guessed.

She reminded me of the dragons who had come to meet us, who in human form gave little clue as to their other nature. Except for their size, with all of them being as tall as the fey, meaning that they topped most supermodels in height, and yet were far sturdier. The fey always struck me as sylph-like and vaguely ephemeral, as if the elements had formed bodies for themselves that they could drop at any moment, dusting away into mist or a fluttering of leaves blown on the wind.

But not dragons. They were undeniably real, solid, and even hefty, with this one looking like a Valkyrie warrior. She had a strong, pretty face, long blonde tresses and a diaphanous gown of ombre silk colored to look like a sunrise, with pale yellow fading into pink and then into the softest of blues. It made my lovely evening dress look boring and one-note.

Better get used to being outclassed in just every freaking area, I thought wryly.

The amazing gown was fluttering in the wind, while her pets zoomed about like overly rambunctious puppies. One of them spied us and tried to come down to investigate, but she pulled it back easily, despite the fact that Fluffy had to weigh at least five hundred pounds. So, Claire's people were strong even in human form.

Something to remember.

But the dragons who really drew the eye were the ones hovering in the vast expanse beyond the balcony, spread out like colorful balloons. If balloons were full of massive teeth and giant claws and enough muscle to rip us apart like tissue paper. But I couldn't deny that they were damned impressive, with colors and textures like nothing in our version of nature. And while I'd thought that the coloring on Claire's dragon form was stunning, pewter and pale lavender were strictly dull things around here, where everyone seemed to be trying to outdo the rest.

It was hard to say who was winning.

I spied another red, like the bastard who had buzzed us, only this one had a belly speckled with dark orange, gold, and yellow, like a scaley sunset. There was a mottled one with skin featuring a dozen shades of blue and a purple belly, with a double barb on the end of his tail. There was one with two mismatched tails, one long and thick and one short and stumpy, but his coloring was so breathtaking that you barely noticed: brilliant green with a bright red belly and what looked like red racing stripes up the sides. There was an ethereal looking all white one, with palest blue on her stomach and the same color along the ribs of her wings.

And those were just the most stunning, with plenty of plainer versions scattered about, if you consider green with purple veining on the wings and gray with brilliant-colored manes to be plain. Still more arrived while we stood there, nosy parkers coming to see the humans like people lining up for a new animal exhibit at the zoo. They weren't approaching, any more than you'd get too close to a grizzly's enclosure, but there were dozens of them.

I was starting to get concerned.

"Let's . . . go inside," I said, because the last thing we needed was an incident. Not that the crowd was threatening . . . exactly . . . but more and more were arriving by the minute, as word spread. And it didn't look like there was much happening 'round the old castle today, because everybody was coming to take a peek.

I saw several perfectly normal-looking men, if overly tall and broad shouldered, dive off of their balconies several stories below and transform in a wink into their alternate forms, to join the growing throng. One looked plain brown from a distance, but his scales sparkled like gold dusted tortoiseshell when he got closer, his formerly loose-fitting clothing now a fancy scarf around the hugely muscled neck.

The other was even more dashing, with a brilliant yellow belly but a jet-black body. There was yellow on his face, too, slashes of it on the side of each eye, like dramatic makeup or war paint. But it was scales instead, small ones in this case, that made an elaborate pattern amid the larger plates on his face and head.

All of the dragons had that feature in some form. Rivers of small scales ran between the larger ones that protected areas that needed to be more flexible, like around the eyes and mouth, and at the joints of the great limbs. The bellies, on the other hand, had the biggest, smoothest scales, while the backs were often ridged in two great lines running down to the enormous spikes that often decorated the tails, and could probably be used like flails in battle.

The way they all fit together was fascinating and beautiful and undeniably real. And unlike the fairytale quality of most other things here, the black and yellow dragon was immediately and violently believable. Immediately because he had come closer than all the rest, and violently because of the scrapes and scratches on the scales of his right shoulder and part of his face.

Some of the protective armor was missing there, showing bumpy, reptilian skin below in the same color. Something had gotten claws into him and then jerked back, something stronger than I could even imagine. Another dragon, or something worse?

I didn't know, but it fascinated me, that these seemingly all-powerful creatures could be hurt. I didn't know why; I'd briefly gotten a knife into Claire once, when I'd thought she was an intruder in her own home. She'd been away for a while and startled me on her return, and startling a dhampir has consequences.

Not that it had hurt her much, although it hadn't done her mood any good. Or mine, once I'd realized that I had a dragon with a sore toe squashed into my hallway. But she'd been little more than a baby at the time, while this one . . .

Definitely wasn't.

He also wasn't female. Even in their altered state, the males were much more heavily muscled and the scaffolding of their wings was noticeably thicker. The black and yellow's huge neck was many times broader than a bull's as it reared over us.

He was so close now that, if I'd dared to lean over the balcony, I could have touched him. He seemed to have the same idea, because an arm thicker than my whole body abruptly reached out, with talons as black as night on the end of the elongated hand, sparkling like black diamonds. I got a really good look, because one of the twelve-inch-long daggers touched a strand of my hair.

And that tore it for Louis-Cesare, who had been tensing more and more at my side. His hand went to his rapier, which he didn't draw, but the creature gave a screech nonetheless, shrill enough to slice through my brain like a cleaver. I staggered back and the dragon wheeled off, still screeching.

And things immediately went south.

I didn't know if the onlookers thought that we'd done something to him, or if he'd simply rendered a verdict that they agreed with. But the tone of the scene abruptly changed. And it wasn't just me who noticed.

"Yes," Louis-Cesare said, taking my arm. "Let's . . . go inside."

Above us, shutters were slamming shut, including the blonde's, who pulled her pets inside and did something that caused a bunch of heavy wooden screens to clatter down from a recessed area above the balcony. I looked up and saw that we had the same sort of set up, only I didn't know how to operate it. And I didn't have time to find out.

Because they were coming, not all of them, but some of them—more than enough. Louis-Cesare drew his weapon, I started to run for my bag, and neither was likely to help. But it didn't have to.

A new group took that moment to burst onto the scene, and I had no idea who or even what they were. They looked like a cross between dragons and humans, but not in the way that Claire did. She had tell-tale signs in human form of her other lineage, like faint lilac in the hollows of her cheeks and over her eyes that had nothing to do with make-up, but for the most part, you couldn't tell.

Not so with these guys.

They were humanoid, although larger by a good two feet and several hundred pounds, but were covered in the bumpy skin that I'd seen under the black and yellow dragon's missing scales. They were subdued in coloring, mostly greens and grays with huge, dark eyes. But the biggest difference was the head.

It was smoother than those of their scaley cousins, without all the intricate crests and ridges. But it was undeniably a dragon head. Which looked exactly as terrifying as you'd expect on a human body.

They also had tails, stumpy little things, and were riding the animal-type dragons with saddles and bridles as if they were horses. They were small in comparison to their scaley cousins, but there were about a hundred of them. And they had long spear-like weapons that seemed to be electrified, judging by the sparks they let off and the shriek that the black and yellow male gave when several targeted him.

It was a shock, not a killing blow, but he wheeled away nonetheless, his cries echoing over the mountains. One of the humanoid dragons paused by our railing, his mount snarling and snorting as it fought against the reins. He was wearing a tabard over his scales, like some sort of uniform, and had on leather gauntlets and boots.

I just stared at him.

"Stay inside," he said, his voice harsh and guttural, but clear enough.

And then we had to jump back as the shutters came rattling down, right in our faces.

I stayed inside, but through gaps in the lattice I watched the guards, which was what I guessed they were, clearing the area. Most of their larger cousins had already fled, but a small group had decided to be belligerent. And for a moment, I didn't know who would win.

Really didn't, I thought, my fingers tightening on gaps in the lattice as one of the guards got knocked off his mount by a viciously swinging tail, and was only saved when another, situated slightly below, managed to snag him out of the air. Several more were chased off by the bright red dragon with the sunset stomach, and another fell along with his mount when its head was bitten off by the red and green version. Blood spurted onto the clear, cold air, bright as rubies against the pale blue sky, and dragons' screeches echoed everywhere.

But the rest of the guards rallied, and circled three of the biggest offenders, shocking the hell out of them with multiple weapons at a time. Causing them to screech and flap and, ultimately, to peel off. The conflict didn't last long, after that.

"Come away," Louis-Cesare said softly.

But I stayed for another moment, to watch half of the remaining guards clear the skies, and the rest start flooding downward, their mounts' wings tucked close to their bodies, their faces impassive.

On the way to retrieve their dead.

"I'm beginning to understand why our host came to get us himself," I said, and then turned and strode inside.

Chapter Three
Dorina

"Let me out! Goddamnit, do you hear me?"

"He is becoming very loud," I said, glancing back at the curly haired man in the cage behind us.

It was quite a sight, as the cage in question was perched on the back of a gigantic land crab like the one that my companion and I were riding. The creatures were used by the local fey for transport, as their home was the same huge forest that we were traveling through, and which they could navigate either on the ground or by scuttling through the treetops. We were on the ground at present, following a trail that was wide and well-known to our companions and was considered safe.

Or as safe as anything here.

"He's an *asshole*," Ray, my partner on this adventure, yelled back over his shoulder. "And an idiot who doesn't realize that he's only making things worse for himself!"

"I've been kidnapped, trussed up like a turkey, and am currently in *prison!*" the man shouted back. "Would you like to tell me how much worse it can get?"

"You're gonna find out," Ray muttered, obviously tired of the constant back and forth.

I did not blame him, as the conversation had been going on for days with no particular point that I could see. The fey were not likely to release a master vampire who they had caught prowling around their lands, particularly the dark fey, who had more than sufficient reason not to trust outsiders. And not when said master, instead of trying to make friends and reassure them, kept trying to escape, forcing them to chase after him.

They had finally dumped him in one of the cages they used for transporting exotic animals, which they occasionally stumbled upon and trapped for the royal court, and were taking him to their queen. They had told Ray that she would decide his fate, which seemed fair. Only he did not seem to think so.

Perhaps because Ray and I were also outsiders, as the captive man continually pointed out, and Ray was another master, and yet we were not trussed up.

"Such is the power of Little Debbies," Ray had said, referencing one of the more popular items he traded with the fey.

He'd been a smuggler for years, although not to the highborn type of fey, which was where most of the trade from Earth went. The great houses who ruled much of Faerie had contacts who supplied them with whatever human items they required. That was technically illegal, but the Vampire Senate was not above such things, and I strongly suspected that the Silver Circle, the leading society of mages, felt the same.

Ray had not thought much of that point of view, as he'd mentioned last night, as we sat around a campfire sharing our evening meal.

"Sure, that's typical," he'd said, waving a roasted bird's leg around. Ray, like all vampires, did not require food for sustenance, but refusing to eat what our hosts had provided would have been rude. I, on the other hand, had torn into the stew, flat bread, and roast fowl as if starving, which I mostly was.

A dhampir metabolism was rarely satisfied, and the novelty of choosing what I wanted to eat was a continual revelation. Indeed, everything was a revelation these days, from the way the moonlight filtered through unfamiliar trees, to the strange rhythm a troll girl was dancing to further down the road, her colorful skirts swirling in the firelight, to the haunting call of a bird I couldn't name somewhere overhead. Faerie was a continual, startling newness around every turn, such as I had never known.

Of course, I had never known a good many things, even back on Earth. My father had long ago separated my and Dory's consciousnesses, to save his daughter from the madness that took the lives of so many dhampirs. In desperation, he had carved off the vampire side of her nature that was threatening to overwhelm her, and locked me away.

Which was where I had mostly stayed for centuries, able to emerge only for short periods when she was unconscious. Until a series of strange circumstances involving a fey queen's revenge, an ancient device, and a kidnapping ended with me being separated from her and taken into Faerie, where spirits are clothed in flesh. Giving me, for the first time in my life, a body of my own.

And how very strange that had been!

Dory had been in charge for most of our lives, to the point that I had never really come to grips with making the most basic of human choices—what to eat, what to wear, who to talk to. I went where she did; I ate and wore and talked as she did. And the rare occasions when I was in control were usually during a fight after she had been knocked out and I had been needed to take over.

And there were few choices to be made then except for who to attack next.

But as we traveled with the Wanderers, as they called themselves, I had learned that all decisions were suddenly mine, and it was a bit dizzying even after several weeks. Like the ale, which they drank in great quantities, and which was flavored in so many different ways. There was the small berry ale, as they called it, which was given to children as it was so low in alcohol, and so highly flavored by the dark purple berries that grew along the roadside, that it was basically juice; the rich, red ale, the color deriving from the sap of a vine that grew everywhere and gave it a buzzing feeling that numbed the tongue; and the regular golden ale, which wasn't flavored with anything, but was so strong that it raised even my eyebrows.

We had a flask of each, so I had to choose between them each time I wanted a drink. It was surprisingly difficult, as I liked them all, and hesitated whenever I went to reach for one. Ray had watched me with firelight gleaming in his eyes, but said nothing, although I knew he'd noticed.

He noticed everything, but although he talked a great deal, he didn't always comment. Yet he was the one who had made sure that we had all three brews, as if he wanted to force the choice on me. I didn't understand why he would do that, but I was grateful.

They were all delicious.

After a moment, I settled on the red, and took a drink. "What is typical?" I asked, as the tingling sensation spread over my tongue. It was quite pronounced, as the vine it came from was also used to make salves for burns, and left me with an urge to giggle.

I did not, but Ray looked as if he knew I wanted to.

But again, he didn't say anything. At least, not about that. He had plenty to say about the great houses, however, and did so at length.

"It's the same everywhere," he scowled, swigging back the strong golden ale. "The little guys have to look out for each other, 'cause the big guys only see us as a commodity. To them, we're the ones to be bought and sold, or our labor is, and do they ever reward faithful service? Oh, hell no. All they do is take, take, take—and make rules meant for you and me that they ignore themselves.

"So, I figured, maybe there'd be some little guys in Faerie wanting to buy from another little guy. Turns out, I was right. Weapons, wards, freaking snack cakes—there's a market for it. Like there's a market in our world for fey wine, which'll get you drunk off your ass even if you're a vamp—or a dhampir," he added, noting the amount I had been drinking.

"This is not fey wine," I pointed out.

"Naw, but they make it with a lot of the same ingredients. Unless you're trying to get drunk? Which, I mean, is none of my business."

I thought about it. "I do not know."

"You don't know if you're trying to get drunk?"

"No." I took another swallow, and let it play over my tongue. The numbing effect grew more pronounced. I swallowed it, and felt the icy sensation carving a path all the way down to my stomach. It was odd, but I thought I liked it.

But I wasn't sure about that, either.

"Well, then maybe you outta lighten up 'til you figure it out," he said, which sounded like good advice. Ray frequently gave good advice, and since we had landed on these foreign shores together, I had learned to listen to him. I put down the skin.

He frowned.

"What is wrong?" I asked. I did not like to see Ray frown.

"Did you want to stop drinking?" he asked, his eyes narrowing.

I hesitated.

"Go on, have another drink," he told me.

I obediently lifted the skin again, which only made him frown harder.

"What is it?" I asked, pausing the motion.

"Put the skin down," he said, sounding annoyed. I did not understand why he would ask me that, when he had just told me to drink, but I did it anyway. Which only seemed to annoy him further. "This is bullshit!" he said, and suddenly got up and strode away from the fire.

I watched him, feeling confused. And was even more so when he abruptly whirled around, came back and got in my face. "This. Is. Bullshit," he repeated, taking my cheeks between his hands. "You get that, right? And it ends tonight."

"What ends?" I asked, finding it hard to talk with my face sandwiched between two rough palms.

Ray was a vampire; he should not have had calluses. But he had not had an easy life before he transitioned. The product of a Dutch sailor—hence his blue eyes—and, as Dory had put it, "the slowest Indonesian woman in her village," Ray had not been wanted from his earliest memory. He had been shunned by the other villagers and had been lucky to survive, and that was before he fell in with a bunch of vampire pirates and began a new existence on the bottom rung of yet another ladder.

He had never really gotten off it, despite eventually rising to the rank of master, partly because of those blue eyes. They made him an outsider wherever he went in Asia, like his scrawny frame, lack of height, and Indonesian features had made him stick out in the West. Ray didn't belong anywhere, which was one reason I found him so relatable.

Neither did I.

That was truer for me even than Dory, who straddled the vamp and human worlds, but would never completely fit into either. She had a position now because the Vampire Senate needed her, but when they no longer did so? Neither she nor I thought that her lofty title was likely to be permanent. And if it was, it would be in spite of her nature, not because of it.

And of the two of us, she was the normal one.

I was still not quite sure what I was, as the longstanding belief that I was simply Dory's vampire half had been challenged recently. Apparently, dhampirs did not have two easily separated halves as Dory and I did. Our dual nature was instead some kind of strange experiment, or so Nimue, one of the queens of the light fey, had told me shortly before her death. According to her, I was not something that was supposed to exist, being a weird amalgam of human, vampire, fey and possibly god blood, intended as an uber assassin.

Well, that wasn't entirely true. It had been my mother who had been engineered in the gods' experiment, who had wanted to find something that could kill other gods in their incessant wars. She had been a failure as the hoped-for prototype, however; whereas I, a product of her affair with my father, a vampire in transition, had somehow solved the problem that even the gods could not. And become the weapon they had envisioned.

But a weapon was a thing, not a woman.

So, what was I?

And how did I live without my other half, who had always been there, navigating the world, dealing with all sorts of people, and making all the decisions? I had once looked forward to such things, had dreamed of the time when I might have some control over the one body that we both shared. But now that it came to it . . .

It was frightening.

Fortunately, I had Ray to help me.

Or perhaps not, I thought, seeing his scowl become even more pronounced.

"See? That's what I was afraid of!" he accused.

I stared up at him, nonplussed, although I didn't know why. He had shown a great ability to read my thoughts in the past. "Afraid of what?" I asked.

"That you're making me a substitute for Dory! I'm not gonna do that; I'm not gonna make decisions for you, and you wanna know why?"

"Yes," I said, because listening to him had been very useful so far.

"Listening ain't the problem!" he said angrily. Before dropping his hands to my shoulders and shaking me a little. "Listen all you want, but you make the call. You make the decision. You got a good head on your shoulders; you don't need to use me as a crutch. And given how dangerous Faerie is, you don't want to. What if I'm suddenly not here anymore?"

I stared up at him, and felt an icy hand grip my heart. "Where are you going?"

"Down something's gullet, like as not," he said, glancing up, as a sound echoed through the forest from somewhere high above the tree tops.

Dragons. I scanned the darkened night sky while the haunting call etched its way across my skin, but saw nothing. We were near the territory of the wildest sort of beast, or so I had been told, although we had seen none up close.

So far.

"I will protect you," I said, my eyes falling again to meet Ray's.

His looked black in the night, with twin flames from the reflected firelight dancing in the pupils. For once, he looked like a vampire. "And if you can't?" he said, and said no more, although I knew what he was thinking. And it didn't take the mental connection we sometimes shared for that.

We had almost died a dozen times since our arrival here. Chased through an already hostile land by the creatures of a power-hungry queen, we had only been saved by the machinations of another one, by my own fierce nature, and by Ray's seemingly unending resourcefulness, although he failed to see how much he had aided us. We had survived, but it had been a close thing.

I was used to thinking of myself as formidable, but Faerie was more so. Yet it couldn't have Ray. It *wouldn't!*

"I *will* protect you," I told him, and saw his eyes roll as he released me.

"Look," he said, scraping black hair off his forehead. "We gotta talk, okay?"

I blinked. "Is that not what we have been doing?"

"No! We've been bullshitting. But right now, we need to *talk*." He knelt down, which was more comfortable than having him loom over me, and looked at me with an odd expression. Part fond, part exasperated, part . . . I wasn't sure. But it was serious. I could see that much.

My hand reached out and cupped his cheek. He hadn't been able to shave in a while, and unlike most masters, he had less than perfect bodily control. As a result, his beard was starting to come in in patches. He had tried shaving it off, because it did look rather odd, with a knife we had borrowed from one of the villagers and a bowl of soapy water, but the result had been less than perfect.

I was glad he had stopped.

I liked his face without a lot of chunks carved out of it.

He grasped my wrist and then just held it, staring at me. "Listen."

"I am listening."

"Good. Then stop trying to distract me."

"How am I doing that?" I asked, confused, and heard him sigh again.

He put my hand back on the ground and kept his on top of it, to hold it there. "You aren't Dory, okay?"

"I know that."

"You are your own person; you are Dorina. And I need for you to get that, and to start acting like it. Don't wait for me or anyone else to tell you what to do or how to think or what to feel, okay? You decide. This is your life now—"

"And when it isn't?"

He frowned, possibly at the sudden roughness in my voice that I couldn't disguise. "What do you mean, when it isn't?"

I swallowed. "What I said. I have a body now because we are in Faerie, and souls always manifest bodies here. But what about when it is time to leave?"

It was a thought that had been bothering me more and more. I raised my other hand, and watched it gleam in the moonlight.

It looked so strong, so substantial. I could feel the blood rushing through it, see dirt in the creases and the ragged state of the nails.

I turned it this way and that, and then met Ray's eyes again. "What about when this just . . . dissolves?"

"It won't!"

"Won't it?" I looked at him almost as curiously as I had the hand. He was flushed, to the point that the stain on his skin was possible to see in the darkness, and looked agitated. "Why won't it?"

"Because it won't! We'll figure something out, and anyway, who knows? Maybe we don't have to. Maybe this is how your kind are . . . are born—"

"I don't have a kind."

"—like Dory was the chrysalis or something, and now that you're here, having come out of her—"

"Ray—"

"—maybe you'll stay. Maybe you'll go back home and just be like that—"

"And maybe I won't," I said gently. "Wouldn't it then be easier not to begin making distinctions—"

"Bullshit!"

"—that won't matter soon?"

"They matter! You matter!"

I stared into his eyes, and they were big and sincere and pained, and for some reason, that hurt me, too. But I did not want to lie to him. I did not like to lie.

"Ray, I don't even know—" I broke off.

"Know what?"

I looked around, my gaze suddenly almost as agitated as his had been. All I saw were tall tree trunks, the muffling canopy far overhead that blocked out most of the stars, and the groups of fey camped in the center of the road and spread out for half a mile in either direction. For there were things that prowled in the night here; things that even the fey had learned to fear.

It wasn't the prettiest sight I'd ever seen, but it was real, solid, and completely unlike the hazy half world I had inhabited in my old form.

Here, I could feel the fire's warmth on my skin, the coolness of the night air, the dirt beneath my fingertips. Could smell the few scraps of meat still adhering to the bones of my dinner, interspersed with the spiciness of the ale. I could taste the latter, too, a memory on my lips, like the faint buzz that still danced on my tongue.

I *wanted* this, wanted more of it, wanted everything I had never had and was suddenly, fiercely afraid that I'd never have again. These last weeks, traveling with the Wanderers, had been the most time I'd known as a person in my own right since childhood, yet it wasn't enough. Not anymore.

I wanted a *life*, but wasn't sure whether I was entitled to one. And whether I wasn't just setting myself up for heartbreak by even daring to think of such a thing. *I don't even know if I really exist*, I thought at Ray, knowing that he would pick it up.

"You exist," he told me in a fervent whisper, his forehead coming down to mine. "And you're very real to me."

Chapter Four

I glanced over at Ray now as we jounced along on crab back, and found him slouched down with a large straw-hat drooping over his face. I didn't think it was for the little bit of sun that made it through the tree cover to splatter the road, none of which would hurt him as the fey sun did not carry Earth's curse. I thought it was more likely to make it look like he was asleep so that Marlowe, the vampire in the cage, would stop talking to him.

But if it was for that reason, it did not work.

"I know you're listening," the curly haired vampire said.

The mop on Marlowe's head was dark to match his eyes and goatee, and he had very long lashes for a man. He was handsome, or was maintaining a glamourie to appear so, although I doubted the latter. It would have been a waste of energy as he was filthy, having been a fey captive for some time, to the point that his features were hardly discernable. The effort did not seem worthwhile.

But he could probably afford the power drain, being a first level master and a member of the North American Vampire Senate. What such an illustrious being was doing here, slumming with the dark fey, was anyone's guess, although he was also the consul's chief spy. Perhaps he was spying on the fey?

If so, it was not going well.

He had told me a story about searching for my father. But since he had also said that my father was in Faerie looking for my mother, who had died centuries ago, I had decided that he was lying. From what Dory had said of him, he did that a lot.

"And you know their weird patois," he added, after Ray continued to feign sleep. "Tell me where we're going and what the hell is going on or I'll keep up a running commentary all the damned way."

He waited.

Ray let out what I guessed was supposed to be a snore.

Marlowe growled. "You asked for it," he said. And then did worse than he had threatened. He began to sing.

I believe the tune was meant to be *Greensleeves*, but it was hard to tell as it was terribly off key and also very loud. Loud enough that it startled the giant crab he was riding on top of, which jumped enough to rock the cage. And then did a strange little scurrying motion ahead and bumped into our ride.

That was a problem as we were not sitting on our crab's sleek shell but rather on something that looked vaguely like an old-fashioned buggy seat, albeit made of hides and furs and ropes, and it was already more unsteady than I'd have liked. That was especially the case as the crabs sometimes headed for the trees when startled, using their pincers to grasp the trunks and allow them to make for the shelter of the canopy above. This one did not do that, thankfully, although it did whirl about and snap at the one that had just bumped into us.

I thought that was more of a warning, a 'be careful there' in crab speech, as no blood was shed. But the other didn't take it that way and immediately snapped back, causing the two to begin fighting. That involved a lot of circling and clicking of pincers, and rearing back in attempts to climb on top of each other, which made our driver curse and whip our mount with the leather strop he carried, not that it did any good.

That sort of thing might have worked on horses, with their much thinner skins, but the crab's shell was as hard as stone and I wasn't sure that it even felt it. If it did, it did not stop snapping at the other one, or slinging us around, or screaming when the larger crab with Marlowe's cage started crawling on top of it. And thus, on top of us.

I reached out and tried to push the creature off, which Ray was also doing on the other side of the bench. Only it weighed more than I had thought and was strong besides, bracing on its sturdy back legs and using the two huge front ones to wrestle with its opponent, while the ones in between kept the fey at bay who had run up to help from all directions. And, all the while, Marlowe sang on.

"Would you shut the hell up?" Ray screeched, holding back a giant pincer with difficulty.

"You really are very bad," I added, trying to shame Marlowe into silence.

Neither approached worked.

But the fey were less kind, sticking spears through the cage bars, threatening to skewer him, I guessed being under the impression that his terrible vocals were what was causing all of the ruckus. They weren't wrong, because the crabs' fury definitely increased with every attempted high note. But reasoning, or even threatening, a master wasn't likely to work.

I decided to try the crabs instead, and the next moment, fell into another world.

It was one of blissfully cool, underground caverns, where water from the spring rains rotted the vegetation that was swept inside and led to a proliferation of tasty worms feeding on nature's largess. And on which mother crabs in turn fed their little ones, for these caves were their nursery. Later, as the young crabs grew and ventured forth into the forest pools outside, they found other delicacies: algae, small fish and frogs to start with, then larger fish in the rivers that flowed here and there, and finally furry or feathered forest creatures, which became prey as the crabs grew big and strong and faster than almost everything else in the forest. And all of that did not count the plentiful vegetation, the rotting corpses of animals—for they were happy to finish off another's kill—and essentially anything they met with.

Well, anything that wasn't fey.

The fey were the one food they avoided, for the strange, two-legged creatures had long sticks, some of which erupted in lightning from the ends that hurt even through the shell. The crabs did not like the lightning and would do much to avoid it, including even serving the fey by carrying them on their backs or helping them to move obstructions from the road with their pincers. The wild crabs did not think much of the servile kind, and sometimes made fun of them, with their cries echoing across the forest at night, urging them to run, run, run and rejoin them.

But our crab couldn't run. He had been easily caught and made a beast of burden, for he had been born mangled, with one side leg small and spindly and curled underneath him, useless. And one of his large back ones, which were supposed to match his great front claws and provide stability in a fight, was withered, although at least he could stand on it. But it had never been right.

As it was currently demonstrating.

He felt it give way, felt himself start to fall, and then felt something else, something new: a startling sense of power flowing through the weakened leg. Warmth and the cessation of his constant pain followed, and then a current of strength such as he had never known. It was glorious!

He could feel the muscle plumping up, the formerly crumpled skin stretching tight, the joints popping into their proper places. And while he was still wondering about that, a sudden sound came from the trees, distant and far away. Not a taunt, as he had heard more times than he could count, but a summons: a female of his species calling out for a mate. She was looking for someone strong and ferocious and capable of defending her and their brood.

Someone like him!

He reared up on two strong hind legs, throwing off the puny creatures clinging to his shell, and roared in the face of his startled adversary. Which a moment before had been sure of victory, and now found itself the weaker one, and began quickly backing down. The winner roared again just because he could, then scuttled quickly away, making for the nearest great tree and the freedom of the canopy, where he called out to his mate with a delighted sound.

He did not know what had happened, only that he had a new life this day, a new life and freedom!

Wait for me, he called to her, and heard her bellow back. She would wait. But she would not wait long, he knew, and thus he raced across the treetops with urgent grace, barely ruffling the leaves around him despite his speed.

* * *

"Well, this is just great."

"I am sorry," I said, for at least the tenth time, but Raymond did not care. Raymond was furious, and rightfully so. I bit my lip.

"Isn't this cozy?" Marlowe asked, grinning at me. He seemed to find the fact that we were all bunched up together in the small cage to be highly amusing. Ray did not feel the same.

"I really am very—" I began again, but a look from under the somewhat battered hat stopped the words in my throat.

I stared back mutely.

"They hanged horse thieves in my day," Marlowe offered. "I wonder what they do to crab rustlers?"

"I did not rustle the crab," I pointed out. "I also did not set it free—"

"Tell the fey that."

"I did. They did not seem to understand. I do not know much of their language yet—"

"They understood," Ray said, and the sound of his voice was odd, perhaps because he was gritting his teeth while trying to talk. "They also felt you healing the damned thing, which allowed it to escape—"

"So, semantics, really," Marlowe put in.

"—so we're fucked!" Ray pushed up the hat, which he was somehow still wearing after our tumble from the escaping crab's back, to allow him to glare at me properly. "Do you get that? These are *dark fey*; and property to them is a Very Big Deal. They lost almost everything they owned when the damned Svarestri or Alorestri or whatever -estri came along and took their homes. Their *stuff*. Everything they had that they couldn't run off with before some badass on a horse ran 'em to ground and killed 'em for fun or target practice! So, losing even more stuff 'cause Pollyanna had to feel bad for a goddamned monster—"

"I am sorry," I whispered again, because I hadn't intended to do this. I had just thought that helping the crab to become equal with its opponent might end the fight quicker, as the other had been pressing its advantage, knowing that ours was weaker. I hadn't thought—

But that was the problem. I *hadn't* thought, wasn't used to having to think, about anything at all much less the consequences of my actions. I rarely took actions, and when I did, it was in battle. I knew how to do that, but this . . .

"Do you still want me to think for myself?" I asked Ray, and saw his mouth suddenly close.

He stared at me for a moment, opened his mouth again as if to speak, and then shut it once more. I did not know why, but Marlowe seemed to find that very funny. He laughed in my face, which was less than pleasant as he was highly odorous, having tried to escape a week ago before being tracked to a farmer's pig pen, where he had smeared himself with muck to confuse the noses of the fey dogs.

He had not confused their noses; they had found him again without trouble. But he was now assaulting mine. I could not help it; my face wrinkled, something that made him laugh all the more, to the point that he was clutching his chest and pointing at Ray.

"She's got you there," he wheezed. "Of course, she already did, didn't she? *'Oh, oh, you're very real to me!'*"

"Shut up!" Ray said.

"Or what? What the hell do you think you're going to do? We're about to be *dinner*—"

"The fey aren't cannibals, you fucking idiot—"

"And we're not fey!" Brown eyes glared at him out of a mask of mud and worse. "So, no cannibalism is required, is it? And who is the idiot? You were my only chance of escaping, but instead of helping me, what have you been doing? Mooning over another monster—"

"Call her that again," Ray said, gripping Marlowe by the front of his shirt.

"And what?" Marlowe spread his arms, as far as the cage would allow. That wasn't very far, which was probably why he scraped his knuckles on the rusty bars and cursed. And then did it again, only louder, when the ward attached to them, which was what was really keeping us all in place, shocked him.

"Goddamnit! You've killed us all!" he raged. "Why didn't you two just *get a room*—"

Which was when Ray belted him.

It was a good blow, enough to rock Marlowe's head back, which was not easy to do to a first level master. But Marlowe had been shocked half a dozen times during his impromptu concert with some of the feared electric spears, which the locals had either purloined from the Svarestri—the light fey clan who had invented them—or jury rigged for themselves. And as I knew from experience, those blasts were not easy to throw off.

As a result, the fight wasn't nearly as one-sided as it might have been, although a lot of the cursing was probably due more to repeated shocks from the ward whenever the two of them rolled into it rather than the blows they were delivering. There just wasn't enough room for a proper fight in here, which was why I didn't try to intervene. I watched the woods pass by instead, eventually start to thin, and finally give way to rolling fields, a gurgling brook and a view into a large valley, which appeared to be almost covered with fey encampments.

All sorts of fey.

"What is this?" I asked a passing troll girl.

She was young, but already tall enough to look me in the eye despite my perch atop the crab. She was also green, although a brighter hue than the crab's mottled greenish-brown, which was true of many of the caravan, most of whom appeared to be related. There were also a scattering of other colors and shapes—dark purple and skinny instead of her soft green roundness, or short with a pinkish hue and tusks like an ogre's. Or perhaps they *were* ogres; I wasn't sure.

There were even a few light fey villagers who had come along, packing up bedrolls and wagons and wheelbarrows after we skittered through their towns and following us. The conveyances they drove or wheeled along were mostly full of food but sometimes also contained homespun blankets, carefully made quilts, and baskets of reeds with hinged tops on them. There were so many items that they looked like trade goods more than personal comforts, although I hadn't seen anyone trading.

I wondered now if they had been waiting for a bigger customer pool, but didn't know whether my curiosity would be satisfied. I was a felon, after all. But the troll girl had brought us dinner the previous night, in thanks for me helping her with some laundry at the last river we'd encountered, and she seemed to have a bit of goodwill left.

She also seemed to be in a jolly mood, picking wildflowers as she walked to twine into her many braids. In fact, the spirits of everyone in the caravan was lifting, with more than one person humming a tune far more pleasant that Marlowe's had been. That did not tell me much considering my very inadequate knowledge of the language, however.

"She said it's the *Turl uh Talat,*" Ray gasped, from underneath Marlowe's arm. Or at least, that's what it sounded like.

"What is that?" I asked, because there had to be thousands of fey in that valley, perhaps tens of thousands, bustling about setting up tents and tables or making fires, as if they planned to stay for a while.

"The dark fey . . . who've lost their lands . . . are nomadic now," Ray gasped, as Marlowe pummeled him in the ribs. "Some try . . . to head into our world . . . but a lot don't want . . . to go. This was their land . . . from time immemorial. Instead of leaving it . . . they just resumed the old . . . way of life . . . before everybody settled down and got civilized—"

"Hunter gatherers," Marlowe said, right before Ray bit his hand. "Ow, you bastard!"

But he didn't retaliate, although I saw his fist clench, because he was now staring past the bars at the colorful tents, distant laughter, music and vendors' cants drifting to us on the breeze, along with the smell of roasting meat. My stomach woke up to complain loudly at the latter, causing Ray to grimace. And then to finally give Marlowe some of the answers he had been demanding.

"No, not like that," Ray said. "More like an extended shopping trip. The Old Path was all about trade: pick stuff up in one place, sell it at another. The light fey had towns, hamlets and cities long before the dark did, maybe 'cause they got some help from their godly benefactors. The same ones who threw the dark fey out as failed experiments who could go hang themselves.

"Only they didn't hang. They traded instead. Each band had a set path they took, and customers who bought from them. Then, once a year, all the different bands met in a central location to exchange news, swap stories, and let the young ones have a go at courting outside of their family group. It only lasted for a few weeks, 'cause the surrounding countryside could only support that many for so long, but it was a hell of a time for as long as it did.

"The *Turl uh Talat* was the name of the meeting. It's started up again with so many dark fey back on the road thanks to the war. I tried to come here once to do a little wheeling and dealing of my own, but was told that only fey are allowed."

"Then why are the three of us being let in?" Marlowe demanded.

Ray shrugged. "Well, since we aren't fey, my guess would be . . . we're the merchandise."

Chapter Five
Dory

Despite everything, we still went to dinner. Claire said that we had to. But none of us were happy about it, including her.

"Hurry up, or we'll be late," she said, as we hustled down a broad stone passageway to a set of too-steep stairs going up.

The main hall in this castle was at the top, rather than occupying a lower floor as in human strongholds, but that would have been okay if the stairs hadn't been made for people with longer strides than I had. A lot longer. They were also deeper, as if meant for bigger feet, leaving me leaping from one to the other more than walking, as Claire was also doing up ahead.

"And I, for one, do not want to make an entrance!" she panted.

Yeah, blending in at some back table in the shadows sounded more like a plan to me. Assuming that we could keep up with our guide, that is, since despite the stairs, she was not letting grass grow. But I was glad we had her, because this place was like no other castle I'd ever seen.

Unlike our room, which had glittered with mosaic and had beautiful designs inlaid into the floors, the passageways were almost completely unadorned. There also wasn't any artwork, carpets or benches to break up the view, just acres of golden stone. And with no niches for lanterns, I wouldn't have been able to see anything if the ends of the halls hadn't been open to the skies.

That let the wind whistle through at regular intervals, tugging at our hair and fluttering our clothes every time we hit another passage, and I supposed explained the missing furnishings, as the weather and wildlife would have ravaged them soon enough. But the architecture still seemed odd, since the whole point of Earth castles was to be defensive. But when you had a scaley wall that could be deployed at any time, I guessed that didn't matter so much.

Lord Rathen's people had clearly prioritized ease of access over protection, and they were using it, coming and going constantly—only not on the stairs.

I watched some of them, who were as late as we were, emerge from their rooms, run down the hallways and throw themselves into the air, changing in an instant and soaring upward. Or coming back from some errand or other, and landing and shifting bodies at the same moment. Making a transformation that appeared as effortless for them as breathing did for me.

That might explain why the shifting was constant, with some doing so merely to avoid the stairs and skip up a flight or two the easy way. And was facilitated by the breezy, halter-style outfits I'd seen once on Earth, with gauzy waves of beautiful cloth cascading from a single magical band around their throats. In dragon form, it was a scarf-like adornment; in human, the filmy folds fell downward as their bodies shrank, clothing them as they changed.

I hadn't seen the constant activity as we approached, since the castle, in the brief glimpse I'd had of it from the road, had seemed rather sleepy. But I imagined that it must now resemble a great birdcage, with the brightly colored creatures who flitted around it like exotic pets. Ones with claws and scales and maws full of teeth, but still.

Stunning.

Louis-Cesare was watching them, too, but he didn't seem so awed anymore. We appeared to be going in opposite directions, with my initial suspicion and wariness leaching onto him, and some of his wonder onto me. His expression was calculated, as if trying to determine the weaknesses in all that armor plating and the best place to strike, if it came to it.

I could have answered that from observing Claire's other form: nowhere.

"We might have dined in our room," he said, with his tone telling me that his thoughts had mirrored mine. "If we are so late."

"No, you couldn't have," Claire said, throwing her bright red mane over her shoulder, and causing it to bounce almost down to her waist. It reminded me of the real mane that her alternate form had, except for being curly and red instead of flowing and lavender, so okay, not at all. But there was something there, nonetheless, some hint at her alter ego that was usually absent.

Maybe it was the violet silk she wore, shot through with silver and almost scandalously sheer. It was also open at the sides except for some silken ties that were loosely fastened so as not to bind her or rip the material if she had to change quickly. It was striking, but it wasn't Claire.

She was normally on the conservative side with her clothing, preferring maillots to bikinis and long skirts to minis. She had a prairie chic aesthetic, with jean jackets over long, flowy prints and boho jewelry. She could have been a model for Valentino if she didn't disdain makeup most of the time, and if she didn't hate high heels with every fiber of her being.

Today she was barefoot, I guessed because shifting into her alter ego was hell on shoes, and looked more like some pagan priestess planning to serve us up on an alter to her god than my old friend. It made me nervous, because everything around here was making me nervous, and I didn't like it. It was hard to know what to be wary of when even my friend seemed strange!

"I beg your pardon?" Louis-Cesare asked, continuing the conversation I'd lost the thread of.

"Cowardice is the biggest sin among the houses," Claire informed him. "Your reputation is everything, so cringing in your room—which is how missing dinner would be seen—would only result in more attacks. You have to brave it out."

"Something that would be considerably easier if we knew why we were being targeted," he commented tartly.

But Claire wasn't listening. Claire had spied the duffle bag I'd brought along despite the fact that it in no way matched my outfit. She hadn't noticed it before since she'd been in a tizzy after returning from teaching her half-brother—the massive red creature who'd buzzed us on the road—a lesson. Only to discover that she'd missed even more excitement back here.

A ginger eyebrow raised. "Really, Dory?"

"Yes." I gripped it tighter. "Really."

"My father will protect you—"

"Your father wasn't there earlier," I pointed out, and saw her flush. It didn't help my mood that the color was more lavender than pink, almost matching her dress and staining her cheeks up to her temples.

"He didn't think you'd be attacked in his own house! Nobody did—"

"Then why were we?" Louis-Cesare asked, because he did not do the usual courtier routine. He might look like he belonged in the salons of a different age, but he had never fit in there, as he tended to be far too direct for most people's liking. Including Claire's, judging by the way her green eyes snapped when she glanced back as we started up yet another stairway.

This one was even more impressive than the interior ones we'd been following, as it wound outside of the castle, like a crazed snake hugging the place. Or a crazed dragon, I supposed, with the stairs being the jagged ridges along its backbone. And, of course, there were no railings, because what did dragons need with railings?

I was surprised they'd had them on the balcony in our room. But even there, they'd been short and more decorative than anything else, and here they were missing all together. Giving us a dizzying view of what looked to be a couple miles straight down into the mist-wreathed valley below.

I could see glimpses of tree-covered slopes, of rolling hills, of cascades and rivers and small flocks of animals, although we were too high up for me to name them. But mostly, I saw mountains and mist, because we'd broken through the cloud line by now. It didn't help with the vertigo, and neither did the wind.

It was even more chilly out here and the "breeze" was savage. I hugged the castle wall as closely as possible while having to jump from massive stair to massive stair, with my hair whipping around and Louis-Cesare putting a subtle hand under my elbow, just in case. That helped with the wind, but less so with the bird I disturbed, which had made a nest in a cleft in the stone. I was pecked as I passed and resorted to sucking on my injured hand and trying not to think at all as we followed Claire ever upward.

"It shouldn't have happened," she was saying, with the wind tearing the words apart almost before they reached us.

"But it did," Louis-Cesare said flatly. "And before I subject my wife or myself to another potential assault, I would like to know why."

That went over about as well as I'd expected, with Claire's flush reaching new heights, even climbing into her hairline as she glanced back at us. "She's your wife, but she's *my* friend! Do you really think I'd have brought her here if I thought there was a chance—"

"I don't know what to think—about any of this. But I need to. Or we will depart and find another way—"

"There is no other way," I said. "You know that."

It was true. I, for one, hadn't had any idea of the scale of Faerie before we came here. I don't know what I'd expected, maybe a nice video game version of a medieval world, with a squat, rundown castle on a hill, a picturesque village at its feet, and a bunch of well tilled fields beyond that. Obviously, I knew its reputation, and I'd met more than a few of its people through the years, none of which would have fit into that happy little illusion.

And yet, somehow, it had remained stuck in my brain. Maybe I'd wanted it there. Because the reality was scary as hell.

This was a whole new world, and one that I knew very little about, with customs, people and—presumably—weaponry that I had never seen and didn't know how to deal with. I'd known I would need help—I wasn't so crazy that I didn't recall the number of people the Senate had sent here through the years who had never returned—but my gallant band of master vamps now seemed almost laughably inadequate.

It didn't help that we'd had to leave Claire's fey bodyguards in New York, as they had flatly refused to let her go on what one had called "a damned fool quest to get herself killed!" It was also a factor that a party of armed light fey would have never been allowed to come here and might well have been attacked on sight. We had therefore resorted to roofying the whole group on fey wine and slipping out in the middle of the night while they slept it off.

That was going to be a fun conversation when we got back.

If we got back.

The only other people on our side were a group of mercenaries who we'd contracted to trace Dorina from her last known whereabouts. But those directions had been provided by a queen who'd been trying to kill her until an abrupt change of heart, so I didn't trust them at all, and anyway, they were weeks out of date. Sure, Dorina might be sitting around a campfire somewhere, drinking ale and chilling, but why did I doubt that?

No, Claire's people were our best bet, which why we were here instead of hacking through the undergrowth with the mercs.

I just didn't know if we were any better off, and Louis-Cesare seemed to feel the same.

"What I know is that staying here is equally problematic," he said to Claire. "You should have warned us—"

"About what?" she demanded, whirling on him. "That there's a war raging across Faerie? That we would be traversing a battle zone by coming here? Were you in any way unclear on that?"

Louis-Cesare looked a little startled to have a furious redhead suddenly in his face, possibly because we'd just reentered the castle, the stairs weaving their way back inside, and his eyes took a moment to adjust from the blinding glare. Or because Claire seemed a little . . . tense . . . today. And we'd just seen what a tense dragon could do.

"No," he said, blinking at her. "But—"

"Then maybe it failed to cross your mind that some people don't want to be involved in said war? And that my father choosing to align with your Senate wasn't universally popular?"

"How could I know that?" he asked, somewhat reasonably. "You have never mentioned it before."

"I didn't think it would matter! There's only three of us. And we're not here on war business. We're just trying to find Dorina and get the hell out—"

"Only some people don't believe that," I guessed, and she nodded, pushing random curls out of her face.

"Our arrival couldn't have come at a worse time. There's a debate raging about the war, with some people wanting to stay out, others leaning toward helping our side, and still more who rumors say have joined Aeslinn's," she said, talking about the light fey king who had started the current hostilities. "A few of the other houses—"

"There are other houses?" Louis-Cesare interrupted.

Claire shot him an impatient look. "Of course. Did you think that we were the only group of dragonkind to have—" She stopped to allow a couple of plump old women to pass by.

Or plump old somethings, because while the two looked like harmless grandmas of the Tweety Bird variety, with wispy white hair done up in identical buns on the tops of their heads and long black dresses with starched white aprons, they didn't move like it.

They didn't walk down the corridor so much as hop, even before reaching the stairs. And when they turned their heads, it was with odd, bird-like motions.

But compared to the dragons, who were seven and eight feet tall with body builders' physiques even in human form, they seemed pretty normal. I watched them head down the stairs, my eyes glad to have something familiar to focus on for a change. And felt my spine begin to unclench somewhat.

Until I glimpsed three-toed bird feet when one of the dresses fluttered up on a hop.

I sighed.

"Harpies," Claire said, following my eyes. "There's a clan that lives in the crags near here, and some work for father."

"Sure," I tried to look nonchalant.

I don't think I succeeded, but she didn't call me on it. "There are numerous houses, with nine great ones, in these mountains," she said instead. "Father has the allegiance of more of the smaller houses than anyone else, making him the first among equals, I guess. But he isn't a king. He doesn't get to say what the other great houses do. Dragonkind are fiercely independent and would never put up with that."

"And what about what his own house does?" Louis-Cesare asked, because the creatures who had attacked us had looked pretty local to me.

"He'll deal with it," Claire said, her jaw tight.

"Here, perhaps. But that doesn't mean we can trust anyone he sends with us. Once they are out of his sight—"

"He'll deal with it!" she repeated, but the uncertainty in her voice echoed in the confines of the passage, which a moment later let out onto the largest corridor I'd seen yet. There was no one there but us, which probably meant that we were very late, and everyone else had already gone into the dining hall, but Claire nonetheless pulled us over by the wall.

"He *will*," she said, sounding more certain.

"Not if he isn't there," Louis-Cesare said stubbornly. "Anyone who doesn't want us here could volunteer to accompany us on our quest, then tell him whatever they liked when they returned alone. There are a thousand ways to die in Faerie, and once we're gone—"

"No one is going to kill you!" she whisper-shouted.

"—who is to contradict them? I am not saying that your father's people are traitors or disloyal," he said, as Claire's eyes flashed dangerously. "But they could dispose of us thinking that they were helping him by keeping his house out of the current conflict—"

"You understand nothing about dragons! They don't think like humans—"

"Then how do they think?"

"—and I'll be with you—"

"As you were today?" Louis-Cesare asked archly, and watched her bristle. But he didn't back down. "There are plenty of ways to separate us, and once you're no longer present—"

"My father's people are not a threat!" Claire snarled, just as a bright green dragon with a pale-yellow belly sailed through the open side of the corridor, changing into a pretty brunette before her feet touched the floor.

She stumbled a bit, uncharacteristically clumsy for one of her kind, but she appeared to be in a hurry. Her cheeks were flushed and her hair, which was almost down to her ankles, was a bit mussed. But it complimented her huge dark eyes, and the ombre blue silk dress she wore, with what looked like a scattering of diamonds near the hem where the darkest color was, as if suggesting the coming of night. She was tying up the sides of the dress as she took off running, her bare feet silent on the slick stone floor, until she slipped—

And Louis-Cesare caught her.

It was an instinctive reaction for a gallant Frenchman schooled in the manners of another age. But it was not taken that way. She stared at him for a second in shock, then started screaming bloody murder and changed back in an eyeblink, filling the corridor so tightly that I don't see how she expected to be able to maneuver to fight. But she managed it, with a barbed tail catching Louis-Cesare a glancing blow, which was still enough to send him tumbling out of the open side of the hall.

He caught himself at the last second, literally by the tips of his fingers, and flipped back inside, right before a wash of flame obliterated the space he'd just been occupying. I screamed, Claire roared in a voice I barely recognized as hers, and I spotted my husband clinging like the proverbial bat to the high ceiling of the corridor, and looking more than a little spooked. Then Claire suddenly changed, too, shoving me behind her and getting into the other woman's face.

Only it wasn't a woman anymore, and I just stood there, unable to believe that we were involved in a second fight in less than an hour.

Fortunately, Claire's presence calmed things down, with the other dragon looking startled as hell as she looked from her to us. And then her expression changed to embarrassment followed swiftly by curiosity, staring up at the ceiling as Louis-Cesare dropped back down beside me. And then peering over Claire's scaley shoulder at us as if she'd never seen our kind before.

And maybe she hadn't.

These folk didn't get out much.

She disappeared after a moment, winking out of sight behind Claire's considerable bulk. "Your pardon," someone said softly, a moment later.

The translation spell we were using, because neither Louis-Cesare nor I spoke any fey language, made everything sound kind of tinny. Like listening to an old-fashioned radio minus the static. Nonetheless, the breathy sincereness in the woman's voice came through, and then her human form peeked around a massive dragon thigh to blink at us some more.

"You were saying?" Louis-Cesare said to Claire.

"Goddamnit," she snarled, and changed back.

Chapter Six

Y‎ou don't like it here, do you?" Louis-Cesare asked me a few moments later.

We were waiting on Claire to check out the Great Hall, where everyone had gathered for dinner, and make sure that we weren't about to be jumped as soon as we went in. In the meantime, she'd parked us in a nearby room that, judging by the dust on the various oversized weapons displayed in it, didn't get used much. It was also dim, with no windows and the only light leaking in from the hall.

So, I wasn't sure that he could see the incredulity in the expression I turned on him. But vamp eyes are good, and he huffed out a laugh. "Fair enough."

"Are *you* enjoying it?" I demanded.

He gave it some thought.

"It hasn't been boring," was the verdict.

"I could use a little more boring," I said savagely, but kept my voice low, because I didn't want to attract attention.

Attention around here got you killed.

"I have rarely seen you this tense," Louis-Cesare said, laying hands on my shoulders.

"It isn't that." He gave me a look, one that said he knew I was lying. "All right, it isn't just that. But it's taken us forever to get here, meaning that Dorina has been lost for over a month, and being here . . . with these creatures . . ."

"Reminds you of how much trouble she's in."

I nodded. "I know she can take care of herself, but Faerie isn't Earth. What if she finally came across something she couldn't handle? This place is at war; the fey themselves are jumpy. And you know how she is—"

Louis-Cesare's arm went around me. "I know she isn't stupid. She'll be careful. She'll survive."

I was glad that he was so sure. I wasn't, even though Dorina was literally my other half. My soul mate, since half of my soul had been sheared off to create her.

I'd been whole once, and as normal as my kind ever got. Until I started having fits, the kind that kill most dhampirs before they have a chance to grow up. Nature's way of stomping out a mistake, I suppose.

But father hadn't cared about nature. He'd only cared about me. So, he'd used his vampire mental abilities to wall off the part of my nature that was literally killing me.

It had saved me, but it had trapped her in a prison of my mind. For centuries, she could only emerge when I was asleep or unconscious, the latter of which usually happened in battles that went wrong. Otherwise, she existed almost like a ghost, a disembodied consciousness that flitted about, observing the world but not truly living in it.

We'd only managed to break that cycle recently, and release her from perpetual confinement. I was no longer a child, and could handle my mental twin just fine. But while we were still trying to get to know each other, and to figure out how to share one body between us, the unthinkable happened.

She was kidnapped by some fey using an ancient relic that ripped us apart. But since Faerie didn't treat souls the same way that Earth did, and clothed any free-floating spirits in flesh, she was currently walking around in a living, breathing body of her own for the first time ever. Which meant that she could be killed.

Louis-Cesare and I had therefore taken it upon ourselves to get a band together and go after her. It had seemed like a daunting prospect—until we got here. Now, it seemed insane.

The only hope we had was that Claire's relatives could help us. Otherwise, I had no idea how we were supposed to scour an entire world, and one at war at that, without ending up as dead as I was starting to suspect that Dorina was. Because if she was okay, why hadn't she come back?

And what would I do without her if she never did?

"It will be alright," Louis-Cesare said, probably watching the emotions flitting across my face. "We'll make sure that it is."

I didn't answer because Claire came back in.

And because I didn't have one.

"I brought you something," she said, handing us both identical looking gauze wrapped packages. "Your clothes were partly what triggered Tamris—"

"Tamris?"

"The woman outside."

"The large green dragon," Louis-Cesare clarified dryly.

Claire shot him a look. "So, I thought that a change was in order. I borrowed Louis-Cesare something from Tanet and Tamris donated yours, Dory. She feels bad."

"She feels bad?" I stared at her. "She almost threw Louis-Cesare to his death!"

"It was a mistake; he startled her—"

"And you therefore get a dress," he said sardonically.

"—and since we don't want any more mistakes, put it on! The food will be served soon!"

I didn't know why that mattered so much, but Claire was looking positively panicked. I decided that I was past worrying about it and unwrapped the dress. It turned out to be a floaty yellow and orange number with speckles of silver, which wasn't the problem.

The problem was that it was almost identical in style to the one that Claire was almost wearing. Louis-Cesare's was the same only in royal blue to match his eyes and with striations of gold running through a slightly heavier, more velvety, fabric. But both were . . . not exactly modest.

Claire saw me noticing. "Oh, for heaven's sake, Dory! This is no time to be prudish! We have to make a good impression."

"We'll make an impression, all right," I said, noticing that the robes were open on both sides, so that a scaley ass had somewhere to go when it shot outward. But for us . . . a belt might help, but not much since I guessed I wasn't supposed to wear underwear with it. Claire didn't, judging by the flash of something further up than thigh that I occasionally got. The amount of fabric was fairly voluminous, since it was expected to cover more flesh than we had, but still. Were snaps out of the question?

But I noticed her glare and swallowed the comment.

She was really good at that.

I put on the dress. It actually covered me pretty well, but only because it was massive. It trailed the ground by at least two feet, and may as well have been a tent. One of those with multiple rooms that slept a family of eight.

Claire looked me up and down and sighed, because no way could I walk in it. I wasn't buckling to the ground only because it was as light as a feather, and softer than any silk I'd ever touched. It felt like wearing a cloud, and complimented my short dark hair and black eyes as if it had been made for me. Tamris had good taste.

But it also made me look like a kid wearing her mother's clothes.

I was swimming in this thing!

"I could run up to my room," Claire offered. "I'm a bit taller, but I should have something—"

"Aren't we late?" Louis-Cesare asked, causing her to turn on him angrily. Those two had butted heads ever since they met, and things had only softened somewhat after the wedding. But this time, her expression shifted into something other than anger, causing me to glance back at my partner and—

Damn.

No, seriously.

Damn.

Louis-Cesare was six feet four, which put him on the short side for a shifter, at least of this variety. But Tanet wasn't fully grown yet, either, being a rambunctious teenager. And the robes that probably left him looking like the gangly, half-grown kid that he was looked . . . different . . . on our resident super model.

They were still too big, but the extra fabric hung nicely off of broad shoulders and fell in rich folds to the floor. The sides were presumably open, but Louis-Cesare appeared to have secured them well, I guessed with more of the little ties, and you couldn't tell. With his wide rapier belt to gird the whole thing in leather, his abundant auburn locks cascading past his shoulders, his strong jaw and keen blue eyes . . .

Well.

"You just need a crown," Claire said, and then she flushed.

"I will take that as a compliment," he said, bowing over her hand.

I didn't say anything. He did look a lot like a medieval king, one of those effigies carved out of marble and lying in prayerful repose in a cathedral somewhere. But he also, surprisingly, looked like a dragon. One in human form, but believable nonetheless.

Unlike me.

"I'm wearing what I came in," I told Claire, throwing off an acre of soft fabric and revealing the wine-colored slip dress I hadn't bothered to take off. "If my five foot two scares anyone, they'll just have to remain scared."

"It's not about scaring them as much as fitting in," she said, tearing her eyes away from Louis-Cesare. "You need to look like you belong here—"

"But I don't belong here. And nobody is going to believe that I do."

"But—"

"Claire. I'm *five foot two*—"

"Mages can be five foot two! It makes no difference to their power level!"

"And it doesn't to mine. If I have to fight, I'll fight, and they won't enjoy it." I hefted my arsenal. "But if they don't start anything, there won't be anything. I just want info. That's it."

"Just . . . don't talk politics, all right? Either of you! Just . . . just don't talk at all!"

"Okay. I'll let you handle this."

Claire nodded, although her expression was very much at war with the gesture. She obviously didn't like this anymore than we did. Which was less than encouraging as we left the little room, walked down the hall, and passed through two of the biggest, tallest wooden doors I'd ever seen.

And into a blast of sound and color and movement that blew my hair back, and after we traversed a short hallway, spilled out into a room that set all others I'd ever seen to shame.

Louis-Cesare looked around for a startled moment, and then laughed, full-throated and throwing his head back, although I couldn't hear him. I couldn't hear anything, and didn't know how anyone else did. But I saw him mouth the words: "Not bored."

And, no, I had to admit.

Neither was I.

There were a lot of reasons for that, almost too many to count. But for one thing, the dining hall wasn't *in* the tower, it *was* the tower. It encompassed the top fourteen or so levels of the highest section of the castle that Rathen-Den called home. And for another, it wasn't set up at all like a human banqueting chamber.

There were large niches in the walls on each story, like miniature caves carved out of the stone of the mountain, a large black swath of which made up more than half of the tower. The niches featured low lying tables surrounded by large cushions where people sat in small groups, and ledges out in front that served as landing pads. Servants with trays of food and garrulous diners who wanted to chat with their friends were flitting between the different levels, having manifested smaller, human-sized wings that allowed them to fly about at will.

But as dizzying as that was, it wasn't what drew the eye. Despite the setting, the diners mostly looked like people in any hall I'd ever seen: seated at tables, eating food off of plates, sloshing wine around in goblets and decanters, and watching children run about excitedly. There was nothing too surprising there.

Unlike the center of the room, where others weren't dining normally at all.

I stared as some sort of large, ibis-type animal with spots and huge horns was dragged through a doorway by a couple of the burly, lizard-like guards. They managed to manhandle it pretty easily despite it being as big as a bull moose and kicking at them viciously, as if it knew what was coming. One hoof managed to clip one of the guards, leaving a red welt across his chin, but it wasn't enough.

The next moment, the guards had reached the center of the room where they sent the creature screaming into the air, chucking it perhaps four stories high despite its size, and the second after that—

"Well. Shit," I said, as a fine mist of blood rained down from on high, where the animal had just become the latest course in a mid-air feast for those who did not want to dine sitting down.

No, they wanted to tear their food limb from limb and fight off other diners while they did it, screeching and clawing and taking up much of the huge space because they hadn't bothered to partially transform. They were in full-on beast mode, with claws out and tails whipping. Which was why the football-field-sized tower felt small and why a slice of red splattered me across the face before I could dodge out of the way.

"Radu would love this," Louis-Cesare mouthed, looking up out of a blood-speckled face.

He was probably thinking of Radu's mage of a chef, who had enchanted some lamb cutlets once to look like miniature versions of their former wooly selves: growing fur, sprouting tiny heads and legs, and running around peoples' plates before attempting to hide underneath the salad. That had been a one-off, done to honor Radu's guest of the evening, who had been Caedmon, a king of the light fey. I wondered now whether Caedmon had really enjoyed his meal, or whether he had eaten it merely to be polite to his host, whose chef may have confused the dining habits of the different types of fey.

But they were loving it here, although I didn't think there was any enchantment going on in this case. Just tartare on the hoof being consumed as rare as it gets, with the same gusto with which a human might have approached a tray of raw oysters. Although at least the oysters wouldn't bleed all over you, I thought grimly—before noticing something else odd.

I was a mess, with a slash of crimson over my face and splotches dotting my gown. But Louis-Cesare looked perfectly fine, despite having been in the same shape only a moment before. Part of that made sense, with a couple of the remaining bloody freckles on his cheeks being absorbed into the skin as I watched. Fey blood wouldn't nourish a vampire, just like the fey sun wouldn't harm them, but he could get rid of it easily enough.

But what was going on with his clothes?

I suddenly realized that there might have been another reason why Claire had wanted me to change. The ochre that was being tossed around as more appetizers hit the air hazed Louis-Cesare's outfit just as they did mine. Only in his case, they quickly formed themselves into bloody tears that were busily weeping away, running down the velvet nap of his robes to drip onto the golden stones of the floor, which in here were less gold and more brown, having been stained from past feasts.

The result was that he became pristine again in a matter of seconds, whereas I . . .

Did not. And that was before I sprawled against a bloody wall when a raucous squealing came from behind us, loud enough to cut through the din. And warning me to leap aside just in time to avoid a whole herd of wild pigs.

They had been released through the massive doorway, with several of the lizard guys driving them. And I guessed they must have been driving them hard, because they stampeded into the room in a full-out run, before scattering and screeching, loudly enough to wake the dead. Right before taloned feet speared down from above, grabbing them and throwing them into the air, and—

Goddamnit!

A full-on rain of red hit me, leaving me looking like Carrie after the prom and I hadn't even been here two minutes yet!

"Come on," I saw Claire mouth, as she grabbed my hand and pulled me out of the carnage toward a nearby, much smaller arched doorway in the stone.

It led to another staircase hidden within the walls that I hadn't noticed, and still mostly didn't, being too busy trying not to slide on the bloody steps or to flinch at the sounds coming from behind us. The dining hall looked and smelled like an abattoir and sounded like a concert of the damned. I'd never experienced anything like it in my life, and I'd lived with some dark fey.

I had never realized how much my old roommates had been accommodating my human squeamishness, I thought. Right before the crowd roared their appreciation at something loudly enough to almost rupture my eardrums. I braced my arms on either side of the narrow passage, wondering if the tower was about to collapse, then followed Claire upward again when it didn't.

We emerged from the stairs just in time to see what all the uproar was about. Two of the scaley diners had grabbed the same struggling morsel and neither was letting go. Until the inevitable happened, and their tug of war ripped the huge pig in two, causing all of the fun stuff inside to fall about six stories through the air before splatting onto the floor below. And me to finally achieve a rarity for a dhampir: a complete and utter loss of appetite.

What a way to start an evening, I thought dizzily, as we finally made it to our table.

Chapter Seven
Dorina

"Pancakes," Ray said, looking under the homespun cloth covering the latest little reed basket.

I perked up. "What kind of pancakes?"

That won me a side eye. "You can't possibly care."

"I care." I reached for the basket, which he pulled away and nodded at the mound of empty receptacles stacked along one wall of our tent.

"Where on Earth do you put it all?"

"It gets burned up." I made a feint to one side and, when he dodged, snatched my prize. "My metabolism requirements are greater than those of most people."

"*Most* people?" he watched me throw off the cloth and peer inside. The basket was small, but packed with many hand-sized rounds of cooked dough, each of which was studded with nuts and dried fruit and topped with what smelled like a honey drizzle. I took a lick. Yes, it was honey.

Very nice honey, too, redolent of the flowers that grew in the mountains near here. I had been smelling their sweetness on the breeze for days, and was finally tasting it. It was just as I had thought: full of captured sunlight, aromatic grasses, rich earth and summer rains, all distilled into an ineffable sweetness that burst on the tongue.

Divine.

"It is wonderful," I told the small old woman who was watching me enjoy her handiwork with obvious pride. I had once believed that the fey did not age, but had since learned that that was not so. They simply did it slower than humans, making me wonder how many centuries the wizened old face with the bright black eyes had seen.

More than me, at a guess, maybe many more. Her skin was as lined as a dried date and had the color of oak bark, but her hair was as white as new fallen snow. But there was nothing vague or faded about those eyes, which were watching me closely, to see if I was worthy of the title of sorceress.

I was not, despite what our one-time host had been trumpeting to all and sundry, but I nonetheless put on what I hoped was a winning smile. "How can I help you today?"

The woman hesitated, and brushed a small amount of that marvelous hair behind a gracefully shaped, pointed ear. But after a moment, she carefully took a fat, pink bellied creature, which I initially mistook for a piglet, from under her cloak and sat it on the table. I licked sticky fingers and watched as she cooed at it, coaxing it to turn over onto four stumpy little legs. And when it obeyed, I was somewhat surprised to discover that it was a dog.

Possibly. The fey had acquired some Earth animals, perhaps in trade over the centuries, including pigs, chickens and sheep, which made sense as they were useful farm animals and could be eaten. But this . . .

I wasn't sure about this.

It was vaguely dog-like, if very fat and very ugly and of an indeterminate breed. It had a squashed face somewhat like a pug, but an elongated body that was more reminiscent of a dachshund. It had tufts of brownish hair running down the spine, but the rest of it was largely hairless and pink from the distention of the belly, which made what little fur there was rather sparce over the stretched skin.

It looked like it had eaten another dog, perhaps two.

"Er, what seems to be the problem?" I asked, and the old woman switched from beaming pride to slightly tearful distress as she described her pet's troubles to Ray, who was tapping his foot and trying manfully not to roll his eyes at her.

"She says it's lethargic and just lies around all day," he finally informed me. "Imagine that."

"Is that not normal?"

"No. According to her, it's usually running about all over the place. Like lardass could do anything but roll around on the sofa."

"Do the fey have sofas?" I asked, as I had never been inside one of their houses. The closest was the tent that we were currently occupying, which was vaguely house-like, but contained few comforts.

"Not that I know of," Ray said, looking bored.

He and I had been at it for hours today already, as well as for some time yesterday, after our arrival at the faire. And although the plethora of exotic creatures I had been seeing had kept me entertained as well as busy, there had been little for him to do besides crowd control. The fey whose ride we had unwittingly released had been doing that initially, but had gone off somewhere this morning, perhaps to advertise his new business venture. And had paid several ogres to watch over his property in his absence.

That meant us. By fey law, we were his until we earned enough to restore what we had stolen, which would have normally involved back breaking labor for months, or being sold to someone else for the same. But he'd seen what had happened on the road, and so my newfound skill with Faerie's creatures, demonstrated on the crab, was being sold instead.

The dog looked up at me pitifully.

"Does it hurt?" I asked, as I slipped into its mind.

Oh. Make that *her* mind, I thought, reliving a rather steamy session with a much larger creature, possibly another dog, although it appeared to have an otter's tale. I thought it might be a *Dobhar-chú* as they were called on Earth, the aquatic dogs of Faerie that I had seen on a few of the rivers the Wanderers had passed over, and had asked the trolls about. But I couldn't be sure, the night being dark and the woman's pet having been, er, facing the other way.

But she had definitely encountered something, about six weeks ago.

No wonder she was uncomfortable; the puppies she was carrying were huge.

I fed her one of her owner's pancakes and she cheered up. And then had Ray explain the situation to the old woman, whose expression shifted from worried to shocked to outraged in quick succession. Apparently, her baby was considered a purebred.

I gave her some advice about a possible C-section being required in another few weeks and sent her on her way.

She and her precious cargo made it out of the tent, but had to dodge the latest cavalcade coming down the busy road outside. That seemed to be a favorite way of advertising here, where people with something to sell loaded up a gaily dressed wagon and paraded it through the lanes, gaining interest as they went. This one was bigger than most I'd seen, with three trolls on top, one driving and the others blowing horns and pointing at the crude, if brightly colored illustrations painted on homespun sheets, which had been stretched along the sides of the wagon.

They were advertising a fight between a gigantic, hulking creature and a tiny person who did not even come up to the first one's shin. But the little one was feisty and was jumping around in the animated way that fey signs tended to do, pausing occasionally to plunge a sword into the larger one's leg. Blood spurted, the little stick figure, for that was all that either of them were, jumped away to avoid retaliation, and then waved his weapon at the crowd to drum up excitement.

It seemed to be working.

"Does anyone have any meat?" I asked Ray, who didn't answer.

He was eyeing up our nearest babysitter, a bruiser with a broken tusk, a scar across one eye, and a ripped, sagging earlobe. But the creature also had a massive, squat body with the approximate strength of a few bull elephants. And one of the feys' terrible spears.

He had paid no attention to the previous carts, ignoring even the bevy of pretty troll girls in a flower bedecked wagon who had trundled by a few moments ago, hawking some kind of beverage.

They'd paused long enough to give the crowd, including the ogre outside the tent who was taking the money, some free samples out of a large keg. But it seemed that something had finally caught this one's interest, because he went to the tent flap and pushed it aside, eying up the latest cart, which had gotten held up by our queue.

To my surprise, he did not seem upset at the snarl of people clogging the road and disrupting our business, but acted more as if he was excited by it—or by the ad. He said something to the money taker, who huffed out what might have been a laugh and answered back. The two kept talking for a moment while gesturing at the sign, which was unusual as ogres were not loquacious.

But it gave Ray a chance to sidle up next to me.

"You could take him," Ray said softly, nodding slightly at the guard.

"We've discussed this," I reminded him.

I had suggested something similar yesterday, but he'd pointed out that Faerie was difficult enough to manage without an outraged fey and his friends on our tail, wanting payback and alerting everyone to our presence. We were racking up a good profit here; it seemed better to pay off our debt and then maybe get some help making it to an area that Ray was more familiar with. Moving with a group was preferable to taking off on our own, something we could do when no longer a pair of felons.

I had agreed with his reasoning, which was why we were still here. Only he seemed to be rethinking things. "Yeah, but maybe we need to discuss it again. There's bound to be—"

Our babysitter turned and grunted, a low, unhappy sound deep in his chest. He did not like us talking, particularly in a language he didn't know. Ray broke off without attempting to argue, as that rarely worked with ogres, and I sniffed the air.

We had not been given a lunch break, or leave to go find something if we had. But that wasn't necessary as most of our customers had baskets over their arms. People paid the fee outside, but some had realized that an offering to the ever-hungry outworlders meant preferential treatment and less time waiting, and word had spread fast.

And the smells coming off said offerings were heavenly: warm pastries stuffed with spices and drenched in honey; stews and soups with thick pieces of meat and vegetables in spicy broths; mead and ale of all kinds, their aromas fighting with each other on the air; and—yes! There it was! The fatty, meaty goodness of smoked sausage, and one recently on a fire, too.

I hoped it had come from the nearby stall whose offerings had teased me all morning, whenever the wind shifted. Sausage and onions and some sort of garlicky spread was being heaped onto fresh baked bread rolls. The fey version of hot dogs had me salivating, and nothing else would do.

I must have one!

"Someone has a sausage," I told Ray, who glanced up absently, his forehead knitted in thought.

"What?"

"But I want one with the onions and garlic, not plain."

It took him a minute. "Can you stop thinking about your stomach for once?" he demanded, glancing at the ogre.

But he had already forgotten about us with the typical disinterest of the breed, and begun talking to his companion again. He appeared to be wagering on the advertised fight, as there was a good deal of haggling and gesticulating, with more animation than I had thought he was capable of. And then I saw money changing hands.

"Are you listening to me?" Ray demanded. "We have a captive senator—"

"Whom you detest."

"—who is probably languishing in a cell right now, or at a slave auction or worse. He could get sold off to . . . to anybody. To the mines or—"

"What mines?"

"I don't know what mines! But they must have 'em. They have to get all that metal from somewhere."

"And you are concerned for him because?" I asked archly. "The last time you met, you tried to gouge out his eyes."

"They'd have grown back. Eventually."

"Which does not answer my question."

"Two things. First, he's a senator. There's bound to be a reward—"

"You are worried about that now?"

"—and second, he came in here through a portal. He probably plans to go out the same way. We rescue him, we go home, without all the tromping through the countryside and possibly dying stuff—"

"I thought you said that you know where some portals are."

"I do, but if this is the *Turl uh Talat*, then none of them are exactly close, and Faerie ain't a place you want to go meandering around if you got a choice. Especially not now, with a war on and us not knowing exactly who is on what side. If there's a portal nearby, we oughtta try for that one first."

I didn't say anything.

Ray frowned at me some more, as if he knew what I was thinking. Which he probably did. I had not perfected a "poker face" yet, as he kept informing me, much less a poker mind, and he had a talent for picking up my thoughts. Most vampires couldn't, but he was sworn to Dory and thus to me, and it seemed to be part of the bargain.

Sometimes, it was . . . inconvenient.

"Look," he told me now. "I know you're worried about going back. But staying here is not a long-term option. And once we rescue asshole, we can decide what's best to do then, okay? We don't have to go back immediately, but it would be nice to have a portal in our back pocket, right?"

I nodded, trying not to show the almost violent reaction I'd had to the idea of leaving this place. I'd seen so little, and Faerie was so vast! There was so much left to explore.

And this was the closest thing to a real life I had ever known.

But I did not want to put Ray in any more danger. I wanted him back on Earth safe and sound, and this portal might be the best chance of that. As to whether I went with him . . .

I could decide that later.

"We can try, but—" I began, only to have the ogre growl again.

The cavalcade outside had finally passed on, and he had noticed that our line was not moving.

"Next!" Ray called out, but I shook my head. The next in line did not have sausages. "Oh, for— Fine!" he jogged off, only to come back with a small girl child with chestnut curls, a large father who looked to be partly human judging by his barrel chest, and a small lamb. And a sausage with everything.

I beamed at her.

She passed over the sausage, which smelled even better close up, although I could not name the meat. And then her father gave me a small lamb. Its leg was obviously broken.

"Caught . . . in fence," he said, rolling the words, which were in English, around his mouth before he said them, as if they tasted strange. "You fix?"

I nodded. It was an easy repair, but there was a problem. "The heart is weak," I told him. "I think it has a hole in it. I can try to repair it, or . . ." I didn't finish the sentence, as I didn't know if the little girl understood. And her big brown eyes were already filled with tears.

But if they were farmers, there were other solutions. A lamb was usually slaughtered every spring for the rennet in its stomach, needed for making cheese. And a fat spring lamb would not go amiss at the table, either, after a long winter with only dried meat.

The father looked like he agreed, but then he looked down. And saw the sadness on his daughter's face. I did not try to read her thoughts, but they came anyway: she had been there when the creature was born, the first birth she had assisted with; she had helped to pull the little creature from its mother, for it was weak and could not assist in the birthing process as its siblings had done; and she had tenderly nursed it for days afterward after the mother rejected it, and now it was her pet.

I didn't ask anything else. I fixed its condition with the application of a small amount of power, coaxing the little hole to close, and she happily carried it away. And I finally managed to taste what I had been smelling in gusts all morning.

But someone else was hungry, too, and the ogre's small eyes had fixed onto my newest bribe with obvious intent. He said something to Ray, who sighed. "Hand it over," he told me.

"Hand what over?" I asked, knowing full well what he meant, and took another bite.

The ogre growled louder, and raised his spear again, but I was not intimidated. At least not enough to give up my prize. Not all of it.

"Tell him I will share," I offered generously—and futilely, because the ogre was shaking his head even before Ray translated.

I didn't know if he had picked up some English somewhere, or had simply guessed, but as Ray confirmed: he wanted it all.

He could not have it all. My stomach grumbled, the food I had eaten being barely enough to replace the power I had been expending all morning. Healing was tiring, and I was hungry. And I did not think that he would shock me.

Not over a sandwich, at least. Not when it might put me out of business for the rest of the day, fey weapons being what they were. And what kind of money would his master make then?

Of course, I could be wrong, I thought, as he suddenly lunged, spear outstretched ahead of him, and faster than his squat strength would indicate.

"What are you—give him the bloody hot dog!" Ray said, grabbing for it. Or maybe he was trying to pull me away from the spear, which the ogre was using more like a fighting staff that for its intended function, possibly not wanting me to drop his dinner.

Not going to drop it, I thought, ducking and dodging and stuffing it in my face as fast I could, which was pretty darned fast. I had learned a long time ago to eat on the run or in a fight, and this was old hat to me. But not, it seemed, to the ogre, who was getting progressively more upset as his dinner vanished in front of his eyes.

"Give it up!" Ray yelled, as the ogre got tired of the game and fired a blast at me, which missed when I dove for the ground and hit the side of the tent instead.

If it had been leather, it might have simply been scorched, but it was not. And the cheap fabric designed to keep the sun off our heads was no match for a lightning bolt. It went up in flames, and not just the side of the tent, but the top as well when Ray punched the ogre and the latest silver blast went scraggling upward.

Fire rained, people screamed, and Ray grabbed the spear. I don't think he'd planned on that—he looked pretty surprised to find it in his hand—but rather it had been a reflex to stop the flood of lightning. Which it did.

It also left him the target of both ogres' ire.

And one of them had another spear.

But Ray was nothing if not resourceful, and he had no intention of fighting creatures three times as big and far more savage than he was. Instead, he turned the spear's lighting on the tent's central pole, which exploded in a hail of wooden pieces, freaking out his vampire nature. Or perhaps that was the bellow of the older troll, who grabbed for him and succeeded in getting his spear back, but lost us in a sudden stampede of people and animals.

The crowd that had formed the line broke in a tangle of running, panicked bodies, part of which trampled the ogres and headed toward us, only we were no longer there. I realized that Ray had grabbed me only when he sat me down outside one of the nearest tents, which I guessed had been caught in that initial blast as well, as it was burning, too. The crowd caught up a second later, and we took off along with them, running at a breakneck pace while I stared back at our former captors.

They were looking around in frustration and bellowing at the sky, while the tent burned merrily behind them.

"We owe a great deal more money now," I observed.

"Yeah, only they gotta find us first."

Ray grabbed a hat off a nearby stall, whose proprietor was distracted by the chaos, plopped it onto my head and towed me into the thick of the faire.

Chapter Eight

The faire was even more extensive than I had thought, when only seeing part of it from the trail. It was so big, in fact, that the burning cluster of tents behind us soon faded from sight, leaving us in the midst of chaos, but a very pleasant chaos. And one full of food!

The vendors' stalls, drinking tents and entertainment venues were closely packed, with no apparent rhyme nor reason for how they had been laid out. It looked like everyone just set up wherever they liked upon arrival, and latecomers had to squeeze in as best they could. The result was a higgledy-piggledy mess of pens of bleating animals; stalls of vendors selling jewelry, fabric, clothes, furs, spices and dyes; blacksmiths doing repairs on old weapons and hawking new ones; buskers singing, dancing, juggling or telling tall tales; and food and drink purveyors of all types.

I abruptly stopped in front of one of the latter, gaping at the massive amount of meat grilling on an enormous rack over a crackling fire. I could only see the wares intermittently, as billowing clouds of smoke were obscuring the entire booth half of the time and explained why there had been no general uproar at our escape. People probably thought that someone was merely having a bar-b-que.

And someone was, I thought in awe, licking my lips and moving closer to the mesmerizing sight. There were ribs, but not of pork. They were in huge slabs, as if they came from a beast far larger than any pig. Or cow, for that matter, although they looked more like beef ribs, being almost unbelievably meaty and dripping with fat.

They smelled spicy, as if some tantalizing sauce had been spread on them, or maybe a rub. Because they weren't finished yet, although a pile of cooked ones towered nearby, being chopped up by another ogre, although this one was far smaller and more friendly looking than our guards had been. His bald head was covered in sweat, he had a greasy leather apron covering his clothes, and a bright gold earring in one floppy pointed ear. And he was wielding a cleaver no less capably than any trained warrior, slicing through the meat and divvying it up in hearty chunks for hungry faire goers.

But that wasn't all that was on offer. Because the little booth also had coil upon fat, meaty coil of sausages, some bright red with flecks of white, some brown and fragrant with spices, some ghostly pale and filled almost to bursting with what was probably fowl. Like the goose-like creatures on hooks in the back of the tent, many still in their feathers, where a harried looking ogre woman was scalding and plucking them as fast as she could. Others, already denuded, were strung on spits over yet another fire for those who liked their lunch whole.

It was hot, to the point that sweat was rolling down my face to match the ogre's by the time I made it to the front of the queue. And then abruptly remembered that I had no money. The vendor looked at me expectantly, and I looked hungrily back, trying to think how to explain that no, I didn't want any when I was practically drooling.

"One of each," Ray said, coming up alongside. And then I guessed he repeated it in the merchant's cant of the marketplace, because the cleaver started flying once more.

"We have no money," I reminded him in a whisper, in case anyone spoke English.

"Babe, we got all the money," Ray said, and flashed me a view of the moneybag which the guard from our old tent had been filling with coins all morning.

"When did you get that?" I asked, surprised.

"When he was distracted with you. I picked his pocket right before I hit him over the head." He thought for a minute. "I knew you could handle yourself. I woulda been there for you otherwise, even if it meant losing the money."

Considering how much Ray liked money, that was a high compliment. I smiled at him as the ogre handed over a tray full of meat. "You did very well."

He grinned. "Yeah. Let's go have some fun."

And fun was had.

While I wandered after him, eating the largest part of an unknown beast, and then letting a couple of stray dogs lick the remains off the thin wooden slats of the tray, Ray spent lavishly. He bought me a necklace of varicolored beads of amber that were as big as the end of my thumb and reached almost to my waist. I liked the green ones best, which looked like the color of spring leaves in the forest. The light sparkled through them, showing off all the little flecks and glints, like the dappled sunlight on the forest floor.

He also bought me a thigh-length, fuzzy, poncho-type garment in a hue that almost matched the green of the beads. It was light enough to be comfortable on a warm spring day but would also be cozy at night when the temperature dropped. It had a swishy bottom with a fringe, and I kept walking funny to make it shimmer causing Ray to laugh and draw me farther into the crowd.

He added a pair of sturdy trousers and several tunics to my growing wardrobe, along with a bright blue set for himself that almost matched his eyes. He also purchased a sturdy leather backpack for both of us, and finished off by negotiating for some boots. But he made me choose my own pair.

I stood there for a moment in front of the little craftsman's booth staring at a wall of leather. There were so many! And size didn't narrow the selection down as it would have on Earth, as a quick spell would fit any to my feet.

"Take your time," Ray said meaningfully, as he was using our shopping trip to chat with the vendors, trying to find out where in the massive market Marlowe might have been taken.

That wasn't going so well, as all anyone could talk about was the upcoming fights, where the Queen's champion would take on all comers, including someone called The Punisher. From what I understood, the new queen was quite bloodthirsty and her champion even more so, giving the challenger little chance. But that only pushed up the odds, providing an opportunity for real profit should the underdog come out ahead.

It also made everyone even less likely to discuss the fate of a rather battered, ill-tempered, and smelly senator than they might otherwise have been.

Still, I *did* need boots, as the soft soled, slipper-type things that Ray had acquired for me from our companions on the road were inadequate to trekking about the countryside. I appreciated them, nonetheless, as he had traded an afternoon of hard labor around camp for them. But it seemed that they had been meant as a stop gap.

Leaving me staring at a wall of gradated colors, everything from earth to jewel tones and from plain to highly ornamented.

"The red's nice," Ray suggested after a moment, and I obediently reached for them. "Of course, so's the blue. That tooling is well-done. And then there's the brown; it goes with everything, don't you think?"

I shot him a glance; I knew what he was doing. "I like the black," I said, reaching for a pair of plain, serviceable looking items with reinforced toes. I would have preferred steel, but these were not combat boots. Yet they were good, thick leather and would probably—

I paused, my eyes landing on a light gray, suede pair with green embossing up the sides in vine-like swirls.

A closer look showed that only the vines were embossed. The leaves were different shades of green leather that had been inlaid into the surrounding suede and then sewn in such a way as to suggest veins. They were also painted overtop to make them even more life-like.

My forehead wrinkled.

The boots had soft sides that wouldn't protect the calves, slouchy tops that would get caught on everything, and the velvety suede would get dirty quickly. Not to mention the excessive amount of ornamentation, which would only draw attention to us. They were dress up boots, the kinds of things you wore to a festival when you wanted to impress.

They were not practical.

I found myself reaching for them anyway, and running my fingers over the supple leather.

I had never chosen my own clothes before. Not even something as simple as a pair of boots. I wore what Dory wore; my taste was her taste. And her taste would have led me to the sensible black pair. They would wear better, be harder to see at night, and the plain sole would leave few prints behind, and those would tell a tracker little, being difficult to distinguish from everyone else's.

This pair had a design incised into the sole, a ridiculous thing that had no purpose except to leave happy little leaf prints wherever you stepped.

Dory would laugh at the very idea, and rightly so. No one in their right minds would consider them, not in a position like ours. I needed to get the black.

So why did I find myself slipping on the gray instead?

The fey had been right; they fit my feet perfectly, without need for alteration, as if they had been made for me. But unlike the slippers, I could no longer feel the scattered stones under my soles or the cart ridges in the trampled down grass. I switched my weight from foot to foot, and then walked in a little circle, and they were easily the most comfortable boots I had ever worn.

"They look good," Ray said mildly, and they did.

They matched the gray of the trousers he had bought me and the green of the poncho. And they had a faintly piratical air about them that made me smile. They were not practical, but they were pretty. And not as slouchy as I had thought, now that I had them on.

"We're running low on cash, and what's left we need for supplies," he added. "You gotta choose one."

"The gray," I said, before I thought. And the next moment, we were walking away from the booth with the sensible black pair still hanging on the wall.

I looked at them over my shoulder in confusion. What was happening to me? I should go back, should say that I'd made a mistake.

I did not go back. And, suddenly, my feet felt good and so did I. I laughed, and Ray looked at me in slight shock.

"Do provisions include candy?" I asked, and grabbed his hand, towing him toward a cluster of booths devoted to rotting the teeth of all races.

I ate some more, until I was finally, completely full, something that was rare in my experience. Including taffy from a light fey seller whose family was enthusiastically pulling it using metal loops set into the wooden back of their booth. It changed colors as they stretched it, from yellow to pale pink to shocking scarlet, and tasted like it changed flavors in my mouth as I chewed.

I next had a bunch of heavily sauced, fried cheese on a stick, some fish jerky dusted with a spicy coating that crunched like potato chips under my teeth, and a highly spiced soup. I wasn't sure whether the latter was supposed to be savory or sweet, as it had elements of both, but it burned on my tongue like fire. So, I also acquired a cool drink with many bubbles that floated up out of the glass and exploded in the air in front of me.

It made me giggle, and the bubbles seemed to giggle, too, as if echoing my sounds. It soon had the fringe on my poncho shimmering, by accident this time, as I wove erratically through the crowd. Until Ray took the rest of it away and belted it back.

And then cursed loudly. "What the hell was *that*?"

Many little bubbles echoed the question as they popped all around us, but I barely noticed. Because I had just noticed something else. Something that made me wonder exactly how strong the feys' brew had been, since I must be seeing things.

But no. I ran unsteadily over to a cauldron that a bunch of small creatures with wings were stirring through the use of a spell, since none of their tiny hands could have made it all the way around the large-handled stick being used as a mixer. It was nonetheless moving inside of the brew, pushing aside a bunch of flowers that were bobbing about, more of which were laid out on the long wooden table alongside.

And all of which appeared to be trying to gut me.

They were thick like succulents, shockingly yellow, and had long, pointed petals that lunged at anyone that came near. They resembled nothing so much as some fell creature's paw, opening and closing and suddenly attacking, with the hard pointed bits on the ends of the petals serving as the creature's claws. That was reflected in the name—Dragon's Claw—which I knew as I had seen these before.

"Oh, shit," Ray said, coming up alongside me.

"Oh shit, oh shit, oh shit," the little bubbles echoed happily.

"What the devil are those doing here?" he demanded, but I had no answer for him.

Until I realized: they were being boiled down and the juice was being made into candy. Honey and spices had been added to the pot, judging by the smaller containers littered around the table, where more of the outraged, claw-like flowers were stabbing at everyone in sight. The ones in the cauldron were acting similarly, causing the whole brew to froth angrily, and a little of it to spill over the side and run gloopily down the pot until it dripped onto the road.

And onto a small, pale purple flower growing by the wayside.

It had somehow avoided the crush of boots and wheels of wagons, and even the heat from the fire under the cauldron hadn't phased it. It bloomed on, small, inoffensive, and beautiful. Like the flowers the troll girl had woven into her braids.

Right up until the mixture from the pot fell onto it, that was.

The orange goop, which had been color changed due to the spices, must have been hot, as it had just been boiling and I could still see steam rising off of it. But the flower was not burned. It was, however, changed, and changed by a lot.

I grabbed Ray's arm and jerked him back.

"What the—" He looked down in consternation as the small flower lunged at his boot. And when it failed to reach it, as he was well out of the way, it picked up its tiny, white roots like an old-fashioned woman gathering up her skirts, pulled them out of the soil, and—

"Don't step on it," I said, as Ray proceeded to do exactly that, whilst also dancing about and screeching.

I didn't blame him. He reminded me of the giant on the cavalcade's sign, vying with a much smaller opponent. One that had just gotten a thorn into him and yanked it back out, along with a gout of blood. Ray cursed and tried to stomp the little thing, but it was faster and, when he attempted to kick it instead, it latched onto one of his new boots with a thorny embrace and appeared to be trying to rip through it.

Judging by Ray's squawking, it was succeeding.

The small creatures—pixies, at a guess—who were stirring the pot looked up in annoyance. And then noticed that Ray's antics had begun drawing a crowd. At which point one of them decided to help the now vicious flower and sent a small stream of magic at it; I could taste it on the breeze as it passed by me but couldn't stop it.

It hit the little bit of flora full on and, oh, the difference that made!

Ray suddenly found himself battling, not a small roadside weed, but a three-foot tall woody specimen with a head of wild purple blossoms, a dozen arms each capped by a familiar-looking claw, and a forest of pale roots sprawling over the ground and moving so fast that I couldn't be sure of the count.

"Auggghhh!" he yelled, as I dropped our purchases and leapt for the crazed sort-of tree.

I landed on its back, judging by the fact that it was facing off with Ray on the other side, although it was hard to tell as I received a bunch of blossoms in the face. They smelled divine, so much so that they almost became another defense, distracting me in a cloud of lush perfume for a second. Until Ray screamed again.

And this time, it was a high pitched, panicked note that I had seldom heard from him, and it sounded terrified.

And then flowers were falling everywhere, limbs were cracking and leaves were raining down on the people who were pushing back from the melee that I was not at all sure that we were winning. Which made no sense, as Dragon's Claw merely transferred attributes from one creature to another. Meaning that the little weed now had some of the abilities of the Dragon's Claw itself, and of the pixie who had helped to enchant it.

And that was trumping a master vampire and a dhampir?

I snarled and upped the ante, but the creature was regrowing limbs before I could finish severing the things. Probably because all of the pixies were now in on it, I realized, shooting little bursts of magic our way, wanting to keep the fight, which had drawn quite a crowd, going as long as possible. For they were suddenly selling massive quantities of their brew, which they had cooked down into little pastilles and stuffed into homespun bags.

And for what? I thought, as a thorn bedecked limb wrapped around me, and squeezed like a vise. What insanity was this, to sell such a concoction in an area devoted to candy?

But it did not appear to be affecting the local fey nearly so much. I saw a child munch on a pastille, and then grip her friend's hand and push a pug nose out of her face that looked just like his. The two of them laughed and pointed, while his hair took on the ashen quality of hers in streaks among his natural black.

The effect was muted, then, unless aided by an outside force, which was definitely the case here. The former weed was resisting all my efforts to break its hold; if anything, it got tighter, as if it would like to see what color sap I had. I was already covered in its pale white version, and then in red before I finally broke the stranglehold that had now reached my neck and beat the thing with one of its own, still-flailing limbs.

And then beat the pixies with it as well, since the nasty, vicious things were the cause of our distress. They did not seem to like that, and while some scattered to the winds, small wings whirring, others chose to dive bomb us in between the mad thrashing we were still receiving from the weed. Which was now more like six feet tall!

But it suddenly went up in flames, why I didn't know unless Ray had gotten a piece of the pot's firewood onto it. I couldn't tell as the former weed began even more wild thrashing, and then abruptly made a beeline for the forest, clearing a path through the spectators as it did so. And I took the chance to send the pixies tumbling into each other and rocketing out of sight as I laid about with two of the creature's still-thrashing limbs.

Finally, they were gone, including the ones at the vendor's table, who had scarpered for less dangerous parts along with their bags of coins. Leaving me panting and heaving, with my pretty new outfit in tatters and the pixies' spell light still buzzing over my skin. But I was okay, if bloody and alarmingly sap covered, and so was Ray, who was lying on the ground and staring up at me in alarm.

"It's okay," I told him, tossing away a thorny limb and reaching out a hand.

"It's not okay," he said, sounding strangled, and shifted his gaze to something behind me.

Something I saw as I turned, but only for an instant.

No, I agreed as I sank to the ground alongside him, after a bolt of far more powerful magic hit me square in the chest.

Probably not okay now.

Chapter Nine
Dory

"You're late." Tanet sounded annoyed as we approached the table.

"Had to climb the stairs," Claire said carelessly. "I'd forgotten how many there were. You remember Dory, and this is Louis-Cesare."

Tanet did not so much as spare us a glance. "You might have given them a lift," he pointed out, all but glaring at his sister.

"I've spent enough time scaley today—"

"Not nearly enough!" he said, and his hand hit the table.

The item in question was a slab of black granite, glittering under the few lamps that swung on chains here and there, and looking like the same stuff that made up this part of the mountain. In fact, it appeared to be still attached where it had grown, with the stone of the dining chamber having simply been carved away from it. Yet he managed to rattle the golden plates and goblets it held anyway, causing one of the latter to tip over.

Claire righted the goblet and ignored her brother's outburst. "Sit down. He won't tell you to," she said to me. Louis-Cesare and I obediently sat, me beside her on her brother's left, and my partner on the only other pillow available, across the table by Tamris, who shot him a shy smile.

I took the few moments while we got situated to reevaluate Tanet. He had changed a bit since we'd first met, while he was on a visit to New York. He'd been thin and gangly then, with his muscles not matching his considerable height or the occasional flash of fire in his eyes. His hair had likewise been short and red, and of a hue not naturally found on Earth, and sticking up in tufts. As if he spent more time in dragon form than in human and wasn't quite sure what to do with it.

That . . . was no longer the case.

He was reclining at one end of the table in a rich burgundy velvet robe with scattered, silver spangles that showed off a well-muscled chest. His hair was now shoulder length and gleamed in loose waves, and he had grown into his features as well, which were lean and hawk-like in human guise. The impression was heightened by the fact that he was eating something which I strongly suspected had been alive until a moment ago, as it had stained his lips a brilliant scarlet.

He looked like an ancient Roman senator who had been drinking too much wine, rather than a teenager who had spent his afternoon annoying his sister. And it wasn't just the outward appearance that had changed. I remembered him as inquisitive and coltish, getting into anything and everything, and then laughing his way out when it landed him in trouble. He'd had an easy sort of charm, youthful, a little bumbling, and yet endearing.

Even Claire's fey bodyguards had liked him, and they didn't like anyone.

But when he met my eyes now, it took actual effort not to look away. I made the effort, holding his gaze long enough to avoid a charge of cravenness, but not long enough to be considered a challenge. I hoped.

I let my lips curve into a smile instead. "You've had a glow up," I told him frankly, and saw him blink.

For a second, he was that boy again, with a faint blush staining his cheeks and a grin splitting his lips. And then he remembered his dignity and frowned, ignoring the hand I had extended. "We don't do that here," he told me bluntly.

"Oh? What do you do?"

He frowned some more, perhaps realizing that he'd trapped himself, and was now going to have to be either breathtakingly rude or greet me properly. But after a brief hesitation, he manned up, reached over to put a hand behind my head, and briefly touched our foreheads together. And since he'd decided to be hospitable, he did the same for Louis-Cesare.

Claire, however, declined, looking around for somebody to fill her goblet. "You already greeted me, remember?" she asked.

"People are watching," Tanet told her quietly. "They'll think we're feuding."

"Aren't we? I still have claw marks on my back."

"You do not! I was careful—"

"Is that what you call it? Because I'd hate to see the results if you weren't."

"Yes, you would," he agreed. "Now, greet me."

He reached for her again, but she pretended she didn't notice and held out her goblet for the servants who had just fluttered in.

There were three of them, which seemed excessive as we already had two, one positioned on either side of the oblong opening onto the carnage. But the latest arrivals had brought food, platter after platter of it, which they artfully arranged on the slab of granite. They got in the way of the guy with the pitcher, who was trying to forge a path through to Claire's empty glass, but he finally managed it.

He filled it with some delicious smelling wine, then moved on to Louis-Cesare and I. Claire tasted the offering, smiled, and finally gave Tanet his greeting. Which did not seem to mollify him much.

"I'm sorry my sister has such poor manners," he told us, as if he hadn't had to be strong armed into playing host. But he leaned into it now, perhaps to show Claire up, and dutifully enquired about our day and how we were finding our accommodations.

I let Louis-Cesare answer him, and wax lyrical about how beautiful we found his realm. He was better at that sort of thing than me—most people were better at that than me—although at least I had managed not to embarrass myself. And they said diplomacy couldn't be taught!

My family history proved otherwise. My father had been known as Mircea the Bold once, a nickname he'd earned by being far more likely to stick a sword in your eye than to offer you pretty speeches. Yet he was now the consul's chief diplomat and famous for his charm.

Maybe there was hope for me yet.

"They're putting on a show tonight," Tanet said dryly, as the two servants by the door suddenly leapt toward the center of the opening, to keep some tasty morsel from splatting in the middle of our table.

The slaughter was ramping up outside, as more and more diners decided to take to the air. It was making the "chefs'" job that much harder, as there wasn't much free space to fling anything into anymore, and ensured that each course that did make it was set upon by a number of hungry guests. That, of course, caused fights, and ended with a good deal of the meal getting tossed about.

I didn't see what they'd accidentally sent our way, as the servants had already thrown it back, which was fine with me.

"This isn't normal?" I asked Tanet calmly.

"No, it's to show off—to you and about you." He shot me a look over some tiny, scrabbling feet.

His dinner seemed to consist of a mass of struggling small creatures that looked like dormice and were trying to climb out of the slick, high sided bowl they'd been served in. One of the tiny, furry faces had surmounted what I assumed was a hill of his brothers and was twitching miniature whispers at me over the rim. I drank some wine, a rich, fruity red, and glanced at Claire, wondering how she was holding up.

Not well, as it happened. That wasn't surprising, considering that she was that most impossible of impossible things: a vegan dragon. Or she was trying to be, having ordered up a bounty of greenery for the table which Tamris was regarding in confusion. But Claire's alter ego had other ideas, and I saw the struggle on her face.

Literally saw it, as her usually smooth cheeks kept flushing with more than color. Faint scales bloomed and shifted across her pale skin—pewter with an iridescent lavender tint—making her look as if a strange spotlight was strobing her. But there was no light; it was her inner turmoil writ large, and everybody just ignored it.

"About us?" Louis-Cesare asked, after a moment.

"Father is trying to use your presence here to shore up support for the alliance with your senate," Tanet elaborated, digging through his bowl. "He's banking on everybody assuming that we're so important to your plans that a pair of senators were sent on a diplomatic mission."

"And you don't approve?" I guessed, although I didn't need to. He wasn't exactly subtle.

He scowled, the latest struggling sacrifice in hand. "I've been to your world. Your senate could give a shit about us, except for how many of us are willing to die fighting your war—"

"It isn't their war. It belongs to all of us," Claire began.

"—and neither do you. You're not here for us; you're here for your sister. And have somehow persuaded mine to help you out."

"She didn't persuade me of anything," Claire said hotly, but Tanet only scowled and ate his latest victim, washing it down with wine.

It mingled with the blood on his chin from his supper, but he wiped it away carelessly with one velvet sleeve. Tamris quickly refilled his cup, without waiting for it to be empty or for a servant to do it. Judging from the way she was gazing at him, it was clear that she was either besotted or planning to be the next lady of the manor.

Or both.

I didn't give much for her chances, as Tanet barely seemed to register her presence. He paid more attention to the servants who occasionally flew by offering struggling delicacies than to the pretty girl in the starry dress. Which I suspected she had worn just for him, as she kept arranging and rearranging it to best effect.

I felt sorry for her, but worse for us. What was supposed to be a quick in and out for a few guides was turning into a more fraught situation than I had expected. I wondered why Claire hadn't warned us.

Maybe because we needed her family's help and this was the only way to get it, I thought wryly. And it was just as well, as Louis-Cesare wouldn't have come had anyone mentioned possible danger to me. He was getting better about his natural overprotectiveness, but that was on Earth.

This would have been a step too far.

But he was realizing the problem now.

"You sound as if you agree with those who attacked us earlier," he said to Tanet, deceptively mildly.

It wasn't mild enough as Tanet's eyes flashed red for a moment, before calming back down to their usual brown. "They didn't attack you, or you wouldn't be here. One of them touched you—a display of bravado that ended up getting a guard killed. You haven't been here a day and already people are dying."

"And you're afraid that more will follow," I said, because clearly.

"Shouldn't I be?"

"Tanet," Claire began, but he ignored her.

"If you want to get yourself killed, be my guest," he told me. "But leave my family—including my sister—out of it."

"You don't speak for me!" Claire said.

"Perhaps not, but someone needs to. And I don't see that harebrained light fey prince you married around anywhere—"

"You know why!"

"Yes, I do. Do you?" he asked archly but didn't give her a chance to reply. "Go home," he told me. "While you still can. You may be a fearsome vampire senate leader back on Earth, but here?" He deliberately ate another struggling rodent in front of me, taking his time, letting me watch the little legs go limp as he bit down and then slurped up the tiny tail. And grinned at me through red-stained teeth. "You're just dinner."

"Stop trying to scare her!" Claire said, furiously. "You know she'll never find Dorina alone—"

"She'll never find her at all. Her information on the woman's last location is weeks old."

"So, we shouldn't even try?"

"Not if living is something you'd like to continue to enjoy," he said darkly.

"I haven't been enjoying it much lately."

"More than you would on the border of Nimue's old lands. Things have descended into chaos over there since her death. Everyone's trying to snatch a piece of the pie before her people appoint another monarch, and until they do, the borders change daily—"

"That doesn't mean—"

"—not to mention that the dark fey court has a disputed succession right now, ever since their king was kidnapped by the Svarestri. At least, that's the rumor; nobody really knows what happened to the old bastard—"

"Aren't you dark fey?" Louis-Cesare asked, trying to keep up, and received a purely vicious look in return.

"We are Dragonkind!" Tanet snarled. "We don't mix with mongrel scum—"

"You liked those 'mongrel scum' well enough when visiting me," Claire said pertly, helping herself to salad. "Olga took you to work so her partner could give you a haircut, remember? And Sven taught you how to play troll chess—"

"I didn't mean them—"

"Who then? The ogres? Because you enjoyed their stew when we visited the enclave, to the point of saying that you'd dreamed about it later, and you played ball with their children. Or maybe you meant the duergars, who fixed your belt for you, and whose skill you highly praised. Or the brownies—"

"I wasn't speaking of the ones who fled to Earth!" Tanet said. "You won't be dealing with them! It's the bastards who are still here that you have to worry about, and you do have to worry."

"Why?" Louis-Cesare said sharply. "What would the dark fey want with us?"

"Nothing!" Tanet said, looking exasperated. "But you're walking into a hell of a mess. The Svarestri took the dark fey king to exploit the rifts in their society, and ensure that they'd end up in a civil war and not be able to spare troops for the greater conflict. And they got exactly what they wanted. Fighting hasn't broken out yet, but it's only a matter of time. You could easily find yourself venturing into a war zone inside of a war zone, looking for someone who's probably already—"

He cut off, but he didn't need to finish the sentence.

We all knew what he meant.

I'd helped myself to something that looked like a spinach quiche but probably wasn't, and had been trying to decide between a salad or some unknown fruit as a side dish, in an attempt to stimulate my appetite. But at that I put my utensils down. I couldn't eat right now, not with anxiety clawing at my insides as efficiently as any dragon.

"Let's change the subject," Claire said, shooting me a glance. And then shied back from a fine spray of blood from the feast taking place in the air outside our little nook.

Her father's expansive dining room was next to ours, visible because of the curve in the wall, and because it took up a third of the space on this level, which seemed to be the most prestigious in the hall. So, I supposed it made sense that the show was being concentrated here. But the screaming, clawing and ripping sounds were less than appetizing, and were only somewhat muffled by the surrounding stone. Along with the roars of the crowd as someone stole someone else's dinner and started a chase around the great space with it.

Pigs literally flew, being carried in massive claws and thrown from diner to diner in an epic game of keep away. Their terrified squeals combined with flowing rivers of varied colored scales, claws and gleaming teeth; with wildly whipping tails and ear-piercing shrieks; with skewing firelight from an ornate lamp on a chain swinging outside of our cave that had been brushed by the battle and was now sending weird shadows dancing over us; and with the pervasive smells of blood and viscera and worse. The combination would have put me off any lingering idea of food if I wasn't already there, and if everything hadn't just been hazed by a mist of red.

I glanced at Louis-Cesare, who was leaning back against his cushion, drinking wine and watching the show. If he was bothered by it, he gave no outward sign. I accepted a refill from a servant and tried to appear equally unruffled.

Tanet, on the other hand, barely seemed to register it, as he must have seen similar displays many times. Instead, he was watching his sister. I expected him to push the go-home narrative some more, but he surprised me, agreeing with her desire for a new topic of conversation.

Only she didn't like this one any better.

"You might enjoy yourself more if you let loose a little." He nodded at her plate, which she'd somehow kept free from the sauce of battle. "Eat the food—not the food's food—"

"I'll eat what I like and go where I choose!" Claire said hotly.

"But you don't like it." He leaned over the table, suddenly enough that it could almost be called a lunge. "You hate every mouthful, or part of you does. Stop eating slop and risking your neck for off-worlders and come be with us. Really *be* with us for once and learn who you truly are. Or are you afraid you might enjoy it?"

"I know who I am," Claire snapped, and aggressively ate lettuce at him.

He sighed and leaned back on one elbow, before deliberately tipping over the bowl with the remaining dormice, allowing them to scatter everywhere.

I reared back slightly, as did Louis-Cesare. Which was a normal enough reaction when a bunch of rodents scarpers at you across a dining table. But Claire . . . did not.

I saw her nose twitch and her eyes flood purple. And the next moment, a dormouse was hanging out of her mouth, its tiny, startled face looking out from between her suddenly sharper than usual teeth. Everyone froze.

That included Claire, who just sat there, her eyes huge and flooding back to their normal green, while the tiny, furry creature started struggling desperately. And then fell to the table and bolted off when Claire abruptly released it. She got up before anyone could say anything and ran off herself, heading for the doorway to the stairs, and I followed with Tanet's voice echoing behind us.

"You can't run forever, Claire. Come back. Come back and join us!"

Chapter Ten

Claire did not go back, nor did she go down. But rather upward, following the stairs on a winding course past numerous rooms filled with rowdy diners, pushing past half transformed servants, and slipping on bloody footprints—both clawed and humanoid.

Until she erupted out of the last stairwell onto the ramparts at the very top of the tower, which were looking out over a magnificent sunset.

I followed, my steps unconsciously slowing because of the view. It made me grateful for my short hair, which mostly stayed out of my eyes despite the wind. Claire's, on the other hand, was blowing like a banner and had turned a brilliant, flame red in the light of the sun's impressive finale.

It was beautiful and she was beautiful, and raw and dangerous and different in this strange new place. I suddenly understood what Tanet had seen below, and why he had buzzed us earlier, to force her to show who she was inside. She hadn't changed, but she may as well have done. Tonight, the human part of her was a thin veneer over something far wilder and more primal.

But I said none of what I was thinking. I somehow doubted that Claire, who had yet to come to terms with her other half, would appreciate it. And considering that I was still figuring out how to deal with my own alter ego after five hundred years, I could hardly fault her.

I rested my forearms on the stone instead, which wasn't like the weather worn stuff everywhere else. This looked as if it had faced a great assault at some point, one that had probably involved dragon fire as it had a melted, lava-like appearance. Burnt and discolored, it dripped down the mellow, golden hued stone like the wax on top of a candle.

We stood there for a while, but nobody joined us. I hadn't expected Tanet to do so, as he'd said his piece and was smart enough to know that you didn't have to plant a seed twice. But Louis-Cesare surprised me. He wasn't the type to let me out of his sight in a place like this, not that we had been in any places like this.

Yet he also didn't come.

Perhaps he suspected that Claire needed a moment. I thought the same and didn't press. We just stood there, watching silently as the sun edged closer and closer to the horizon, deepening the purple hues in the valley below and lending the clouds pink and lavender underbellies that inevitably made me think of my friend's other half.

She must have been thinking about it, too, because when she glanced at me, her eyes were wet. "I'm sorry," she said, blinking. "I . . . didn't mean for you to see that."

"See what?" I asked, assuming that she was talking about the tears. "You have every right to be upset. Your brother was being a dick."

"No—or rather, yes, he doesn't approve of basically any life choices I've made. But that wasn't what . . . I mean, I didn't want you to see . . . you know . . ."

"I know . . . what?" I asked.

"You know! The thing."

"There were a lot of things," I said, thinking about the strangest dinner I'd never had a chance to eat. And doubted that I would.

I wondered if they had room service, and what the menu would look like if they did.

"Stop it, Dory!" Claire said, frowning. "You know what I'm talking about. The . . . rodent."

The last word was said in a whisper, although I didn't know why. She'd let it go, after all. "What about it?"

"What about—" she broke off. And then she just stood there, glaring at me. "I almost ate it!"

"Yes?"

"What do you mean yes? Aren't you concerned about that?"

Judging by her tone, I was supposed to answer in the affirmative. But I still didn't get it. Of all the things to be worried about today, a furry appetizer was pretty far down on my list.

"I eat steak, Claire," I pointed out. "Rare."

"But not alive!"

"And my father's family regularly dine on blood—the human kind. I don't think I have a right to judge."

"I wasn't talking about you judging me! I know better than to think that."

"Then what?"

She turned away and stared out over the mountains some more. "I am in control," she said after a moment, with an undercurrent of savagery in her voice. "*I* am. Not whatever . . . not my other half. Alright?"

"Okay," I said, which was apparently also the wrong answer, because she whirled on me. It was a shock, but not because of the temper on her face—Claire was kind of known for her temper. But because that motion hadn't been normal.

Some of the few perks to my condition were excellent reflexes and senses as sharp as a vamp's. I was supposed to see everything, yet I hadn't seen her move. Hadn't tracked it with my eyes, felt the rush of air as she moved, or heard a change in her breathing. Yet suddenly she was there, all of half of an inch away, her eyes full-on purple with yellow flames in the centers, and her breath hot, hot, hot on my face.

I instinctively moved back, putting some distance between us. Maybe more than I'd planned, because she stopped and just stared at me, as wide eyed and frozen as she had been in the dining hall. Before suddenly crumpling to the ground and beginning to sob.

For a moment, I just looked at her, nonplussed, and then went down onto my haunches and awkwardly hugged her. I wasn't a hugger and Claire knew it, which was probably why it worked. She looked up at me out of tear-flooded green eyes and a flushed face caught between pain and anger.

"Oh, stop it, Dory! I know how you hate that sort of thing!"

"I don't hate it," I said, sitting beside her to put our faces on a level, and brushing back a lock of that glorious hair. "And you looked like you needed it."

"I need a lot of things," she said, suddenly vicious. "Mostly, I need to get out of here!"

"Then why don't we? We came for guides. Let's get them and go."

Claire's impatience ramped up a notch. "You know it's not that simple!"

"Do I?"

"You heard Tanet!"

"And your father needs to show us off that badly?" I asked, troubled.

Claire shot me a glance, as if she'd heard the slight change in my tone. But she didn't lie to me. "Frankly, yes. Few people at court are happy about this alliance."

"Enough to attack us before we barely set foot in the place?"

She sighed and leaned back against the stone, her shoulders slumping. But she shook her head. "No. Tanet was likely right about that—it was bravado that got out of control. Antem, the one who touched you, has a mother from Vitharr, a rival clan who is rumored to have joined the other side in the war. He probably wasn't happy about us coming here."

"You're the chieftain's daughter," I pointed out. "Who cares whether he's happy?"

"It's not just him." Claire's hands knotted in her lap. "I don't belong here and everyone knows it. I couldn't stick out more if I tried. Dragonkind don't normally travel far from their mountains, so my father's interest in other lands, foreign cultures . . . it's always been viewed with suspicion and distaste. And then to have him bring back a half human daughter—"

"He's lucky to have you!"

Claire shook her head. "A normal child, yes. That's always a happy day for a people who welcome so few children. But in my case—"

"Then they're stupid—"

"Are they?" Claire shot me a glance. "Think about it from their point of view. Father's half alien bastard comes bringing war to their doorstep—"

"That's not what you're doing!"

"But it is, from a certain point of view. I'm asking for help and giving it could be regarded as choosing sides. Something they don't want to do, that many of them have carefully avoided doing, up until now. But by hosting us they are tacitly giving support to the alliance even if they don't agree with it. They see our coming as making them a target, and father as forcing their hand.

"Which, frankly, he is. He could have helped us quietly, without all the fanfare, but—"

"Why lose an opportunity?"

She nodded.

Our fathers seemed to have a lot in common, I thought wryly.

"Then should we just go?" I asked. "With or without guides?"

Claire sighed again. "It's too late for that. By coming here, we inserted ourselves into the middle of the argument raging among the clans about the war, and there's no getting out of it now. Father thinks they're being naive, that staying neutral doesn't work in times like these, and that eventually, they'd be drawn into the conflict anyway. But others don't agree and everyone is tense as hell—"

"And then we show up."

She nodded. "It's my fault. I shouldn't have brought us here. But I didn't fully realize the problem until I talked to him after we arrived—"

So that's where they'd been while Louis-Cesare and I were being attacked in our room. I wondered if someone had noticed and taken advantage of that. Or if it really had been just a silly display of bravado.

It didn't reassure me that I had no way to know.

"—and we have a lot of ground to cover," Claire added, "and most of the people who could help us are . . . elsewhere . . ."

She didn't finish the statement, but I knew she was talking about Heidar, her husband and a prince of the Blarestri, a leading light fey house that were currently making a bid to rule a lot more than their ancestral holdings. War had given Caedmon, Heidar's father, a chance to greatly increase his territory, and Heidar was helping him by some espionage that I wasn't very clear on. But the point from Claire's perspective was that he had chosen his father's desires over hers and wasn't around when she needed him, something that had been true for most of their married life.

"I don't know what I'm doing here, Dory!" she said suddenly, passionately. "I don't know what I'm doing anywhere. It's just like at the Blarestri court, everyone side eyeing me all the time, waiting for the monster to emerge. While here it's the monster they're looking for! They take me for weak, and maybe I am—"

"You're not weak," I said flatly. "You're the least weak person I know."

She laughed suddenly, and it was bitter. "You can say that. You who never had a moment of weakness in your life!"

I blinked at her for a moment, wondering how things could look so different to other people—and how wrong.

"I was never the strong one," I finally said. "That was Dorina. And now she's gone."

Claire looked up at me, and her face changed, because she was nothing if not kind and realized that she'd wounded me. But she didn't seem to agree. "That's ridiculous!"

"It isn't though," I said. Because it was something I'd had plenty of time to face up to, in the last month or so. "I tried to tell myself otherwise, to tell Louis-Cesare otherwise, ever since Dorina disappeared. I was still dhampir, still had my expensive toys, still had hundreds of years of experience—"

"Which you do!"

"Yes, but this place," I paused and looked around, although all I could see from our current position was melted stone, since the ramparts blocked the view. But I didn't need it. That vista was the kind of thing that stayed with you, possibly forever.

Faerie had that effect.

It had another one, too.

"I'm on the senate," I finally said, "but I'm not strong enough to do most of the jobs they have open. And the more diplomatic ones, the ones they keep assigning me because of father's reputation . . . well, I'm trying. But they're not exactly my forte, either, and anyway, no one respects a dhampir—"

"Well, they should!" Claire said, her tears drying on her cheeks. Because nothing rallied my best friend like someone else hurting. Especially me.

I didn't know what I'd done to deserve her.

"But they don't," I said gently. "And now I'm here, and every day just reminds me how . . . inadequate . . . I am. I've spent my life running down revenants, dragging back low tier threats to the senate, and taking freelance jobs for losers who forget to pay me half the time—and who don't even call these days because you can't forget to pay a senator! I don't know who I am anymore, and without Dorina—"

"We'll find her," Claire said, and it wasn't a question. There was a thread of steel running through her voice, and it scared me. It scared me a lot.

"Maybe we shouldn't," I said, voicing the thought I'd been pushing away for weeks.

"What?" Claire stared at me, caught off guard, and her fingers tightened on my arms.

"I don't want to lose you, too," I said roughly. "Or Louis-Cesare or any of the bastards crazy enough to sign on to this . . . this . . . this shot in the dark or whatever it is! I don't want to be the cause of your deaths—"

"You won't be. That's absurd—"

"Is it? Tanet seems to think otherwise." Claire tried to interrupt, but I talked over her. "And he knows this place, Claire. He's lived here all his life. What if he's right? What if she's already dead, and all I'm doing is dragging the rest of the people I care about into danger? I don't know what I'm doing, and without Dorina, I can't protect you. I'm not even sure I can protect myself anymore and—"

"Dory!" Claire's usually soft tones suddenly cracked like a whip. It was so unusual that it actually shut me up, something I was extremely grateful for. I hadn't expected every insecurity I had to come tumbling out like that, and especially not to her. I had come up here to comfort her, and what the hell was I doing instead?

I must have spoken that last part aloud, because she suddenly hugged me. Claire was a hugger, and a good one, and for a long moment, it felt like she would never let me go. But she did, and when she sat back, her face was still tear streaked, but also calm and resolute.

It seemed like I'd done what I came up here for, although not in the way I'd planned.

"We *will* find her," she told me staunchly. "I don't give a damn what anyone thinks, including my brother! My father has offered assistance, and no one at court is going to go against his decision."

"Even so, you just said his people don't venture far from their mountains. Will they even know how to track her, or who to ask—"

"*I'll* know," Claire said smiling, but there was an edge to it. "I have a foot in both camps, whether I like it or not: Blarestri princess and monster's daughter. Between the two, everyone will want to cultivate me or fear me too much to say no. Father's people are just coming for security."

I laughed; I couldn't help it. "So, you're going to intimidate the whole of Faerie into turning her over!"

"Why not? My position never helped me before, so it's about time. It's about time for a lot of things," she added, her expression darkening.

I wisely didn't ask. "So, what do we do now?"

"We go back down to dinner and wait for father's announcement. He's going to ask for volunteers, and he'll get them. He wouldn't risk it otherwise—"

"He's already talked to them then."

She nodded. "Probably. Or he knows them well enough that he doesn't have to. And this way, no one can say anything, since dragons do what they want. He isn't forcing anybody to take part; he's merely asking for help for his daughter."

I frowned. "But how does that help him, if he's trying to use our presence here to drum up support for the war?"

She shrugged. "I don't know exactly, but I'm not a three thousand year old master manipulator, either. Father has been handling the clans for most of his life, as he inherited the position young. And Eddred wasn't the leading clan then; we weren't even in the top five. But he made it happen, and he's held onto it, mostly because of the respect the other clans have for his judgment. So, I trust him . . ." she grimaced. "Mostly."

And that was as good as we were going to get, I thought.

"Well, I *am* still hungry," I said, after a moment.

"For rodents?" she asked dryly.

"No, but I'll take some of that salad, if you have any that hasn't been—"

I stopped talking, because Claire was no longer listening. She was on her feet, in another of those too-fast-to-track movements, staring out into the gathering twilight. I didn't notice anything when I rose back to my feet, but the same was obviously not true for her. She was stiff as a board, all except for her right hand, which was crumbling the molten rock as if it was used charcoal.

"Claire?" I said, my eyes scanning the huge space, but still seeing nothing. "What is it?"

"Vitharr, coming in force. And coming fast."

Chapter Eleven

The steep stone staircase was even more crazy when we reentered it, with a blaring siren and an orange tint flashing on the walls, although I saw no source for it. Some kind of ward, I assumed, but couldn't ask as I couldn't hear myself think over the alarm, the cries of panic from running servants, and the screaming invective being thrown at a massive dragon that had parked its blue-gray behind in the middle of the stairs. And had completely blocked the way down in the process.

I didn't think that was deliberate; the poor thing seemed terrified, with its huge, clawed hands clamped over its head, and only the great snout sticking out. It was also trembling, sending massive, blue-tinged wings sliding along the walls, cutting gouges in the stone and bringing little tricklings of rock down on our heads. And howling, although I couldn't hear it over all the rest.

But I could see its distress ruffling the skin around the great mouth, and flooding the one huge, yellow eye that was visible between all the scales with panic. Invective or no, the creature wasn't likely to budge, or to stop blocking our way. We could be here forever, I thought, having no idea how to budge a dragon.

Luckily, somebody else did. A second later, an equally large dragon, pewter and lavender and very familiar, took up most of the remaining space on the stairs and roared at him. Or, no, that wasn't correct; Claire didn't just roar. She *roared*, shaking the building and stunning into silence the surrounding servants, including a few harpies who had been screeching in the air overhead, their usual grandma personas having given way to gaunt, ashen-colored hags with long, tangled hair and glowing orange eyes.

But even they shut up when Claire slapped the hell out of the cowering dragon with a huge, clawed hand.

He went silent, too, and dropped his paws to stare at her. And then dropped his alter ego when she roared again, melting into a small, balding man in a scrap of fabric that strained to contain a prominent beer gut. He looked like a chef, although I had yet to see much that was cooked at this feast.

And probably wouldn't now, as Claire batted him into the wall, hard enough that he was still sliding down it when she transformed on the run and headed back down the stairs. I followed and burst into her brother's banqueting chamber only to barrel right into her, since she'd stopped just inside. And was staring around at a frozen tableau.

Tanet was on his feet and while he hadn't yet transformed, it was obviously coming. He'd dropped the robe and his hand was on the laces of the black silk tunic he wore underneath, which I hadn't noticed earlier as it was open to the waist. It showed a chest covered with the same moving, mottled appearance that Claire's cheeks previously had, with vague patches of scales blooming and shifting across the skin.

Other people were standing, too, with their hands also on their lacings. It reminded me of a bunch of gunslingers fingering their Colt .45s but not yet drawing them. But expecting to do so, just any time now.

Moving forward, I caught sight of the problem, which seemed to be the group of tall, broad-shouldered men and women who had just entered the bloodstained floor of the dining hall below. They hadn't transformed, either, although there was no doubt as to what they were. The huge torches by the door guttered as they finished filing past, as if massive, invisible wings had brushed them.

I also thought I saw strange shadows painting the floor around them, with two dimensional depictions of clawed feet, whipping tails and those same, oversized wings. But I couldn't be sure since the gnawed ribcages and scattered bones underfoot were casting weird shapes in the flickering firelight. Like the columns of bumpy-skinned, humanoid guards who ran in a moment later, surrounding the newcomers with spears out, and were either completely ignored or favored with a few contemptuous snarls.

Tanet was doing the same to the uninvited guests, his mountain of red hair crackling like dancing flames and his muscles bulging and retreating in his back and arms in ways that a human's simply couldn't. He looked like a man who really wanted to tear someone's throat out, and then possibly eat him. He looked full-on savage.

Which made it even more surprising when his father stood up, walked to the front of his dining chamber, and smiled.

In human form, Lord Rathen was a seven-foot-tall, muscular man with strong, handsome features, blue eyes and burnished red hair a shade darker than his son's. He kept it cut short in a human style that matched the careless scruff on his face, and in the right clothes he could have walked the streets of New York and never turned a head except in admiration. And from what I'd heard of him, he'd probably done so.

He looked to be a very well kept fifty or a rough and tumble forty. But either way, most women wouldn't have kicked him out of bed. Or most men, either, probably, as that smile was a charmer. It crinkled the corners of his eyes and lit up his face with every appearance of pleasure. He looked like a man greeting friends or long-lost relatives that he hadn't seen in a while. As did his body language, when he threw out his arms, a goblet in one hand and a huge ruby ring flashing on the other, the latter matching the wine-deep color of his robes.

"Steen-Ryn of the honorable Clan Vitharr," he boomed, his voice echoing around the room's excellent acoustics. "Your presence is as unexpected as it is welcome. Join us in the feast to celebrate the arrival of my daughter and our off-world guests to my home!"

An older man stepped forward from among the new arrivals, with sapphire robes over a pure silver sheath, and like Lord Rathen, he was smiling. I couldn't tell if it reached his eyes because of the distance, and because of the huge beard he wore, which cascaded almost to the floor. It distracted me from everything else, since beards on Earth simply never grew that long or that full. Or that silver, with the color mixing with that of his equally long hair and the sheath he wore to the point that I couldn't tell where one ended and the other began.

And then I was distracted once again when great, shadowy wings rose up behind him, casting the other newcomers and half of the hall into shade. They caused torches and lamps dozens of yards away to flicker and a few to go out and sent a definite chill across the diners. I saw several people shiver and others, on the edges of the shadow, deliberately move out of its path.

I didn't blame them. And the voice that came out of the man's throat a moment later was no better. It didn't sound human, but neither did it sound like Lord Rathen's when he was transformed. I wasn't sure what it sounded like, but if it had been written out, the letters would have had scrawling edges that bled blackly across the page. There were screeches and screams and howls somewhere behind the words, like far off damned souls tearing at them as if at the bars of a cage, trying to get out.

It made my skin crawl, and that was before I realized what it was saying.

"To welcome your daughter, surely; I have heard tales of her beauty," the terrible voice said, causing Claire to make a startled, unhappy sound. "But of the others..." his face turned unerringly toward our box, as if he'd known exactly where we'd be. "One of them has had dealings with my house. I would take her and go, and trouble you no further."

A murmuring went around the great space, and Louis-Cesare looked at me. I looked back, shaking my head; I had no idea what he was talking about. I was the only other woman in our party besides Claire, but I'd never seen Steen before in my life.

And that included his alter ego "Ryn."

I watched it in the shadows behind him, acting almost like an independent entity. Even his own men stiffened when its shade fell across them. And those completely in its shadow seemed to shrink, falling into themselves, and failing to show the bravado of their companions on the edges.

But Claire's father didn't seem to notice.

"Her?" Rathen-Den sounded slightly puzzled. Tanet had jerked his head to look at me, as practically the rest of the hall was now doing, but his father never so much as glanced my way. "I'm afraid I'm at a loss, Lord Steen. The only woman in my daughter's party is an off-worlder who has never before visited our fair lands. You must have her confused with someone else."

And suddenly, belatedly, I got it, at the same moment that Louis-Cesare did. Our eyes met, and our lips formed the same word: Dorina. What did you do? I thought, alarmed.

And then I thought about something else.

"I beg to differ," Steen was saying, and his terrible voice had sharpened to a knife's edge. "She has done me an injury. I will have recompense. And I will have it now."

Dragons did not appear to share the senate's love of discourse, and of following carefully veiled threats with more and more obvious ones for some time before exploding into action. Because that was it—that was literally everything that was said before the people around Steen were on the move.

They shifted all together like a tide, or like a sudden storm if storms were made up of scales and teeth and giant, dhampir-spearing claws abruptly boiling in my direction. But I was moving, too, only not away. Claire was screaming something about the stairs and grabbing for me, and with her newfound speed, she should have caught me.

But I had speed, too, when I chose to use it, and an intense need to talk to the only person who might be able to tell me where my sister was.

And his people had just left him alone.

Of course, the reason they had done so was to attack me, but Rathen-Den didn't like that, and his people were moving, too. They changed in an eyeblink, flying off perches all over the hollow tower to meet Steen's forces in a deafening clash in the air. But they didn't meet me, because I'd already jumped down, hit the blood-slick floor, rolled and was off—

And Louis-Cesare was right there with me, trying to grab hold, and he was faster than Claire. He was faster than anyone I'd ever met, but a screaming group of bison-like creatures, shaggy and meaty and panicked, who I guessed had been the next course, took that moment to stampede across the floor, separating us. And buying me an extra second.

And a second was all I needed.

Because a second is just a second, unless it's in slow-time, the altered reality that dhampirs and vamps can fall into during combat, which makes it seem like everything is happening in slow-motion—except for you. Which is why I was treated to the sight of a squirming mass of scales in a rainbow of colors overhead; to a torch flinging sparks in a parabola across the scene, knocked out of its bracket by a lashing tail; to a glimpse of Claire transforming in the fighting mass overhead, right before she was crashed into by a dark purple dragon twice her size; to Tanet, his alter ego finally unleashed, changing and turning and ripping into the beast on top of her with every evidence of relish; and to a wash of flame from someone's open maw hitting a silken banner hanging from Lord Rathen's dining chamber, setting it alight. "Wel Com Of-Wurlled

Gests" it had proclaimed in lively, golden embroidery, a kind gesture that I had failed to notice on my arrival, being too busy watching entrails raining down from the sky.

I wasn't watching that now, but only because the sides were evenly matched, at least in the toughness of their scales. But Steen's people were seriously outnumbered, which had me wondering what he was thinking coming here. I didn't wonder for long.

A bunch of dark shapes appeared in the windows scattered around the half of the tower that wasn't mountainside, silhouetted against the stars. And then crawled in, hunching down, making themselves compact enough to fit through the great, elongated rectangles, but not bothering to transform back into human shapes to make it easier. Those that couldn't fit busted through the thick slabs of rock instead, shattering the stone inward and peppering the fight with flying shards.

I avoided the spray by keeping the battling pairs above me as a sort of shield as I darted across the floor. And rooted around in my big, black duffle bag for the magic it contained, which I really hoped my opponent had never seen before. Because otherwise, I was screwed.

But I couldn't just run away and let others fight, and possibly die, for me. And I couldn't lose what might be my only chance to find out where Dorina was and what she'd been doing recently. A location could make all the difference in the world to this crazy venture, and get us all the hell out of here before anything else went wrong.

It was worth a risk.

So, Lord Steen it was, and while he was big and bad and terrible, especially now as he'd just transformed into a huge black dragon with jade and purple iridescence on his wings and burning green eyes, he was still the job. And I'd spent a lifetime doing the job. And taking down things that scared me almost as much as he did.

Let's see what five hundred years of experience gets you, I thought, right before a golden bullet co-opted me.

Even in slow-time, it took me a moment to realize what had just happened, it was that fast. And once I did, I still couldn't really track it. I vaguely understood that Lord Rathen was displeased about Steen crashing his party and trying to drag off one of his guests, but all I saw were slashing claws and snapping teeth and tails as big as other dragons' whole bodies swiping left and right and clearing a large patch of the floor around them.

Servants were running or flying or swinging on banners out of the way; buffalo were getting squelched underfoot, adding to the slippery carnage on the floor; and the gallant guards had their spears out and at the ready, only they couldn't reach the fight without their steeds, as they had no wings.

Which was probably just as well, considering how those who did manage it were fairing.

And then Louis-Cesare caught up with me.

He was furious, and he'd bloodied something; his clothes were running with the evidence. His face was also splattered with it—for an instant, before he absorbed it and grimaced, because fey blood tastes nasty. And then he grabbed me.

"I need to talk to him," I said, indicating Lord Rathen's fight with Steen, right before it came our way and Louis-Cesare jumped us both over a swinging tail.

"I know!"

"Before Rathen guts him," I added, in case I hadn't been clear.

"*I know!*" he glared at me.

"Well, what's the plan?"

"The plan? You mean to say you came down here without a plan?"

"Kinda thought I'd wing it."

"Then let's go with that," he said grimly, and disappeared.

Louis-Cesare's master power, known as The Veil, allowed him to slip out of phase with the world for a short time. That rendered him both invisible and untouchable to anyone still inside real space and worked amazingly well in combat for obvious reasons. It was one example of why he was so feared as an opponent.

But it wasn't working so well this time. Or rather, it was, as I saw when he abruptly jerked me in beside him, likely so that we could successfully catch up to the fight between the chieftains that was rapidly wrecking the room and endangering anyone in their path. Only that wasn't what we did.

Because we weren't alone.

I had no sooner stepped inside the hazy, pale and washed-out world of The Veil, which looked like someone had thrown a piece of white gauze over reality, when I realized that things worked differently in Faerie.

Very. Differently.

"*Merde*," Louis-Cesare said, as a dozen heads suddenly swiveled our way.

They were human heads, attached to human bodies, but they weren't human. We could tell, since around each one the hazy figure of a dragon loomed, one thrashing and fighting and snarling and wreaking havoc in the real world. While here . . . their human halves languished, unable to join in the conflict except vicariously, because dragonkind had a sort of Veil, too, didn't they?

And we had just made the mistake of bringing the fight to them.

"*Merde*," I agreed, as the group lunged for us.

We didn't know how to fight this way, which was why Louis-Cesare abruptly dragged us back into the real world. The transition was quick enough to make me dizzy and didn't even help. Because the group's dragons promptly turned away from their own fights and freaking leapt for us—again.

"*Merde!*" we both said in unison, right before a plume of fire the width of the room erupted from a dozen throats.

I found myself back in La-La Land, because at least The Veil didn't have anything that breathed fire, which was anathema to vampires. But we only had a short time here, because Louis-Cesare had maybe two minutes of access once he pulled that particular trigger, and the clock was ticking. And once it ran down, he would not be able to access the Veil again for a day or more.

Which was a problem considering that a bunch of murderous bastards with evil intent jumped us as soon as we came through, because they'd expected it. That was what all the fire had been about. And this wasn't much better than roasting to death, I thought, as somebody throttled me, several somebodies pummeled Louis-Cesare like he was a punching bag at the gym, and then the rest jumped us in a rush.

Right before we hit the ground outside of the Veil, and halfway across the room, because I'd just used my portable portal.

It didn't take us out of Faerie, and probably wouldn't work to take us much of anywhere inside of it, either, knowing how incompatible human and fey magic were. But it had succeeded in throwing us across the room, and I guessed Louis-Cesare must have pulled us out of the Veil at the same time, because we rolled onto the floor beside a bunch of panicked sheep who decided that we were the last straw. And trampled us.

But being trampled by a flock is a lot better than being beaten to death by a group of seven-foot-tall humans. Or roasted by their dragons. Or crushed by a couple of battling chieftains, the latter of which was about to happen anyway, as they were headed this way!

Louis-Cesare flung us back inside The Veil just in time to miss them, landing us in the middle of the fighting chieftains in human form who crashed into us a moment later. That still wasn't fun considering their size and savagery, but my husband threw himself in front of me, looking more wild-eyed and panicked than a senator had any right to. And I got an idea.

Because he didn't look like a man who knew what the hell had just happened, which meant that maybe he hadn't taken the exact moment that I opened the portal to decide to shift us back into normal space, after all.

Maybe the portal had done that instead, all on its own, and if that was true . . .

Well, let's test a theory, I thought, and opened it again.

As a result, the four of us tumbled back into the real world, with the two of them gripped by Louis-Cesare, who was trying to hold them away from me, and me throwing my arms around the threesome at the last second. And that seemed to be all it took to force a change on a dragon. Well, alright then.

My butt hit down on cold stone once more and I spun, getting behind the bearded man I'd been clutching, grabbing him by his now very human throat, and getting a knife against it.

And, suddenly, the room stilled.

There were some battles going on at the peripheries, others on various balconies, and a few more that seemed to be taking place inside of the walls, judging by the pieces regularly being knocked out of them. But all of the fighting in the main part of the room ceased. Leaving me panting and cutting a line of red into the hairy throat of a startled and uncomprehending dragon who had just been thrust unceremoniously back into his human guise.

And wasn't liking it.

But I wasn't liking much right now, either, and there was one thing, and one thing only, keeping me from ending him.

"Where," I gritted into his ear. "Is my *sister*?"

Chapter Twelve
Dorina

"At least we found Marlowe," I said sometime later, and received a purely vicious look in return.

I did not object, for I knew it was born out of fear. Ray had grown up rough, in places where it was unwise to show his true emotions, so he tended to cover them with belligerence. I did not take it to heart.

And he was probably very afraid now, as we were currently back in jail. Only this was a better jail than the one we had experienced on the road. It had a water bucket, another container for refuse, smelled clean, and the walls were merely tent panels, albeit ones with strong enchantments on them. We even had a bench to sit on, which would have been more comfortable if we hadn't been sharing it with our fellow prisoner.

And if we hadn't been about to die.

"Should have known," Marlowe snarled, pulling on the chains that our captors had seen fit to put him in, after he escaped them twice. "They'll come any time now," he said sarcastically. "They'll rescue me. We're both on the senate, after all; she wouldn't merely leave me to die!"

I received a malevolent glare from him, an order of magnitude stronger than Ray's, although I didn't see why.

"We were coming to rescue you," I pointed out.

"You call this rescuing, do you?"

It was truly amazing, I thought, how much venom he could put into a single sentence.

"We were interrupted by the queen's guards."

"You're a first-level master and a *dhampir*. You can't handle a few goddamned fey?"

"Oh, yeah," Ray said, piping up from behind me. "'Cause you've been doing so much better. You had what? Two days here and three on the road to escape, and where are you now? And why do you still smell like pig shit?"

Marlowe roared and lunged at Ray, who just sat there while the enchanted chains pulled the enraged senator back before he could reach him. Ray was on the other side of me, on the end of the bench, which was probably just as well. I shifted position slightly to block Marlowe's view of him.

"No one seemed to know where you were," I said. "Or had even heard of you. The only thing everyone talked about was an upcoming death match with someone known as The Reaper—"

Marlowe said a bad word. "Yes! That's what they're calling me—"

"Wait, what?" Ray asked, peering around my shoulder.

"—and they'll dream up some stupid name for you, too, for both of you! Don't think they won't!"

"Wait. You're The Reaper?"

"You volunteered to fight the Queen's champion?" I added, because that seemed very unwise.

Marlowe cursed again. He did that a lot. "Volunteered! If you call being told it was that or the axe, then yes, I volunteered! They wanted some new experience to excite the crowd, since this bastard has apparently killed everyone he's gone up against. They can't get any bets against him, so nobody makes any money. Until they had the splendid idea of having him fight some crazed off-worlder, which is how they've billed me—"

I didn't comment. He *was* looking a bit crazed at the moment, with wild eyes staring out of the mask of mud and less savory things that he still wore, as no one had apparently allowed him to bathe. His hair was likewise clumped and matted, and his rags covered less than the mud, having been shredded by multiple fights.

I supposed it all added to the wild man persona they had assigned to him.

"—and how they'll bill the both of you if we don't work together!" he declared. "Help me and I'll help you. Otherwise, it'll be an outworld double feature and we'll all be royally—"

He broke off as Ray suddenly jumped to his feet and went over to the tent flap, which was serving as a door, and looked out. "Hey!" he said to someone out of sight. "Hey, you. Yeah you, tusker face. Get in here!"

"What . . . are you doing?" Marlowe asked, his voice suddenly low and reasonable.

"Getting us outta here. They wanna feed you to their monster, that's fine. But not me. And not Dorina!"

Marlowe sneered. "I might have known. All that was necessary to get you off your arse was a threat to the little woman—"

"One more word, and I will personally beat you to death."

"You and what army?"

"His," Ray said, hiking a thumb at the enormous specimen who had just torn aside the curtain and was peering in at us through tiny eyes.

They were the only tiny things about him.

I thought at first that he was merely a larger-than-average troll, as the muscles on his muscles would seem to suggest. But ogres were the ones with tusks and he had two of them, massive, cracked, yellowing things framing a large, jowl-filled face. He also had whiskers, although I had never seen an ogre with a beard. Trolls could grow them, however, and his towering bulk was also more indicative of that breed. A hybrid perhaps?

I didn't know, but it seemed that, like the liger, a hybrid of a lion and a tiger, the result of a troll-ogre cross was larger than either of his parents. Which was a concern as he did not seem pleased to have been summoned. And was even less so when Ray skipped back a few yards and began saying something in the local merchants' cant which did not sound complimentary.

"He is going to get us all killed," Marlowe said, in that same eerily calm voice.

"Ray," I said, but he flapped a hand at me.

"Yeah, you understood that all right, didn't you?" Ray asked, his voice muffled slightly as he was stuffing something into his mouth. "I said your daddy musta been a wild boar, to give you tusks like that. So, what was mamma, huh?"

"Ray," I said, a bit more urgently.

"I'm thinking bear, considering how hairy you are. Was that it? Was your mamma a hairy bear? You sure stink bad enough—"

The guard seemed to know some English, or perhaps he merely resented Ray's tone, which was no more respectful than his words. Either way, he abruptly threw back the curtain and entered the room, thus breaking the ward, which I supposed was what Ray had wanted. Although why he had wanted that, I wasn't sure.

Until I saw him swallow whatever he had been eating, shoot me a triumphant grin, and grab the troll by the arm.

And abruptly had his formerly patchy scruff become a lush, full beard that cascaded halfway down his chest.

"What is happening?" Marlowe asked me, as the troll creature snatched Ray up by the neck and shook him like a maraca.

"I think Ray is under the impression that the Dragon's Claw he just consumed will lend him the guard's strength."

"Will it?"

"No," I said, and leapt.

The subsequent fight was hard, prolonged and vicious, and involved the troll snatching me off his back to use as a club to bash the other two prisoners. But Ray jumped back up, grabbed the bench and smashed it into the creature's skull. And Marlowe proved the feys' estimate of his sanity correct when he roared again before headbutting the creature considerably below the belt, causing it to drop me and grab him.

Ray and I managed to wrestle the guard to the floor before he could do what he clearly had in mind and rip Marlowe apart, and then I slammed my fist into the massive face a few dozen times, until he finally passed out. It felt like hitting solid rock and left me with bloody knuckles, a sore arm, and a renewed appreciation for fey resiliency. If defeating a simple guard was this difficult, what would their champion be like?

I decided that I did not want to find out.

We left the guard in his own cuffs, his arms trapped behind him and a gag in his mouth, and exited the tent. And by we, I include Marlowe, although I was soon regretting bringing him along. He was an intensely unpleasant man.

"Get me out of these cuffs!" he demanded, as he ran awkwardly beside us.

"I already tried," I reminded him. "The guard breaking the ward released you from your tether to it, but the cuffs themselves are spelled."

"Then get the key!"

"The guard didn't have the key, dumbass," Ray said, through an alarming amount of hair. Which still seemed to be growing.

"Then find one!"

"This isn't Earth, okay? You don't get to order people around—especially me."

"Oh, look, Cousin It disapproves."

"*Bite me.*"

"I can't. You're wearing the equivalent of a pelt. And speaking of dumbasses—"

"Don't go there."

"—did you really think that was going to work? That they sell *candies* in the open marketplace that could let you steal another being's magic—"

"It was worth a shot!"

"—and that the guards wouldn't have taken them from you if they did? Are you really that thick—"

I didn't think Marlowe was done speaking, but Ray suddenly snapped, slamming him up against a tent pole hard enough to crack it and causing a momentary pause.

"I thought it might allow me to get us all out of here," the smaller man hissed. "Which is more than you have been doing!"

"Getting killed might technically be an escape, but it isn't one I wish to experience—"

"Then shut the hell up! We're the *rescuers*; you're the *rescuee*. You do as we say!"

"Fine." Marlowe stared at him malevolently. "Then what is your great plan, after getting into a pointless fight and thrown into jail? Where do we go from here?"

It was a good question. I could hear the roar of a considerable crowd, but not see them. The only thing I *could* see was a maze of fabric walls. And when I pushed past them, I was confronted by more of the same.

We were in a forest of tent poles, brown homespun and a few ropes holding it all together.

One that never seemed to end.

"Maze spell," Ray scowled, having followed me through one set of walls and into another, identical corridor. "No wonder they only had one guard."

"How do we get out?" Marlowe demanded, staring around.

"We don't. The only way out of a maze spell is to go through to the end."

"The end?" He stared at Ray. "As in, where they were probably planning to take us in the first place? Where we are set to be executed? *That* end?"

"Unless you wanna wander around in here forever, yeah." Ray looked at me and his scowl grew. "Come on. And stay behind me."

I did as I was bid, as experience had proven that his knowledge of the fey was considerably greater than mine. Or than Marlowe's it seemed, although the irate man had at least stopped talking. Perhaps because Ray was navigating by sound and he didn't want to interfere with it.

Or perhaps because he had left us to take off on his own, I realized, when I looked back and he was not there.

"Let him go," Ray said, noticing his absence the same time that I did.

"I thought you wanted his portal—"

"*Sod* his portal. I want you out of here alive. If he causes a distraction doing something stupid, it may help us."

It did not help us, but not because Marlowe didn't do something stupid. But because long minutes of wandering through claustrophobic, fabric-sided corridors only led one place. And it wasn't somewhere we wanted to go.

"Alright," Ray said, licking his lips as we stood in a short tunnel leading into a huge arena.

I did not understand where it had come from, as everything in the valley that I had seen had been temporary. Tents and open fronted, collapsable booths had been the order of the day for those not merely selling out of the backs of their wagons. So, I did not understand why I was currently looking at a large arena of pitted, off-white stone, massive blocks of which had been used to construct towering rows of seats surrounding an open space filled with golden sand.

The arena had bright, red and white, striped shades over parts of the stands, hawkers selling refreshments and people waving banners in languages I didn't know to cheer on their favorites. Or I should say, their favorite, as they all looked like the art that I'd seen on the side of the advertising wagon earlier. And I was starting to think that perhaps the size disparity between the combatants depicted had not, after all, been artistic license.

Because something was stomping about out of sight thanks to the high walls of the tunnel.

Something big.

The ponderous footsteps were audible even over the roar of the crowd, and heavy enough to shake pebbles loose from the gravel fill in between the large stones of the wall every time one hit down.

But the crowd roared again, nonetheless, and it was deafening, and that was before a mud-covered savage ran past the opening. It seemed that Marlowe had entered the arena through another gate while we were lost in the maze and did not look to be enjoying it. And neither did Ray, who turned on me with huge eyes.

"Alright. I'm gonna grab that guy," he said, pointing at a massive, troll-ogre hybrid ahead of us. "You just stay here, and I'm gonna go get him."

I blinked at him. That seemed . . . unlikely. The creature was even bigger than the one in our cell had been, not to mention that there were two of them, one on either side of the entrance.

There were dressed in shiny suits of armor they did not need, since troll flesh was as hard as steel, as I had cause to know. Fortunately, they hadn't noticed us yet because they had their backs to us, facing out. And because of the noise. And because they were enjoying seeing Marlowe being thrown around the sand.

Ray watched as a first-level master was tossed through the air like a frisbee, slinging helplessly around and around as if blown out of a cannon, and then turned to me and began speaking rapidly. "As soon as I attack him, you zoom past and climb the stands before the other bully boy can react, okay?"

I looked at him some more, wondering if I had misheard. "And what are you going to do?"

He did not answer me. "They're not nearly as fast as you, so you got an advantage. Find the entrance, battle your way through if you can, or better yet, blend in with the crowd. Keep this up—" he pulled on the hood to my ripped poncho-like garment until it covered my hair and ears. "And keep your head down. They won't be able to tell you from a fey. You're short, but there's a lot of half breeds around here, product of some of the Green Fey's slaves who ran away and intermarried with the locals—"

"Ray."

"—so you'll blend in fine. Just a spectator who got tired and decided to go home early. No big deal—"

"It is a big deal," I pointed out. "I would be leaving you behind."

But Ray was not listening. "And don't look back. Just run. Find a village called Denhall in the Blarestri hinterlands. It's got a big mill there; everybody knows it. There's this guy—"

"I don't care about that."

"—named Penton. He runs the mill and he's an ass, but he has a portal—"

"I am not doing that."

"—in the basement and he'll get you out, okay? Tell him the senate'll make him rich for your return and he'll do whatever you want. I know it's a long way, but you're smart. You'll be alright—"

"I will not, because I will not be going."

And, finally, something seemed to get through.

"You damned well will!" he said furiously, blue eyes snapping. "Look, I'll find you, okay? I'll get out. Marlowe is a bastard, but he can fight, and so can I when it comes down to it. And two is better in a brawl than one—"

"And three is even better than two, is it not?"

"No! Not if one of the three is you. Just *go*—"

"No."

He stared at me, and for the first time, he didn't look merely afraid. He looked terrified. "Please, do this for me. Just—please, Dorina. You have to, okay? I—you have to."

"Like you left me when I was injured and could not walk, and we were in a cave being pursued by Svarestri warriors? Because I do not remember it like that."

"*Please—*"

"Or when they caught up with us on the river, and I still couldn't walk, and you could have escaped but chose to stay with me instead?"

"That is not the same thing!"

"How is it not?" I tilted my head curiously. "The Svarestri were not chasing you; they were after me. You could have easily taken off and left me behind, and they would not have pursued you. But you did not."

"Dorina—"

"You stayed and fished to feed me, when you did not need such food yourself, and built a boat for us so that we could float away. And when they found us anyway—"

"Goddamnit! Stop talking!"

"—you stayed again and fought by my side. Do you really think that I would leave you now?"

"Yes!" He looked at me wildly. "You have to!"

"Then, Raymond Lu, it seems that you do not know me as well as I thought," I said, and headed for the arena.

Chapter Thirteen

One of the guards had another of those strange fey spears, so I grabbed it as I ran past. The creature seemed surprised, perhaps because Marlowe's fight was scheduled to be a one-on-one, although the crowd seemed happy enough to see me. Although that might have been because the great off-world champion was getting his arse kicked.

Badly.

That wasn't surprising considering that, if anything, the depictions on the ads I had seen had downplayed the situation. He wasn't merely facing a giant; he was facing a colossus with hands larger than my whole body and legs like tree trunks—if the trees were sequoias. And when the creature's body passed in front of a section of the stands, it shaded more than the awnings did.

The spear I had grabbed suddenly made me feel less secure.

The only good thing was that the giant had yet to notice me. Its shaggy head, covered with a matted mass of dark hair and a scruffy beard, was high enough that the roar of the crowd likely barely registered, and it was distracted, being busy trying to stomp Marlowe like a bug. The footsteps that had reverberated in the corridor were now creating concentric ripples in the sand big enough to threaten to throw me off my feet each time one hit.

I stared upward at the huge mass backlit by the sun, or whatever star burned in the fey sky, and felt confused. I had never fought such a thing; never so much as seen one. Where to even start?

Before I could decide, someone grabbed me.

"You're crazy!" Ray yelled, so loudly that I heard him above the crowd's screams and the giant's stomps. "Let's *go!*"

He was pointing violently at the stands, I supposed with the same idea as before only now modified to include both of us. And it required a quick decision, as the guards had overcome their initial shock and were headed this way. But sand waves kept knocking them back, giving me a moment to choose.

I looked back at Marlowe.

I had been content enough to let him solve his own problems when there was anything like an even playing field. He was a first-level master and a senator. He did not need me.

Until he did. Because this was not level, and I could not leave him there to be smeared across the sand like so many others clearly had been. This ended now, for all of us, and the only way to do that was to bring the giant down.

"Stand clear!" I told Ray.

"What?" His hearing did not seem to be as good as mine.

"Stand out of the way when you see it fall!"

"*What?*" And perhaps I was wrong about the hearing, I thought, as his eyes widened and his fingers, which had wrapped around my forearm, abruptly tightened.

But I did not have time to argue, so I shook off his hold, tightened my grip on my spear and took off at a run, jumping over waves of sand and heading straight for the nearest huge, hairy leg.

The giant did not have many clothes, as it would have taken the wool of an entire flock of sheep merely to make him a tunic. As a result, he wore only a brief loin cloth instead. Leaving his flesh unprotected and vulnerable, including that over his Achilles tendon.

A huge leg came crashing down, aiming for the man lying mad-eyed and desperate in a canyon of sand that previous stomps had created. I leapt, jumping off of the opposite foot and striking while still in the air. Fortunately, the spear was easy enough to use, with a small lever that activated the energy blasts, one of which I sent straight at the massive calf above me.

I did not see whether I hit my target, but I hit something. Before my back slammed down onto the sand, a wave of blood shot over me, black as midnight, and the creature roared in pain and what sounded like outrage. And all but deafened me in the process.

I did not know how the crowd reacted, because I could not hear them anymore. I did not know whether the creature had been seriously injured, because more blood had just drenched me and cut off my vision. I did not know much of anything except that someone had grabbed me and was hauling me away at a rapid pace—

And it wasn't Ray.

I wiped an arm over my eyes and looked up, expecting to see Marlowe or one of the guards. And instead, saw my father, staring down at me. It was a shock, as I hadn't really believed

Marlowe's explanation for his presence here, as it had seemed incredibly unlikely considering what I knew of my sire.

But it was undoubtedly Mircea.

His dark hair was as perfectly groomed as usual, shoulder length and lustrous, and caught back in a clip at the base of his neck. He wore a fey tunic and leggings, luxurious things in gray with a nap like raw silk, the local equivalent of his normal, elegant attire. But there was nothing normal about his expression.

It was something I had never thought to see on his face, not when directed at me. He was shaking me while shouting words I couldn't hear because I couldn't hear anything. But he looked terrified.

Oh, I thought, as realization hit.

He thinks I'm Dory.

And then I didn't think anything else, because something was happening.

I looked up, almost blinded by the sun, and saw the great shadow in front of it wavering. That was not a surprise; I had hoped to topple the creature by my stroke, getting its vulnerable bits closer to the ground and my weapon. But after a moment, I realized that I had done more than that.

Marlowe was gaping upward, while drenched in black like someone who had fallen into a tarpit. Which it almost looked like he had, as the crater was now full of black blood that gleamed in the intermittent sunlight. And then blew up like a volcanic eruption when the enormous body overhead suddenly collapsed.

I did not at first understand what had happened, thanks to the tsunami of bloody sand that hit us, almost throwing both Mircea and me off our feet. But we braced and stood our ground, and when the storm passed, I was left blinking in surprise at the unmoving body of the feys' champion. Who was now very clearly dead, although I did not know why.

Until I noticed the gouge mark, like a lightning blast, that scrawled around his massive leg.

It had not severed the tendon I had been aiming for, but rather the femoral artery in the thigh above. Well, that explains it, I thought, impressed at the power of the spear. I had not thought that it could reach so high, or I would have tried for that outcome in the first place, but I seemed to have gotten lucky.

Or not, I realized, noticing the furious faces of the audience in the stands.

They did not seem to like their champion's demise. They may have been cheering me when I first arrived, but that was when they thought I would merely provide additional sport. I did not get the impression that challengers were supposed to win.

And I didn't think that Mircea did, either, judging by the way his arm abruptly tightened around me.

I am Dorina, I told him mentally, but received no response. Perhaps because there was no time. The giant's fall was still sending waves of sand to crash against the sides of the arena when the first fey jumped down into it, teeth bared and weapons flashing.

"Oh shit, oh shit, oh shit," Ray said, running up as the same thing started happening all over the great space.

Fey of all descriptions were surging down the steps, were washing up against the barriers, were baring teeth and weapons at us. Most appeared to be trolls, but there were a fair number of ogres, light fey, brownies, goblins, and pixies in the mix, the latter so numerous that they looked like dark clouds against the day. Not to mention hybrids of all descriptions, many of the latter of which looked reasonably human, at least from here.

Ray had been right; we could have gotten away.

One of these days, I was going to learn to listen to him, I thought, gripping my spear, as hundreds of enraged onlookers started leaping across the barrier and spilling into the arena to avenge their fallen colossus.

"Oh, I see how it is," Marlowe yelled, as my ears popped. "I die and everything's fine. My opponent dies, and there's a riot. Is that it?"

"I think that is it," I said, and had him glare at me out of his mask of blood.

"We bookend them on either side," Mircea said crisply, and I assumed that he was talking to me. But Marlowe seemed to have had the same thought about himself, for he answered.

"And go where?" There was some outraged arm waving. "The tunnels all lead to an infernal maze that's impossible to break out of, and the stands are full of more people who want to kill us! Where in the hell do you expect us to go?"

"The royal box."

"The what?"

Mircea nodded his head toward a built-up and covered area of the stands at the far end of the arena, where a canopy of bright gold, and banners of white and red, shimmered in the sunlight. It was very pretty, but I did not see how it would help us, as presumably the queen, or whoever was inside, had been enjoying the festivities right along with everyone else. Why save us now?

Not to mention the obvious fact that we would never get there alive.

"We'll never make it!" Marlowe said, echoing my thoughts, with the surging crowd already almost upon us.

"We'll have help," Mircea said, and then we were swamped.

But not by the fey.

A dozen old cars suddenly appeared, their butts sticking out of the sand like the boulders at Stonehenge. One was close enough that I could see myself in its rusted fender; others were scattered about haphazardly—and uselessly, as they did nothing to the approaching throng except to confuse it. They confused me, too, as they had literally appeared out of thin air.

But not Marlowe, it seemed.

He was staring around wildly, and then at Mircea. "Is she—"

"Yes."

"Then why doesn't she shift us bloody well out?"

"Her power is tied to Earth. It works only intermittently here, when the distant portal churns to the location of our world. And even then, what she can do is limited."

"Wait," Ray said. "The Pythia is here? That's who you're talking about, right? Is she here?"

Nobody answered him, or even acknowledged that he had been talking. And neither did I, although that was due to having to fight off an attack by three trolls, which I did by turning my weapon on them. They dove into the still churning sand, a line of which glassed over top of them, and I punched another in the face who had thrown himself at me while I was distracted.

"So, tell her to get us as close to the damned portal as she can and we'll run for it!" Marlowe yelled, slamming his elbow back into an ogre who had just grabbed him over the top of a rusted-out Chrysler. "Or just out of the damned arena!"

"It doesn't work that way," Mircea said, knocking two more ogres' heads together.

"Then how does it work?"

Like that, I thought, as a path was quickly formed for us toward the distant royal box by what looked like the contents of an entire junkyard. I did not understand how, but everything but the kitchen sink was being thrown onto either side of a slender alleyway. That included old stoves, bedsteads, couches and refrigerators; a mountain of old tires that bounced everywhere; giant coils of barbed wire, rusty and looking like colossal tumbleweeds; more cars, none of which appeared to be in drivable condition; heaps of scrap metal; and a combine tractor.

And a kitchen sink, which landed in front of us as we started to run, causing me to have to jump over it at the last second.

The fey were not so lucky, and I saw several of them go down under the weight of dressers with cracked laminate, broken mirrors, an old treadmill, a hail of moldy bricks big enough to have built a house, and a rusted-out school bus painted a bilious green. None of these things were whole, and some of them were as mangled as if the giant himself had been chewing on them. And I belatedly realized what my father had meant about the Pythia's power "not working that way".

I had faced her in battle once, the chief seer for the supernatural world, and although the memory was hazy, I recalled clearly how easily she had evaded my attempts on her life. She had a power I did not understand, one allowing her to move from place to place without covering the ground in between, a shocking sort of magic even to me who had seen many. But it was usable only when the portal they must have come through flashed by Earth in its churning, ever changing rotation.

And if she attempted to move something here and was cut off when the portal changed to a new location . . .

Well, that happened.

I stared at what looked like a modern sculpture made out of metal as I passed by, but which had probably been another car at one point in time. But it was honestly hard to tell. The piece looked like it had been turned inside out and then . . . scattered, for lack of a better term.

A headlight, just the one, resided atop a long stalk of strained steel, like an eye on top of an alien creature. A fender had feathered into a thousand tiny filaments that blew and chimed softly on the breeze. A door and what might have once been the front windshield had blended, to the point that it looked like the glass had been smeared by metal, or perhaps the other way around.

I couldn't tell anymore; I just did not want to have the same thing happen to me.

And I supposed that Marlowe felt the same, because I saw him staring about, too, and he did not ask again.

But some things got through unscathed, including a boat. It was a smaller type used for fishing, but its holey hull still seemed to enrage the fey that it fell on, who busted through the side a moment later with a sword in both hands. I blasted him back into the darkened recesses with my spear, because he was one of the huge troll/ogre hybrids and I did not feel like fighting another of those. It worked, but when a regular ogre jumped for me a moment later, the staff did nothing but sputter at him.

So, I bashed him in the face with it, instead.

"Augghhhh, augghhhh, you bastards!" Marlowe was screaming, while staggering under the weight of half a dozen fey.

I pulled several off him as we ran, and Ray grabbed another, a rabid-looking brownie, who did not appear to have expected fangs. He had been making up for what he lacked in size with magic, but he lost his nerve when Ray grabbed his bag of tricks away and snarled at him. And Marlowe managed to clear the rest on his own, while still running.

And then he and Mircea were throwing the rusty pieces we had been provided with at the fey, attempting to keep the corridor ahead of us clear.

They were doing a good job.

A heavy-duty hubcap bashed a troll in the face, and despite the fact that he was another hybrid, hit hard enough to throw him off his feet. A second later, Mircea had the creature's weapon and was laying waste with it, sending lightning bolts into the sides of the makeshift tunnel, much of which was made out of metal.

That sent a load of fey vibrating and then falling backward off the top, although it did not do much to those who had already jumped down in front of us.

But Marlowe was hacking a passage through them, emulating the boat fey with a sword in each hand, and Ray was lobbing spell bombs from the bag he had taken off the brownie. I realized that I was the only one with an inadequate weapon, and looked about to exchange it. But all I saw was a new wave of fey coming up on our rear.

That included several of the champion's friends or possibly family, who had taken a moment to react, as they did not seem to have the intellect to match their size. But they had that, I thought, as one of them picked up the combine tractor, which must have weighed four or five tons, as easily as I might have grabbed a convenient stick. And threw it at us like a man lobbing a baseball, except that this one would have broken records, as it was traveling at approximately the speed of a bullet.

That stopped everything, both for us and our attackers, as people abruptly dove for cover. I jerked Ray down at the last second, and Marlowe tackled Mircea. He was just in time.

The great projectile screamed by overhead, stirring up a whirlwind of sand and dragging a couple dozen pixies helplessly in its wake. Before crashing into the ground a dozen yards in front of us and sending a stinging blast of sand radiating outward that I thought might flay the flesh right off of my bones. And it might have, except for Ray, who had somehow had the presence of mind to throw a shield spell in front of us.

I assumed he had taken it from the brownie's pack as we had not had it before. And it was powerful, wavering in front of our eyes like a mirage in the desert, showing us nothing but whirling sand on the other side for a moment. And then Mircea and Marlowe emerged from the chaos, now both blood-covered savages, only this blood was theirs.

I screamed and ran into the ward, unthinking. And then found myself thrashing about in its clutches, unable to break through no matter what I did. Until I finally tore a small hole and then shredded it and was out the other side.

In time to see that Mircea had already healed, his outfit ruined but his torn skin smoothing out under the blood that he was quickly reabsorbing. I didn't see what Marlowe looked like as I wasn't looking at Marlowe. But I did see . . .

My thoughts petered out at the sight of a field of bloody and now completely deranged fey digging themselves out of the sand; a missing barrier, as the junk walls ahead of us had been pulverized or knocked out of the way; and a large contingent of the armed, troll/ogre hybrids pouring out of every tunnel leading into the arena.

No way could we handle all of that.

But before they could attack, something else unexpected happened. Something I didn't understand any more than I had most of the things that had taken place recently. But everyone else certainly seemed to.

Because a screeching cry rang out over the arena, and a group of dark shadows rippled across the ground. And, suddenly, everyone was moving again—in the opposite direction. The entire area was abruptly churning with screaming, running figures, many of whom left their weapons behind in their desperation to get away.

But not from us. From whatever was now circling us, sending a whirlwind of shadows chasing each other across the sand. Its identity was hidden from sight by the sun and the particles in my eyes, but not, it seemed, from Ray's.

He was staring upward and appeared to be trying to grasp my arm but kept missing. Since he was a vampire, that was very odd, but not as much as his expression. Which I had never seen before and couldn't name.

"What is it?" I asked, but he did not seem to be able to answer.

"Ray?" I said again, not understanding why he was acting this way.

Until something landed in front of me, the size of a giant but in a very different form, and shaded my eyes by a pair of massive, leathery wings.

Oh, I thought.

That was why.

Chapter Fourteen

The creature in front of me was beautiful. That was all I could think of for a moment, staring in awe at the royal purple color of the scales that covered the hugely muscled body. The ones over the breastbone were so large and shiny that they showed me back my own bedraggled form, and were topped by a surprisingly elegant head with massive, curled black horns framed by huge, leathery black wings.

I recognized what it was, of course; Dory's friend Claire could turn into something like this, only her dragon form was considerably smaller and more delicate. This one would have made six of her and was easily the most imposing creature I had ever seen. The giant had been big, but even while attempting to kill Marlowe, it had not been nearly so menacing.

This was danger given form, and its savage beauty was that of a force of nature: a surging sea, a churning tornado, a wildfire burning out of control.

I was utterly entranced.

Right up until the creature threw out a careless claw and knocked Ray, who had been standing at my side and frozen in shock, almost the length of the arena.

I didn't see where he landed; there was too much junk in the way. But I heard his scream in my head, one that was abruptly cut off.

And then all I saw was red.

I heard someone scream "No!" Felt fingers brush my arm, grasping for me with lightning speed. Smelled someone's fear on the air, but it wasn't mine.

I eluded the grasping fingers, grabbed a metal pipe with a jagged end, and struck. Not the scales, which I instinctively knew I had no chance with, but rather the softest target available: the wings. Or to be more precise, one wing, which was shortly thereafter a torn and tattered sail.

The creature screamed and reared back, spilling ruby colored blood onto the hot, sunlit air. It did not seem to have expected the attack, although why I did not know. It would receive more of the same soon, and if Ray was dead . . .

Then I would have killed two new enemies in a single day.

But that would have to wait, as the next thing I knew, I was flying after my Second.

The blow was stunning, and so liquid fast that I had not seen it coming, although I should have expected it, too. It seemed that this creature and I were constantly underestimating each other.

It would not happen on my end again.

I landed hard, or as hard as one can in sand, before rolling back to my feet and shaking off the blow. My ribs felt caved in on one side, where the creature's clawed hand had caught me, but it was a bruise not a break. My bones were hard to shatter, and although the creature had tried, it had failed.

I dragged in a rough breath, then two. And had the air crushed out of me again when someone grabbed me from behind. It hurt, but it was Ray, so I allowed it.

"Are you alright?" I asked him.

"Me? *Me?* I'm not the one dueling a goddamned dragon!"

Neither was I, I almost said, only to realize that that wasn't exactly true.

There were a number of the creatures, I saw now, which would explain the multitude of shadows that had rippled over the ground. But most of them were standing back, were staring at the great purple one, were doing nothing that I could see. He, on the other hand, was coming at me down the length of the arena.

And he was coming fast.

I did not know how to fight him, and my weapon no longer worked except as a staff, and I seriously doubted that it was going to be enough. But Ray had an idea. I did not know what it was and there was no time to ask, but he was putting something inside my hand, was raising it to my lips, was saying "trust me."

I did trust him.

And I had learned the hard way to listen to him.

I swallowed whatever it was, and then creature was on me.

It tried to roast me with its breath, which was hot enough to scorch multiple lines in the sand, blackening the gold underfoot and creating a crazy pattern as it followed my leaps and bounds. I stayed ahead of the blasts, if only just, but that would not be the case for long. If I faltered, I was dead, for we were well matched in speed and there would be no time to recover from even a single mistake.

So, I did not make one. And I did not stay in front of it, where it could burn me. I caught hold of its tattered wing instead, part of which was trailing after it through the sand, and vaulted onto its back. It did not seem to like that; it screamed again, perhaps because I had torn the wing even more in the process.

I did not mind the scream, but the bucking-far-worse-than-a-bronco that I suddenly found myself riding was a different story.

Ray was running alongside us, yelling something, but I wasn't sure what; I couldn't hear him over the pounding of my heart. And that was despite the fact that the arena was suddenly, eerily quiet, even though the stands remained full of fey. The stadium was large and would not empty quickly, but most people no longer appeared to be trying to get away.

They were just standing there, staring at us with blank expressions that I couldn't read and did not have time to worry about, as the creature I was fighting was clever. When it could not overwhelm me one way, it tried another. And changed form, shifting from dragonkind to its alter ego in an eyeblink, and causing me to suddenly find myself rolling around on the sand once more, wrestling an eight-foot-tall fey with the strength of ten men.

That would have been a problem, except for one thing.

I am dhampir.

The dragonkind seemed surprised to find that I matched him in speed and resiliency. And even more to discover that I hit as hard as he did. It was an even fight, something that was refreshing, as Dory had faced impossible odds more than once.

I was used to waking up surrounded by hostile mages, their hands already wreathed in spell fire. Or an army of torch wielding humans with stakes at the ready. Or a master vampire ages older than we were, who was furious and looking for blood.

Ours.

I had survived them all, even if I had not always won the fight, and had gotten both Dory and me out of there in one piece. Through the years, long odds had become normal, and I no longer feared them. The same did not seem to be true for my opponent, however.

He had an equal chance to best me, but I formed the impression that he was used to easy victories and did not know what to do with either pain or fear. So, I made him feel more of both, hoping that he might flee the field. Instead, he fled back into his stronger form, which was not much of a surprise, as I had expected it.

I had not expected what happened next.

His blood, now liberally smeared on my hand, sank into my skin with a golden flash. And I began to feel strange. Very strange.

"Yeah!" Ray yelled, from somewhere behind me. "Yeah! *Kick his ass, Dorina!*"

I did not know why he was yelling so loudly, as if he possessed the world's largest bullhorn, but it was distracting. As were the other, suddenly magnified sounds all around me. Suddenly, I could hear *everything*.

That included the wind blowing across the sand in a thousand tiny shushing noises; the *creak-creak-creak* of a metal windmill—somebody's junked lawn ornament—slowly turning half an arena away; the nervous shuffling of the previous, almost silent crowd; the caw of a bird far overhead.

And then it accelerated, with sounds rushing at me like speeding bullets from all sides: the liquid from someone's spilled wineskin glugging away over the sand; the *yip, yip, yip* of a small dog, confused about what, exactly, was going on; the banners around the top of the arena snapping; the sudden shocked, indrawn breath of hundreds of people, almost in unison; and a screech from one of the dragonkind that sounded like human screaming.

I looked down at my arm, and all consciousness of my surroundings ceased. Something was happening to me; something strange and potentially very bad. And new—in five hundred years, I had never encountered anything like it.

Fear of the unknown caused a red haze to descend over my vision again and for me to grab the creature who had spelled me.

"What is this?" I heard myself snarl in a voice not my own. "What have you done?"

But he either didn't understand or did not deign to reply, because he started struggling in my grasp, and screeching something in a language I did not know, and trying to back away with his eyes blown wide and alien in his face. He had started to change, but seemed to be doing it very slowly. Or perhaps the time-distortion was mine.

Either way, I saw when scales cascaded down his arms; when his color shaded from peach to lavender to iridescent purple; when his body blew up and then apart, reforming itself into a different and much larger shape; when his shoulder blades erupted with massive black wings, now healed from the damage I had inflicted; and when the no longer human face turned on me with a maw of huge teeth, bared and snarling.

And were met by my own, along with a burst of fire out of my no-longer-recognizable mouth, as my own now huge body came off of the sands in a lunge and tore at his throat before the flames had ended.

I felt scales crushing under the weight of my new maw, felt fangs sinking deep, felt blood filling my mouth and then vaporizing immediately under the heat generated by both our fires. He was trying to incinerate me, with flames rushing all over my body. And sloughing off as easily and harmlessly as raindrops, blackening the sand around us but leaving me untouched.

Because I had scales now, too, rivers of them stretching over a form easily as large as his. Indeed, it seemed to *be* his, or a copy of it, with hugely powerful black claws on the ends of my arms, thrashing black wings in the air above me, and everywhere I looked, deep, dark, iridescent scales, all in the rich purple I had so admired.

And had just stolen, I realized, as I finally understood what Ray had done.

Because this had happened to me once before, or to be more accurate, it had happened to Dory. The flower known as Dragon's Claw allowed someone to absorb certain aspects of another creature for a short time. Normally, the changes were minor, as had been the case with the children eating the candy in the marketplace. Or with Ray, suddenly becoming far more hirsute than before.

But he had had a reason for thinking that he might get more than that; that he might take on our guard's complete form, giving him an equal chance in a fight against him. Because he'd seen it happen before. He'd seen it happen to Dory.

She and I seemed to have an affinity for the plant far greater than what was normal. Enough that she'd once taken on the form of an Irin, better known as a fallen angel on Earth, long enough to defeat a powerful demon lord. And enough that I had now mirrored the form of my opponent, giving me a brief chance against him.

One I had better use, because I did not think that this would last for long.

And when it failed . . .

I did not think it would be a good idea to be here when it failed.

I renewed my efforts, ignoring the flames, the claws that raked harmlessly off of my scales, and the creature's desperate thrashing. I had him by the neck, my powerful jaws clamped tight on the smaller, more flexible, and more vulnerable scales there. And I discovered that there was one thing that could hurt a dragon: another dragon.

But he knew that, too, and tried everything to get a grip on me. Including grasping me hard by all four limbs and dragging me off the ground, his massive wings shredding the air as they fought to carry both of us skyward. I heard Ray curse as he was tossed head over heels by the gale-force winds, saw the sands underneath us recede as the creature took to the heavens; felt my huge tail whip about uselessly beneath me, like my legs, which were suddenly scrabbling for purchase on absolutely nothing.

But I did not let go. I did not know this body and could not afford to lose the advantage that surprise had given me. I had one chance to defeat him, one brief moment in which to snatch victory from defeat and death. And I was taking it.

So, I ignored his flailing, his fire, his claws. I wrapped my useless tail around him instead, squeezing the great body as hard as I could and making sure that I could not fall away. It was like an extra arm, one far larger than the other ones I had, increasing my grip considerably.

And allowing me to savage him.

I tore at the great neck, mauled it, shredded it. Felt the scales come away in my mouth, enough to threaten to choke me, but still I held on. I used fire to blast them, activating it with a thought, and blowing them out of my throat like ash. And sank my teeth ever deeper, into meat unprotected by any armor, into flesh that gave and gave and gave under my assault, into blood that gushed and spurted and filled my mouth with something far more delicious than scales.

And then we were falling again, with no warning from my suddenly weakly moving companion except for the ground rushing up to meet us. We hit with a terrible crash, thudding my bones and almost making me lose my grip. But if that had been the plan, it failed.

My jaws felt like they were locked in place; I wasn't sure I could have let go had I wanted to. And I did not want to. I wanted to rend, to tear, to bite through the great throat entirely and watch the head bounce away onto the sand. I wanted blood, more and more of it, drinking it down now as if I could never get enough. I wanted *everything*.

I had heard of the blood lust of vampires all my life but had never felt it. I was feeling it now, only this went far beyond that. It was a blood frenzy, such as the old legends spoke of; when masters became crazed in battle from the carnage being wrought and the blood being absorbed by them and their families. Until it was all they could see, feel, smell, or want.

Until it became their whole world, and they would continue until the battle ended or they were dead. Nothing else could stop them. And nothing was stopping me.

I felt my opponent fall from my lips, whether in one piece or two I didn't know and no longer cared. For he was dead and there was other prey to be had. Half a dozen of them had come with him, and were now looking at each other, and screeching in their strange voices as a blood covered savage with a dripping maw charged at them from across the arena. And called out a mind-numbing cry as she did so, the master power I possessed.

The one that froze my prey in place for a long moment while I brutalized them.

And brutalize I did.

One got away, one who had already taken off before I reached them, one who spiraled into the sky in a limping sort of flight, as if the call had almost caught him, too.

But he was too far away; he shrugged it off and fled, becoming a distant speck in a moment.

But the rest were mine.

"Dorina! Dorina!" I heard someone calling my name, and felt my father's familiar power flowing across my mind. On Earth, it might have been enough to rein me in; even here it might have, as he had always been stronger. But it seemed that my mind had changed, too, and he was unfamiliar with its new makeup.

So, I threw off his hold and *feasted*.

Blood spurted, scales flew, claws raked me again and again as paralysis broke—too late. I felt the meat of my body torn, felt bones hard as iron shatter and buckle, felt pain—but I was used to pain. I wasn't used to this, this exhilaration that came from literally consuming my enemies, or the power that their blood lent me, which healed my wounds almost as soon as they were created, and fed the blood lust that had been sleeping for five hundred years and slept no more.

And then it was suddenly over.

I paused, looking around and heaving, my body blood covered one minute and pristine the next, as all of the fey blood was absorbed in an instant.

But there was no more. None living anyway. The dragonkind were torn asunder, with pieces of their flesh gone as well as their blood drained. They lay steaming on the blackened ground, the fires they had used against me still burning in places, and their bodies twitching but not with life.

And I suddenly found myself exhausted, falling back onto human knees that burned as they hit the smoking ground. I cried out softly, not understanding, and then they were there: Mircea, gathering me up in his arms; Ray, yelling something I couldn't understand; Marlowe, staring at me as if he had never seen me before; and fey, hundreds, perhaps thousands of fey, screaming one thing, over and over into the midday air: "*Dorina, Dorina, Dorina!*"

Then darkness overtook me and I knew no more.

Chapter Fifteen
Dory

Okay, that might not have been the best move I ever made, I thought, as all hell broke loose a moment after I grabbed Steen. The worst of it was that I hadn't considered the fact that dragons could partially change. And that if the human-looking waiters could sprout wings out of their backs, the chieftain of Vitharr could probably grow scales over his neck.

Like in the area directly under my knife.

That would have been bad enough, but he didn't stop there. He transformed in an instant, going from human to something else faster than I could blink. And sprouting a tail in the process that he used to fling me across the length of the tower, in a blow that felt like it broke my back.

I immediately fell back into slow-time, since anything else would have meant instant death, and even that didn't help much. Blurred shapes leapt for me from all sides, moving so blindingly fast despite the warped time perception that my eyes couldn't follow them, forcing me to rely on blasts of flame and displaced air to even guess where they were. And my other senses weren't doing any better.

All I could smell was fear—familiar, skin-ruffling, sweat-inducing fear; all I could taste was blood on my tongue where I must have bitten it, harsh and penny bright and bitter; and all I could hear was indescribable. Dragons could move silently when they wanted to, despite their huge size, but these had no reason to want to. And the infernal screeches were so loud in the enclosed space, and so stunning in their intensity, that it felt like being in the midst of a hurricane—just an endless, deafening roar.

I hit down, a stunning blow against the far wall, but nowhere near any stairs or doors out of here. And immediately launched myself off the stone and back into the room, getting space to maneuver. But it wasn't easy.

In seconds, the world had been reduced to fire, scales, screams and claws, leaving me unable to think. I could barely even breathe, and was surviving off of instinct alone—and speed and agility that they hadn't expected from a human. But it wouldn't last, and it wouldn't be enough.

I was as far outside of my league here as a guy off the street facing a master vampire, and was likely to end the same way.

And soon.

Someone scraped claws down my arm, lines of fire that barely connected or they would have torn the whole thing off; someone else threw a blast of flame across the space where I'd been a second before, catching the trailing hem of my pretty new gown on fire; and another blurry form hit the ground in front of me, cutting off my escape and shattering the stone under its weight, shards of which flew up into my face as I turned—

Straight into the path of a pair of gigantic jaws.

I had half a second to see them swooping down from above, so large that they blocked out my view of anything else; to watch firelight glinting off of rows of blood-stained teeth; to smell fetid breath washing over me in a vomit-inducing wave—

And then I jerked my duffle bag over my head and felt the familiar, disorienting flip into another world.

There was a sudden, eerie silence as I lay sprawled on the concrete steps leading down into my arsenal. I could hear nothing except for the echoes of another world ringing in my ears. That lasted longer than it should have, as my hearing usually repaired itself quickly, but then, it wasn't usually blasted by decibels loud enough to feel like body blows, either.

It was enough to make me wonder if I even had eardrums anymore. But after a few moments, the ringing resolved itself into sounds: my own desperate breathing, the ceiling fan creaking slightly every time it revolved, and the crackle of flames.

I didn't understand the latter until I realized: I was still on fire.

I leapt for a nearby shelf, grabbed a suppressant potion, and smashed the fist-sized globe into the center of my chest. It broke, allowing the cool contents to splatter all over me. And then to run across my body in a glistening coat of blue-tinted gel that suffocated the fire and soothed my blistered skin.

It didn't sooth enough.

My body felt like a giant wound from the searing pain of burns, too many to count; I couldn't see much through the billowing steam; and my ears were still being assaulted by hissing sounds as the suppressant battled the fire. But the senate's stash proved its worth, and in the end, the fire lost. And I collapsed back onto the steps, unable to cope for a moment, even to assess the damage.

I just lay there instead, trying to pant my way back to something like coherence, while spent blue goo slowly dripped off my body and down the stairs, making a small puddle at the bottom. I watched it blankly, wondering what the hell. And whether my duffle bag was currently getting batted about the hall by massive claws or crushed underfoot.

I wasn't worried about that so much, as I'd paid a mage a fortune to layer protections on the thing, enough that even a dragon's weight shouldn't bother it. The big question was, had they seen me disappear into it? I was in slow-time when it happened, so it should have looked like I simply vanished, disappearing in the blink of an eye with the dark colored bag falling unnoticed to the floor thereafter.

Should have.

But what if dragons could do slow-time, too? I'd never thought to ask Claire. Seemed like kind of a glaring oversight at the moment.

And if they could . . .

I stared up at the ceiling, wondering if my squeaky fan would get fixed by the simple method of a bunch of enraged dragons tearing it apart. My overstimulated brain even had me jumping at literal shadows a few times, as the elongated, moving fingers of the fan blades mimicked dragon claws ripping through the concrete. The third time my heart almost leapt out of my chest I decided that I had to know what was going on, regardless of how bad it was, rolled over and got to my knees.

And winced when the movement stretched damaged flesh to the splitting point. But my body supported me, however unwillingly. And I ignored the large burnt patches on my legs where the burning skirt had slapped me, some of which looked well and surely cooked, because I was still in battle and you didn't stop in battle unless the wound was mortal.

Or else you'd likely acquire one that was.

Instead, I cracked open the door at the top of the stairs to see what was happening outside. It looked like an actual door on this side, with a knob and everything, and a round hole on the other where the portal let out into the real world. I stayed well back, as getting too far through the door would activate said portal and dump me out somewhere that I probably didn't want to be. But that limited my vision, and all I saw was . . . nothing.

Just nothing.

A wall of boiling blackness met my eyes, without the tiniest fragment of light to help me out. I killed the fluorescents overhead by dragging a bloody hand across the switch by the door, but it didn't improve things. Now all I saw were leaping after images.

Yet I could feel, and the air was warm, humid and strangely heavy. And I could smell, although I wished I couldn't as whatever was out there was nose-wrinklingly rancid, like rotting meat mixed with sulphur mixed with . . . I didn't know. But it was awful enough to make the abattoir of a hall seem perfumed by comparison, and to leave me teary eyed and thus even less able to see anything!

I could hear, however, only I didn't know what, exactly, I was listening to.

Instead of the scrape of huge claws over stone, the flapping of giant wings, and the unearthly, mind-numbing, almost-a-weapon-in-itself screeching, there was . . . I wasn't sure. It sounded like a giant kettledrum, beating loudly from somewhere nearby. And a rushing wind that was even louder, almost gale force in its intensity, although I could feel none of it. And underneath it all, the faint lapping of waves . . .

I was still trying to puzzle it out when one of those unearthly screeches tore through the air, sounding muffled and far away, yet echoing so loudly that it pierced my body and threatened to jolt me apart. I clutched the stair underneath me and the nearby wall, holding on despite the fact that the room wasn't moving, being in another dimension from whatever was happening out there. And despite the fact that it didn't help; I continued to feel like a pancake that was being flipped a dozen different ways.

Until the hellish sound broke off, as abruptly as it had come, leaving me panting again and more than a little freaked out. As soon as I could move, I grabbed an industrial-strength flashlight and aimed it out of the door, trying to see something, anything. And I did, although nothing I had ever expected.

Instead of the Great Hall, what appeared in the flashlight's thin beam looked like a cave, albeit a weird one with a floor of liquid sloshing against strange, curved walls. The liquid appeared to be the source of the stench, sending foul streams of gasses floating upward and bubbling alarmingly as it hit the sides of the cave. The rounded walls bowed inward and did not appear to be made out of rock. Instead, they glistened pinkish red and wrinkled, and pulsed slightly, almost as if—

My thoughts stuttered to a halt and I stared at the walls some more. Then let the light slowly trace what looked like dark veining running through what was definitely not stone. And finally splashed some illumination around the extent of the "cave" while I adjusted to my new reality.

Yeah.

Yeah.

Okay, then.

I closed the door carefully, so that none of the wetness sloshing about a few feet below the frame would get in. And started digging through my arsenal while ignoring the beating of my own heart, which was more like a snare drum at the moment than a kettle, and the rapid rushing of air through my own lungs, and the sudden cramping in my own stomach. Because if ever there was a time to break out the good stuff, it was after having been swallowed by a dragon.

One who was about to have a very bad case of indigestion.

I'd lost my portal in the confusion, probably when Steen smacked the hell out of me with his tail, and wasn't sure I had anything in stock that would work on dragon scales. But fortunately, I wasn't dealing with dragon scales. Unless the creatures had them coating their insides, too, and it hadn't looked that way.

In any case, the game plan wasn't to bust out of here; it was to get the beast to vomit me up, and then go HAM on anybody who objected to my continued, non-digested state. Which was why I went with potion grenades, grabbing a couple of the largest I had and lobbing them out the door before slamming it shut. And waiting.

Some vague noises made it to my ears, but I couldn't tell what they were. If the beast was bellowing in agony, it was being subtle about it. So, I threw out a few more bombs, and then a few more, all with the same effect—not much. I stood there after a moment, nonplussed and gazing about, and wondered what to try next when the damned creature's stomach acid just absorbed whatever I gave it, as if I was feeding the thing instead of hurting it!

And then I noticed: I had a bigger problem.

Way bigger.

Because I wasn't actually in anything's stomach; the door to my portal was, having been swallowed along with my duffle bag by a bastard of a dragon. But said door was starting to look a little ragged around the edges, despite the layers of protection on it. It was supposed to be impervious to just about anything—except dragon stomach acid, apparently.

And if it went, so did I. Not for a meal, but for an eternity in a little concrete box, because without a gate, no one could find the portal I'd made for myself in non-space. Leaving me stuck here until I suffocated or starved or offed myself with one of the many available weapons, because the alternative was—

Not happening, I thought, breaking out of my moment of stunned realization and grabbing one of the big boys. Because *fuck* dying alone, lost in a little capsule in nothingness. Fuck that right to hell!

Along with the goddamned creature who'd swallowed me.

I flung open the door, a new weapon in hand. It was experimental, a bastard of a thing that didn't even have a name yet, but which I had dubbed The Liquidator since that was what usually happened to anything that encountered it. It was basically an acid grenade launcher on steroids, and in trials, I'd seen it dissolve a Mack truck.

Here's hoping, I thought, and let loose.

And, okay, *that* was doing something, I realized, as the whole arsenal abruptly began rocking hard enough to throw me off my feet. It wasn't supposed to do that, but maybe the rules changed when you had the door open and were actively connected to another world? Or maybe the damage was worse than I'd thought, and the whole thing was about to collapse on top of my head!

I didn't know, and didn't have time to ponder the possibilities. The mad thrashing sent me tumbling off the stairs, hitting the ground, and dodging to avoid a shelf full of small arms that smashed into the concrete beside my head. And then crawling back up again, to wedge myself into the doorway and keep on firing, despite the whole place feeling as if it had been caught in an earthquake.

Only there was no earth here, just dragon flesh, which it seemed wasn't impervious to everything, after all. But I couldn't tell how much damage I was doing because I couldn't see. The Liquidator didn't have a tactical light and I couldn't hold it and the flashlight both.

And couldn't spare time to give a damn, because the movement was causing waves of stomach acid to slosh over the doorframe! As if I didn't have enough problems right now! Even worse, the damned stuff was almost as good as what I was shooting, etching the stairs at it flooded downward, and eating into the soles of my shoes.

I cursed, grabbed another suppressant, and smashed it on the stairs to stop the liquid from dissolving the concrete. But I still had to duck behind a warded cabinet to keep from being immolated by my own stash, some of which the flood had set off in the room behind me. So much for my wardrobe, I thought, as it went up in flames after one of my own firebombs hit it.

What hit me was a sudden beam of light from the darkness beyond the doorframe. Smoke was billowing everywhere inside my arsenal now so I still couldn't see too well. But I kicked off my shoes, grabbed some thick soled boots before they went up in flames, shoved my feet inside and made my way back up there.

And saw a hole in the "cave" wall not too far away, a big one. But it didn't show me the dining hall.

I couldn't see much of anything beyond the ring of fire, with fluttery bits of burning flesh around it and a smaller hole further back which I guessed was to the outside? I couldn't tell as it opened less onto light than onto slightly softer darkness. It seemed bright down here in the depths, but it really wasn't.

That didn't make sense, as the hall had been filled with color and light and noise only a few moments ago. So, maybe I hadn't torn through to the outside, after all. But then, where was the light coming from?

I concentrated, but heard nothing now, except for the whistling of the wind. And I was pretty sure that it *was* wind this time, and not the labored breathing of the dragon's lungs, because I could hear that, too. But this was louder and constant, not in and out, but almost as if—

I didn't get a chance to finish the thought before another screech tore through the darkness and my vision suddenly skewed. Now I was looking at a light, all right—a moon, shining through the two gaping, burning holes. Not Earth's moon, with its familiar craters and valleys, but *a* moon, nonetheless.

One spreading light across the open sky and inward through the wound I'd made, because we weren't in the tower anymore. We'd left it behind and were airborne, me and the creature who had decided to swallow me. I saw a few snow-capped peaks, silvered by moonlight, for an instant, before we slung around in another direction.

Only not for long.

Because it looked like The Liquidator had done its job, enough that the beast carrying me across the heavens was struggling. I could hear its screams constantly now, muffled by the surrounding acres of dragon flesh; could see the visual in front of me changing repeatedly as the beast writhed across the sky, fighting to stay aloft; could feel the sudden jerk and accompanying weightlessness when it failed.

And *shit.*

Chapter Sixteen

I jerked back inside the arsenal as we began to plummet and slammed the door. And stood there for a second with my back to it, arms splayed and mind racing, wondering if my already tattered gateway would hold up to a mile long fall onto rocky cliffs while encased in a few thousand pounds of dragon flesh. And what would happen to me if it didn't.

Then I grabbed what I could, including my bug out bag, any weapon with a strap I could throw over my back, and a personal shield. I slapped the latter around my wrist before flinging open the door, preparing to jump and take my chances. But something had happened in the brief time I'd been away.

Something I didn't understand, because the only light I had was being slung around wildly and obscured half the time by something else. Something that I couldn't see, even when I shone my flashlight at it, because it didn't stay put long enough. And because the dragon I was riding in was pretty damned active for a corpse!

I finally realized that my dragon wasn't responsible for the contortions; that was down to those who were currently fighting over it. I couldn't tell exactly what was happening, except that it was taking place hundreds of feet up and involved deafening screeches, massive claws and flying blood. And left me being slung about as the body I was riding in was jerked back and forth.

After a moment of silently cursing, I decided that this changed nothing. And to go with the initial plan of getting the hell out of there, because part of surviving a fight is knowing when you are outclassed. And being smart enough to swallow your pride and run.

I had no problem with running, but I did have a problem getting to the opening to allow me to do so.

The fight had caused the stomach acid to begin sloshing about like waves on the ocean—toxic, acidic waves. And while it shouldn't have been able to get through my shield, I'd just seen the stuff eat a dozen potion bombs while barely burping. I stared at it, watching it froth and foam a few feet below the doorframe, and did not feel confident.

But there was nothing for it, so I stuck in a toe, and when it failed to get eaten off, jumped down into a sea of foul-smelling liquid. It was thicker than water, and darker; when submerged, I couldn't see a thing, which did not help with the disorientation. I couldn't even see the indicator light on my shield, which was supposed to protect me for a full half hour but that was under normal conditions.

I had no idea how well it would work in these, and decided not to find out. I kept my eyes fixed on the jagged hole of slightly less dark up ahead and fought my way through the surf—and the leftovers of the dragon's last meal, the bones of which were large enough to have not completely dissolved and kept slamming into me like trees in a rapids-filled river. I went down more than once, my head spinning, but kept on fighting, because what choice was there?

Finally, in pain and nearing exhaustion, I made it to the edge of the no longer burning hole. And grasped hold of the ragged top, which was hot enough to make the shield smoke and hiss. And hiked myself up enough to get out of the acidic flood, while I fought my way across the gap from the ruined, rubbery stomach to the ruined, fleshy hide.

And then lay there, on a ledge of smoking meat and fat, gasping and laughing and half disbelieving that I'd made it this far.

Only to look over the side and almost immediately wish that I hadn't.

Because my captor hadn't been challenged by a single dragon, or even two. He and his people had been pursued by what had to be half a castle's worth of them, all of whom had just caught up with us. And were lighting up the night with glowing eyes and bursts of flame that seared my vision—and my skin.

None of the flames touched me, as I was merely an insignificant, dark lump clinging to the side of the great creature I rode. But I was quickly sweating anyway, both from panic and from the amount of heat that was being tossed around. And which was being fanned by the speed of the bodies whizzing by so close as to almost blow me off with the wind of their passing.

Yet I couldn't tear my eyes away. Giant wings were silvered by moonlight as they sliced through the air, throats and eyes glowed golden yellow and fiery red, and scales glittered like shards of precious jewels in the firelight—ruby, dark emerald, sapphire, amethyst and topaz. But they moved as sinuously as the flames themselves, set against a backdrop of night and moon and snow-covered mountains framed by pale green, diaphanous scarves of what looked like aurora borealis.

Fire made flesh, I thought dizzily. Claire had told me that her people were called that by other fey, and I'd never seen a clearer demonstration of why. They looked like sparks darting up into the sky from a campfire, just as fast, just as deadly, just as beautiful.

I would have probably sat there for longer, transfixed and in awe, with their heat and the cold wind alternately freezing and cooking me—except they decided to play a game. Suddenly, I knew how the pigs had felt at dinner, when the corpse I was riding was snagged by something I couldn't see, except for a massive, reaching claw. And flung across the heavens like a fleshy football.

I was caught by someone else before I could so much as gasp out a breath, who was almost immediately attacked by a dozen others. So, he threw his prize to another player in this weird game of keep away, or maybe hot potato, because nobody kept me for more than a minute. In quick succession, the dragon's corpse was flung to a third and then a fourth combatant, twisting and turning all the while as if trying to shake me loose.

And doing a damned fine job! Some of the scales around me were blackened and broken, or melted by the blasts I'd shot at them, but not nearly as many as I'd have liked. They were strong and slick, and hard as hell to grasp, with my only saving grace being the shield, which allowed me to grip the knife-edged shards without slicing myself to pieces.

It ensured that I was still in place when another screaming behemoth latched hold.

He was enormous, this one, a scarred old bastard that looked as ancient and rugged as the hills. Some of his scales were missing, cut away in long furrows down one side as if something had gotten claws into him and gotten them in deep. But that must have been years ago, as the healed skin underneath looked as gnarled and solid as stone.

He was hard to see except for those scars, as his coloring was mostly green, but not sleek and shiny like the others. More like a dragon shaped piece of the mountainside had been cut out and molded onto his hide.

There were ridges everywhere, not in any neat alignment, but as haphazard as the striations and fissures in rock. And the mottled color, which varied from every shade of green through every shade of gray to black in the crevasses, gave off a very convincing mossy vibe.

I could imagine him lying in wait on a mountain somewhere, unseen by his prey, until they literally stumbled across him, and maybe not even then.

But there was nothing subtle about his eyes, which were a blazing yellow that shed a radiance onto the space around them like twin suns. I got a good look at them when he suddenly curved the great neck around to stare at me, as if he'd known exactly where I was. I stared back, at flaring nostrils larger than my head; at red-tinged teeth longer than my body; and at glowing, sun-lit eyes that were going to enslave my mind, any second now, if I didn't look away!

Yet I found myself unable to, even though staring a dragon in the face was as intimidating as hell.

I'd done it once with Claire in her transformed state, but this was worse since I didn't know whether I was facing friend or foe. And still didn't, when the eyes narrowed and hot, hot breath washed over me, like a blast straight off a furnace. But if he was an enemy, he could have eaten me already and there wouldn't have been a damned thing that I could do about it, so I must be looking at a friend.

Right?

I guessed so. Because a voice rumbled through me a moment later, so deep and dark and primal that it felt like a mountain was speaking. "Hold on, little one."

I held on, completely incapable at that moment of doing anything else, including answering back. But that seemed to be enough. The huge neck curved away and he took off for the castle, the immense black wings above us rending the sky as if they were giant claws themselves.

Yet this time, I didn't feel as if I was about to fall to my death. He was huge, just mind-numbingly big, and he moved like a bat straight out of hell. But he managed to do it with a serpentine grace that made it possible for me to cling on despite the ridiculous speed.

We outpaced everyone else, with me getting the definite impression that the others didn't want to mess with this one. Two smaller dragons scattered in front of us, contorting their bodies in almost comically undignified movements to get out of the way. And another, who was closer to our size, sailed off with a bit more elegance but no less speed, becoming a speck on the horizon in the time it took for me to blink.

For brief moment, I thought we were home free, as it seemed that nobody was willing to take on my champion alone. And they didn't. They took him together, with three of them attacking at once from different directions, and a fourth joining a moment later, claws out and shrieking, from directly overhead.

And I guessed that last one was too much, even for my behemoth of a rescuer.

Because a second later, he dropped me.

I would have screamed then, if I hadn't been choking on my stomach, which was suddenly trying to leave my body through my throat, and if there'd been any point. But I'd had so many shocks today that it seemed almost trite. Like, you're screaming *now?*

Instead, I clutched a protruding rib and hung on for dear life as the huge corpse slowly rolled over. The enormous spine, which I guessed was what the dragons had been latching hold of, was heavy enough to flip us. And leave me clinging to my rib bone upside down as the ground rushed up to meet me.

Even worse, the dead dragon's wing, which had been protecting me a little from the winds in front, wrapped around the body and flapped upward, doing exactly nothing except deafening me from the ungodly sound. And knocking against me painfully, jolting my body and making it almost impossible to focus on my indicator, the lighted, watch-like piece on my wrist that paired with the shield and told me how much protection I had left. And when I finally did catch a glimpse . . .

Shit!

I switched off the shield, because fifteen seconds weren't going to help me much right now, but would be needed in a minute when this crazy ride ended. Until then, I'd make do. After all, how much worse could it get?

I got my answer a second later, when the residue of already committed magic faded from my protection, and the wind hit me with its full force for the first time.

And son of a *bitch!*

It was immediately staggering, furious and painful, like a constant uppercut. I was almost blown off my perch so many times that I lost count, with my body rattling painfully against the rib bone, my hands sliding desperately on half-dried blood, and my legs being sliced to ribbons while trying to cling to the damned scales of the seat.

One that was now above me!

It made spotting a good place to land almost impossible, but I had no choice. I had to separate from the giant body I was riding or die. I had all of fifteen seconds of protection left to keep my brains from decorating a rock in Faerie, assuming that I could time things right; they wouldn't also protect me from being crushed by tons of scale-covered blubber immediately thereafter!

But it was hard to see anything with the wind slapping me in the face, tears running down my cheeks, and a jutting ledge sticking out of a cliffside and almost sucker punching me in the head.

I jerked back, then tried desperately to catch hold of it, or at least of one of the pine-like trees bristling outward from it at weird angles. But they were gone almost before I'd realized they were there, flashing by in an instant. And the only thing around me then was—

That, I thought, as my ride was grabbed and jerked upward by another screeching monster.

It flipped us, I guessed to grab hold of the spine rather than the huge, shiny plates over the stomach, which offered little purchase. And would have sent me flying in the process, except for the damned wing. It redeemed itself by crashing into me again a second after I lost my grip, flinging my suddenly airborne body back against the scaley hide, which I finished ruining my hands scrambling to grasp.

I managed it—somehow—and was rewarded by the hot potato game starting up again, because the whole battling group appeared to have caught up to me at the same moment. I didn't bother keeping track of the score this time. It took everything I had just to hold on while my hands and legs were shredded, my breath was continually cut off by vertigo-inducing movements, and my body was battered by the damned, infernal, godforsaken wing!

I clung nonetheless, bleeding from a hundred wounds but not letting go. Because diving off the side and taking my chances with the shield had just been ruled out. Sure, it might help with the dashing-my-brains-out-on-a-rock thing, but I didn't think it would do much for the being-ripped-apart-by-apex-predators thing that was likely to happen first.

Dragons peppered the sky everywhere I looked, moving like quicksilver and seemingly more at home in the air than on land. Bash my head in hell, I thought desperately, watching them. I'd never make it to the ground to have that chance.

And then it got worse, when the scaley football I was riding was intercepted yet again—by Lord Steen.

It had to be him; it was too big to be anyone else, and no other dragon had that particular black with iridescent green and purple coloring. He reflected the moon and the night and the aurora borealis like a mirror, and was honestly hard to see even this close. But I had plenty of chances to try because he didn't take off with me like the others.

Instead, he began ripping through the corpse, ignoring the still burning and smoking parts, literally butchering his own creature mid-air. Limbs and the opposite wing went flying, but I think they were accidental, because he was focusing his attack on the torso. He was digging for me.

Even worse, his dragons were keeping my would-be rescuers at bay. They couldn't get close enough to save me, not before Steen finished tearing me apart. I was on my own.

And then, as if to underscore the point, my ride suddenly acquired a sunroof.

I felt my stomach cramp, and my breath start coming faster and heavier in my throat as panic swept over me.

It wasn't something I normally felt. Normally, when things got this bad, Dorina came out and saved the day with some of her patented, cutthroat savagery. It might get wicked, it *would* get bloody, but it would work; it always had.

Only Dorina wasn't here. And without her, I was falling apart. My hands were shaking, sliding on my own blood as I gripped what were essentially knife blades to try to stay put; my heart was beating, but erratically, as if it couldn't decide between fight or flight since neither was an option, and kept flipping between the two; and my mind . . . was fog.

Just fog. Just panic. Just nothing useful at all. I couldn't think, could barely breathe, and was absolutely, positively, flat out of ideas.

But someone else wasn't.

Someone else had plenty of ideas. Not good ones, mind you, but ideas. And they were being put into effect in the middle of the craziest, most dangerous battle I had ever been in, because my husband was *insane*.

And the fact that he did not have wings had not stopped him from flying.

I assumed he had hitched a ride with somebody to get this far, but didn't see who. All I saw was a tiny Louis-Cesare getting rapidly bigger as he sped toward me like a bullet. An unshielded bullet who was about to take an acid bath when he plunged through the gaping wound and into the damned stomach and *no, no, no!*

He was moving too fast for me to do anything but brace myself, and try to catch him on impact. And restart the shield around us both at the same time, for whatever tiny advantage that might give us. But he'd been flung at approximately the speed of sound, and I could barely see him much less—

I didn't even feel him hit. I had a second to understand that I'd just gone airborne, to see the reddish "cave" looming up around me again, to feel Louis-Cesare's arms engulf me, tight, tight, so very tight, like he wanted to fuse us together. And then we fell, unshielded since I hadn't had a chance to reactivate a goddamned *thing* before we slammed down—

Into an empty cave.

The impact with the spongy surface was hard enough to rattle me. And between that and the punch that my husband's body had just delivered, it took me a moment to understand what had happened. Namely that the ocean of stomach acid had drained away, probably through one of the many gashes Steen had been making.

The bastard trying to kill us had just done us a favor, which would have been great, which would have been *awesome*, if not for one thing.

One very, very big thing.

I had landed on my back, bouncing slightly on the trampoline-like surface of the ruined organ, giving me a perfect view of a vividly green eyeball the size of the moon. It was peering down at me through the tattered remains of the ribcage, where pieces of red meat and yellow fat clung to the bones that arched upward on both sides like a closed fist. A large flap of skin fluttered in the breeze, half obscuring the scene, like a macabre flag, but all I could see was that eye.

And it saw me, too. The head jerked back slightly and the pupil contracted at the sight of the two tiny creatures that had just tumbled into view. It was close enough that I could see myself, a helpless, nothing of a creature, lost in the great mirror above me.

Louis-Cesare was staggering to his feet, was trying to orient himself, was yet to notice the night sky above us, hung with stars, featuring a breathtakingly beautiful death. And I couldn't tell him. For one of the few times in my life, I experienced a moment of complete, frozen immobility.

I wasn't sure if it was the almost hypnotic quality of the dragon's gaze, about ten times greater than Claire's had been, or the sheer, unadulterated terror coursing through my veins. But I may as well have been glued in place, lying there feeling the remnants of the dead dragon's stomach acid burn my skin. And watching a brilliant orange light suffuse the throat and spill out of the maw of the creature above me.

Fire made flesh, I thought again, and then I *did* scream, because it worked the other way, too, didn't it? Louis-Cesare and I were about to be roasted alive, cooked in our own juices until our flesh dripped off our bones and our ashes blew away on the wind. Flesh made into fire in the most visceral way possible.

"Dory! Dory!" Louis-Cesare was shaking me, because he still didn't see it. And I didn't have time to say anything, even if I could have managed it, before a blast of hot air hit us like something straight off of hell.

And finally, my paralysis broke.

I scrambled to my feet as flames formed a fireball in the great mouth, as they danced off the sides of the ruined "cave", as they scorched my skin even this far away. And as Louis-Cesare finally caught a clue, staring upward for a split second with the same disbelief written on his face that was probably on mine. And then he snatched me up, preparing to demonstrate exactly how fast he could move.

Which, for once, wasn't fast enough.

Chapter Seventeen

Fire exploded all around us, in a rain so thick and intense that I could feel the heat even through the shield I'd managed to raise again, battering and clawing at the surface like a live thing. One that was as furious as its master, throwing us off our feet and across the floor, with the sheer force of the blast enough to have killed us without protection. And even with it, we were tumbling in an endless sea of red, with no idea where the doorway to my arsenal was, our only possible refuge before my fifteen seconds were up and our barrier cut—

Out, I thought, as the ungodly heat abruptly stopped.

For a moment, I thought that my nerve endings had been seared away, and that I simply couldn't feel it. But Louis-Cesare's hand was in mine, hard and strong and undeniably real, and it would have dusted to ash by now had those flames so much as touched us. I stared around, my heart trying to pound its way out of my chest, my mind confused and my eyes completely blind in the pulsing red aftermath, my retinas having had enough and peaced out.

Until Louis-Cesare used the link between us to calm me, and to let me see through his eyes, something we hadn't done for some time now.

Only what I saw didn't make sense.

Well, part of it did, namely the blackened and partially missing floor, the steaming walls, and the air so dry when the last of the shield finally gave up the ghost with a *pop* that it was hard to breathe. Making the burnt-out husk of an organ around us smell like nothing, just nothing at all. But the rest . . .

"What's happening?" I tried to say, only my vocal cords didn't seem to work, with the words coming out only as a faint rasp.

And then I didn't have to ask, when a new cry tore through the heavens, one so loud and so terrifying that it stopped my heart and almost sent me back to the floor. I thought I'd become inured to dragon cries, having heard almost nothing else for long minutes now. But this was different. This shook the *world*, as well as the air all around me, and had my bones wanting to liquify in my skin in sheer goddamned terror.

And judging by how still he'd suddenly gone, this most apex of all predators, at least in our world, Louis-Cesare felt the same. But he held on, nonetheless, although the soothing vibes he'd been sending me abruptly stopped. Along with the blood in my veins, the pounding of my heart, and every other thing in this world, as if the entire realm held its breath for an instant.

Until a colossal golden dragon tore out of the sky and barreled straight into Steen.

Lord Rathen had arrived, and he was *pissed*.

Louis-Cesare was yelling something, but I couldn't hear him over the terrible screeching, from both Steen and Rathen. I couldn't hear anything except for my heart, which had started up again with a lurch and was pounding a thudding beat in my ears. And my brain, some part of which had stayed sane in all this, and woke up to observe that dragons must be able to control to a degree how big they became when transformed, like vampires could decide how much of their power they called up.

Because no way would that behemoth have fit into the tower where we'd dined.

Or that one, I thought, as Steen's form suddenly boiled in the air, as if calling dark shadows to come and join it. And come they did, flying in so thick and fast that they blocked out the moon, like a lightbulb had suddenly been switched off in the sky. It would have been unnerving if I'd had any nerves left, and would have mattered more if I wasn't looking at the world through vampire eyes.

But Louis-Cesare could still see perfectly, if in dark blues, blacks and silvers instead of the vivid colors of a moment ago. Clear enough, anyway, for me to spot the fact that there were suddenly two monsters bigger than jumbo jets hanging in the air above us. And while I wasn't clear on what passed for a code of manners in dragon-land, having been here less than a day and been busy almost dying for much of that, it was safe to say that Steen had shattered it all to hell.

And Lord Rathen, or Lord Den I guessed, since he was currently a massive, screeching, golden hunk of impossible, was annoyed.

Very annoyed.

To the point of immediately trying to eviscerate Steen.

Go get him, I thought dizzily, as the world tumbled around us, sending us rolling again. Our dragon was still clutched in one of Steen's giant claws, which meant that we were caught up in the biggest, baddest, no holds barred throwdown in, well, my history anyway. Which was saying less than it used to, I thought, as I lost my grip on Louis-Cesare, fell what felt like at least a couple stories as our ride did a loop-de-loop, and bounced off of a rubbery wall.

And then was jerked against a possibly genuinely insane man, who was about to shake me to death one minute, and was hugging me so hard the next that I thought I might burst.

"No time," I gasped out, right before the shaking recommenced.

"*Did you hear me?*" Louis-Cesare yelled—straight into my ear.

"Ahhh! No! What?" I stared at him, but only saw a vision of my own, very wigged out expression looking back at me, since I was still seeing through his eyes.

"*—chute, chute, we have to get to the chute!*"

"What?" It was really hard to concentrate, since we should have gone rolling again, and falling, and slapping ourselves silly ricocheting off of walls because the fight outside appeared to have escalated. But Louis-Cesare had buried one foot in the flesh below us, as well as most of his sword, and when he pulled us into a crouching position, we stayed there. Even though I could only tell which direction we were facing by which way my hair was falling.

And then the shaking recommenced. "The parachute!"

"What? Oh. I don't have one!" I screamed, because the battle taking place outside was so loud that I could hardly hear myself think.

"*Quoi?*"

"I. Don't. Have. One. Or don't you think I'd have used it by now?"

"Yes, you do!" the stubborn man said. And then he *moved*, somehow keeping to his feet and towing me behind him as we tore across the wildly bouncing floor, which was less like a trampoline now and more like rubber waves on a wildly thrashing sea.

But we made it, as well as through the small opening of the portal that was somehow still holding together, and into my arsenal. Where I stood, barely keeping to my feet although the bucking and twisting was a lot less pronounced in here. But it wasn't gone, meaning that we should probably get away before this whole thing collapsed.

It was something I tried to point out, but kept falling on my ass before I could. Although that was less because of the shaking of the room and more because my senses were messed up by the dizziness of that headlong plunge. And because I still couldn't see!

Except for what Louis-Cesare was looking at on the other side of the room, which was a quick succession of items from my formerly orderly treasure trove. He was digging them out of the jumbled mess, cursing and muttering and staring at things for less than a second before throwing them away. Which was fair, as half of them were on fire.

At least that explains the quality of the air in here, I thought, and finally managed to wheeze out a piece of advice. "Hurry..."

Louis-Cesare said something in French that I didn't bother to translate, as it didn't sound complimentary. But then he obliged anyway, emerging from the shadows with something in his hand. I couldn't see it, since it was currently below the line of his vision and therefore of mine.

He seemed to realize that after a second, and held it up in front of his eyes.

And, yes, that appeared to be a neatly packed parachute.

"Where did that come from?" I demanded, grabbing the wall and getting back to my feet for the dozenth time.

"I brought it!"

"And you didn't *tell* me?" My freaked-out face suddenly looked pissed, which Louis-Cesare took exception to.

"You argued with Claire over food!" he said, gesturing about, because the French talk almost as much with their hands as the Italians. Or, at least, mine does. "You wouldn't even bring a small pantry as it would displace some of your precious—what are you doing?"

He broke off, probably because I was feeling about on the wall, trying to remember where—

Yes! There it was. I flipped a small switch before spinning on a dime—

And almost falling over again, only Louis-Cesare was there to catch me. "Dory?"

I couldn't see his blue eyes at the moment, only my own, slightly unfocused dark ones. But I knew they were worried, and that there was a little line in between them. I grasped his hand and pressed it reassuringly.

"Running," I said, and pulled him toward the door.

He pulled back. "What?"

"You asked me what I was doing. Running."

"Why? We have a moment to put this on—"

"We have ten seconds."

"What?"

"I hit the self-destruct. Eight seconds."

"*Merde!*"

We ran. And, ladies and gentlemen, when a motivated dhampir and a master vampire run, they do not let grass grow. Not when there was a chance to actually survive this. Because there's nothing like a reprieve from certain death to get the mental juices flowing.

And I'd finally had an idea.

The parachute changed everything and nothing, because as soon as it opened, we'd be spotted sure as hell. Unless everyone was too busy looking at something else, that was. Something *big*.

"Find us in *this!*" I yelled as we jumped into the void, without looking or caring where we were going, because anywhere was better than here.

Especially now, I thought, as the heavens exploded behind us.

I felt the heat on my back, felt us be thrown forward from the sheer force of all the magic being unleashed; felt something slice another piece out of my arm as debris speed by, some of it on fire; and heard Louis-Cesare grunt when another something hit him in the back.

"You okay?" I screamed, only to have the words be snatched away by the wind, before even vampire ears could hear them.

Or maybe he was just busy. We were falling fast, not having had time to open the chute yet, which he was shrugging into while I clung to his chest like a monkey. But even so, it felt like we were *right there*, at the heart of what was probably the biggest demonstration of human magic ever in Faerie.

We did Earth proud, I thought, as Louis-Cesare slammed the last buckle home, got a grip on me and jerked the rip cord.

It stopped our rapid descent but left us tossing and turning in the waves of magic being thrown around, even this far away.

But it was better than what Steen's people were doing. A whole lot better, I thought, staring upward past the wildly whipping chute.

It looked like the biggest fireworks display in history, one that was trying its best to consume a butt load of dragons. Who were too angry at the snarling, snapping, eviscerating magic all around them to do the one thing they needed to accomplish right then and get the hell out of range. Or maybe there was another reason for that, I realized, when one did break away and headed for open sky—

Only to be turned back by a vicious assault from Lord Den's people.

He had screeched a warning when the fireworks started, and shielded them with his body until they were clear. His hard golden luster had run with the multicolored energy trying to consume his foes, but as far as I could tell, nothing got past him. Allowing his dragons to put some distance between themselves and the mid-air conflagration, and to wait at a safe distance to pick off any stragglers.

That left Steen's people caught between an exploding rock and the hardest of hard places, and it showed.

A dragon fell out of the sky with his wings burning, leaving trails of boiling black smoke in the air behind him. Another was hit by a giant-sized dislocator, a notorious spell that rearranged body parts into formations not typically compatible with life—if you were lucky. This one attached his head and neck to another dragon's body, who shrieked in horror and flew off, while the headless corpse followed the fiery one to the ground.

That ground was shrouded in mist just inside the tree line, so I didn't see them land. I wasn't so lucky when a flying potion bomb smashed into a third, coating him with a glowing orange sheen. It ran over his scales, obscuring the dark aubergine, until it reached the very tips of his tail and the barbed points on his wings.

And turned him inside out.

The whole mashed up, bloody, pulsating mass fell past us, somehow still screaming despite the fact that the great lungs were currently on the outside of the body, and I seriously thought about passing out.

"*Merde*," Louis-Cesare whispered, in awe this time, and I nodded silently.

The display seemed to have made an impression on Steen's people, too. More of them broke and ran, preferring to take their chances with a fight they understood than with off world horrors they didn't. Steen was among them, despite the fact that he'd started all this.

I saw him wheel off into the night sky, followed by half a dozen outriders who looked mostly intact, although a few had tattered wings or shattered scales in places. But the same couldn't be said for the rest, the ones who were a little late clawing their way out of the still-exploding magical cloud only to be met by another—of teeth and claws and wildly whipping wings. They were set upon by Den's group in a very visceral display of what, exactly, happens when you lose a battle to a dragon.

Something that Louis-Cesare and I were about to discover, I realized, as a bright green dart came shooting at us across the sky.

I reached for a weapon, any weapon, but our attacker was too fast and I was too slow, having been burnt, battered, and possibly broken, because it was hurting way too much just to breathe. And nothing I had on me was likely to work anyway. I felt Louis-Cesare's arm tighten, acknowledging what I already knew.

We weren't going to make it.

And we wouldn't have, except that a lavender streak took that moment to tear through the night, moving so fast that it was literally only a blur across my vision for a split second before plowing into the other dragon.

No, not it, I thought. She. Because it was Claire and she was savage, in a way that I had never seen nor dreamt of.

The green was larger again by half, perhaps more. It was difficult to tell when they were nothing but a fighting, screeching, mad ball of fury. But I thought it was larger.

It lost anyway. I think most would have, save possibly the biggest. Not because Claire was stronger or faster or better, but because she was simply scarier, with no quarter asked for or given. She intended to kill or die and gave the impression that she didn't much care which. I supposed the green had different thoughts, because it tore away—literally as it lost part of a wing in the process—and darted after its chieftain in the distance.

And Claire followed.

"No!" I screamed, because I wasn't sure that she was rational enough to let him go. If he caught up with the others and she was still following, they would tear her to pieces. "Claire!" I yelled again, but someone else had seen.

Not Den, who was savaging an enormous blue-black specimen up above, with crunching sounds that made my spine clench. And not the smaller, dragon riding castle guards, who had caught up belatedly and were diving after battling duos and trios, adding their numbers to their masters' power. But nobody noticed Claire.

Except for one, and in this case, one was enough.

A brilliant red streak tore after her, fast, fast, so unbelievably fast that he looked like nothing more than a smear of light on the horizon, one last gasp of a sun that had already set. Tanet, I thought, watching him with my heart in my throat. Because he'd started so far behind her that I wasn't sure—

But I hadn't even finished the thought before he caught her, desperation lending him speed and then power as the fluid body wrapped around hers and held on, even as she clawed and fought and twisted and turned, as frantic to get away and after her prey as he was to make sure she never did.

They fell into the tree line and out of sight, still battling each other, along with a dozen other pairs. We drifted down slowly behind them, while the forest burned, the wind whipped my hair into my eyes, and golden cinders fell all around us, turning the blue-black darkness into a fantasyland. The moon silvered it all, including the great castle behind us, shimmering in my borrowed vision as darkness finally claimed me.

Chapter Eighteen

"Mar!" Someone was shouting, as I fought my way back to consciousness. "I am not Tanet! I am Tanet-*Mar* and so I ask again—*who are you?*"

"Let go of me." The voice was low, guttural, and unfamiliar. I tried to place it, but my brain stubbornly refused to come fully back online.

I think it was scared. I hurt all over, like a thousand pulsating suns eating their way across my body. I had been in pain before, plenty of times, and usually dealt with it pretty well.

But not now.

"Tanet-Mar!" the voice roared again. "Son of Rathen-Den and heir to House Eddred! I know who I am, but you—you do not even know your name!"

"I know my name—"

"Then tell it to me! Not the human one you hide behind, *your* name, my *sister's* name." And suddenly, the voice changed, from anger to something approaching horror. "Do you even *have* one? Have you *even thought about it?*"

"I'm warning you—"

"Of what?" The question echoed through the forest, along with a laugh that had no humor in it. "We're at war with Vitharr, having killed a dozen of their people! Everyone will have to choose sides now, they'll have no choice, and what poison do you think that bastard Steen is pouring into their ears at this very moment? We don't know what they'll choose; we don't know what we're up against; and my sister, my *blood*, is half out of her mind and looks like *that!*"

"Get out of my way," Claire said, and it *was* her, although I could barely tell. She didn't sound like herself at all, and I was having trouble thinking clearly. The adrenaline from that crazy fight had completely run out, and my ability to stave off pain along with it.

My world was fire.

I automatically reached for a weapon, any weapon, but preferably my Smith &Wesson. Bought in the eighties, it was the 29-2 model and almost comically massive, dwarfing a Desert Eagle in size and looking like a prop gun off a movie set. In fact, it had been: it was Dirty Harry's gun, and loaded with the same .44 Magnum rounds he had supposedly used. I hadn't bought it for that reason, but had to admit to asking a few people if they felt lucky.

None had.

Maybe because, while it wasn't the most powerful handgun in the world anymore, it was enough to drop a charging rhino and to make the average vamp rethink his priorities. I frankly doubted whether it could do the same to the kinds of things I faced now, but I still needed to touch it, like a child reaching for a favorite blanket and the reassurance it provided. And maybe it would have—

If it hadn't gone missing.

That happy little fact jerked me the rest of the way out of slumber. I'd jumped with as many guns as I could carry and still move, and that one should have been in a handy holster beneath my armpit. But only cloth met my hand when I felt for it, the silky, burnt remains of my once expensive gown, and when I opened my eyes, I saw only darkness.

For a moment, I panicked, thinking that I was still blind, and that maybe it was permanent this time. And while there were other clues to my location—loamy, damp soil under my fingertips along with the occasional forest litter; wind in the treetops outside, moaning a lonesome tune; and the smells of resin and pine—I didn't calm down until light met my desperately searching eyes. Even if only tiny glimmers of it.

Some type of dark fabric was above me, I realized, draping the world in shadow. I was only able to glimpse anything else through some broken strands in the weave, which let in a few crisscrossing lines here and there of slightly less dark. They told me nothing, yet immediately consumed all my attention, cutting out every other thought.

It wasn't a shroud—stop it, Dory! It was too high above my face and too heavy, to the point that it barely ruffled in the breeze. For a brief, frozen moment, I stared at it, not sure what it was.

And then my sluggish mind figured it out, and it felt like every bone in my tortured body liquified. Because it was a tent. Just a tent!

I fell back the scant half inch that I'd risen off the ground and just breathed for a moment.

"Do not try to lay this on us." Louis-Cesare was saying from somewhere outside. My heart leapt in my chest at his voice, although he wasn't sounding happy. He rarely shouted, but when he was pissed off, his voice got progressively flatter and flatter. And this was as close to robotic as I'd ever heard it. "We have done nothing—"

"Nothing?" Tanet repeated. "Your woman charged the chieftain of Vitharr!"

"Who was threatening her life! What would you have had her do? Run away from a direct challenge? Slink off with her tail between her legs?" And, okay, the voice was less robotic now. "If so, you do not know her—or us—very well."

"And wish I knew less," Tanet hissed, although it was getting hard to understand him. His voice had an overlay of what I assumed came from his alter ego, a dark rumble behind the words that was enough to raise the hair on the back of my neck and to have me feeling for the tent flap to back up my partner.

Only to have someone else open it before I could.

I glimpsed Claire's features limned in a dim, greenish light as she ducked inside. I felt myself relax again until I realized—the light wasn't coming from the aurora borealis in the skies outside, as I'd first assumed. It was coming from her eyes, and the things it showed me—

Her hand clapped over my mouth before I could let out the scream that was rising in my throat. So, my gut reaction just stayed there, getting progressively more and more insistent and more panicked but with nowhere to go. She was stunning, some part of my brain piped up to say, while the rest of me was busy screaming "run!"

But I wasn't going to run, because the changes in Claire weren't just cosmetic. I literally couldn't move, and I was not weak, even as damaged as I was. But she was stronger, and so we just remained there, staring at each other, while the two men argued outside.

"—two natured, but she's been suppressing it for most of her life!" Tanet said viciously. "No one has ever heard of such a thing; no one knows what it does! I wanted her to come here and learn about us, about herself, before it was too late—"

"It seems she understands a great deal," Louis-Cesare said. "She was magnificent—"

"She understands nothing!" Tanet snarled, and with his other half's voice echoing his own, it sounded like a lion's roar. "She was overwhelmed by her other nature tonight, consumed by it—"

"She saved our *lives!*"

"Yes! And in the process may lose her own!"

I stopped struggling at that, in favor of staring up at the alien creature above me. She didn't look human anymore, although she had the vague shape of one, and was still garbed in her elegant gown from dinner. But she didn't look like a dragon, either. I didn't know what she looked like, but it was nothing like the dragon headed servants, which must be another species.

Because this . . . was something else.

The hair was the same, brilliantly red and plentiful, only seeming to flow on invisible air currents around her face. And the eyes—the eyes were green, if so bright that I almost couldn't stand to look at them. And her facial features, the slim, delicate, slightly elfin ones I knew, remained, but everything else . . .

I took in the changes slowly, and she let me, even removing her hand from my mouth when I stopped struggling. But there was something vulnerable in her eyes, as if she didn't want me to see her this way. Yet she didn't move even though I didn't hurry.

My head was still swimming, and there was a lot to take in.

Her skin, usually pale, was pure silver-white now, except where tinted with lavender in the hollows. Her eyebrows and lashes were likewise pinkish-lavender, as were her lips. But that was nothing next to the tiny scales feathering out from the sides of her eyes: purple and pink and iridescent green, and growing larger as they met up with those framing her face and running down to interlocking plates on her neck.

As far as I could tell, she was covered in similar plates all over her body, mainly silver in color but with a prismatic quality to them. She could seemingly shade them any color of purple or green that she chose, or leave them a polished mirror reflecting her surroundings. She did that several times as I watched, flushing through the limited spectrum before going dark like the tent, and almost disappearing until she made herself come back so that I might see.

And she was worth seeing, I thought, my wonder finally overriding my fear. The scales created a full, figure-hugging, liquid-looking suit of armor, fitting together so tightly as to be almost seamless. Especially at the joints, where tiny, more flexible scales allowed for ease of movement. And then, to top it all off, was what looked like a literal crown of rough, bone-like scales, starting in a deep vee on her forehead and ranging upward to form two, perfectly curled horns.

I don't know what was on my face, probably shock as I had just woken up and this was not the view I had expected. And I guess that wasn't the right response, because in less than a minute,

Claire's eyes were welling up with tears. The two men were still arguing outside, but I didn't care anymore.

She was hurting.

"It's okay," I told her, cupping her cheek, and feeling the tiny scales framing her jawline against my fingertips.

"It's not okay." She covered my hand with hers, but didn't pry it off. "It's—it's what can happen, when my kind don't let their other side out enough. Sometimes, it doesn't want to go back into hiding and it fights you."

"It?"

Claire closed her eyes. "She. I know it's a she. I just . . ." She trailed off.

"Does she have a name?" I asked, after a moment, remembering what Tanet had said, and her eyes flew open.

"You heard that?"

"As in a dream. I'm not entirely sure I'm awake now."

"You are." Her eyes darkened. "You're just very injured. You almost died, Dory."

"Lucky that I have my healer best friend here then, isn't it?"

"I didn't do much," she admitted, frowning, and putting down a small pot of something stinky and green that I hadn't noticed her carrying because there were so many other things to notice right now. "You're alive because of your own healing abilities, and Louis-Cesare's."

"He doesn't have much," I reminded her. "The family gift skipped him, like it did me."

"But you're tough as nails," Claire said, and then she sobbed suddenly and tried to hug me, only to realize at the last moment that she couldn't because there wasn't enough uninjured skin left to work with.

"I can't take the dress off," she whispered. "It's . . . I'm afraid your skin will come with it."

"Good thing it's a nice color on me," I said, trying not to writhe. "If I'm going to be wearing it for a while."

"Dory!"

Claire had been whispering, but that last had not been a whisper and had cracked like a whip. I stared at her, not understanding what I'd said that was so wrong, and a second later, Louis-Cesare was peering into the tent flap. He didn't look like he understood, either, but he didn't like it.

"Get out," Claire told him, without turning around.

And he liked that even less. So did I, because her tone had gone from more or less normal to knife edged. It sounded a lot like her brother's half transformed voice suddenly. And then I noticed her eyes.

Which were no longer green.

Louis-Cesare started to say something, but I quieted him with a gesture. I didn't break eye contact with Claire—or whoever this was—but not because I didn't trust her. I didn't trust her, as it happened, not if her alter ego had decided to interrupt our conversation, but I kept her gaze for a much simpler reason than that.

I literally couldn't look away.

Oh, yeah. Not Claire anymore, I thought, as the striations in those vividly purple and yellow eyes seemed almost to move. Not Claire at all.

"It's okay," I heard myself say. "Do as she says."

But Louis-Cesare didn't take orders well, even when they came from me, and that hadn't sounded like me. It had been my voice, my lips moving, my tongue forming the words, but they weren't mine. And damnit, this wasn't helping!

I made a Herculean effort and wrenched my eyes away from hers, and ended up panting with the effort that simple move had taken.

"Dory," Louis-Cesare said flatly, as if he suspected something, too. "I do not think that is wise. You are injured—"

"And if I wasn't?" I asked harshly. "If she wanted to attack me there would be nothing I could do about it, no matter what shape I was in." And neither could you, I didn't add, because he wasn't likely to respond to that well. "Please. Give us a moment."

Louis-Cesare and I locked eyes. He was still very much Not Happy, a facial expression I rarely saw. Despite being stubborn bastards who both liked to be right, we actually didn't fight all that much. Probably because we were stubborn about different things.

Unfortunately, one of his triggers was danger to me, partially resulting from a time when he had been possessed by a vengeful spirit and had been the one supplying the danger. He had done me a serious injury and had never forgiven himself for it, despite it not being his fault. We'd been working on the paranoia from that event ever since and some progress had been made, but right now, he was right.

There was danger here.

I could feel it, crawling over my skin like a colony of ants, buzzing in the air, shivering along my skin. A weightiness came with it, as if a heavy blanket had been draped over me, or a few extra atmospheres had suddenly muscled into the air and were making it hard to breathe. But I didn't think the danger was to me. And if I was wrong...

I didn't think there was anything anyone could do about it.

"*Please.*" I made it emphatic.

Despite the male model good looks, my Hubby wasn't stupid. He had done some mental math, too, and hadn't liked what it told him. I saw his hand clench on the fabric of the tent flap, as if to keep from drawing his sword. And then suddenly he was gone, and I heard him and Tanet having a low-voiced conversation somewhere outside that I couldn't decipher.

But Claire obviously could.

"They are deciding what they will do if I become . . . annoyed," she told me.

The new voice was rich, dark, and slightly grating, but not unpleasant. I felt it flow over me and the pain seemed to ebb slightly along with it. Or maybe I was imagining things.

Nothing would surprise me right now.

"Is this . . . permanent?" I whispered.

"That is what Mar is afraid of," she told me calmly. "That I will end up a hybrid who cannot shift. Trapped forever betwixt and between and useless to them. There are legends of such things, although no one who lives has seen it."

She picked up the pot and breathed on the salve or whatever it was that it carried. I assumed Claire had made it, as she was a decent herbalist who was more than conversant with fey plants. But she couldn't do *that*, I thought, as the gunk in the bowl began to glow.

Little pieces of what looked like green starlight began to roam around the inside of the pot, as if looking for a way out. And after a moment, they found one, circling up into the air and shedding faint light shadows onto the tent, the forest floor, and my body, which was in worse shape than I'd thought. I still couldn't see it too well, for which I was grateful, but there were dark patches all over me, blood and burnt flesh and—

I looked away, not really wanting to see. I wasn't sure this amount of damage could be healed, and if it could, it would take ages. Ages in which Dorina would be alone and facing who knew what kind of dangers. Ages when I couldn't find her, or try to help her—I couldn't even help myself right now! The moment of hopelessness I'd felt on the castle ramparts suddenly returned and multiplied by a factor of ten, to the point that I was gasping in panic, was choking on it.

What if I'd killed her? What if my stupid bravado with Steen had cost us whatever advantage we had left, and we'd never find her? She had been there for me, so many times, whenever I'd needed her, and yet I wouldn't be there for her—and it was my fault! It was all my—

"Calm yourself," Claire, or whoever I was dealing with, said. It was the dark rumble again, so I assumed it was her other half, but didn't know; didn't care. It was still Claire; she was in there somewhere, and might be my only hope. I grasped her arm, which seemed to startle her slightly, but she didn't try to pry me loose.

"Dorina," I gasped out.

Her head tilted. "What about her?"

"You can still find her. If I don't . . . if I have to be left behind, you can still search—"

"Not like this," she began, but I didn't let her finish.

My hand contracted, even though I didn't tell it to, but despite the fact that a dhampir can bend steel, it didn't so much as dent the slick scales covering her arm. "Please! I was an idiot to attack Steen—"

"You were that."

"—but she shouldn't have to pay for it! And I think your brother was right; I don't think anyone else can find her. But you—"

"Why do you care so much?" she asked, and the eyes were pure purple now, and strangely intense. "Wouldn't it be easier with her gone? Wouldn't you prefer to be alone in your skin, to not have to share your body, to have no more fits or vacant moments and be in control all of the time?

"I would think you might prefer her dead—"

And then I made the second dumbest mistake of that evening, and possibly of my life. I slapped her. And in my anger and outrage, I put some force behind it, enough to snap her head back for an instant.

The move also sliced my palm open, which was already crisscrossed with wounds from the battle, and the pain brought me back to myself a little. Dear God, I was crazy. And this wasn't going to help Dorina!

"I'm sorry!" I said, almost before I'd finished the motion. "I'm sorry! Don't take it out on her! She's done nothing—"

I cut off abruptly, because that is what you do when a dragon gets in your face. This wasn't one, not completely, but this close, with those mesmerizing eyes staring straight into mine and those scales ruffling up around her like a thousand tiny knives, it was hard to remember that. Yet, she didn't attack me.

Instead, she looked more curious than anything, searching my face for something from barely an inch away, something she seemed to find, although it puzzled her. "You love her," she finally said.

The words shivered over my skin like a living thing, which would have been disturbing enough on its own if today hadn't rewritten my definition of the word. "Of course, I love her! She's my *sister*, and I can't—but *you* can help her, you have to help her! Please, don't let her die out there! Not for some stupidity of mine—"

"Shhh." She sat back and put a finger against my lips, and it was cool. I didn't know why that surprised me. We stayed like that for a long moment, with her gaze unfocused and her scales slowly settling back into place. Then she spoke again, and I didn't understand that, either. "Lýsa."

She removed her finger and began smearing me all over with the glowing salve.

I watched her, uncomprehending. "What?" I finally asked.

"It means 'light' in the old tongue. Claire means the same, yes?"

"I . . . think it means 'bright'," I said, because at that moment, I couldn't think of anything else.

But she seemed to like my answer for once, and nodded. "That is even better. We make each other's light brighter, you see?"

No, I didn't see. I didn't see a goddamned thing. I also didn't know what was happening to me, until I looked down. And saw all that green light sinking into my skin, lessening the pain, and knitting up the worst of the wounds.

I looked back up at her, and she had the strangest expression on her face. It took me a moment to realize that she was laughing at me. "You will not die, Dory of House Basarab. And you will find your sister for yourself. But perhaps, I will come along as well.

"There may be much that we can learn from each other."

Chapter Nineteen

The next morning dawned clear and cold, enough of the latter for me to feel it despite being wrapped in a huge, silken fur that I'd been brought overnight. We were still in the field, although it was starting to look more like a real camp and less like someone's cloak that had been draped over a stick. I did not know why we were out here, but here we were, with 'we' meaning me and Claire, because everyone else had flown off while dawn was still staining the sky.

But I saw it all because Louis-Cesare was letting me look through his eyes, which is how I watched the running takeoff Lord Rathen made as if I was experiencing it from atop his back, while being only too happy that I was not. After last night, I'd be just as glad if my feet never left the ground again. Which was why

I was gasping in my tent as we soared into the heavens, with nothing but clear, bitingly cold air all around us.

The images cut out a moment later, as it would have been disorienting for me to go around all day seeing double. But it was the only way I could follow the events where they were going, being in no shape to travel myself. Claire said it might be days before I was able to hobble around properly, and considering how I felt, I believed her.

Louis-Cesare hadn't wanted to leave my side, where he'd slept all night, curled up protectively beside me. I'd healed enough that he could drape a long arm across me without causing me agony, and there it had stayed, like an iron band. It should have been uncomfortable, but instead had given me the reassurance I needed to fall headlong into one of the deepest sleeps of my life.

My Hubby had seemed to enjoy finally getting to protect the little woman, and for the moment, I had enjoyed being protected. It was a lie, of course; neither of us was actually safe out here, or anywhere in Faerie. But it had felt that way, especially when dragon calls sounded in the distance all night, as if patrolling the skies around us.

Perhaps we'd been safer than I'd thought.

And the next thing I knew, I was yawning into the sunlight streaming through the propped-open door flap of my tent, and soon thereafter having a hearty breakfast around a cold campfire.

"How did you make it with no heat?" I asked Claire, because the logs had burned down at some point in the night and nobody had relit them.

She crouched beside me with a brown cloak thrown over her unusual form, which was even more startling by daylight, although she had ditched the evening dress. I guessed when you were covered in harder-than-steel scales you didn't need it, and it might catch on the underbrush. Which was a concern as she was obviously planning to venture deeper into the forest, judging by the basket she'd thrown over one silvered arm.

"Eat," she said, in that guttural tone that no longer worried me.

I ate, leaving it up to her whether she answered or not. I had discovered last night that that was the best way to get more speech and less grunting out of her, along with doing as she ordered. Claire's other half was bossy, too, it seemed.

So, I concentrated on shoveling in a great quantity of actually cooked food—sausage and bread and some kind of porridge—while she smoothed down my unruly hair. It felt a bit like a pet, the motion you'd make on a good dog's head who had obeyed a command, but I had my mouth full and failed to point that out.

I likely would have failed anyway, as I had more to steal my attention than food. Dragons were flying everywhere this morning, zooming about in all directions. That and our continued presence in the middle of the woods despite a much more comfortable castle being a short flight away told me that something was happening, but I had no idea what.

"They come," Claire said suddenly, indicating a somewhat low-flying dragon—a brilliant, pure yellow with a white belly, who had just leisurely sailed over our treetops. It had been low enough to bend some limbs, yet hadn't tried to land. But I got the distinct impression that it was staring at us, having the same crawling speed and craning neck of looky-loos passing a highway accident.

I felt like waving back, but wasn't quite that brave. But I was feeling a bit steadier as I got more of the feast for twelve in the massive bowl down my throat. So, I decided to try another question.

"Why do they come. And who are they?"

It was a compound question, which dragons—at least this one—didn't seem to like. But I got half of it answered, anyway. "Other clans. Different houses. Some pledged to House Eddred, others not. Some even hostile."

"But not last-night hostile," I guessed.

"No." Claire decided I was warm enough and eating enough and that her work here was done. "I go."

"Wait." I caught her hand. "Why do they come?"

"To talk."

She left.

I watched her disappear into the forest, shimmering away into the foliage like a part of it, and almost immediately invisible courtesy of those kaleidoscoping scales. And wondered what I was supposed to do if someone was more Steen-level hostile than they seemed. I had my Dirty Harry gun, which I'd gotten back from Louis-Cesare this morning, along with a couple of knives that I'd hidden under the fur, although they were less than reassuring as I ate alone in a dragon buzzed campsite in Faerie.

But I didn't stay alone for long.

My spoon was just scraping the bottom of the massive bowl when I looked up and saw a very large, very unknown man striding toward me across the clearing. Shit! I tried to get up, to at least meet him on my feet, but I was as weak as a kitten and the giant fur was heavy as lead. And I somehow ended up tangled in it, to the point that I couldn't even get my gun free to—

And then I noticed: he had stopped halfway across the glade, apparently seeing my struggle. He watched me fight with the fur for a moment, but neither laughed nor took advantage of the situation. Instead, he put a hand out, palm up.

And then politely waited to see what I would do.

That would have been great, only I had no idea what to do. So, I just stood there, trying not to waver noticeably on my feet, clutching my gun and wiping porridge off of my lips. It was a less than intimidating display.

He nonetheless kept his distance and then bowed, rather competently, even though dragons didn't. At least, dragons who had never been to Earth didn't. But he looked old enough to have made the trip, possibly at a time when that sort of courtly gesture was still the norm.

I stopped panicking quite so much and checked him out.

He was eight feet tall, or possibly slightly more, but in no way resembled a slender basketball player. He was massive in every way, with a musculature that could only be described as gargantuan, and which was emphasized by the fact that he was dressed like a medieval knight. Or so I thought.

I changed my mind as he cautiously approached, hands still out where I could see them, which less reassuring all of a sudden because that . . . wasn't armor.

I blinked a couple times, but the view didn't change. It still looked like he had partially transformed, morphing his body so that big, plate-like scales had thickened and expanded over the more vulnerable parts.

It left him looking like he was wearing a chest plate, a set of pauldrons, and heavy greaves, and had scale armor running everywhere else, connecting them all together.

It was amazingly authentic looking, not only because of how it was put together, but because the stuff that was in common use when I was growing up wasn't the shiny, perfect pieces on display in museums.

Most of the armor that had survived the centuries to be oohed and awed over by modern audiences was the spectacular, parade-ready variety worn by kings and noblemen. It was buffed to a high shine, or covered in elaborate etchings and inlaid with gold, because it was a status symbol, like driving a Ferrari. It was meant to impress.

But the kind of thing worn into actual battle was a little different. It looked more like this, being rough from a thousand little nicks made from arrow heads and larger ones left by spear and sword blades. It had dirt in the creases that never got washed out and a patina of age that—

That in this case, was very familiar.

"I know you," I said suddenly, and the man smiled.

It was a small expression, but it transformed the rugged, bearded face. The beard was short, unlike the ridiculous Santa-and-then-some thing Steen had had going on, as was his hair. Both were salt and pepper with mostly salt, matching the deep laugh lines around his eyes. But he had been handsome once, and in some ways, still was. The eyes alone would stop you in your tracks, being vividly blue and piercing, as if the sky had suddenly decided to take an interest in one of the small creatures roaming around underneath it.

"You do." He had crossed the rest of the distance between us while I stared rudely, and now bent over my hand. Which I had unwittingly extended because he was that kind of guy. He kept it briefly, looking at me again with a somber expression once more. "I am Regin-Lar, my lady, and I failed you. That will not happen again."

I had a sudden, vivid memory of the great, mossy backed dragon who had briefly rescued me, and had only let me fall because he was attacked by a whole squadron of Steen's people. "Are you alright?" I asked, and saw his smile grow.

"Yes, and so are you, although none of us can quite believe it." He let my hand go and made a small gesture at the space beside me. "May I?"

I sat back down because it was either that or fall down, and patted the log. It was somewhat crumbly, having been here a while, and I wasn't sure that it would hold what had to be six hundred pounds of muscle. But there wasn't anything else.

He must have had the same reservation, because he settled onto the ground in front of my perch instead. I mulled over the fact that, even in human guise, he made me feel alien—a flimsy, weak, tiny creature who had no business being in this world of giants. But he did not appear to be thinking the same.

"I am the head of my lord's guards, and am to stand in his stead today," he informed me once we were settled. "Would you lend me your strength?"

I blinked at up him, because even sitting on the ground he was taller. "I don't have any strength," I said, which caused him to smile again. And then to chuckle, as if I'd said something witty instead of the stark truth.

"Your presence should be sufficient," he declared gallantly.

"My presence for what?" I asked, as people began to appear at the edges of the clearing.

"Some of the smaller houses are considering joining with us against Lord Steen, after last night's betrayal."

"Betrayal?"

"There is an understanding that our people do not fight each other. When there are disagreements, they are settled by the clan council, something that has been true for generations. Why Lord

Steen felt it necessary to violate this tradition is a mystery, but in doing so he killed two of our people in their own home. That is infamy, and it will be answered."

"I thought it was answered last night," I said, thinking that Steen must have lost people, too. A lot of them.

But Regin shook his head. "It was fought off last night. It was not answered. Allowing Lord Steen to break the authority of the council would bring anarchy back to the houses, along with constant warfare. Perhaps he needs to be reminded of how it was in the old days, before he drags us back into them."

Well, that sounded ominous, I thought, before I thought something else.

"Two?"

"I beg your pardon?"

"You lost two? Which two?"

He frowned. "One was a guard, one of our Taloi, sworn to our service from time out of mind. The other was Tamris, daughter of the chieftain of a closely allied house."

"Tamris?" I felt my stomach drop. "The woman I was dining with?"

"She was the lord's long-term guest," Regin confirmed. "There was some hope of a match between her and the lord's son, but..."

But not now, I thought, feeling sick. I remembered the curiosity with which she'd regarded Louis-Cesare and I, and the pretty dress she'd offered me. And the special, starry one she'd worn for Tanet.

No wonder he was on a rampage.

And no wonder much of it had been directed at me. I'd endangered his sister and gotten his potential lover killed, along with a running tally of two guards. Three people in less than a day, and who knew how many wounded, and I was no closer to finding Dorina than when I got here!

"This has been brewing for a while," Regin said, watching me. "After Lord Rathen allied with your senate for the war, it was rumored that Lord Steen did the same but on the other side. He has long envied Eddred's prominence, and the war gives him the excuse to attempt to unseat us. This was inevitable, whether you came to our mountains or no."

"Tanet doesn't think so."

"Tanet is young. There is much he does not yet understand."

"But Lord Rathen does. Yet he took Louis-Cesare and I on an extended flight about your lands before taking us to our room." I met those piercing baby blues. "He wanted us to be seen."

"Perhaps." Regin didn't bother to deny it. "There are always spies watching us, as he is well aware. But he had no way to know that Lord Steen would take such drastic action. And if he was going to attack you, better that it be here, where you had protection, than on the road. His decision turned out to be fortunate."

Yeah, maybe. But it had also resulted in exactly the outcome Rathen had wanted, hadn't it? He may not have expected Tamris to pay the price, but he had wanted a *casus belli*, a reason for others to rally to his side for the war, and now he had one. The dragonkind were having to choose sides whether they liked it or not, and the price had been the life of a few guards and a girl not even from his own house.

Most of the kings I'd met would have considered that an acceptable loss, even a good deal. I wondered if Lord Rathen had. Or if I was being paranoid, and he had genuinely not expected Steen to come in such force, or to attack him in his own home.

I didn't know, like I didn't know anything here. Except that the politics in Faerie were as complex and cutthroat as the ones back home, and I had somehow ended up in the middle of them. And House Eddred seemed to want to ensure that I stayed that way, because they were coming now, the leaders and representatives of the smaller houses, and Regin kept me by his side as he greeted them on behalf of his lord.

I didn't understand that, either. I was hardly a stalwart looking ally at the moment. I hadn't even had time to wash the sleep out of my eyes or to comb my hair, I was garbed in tatters, dirt and a ridiculously large fur, and my hand had dried blood under the nails and shook when I presented it, over and over. They didn't come close enough to touch foreheads, these hulking men and women garbed in silks and velvets, with glorious hair that dragged the ground behind them, betraying their age. Despite being accompanied by guards who, in some cases, dwarfed even Regin.

The guards hedged their masters closely while giving me a once over, and then often did it again, as if they couldn't believe that this scrawny, beat-up, tiny thing was a threat. I didn't know what they'd been told to expect, but I was clearly a massive disappointment. Their masters seemed to agree, although their faces betrayed nothing, but their touch was as tentative as if they were holding a soap bubble and were afraid they might break it.

I started making a conscious effort to look less pathetic, as I was representing my senate. I hadn't expected to—I was supposed to be here on personal business—but Lord Rathen had made other plans. And if I didn't manage to impress somebody soon, there was a chance I could screw up our entire alliance before it got off the ground.

I sat up straighter, realizing that, whether I felt comfortable or not, whether my title was even entirely real or not, to these people, I was a senator, and they were betting their lives and their houses on mine and my senate's abilities. Or they would be if they joined us. But it was looking like that was far from a sure thing.

Nobody was smiling, and some were talking behind their hands, shooting me glances that were variously sympathetic, pitying, or angry, as if a few of them were insulted at being offered such an ally. Although a lot of the clan leaders just seemed . . . confused. It was starting to look like Regin's gamble had backfired.

Then a ratty old fellow in tattered leathers instead of silks, gray dreads instead of shining locks, and a grimy ring on one hand that looked like it had come out of a Cracker Jack box, roughly grabbed my chin.

"Doesn't look like much to me—" he began.

And then cut off abruptly, maybe because my Smith & Wesson was pressing against his sternum and my knife was denting the skin of his neck.

The clearing held its breath, as everyone froze in place. That included Regin, who didn't even twitch, just sat at my side looking expressionless. And me, because I hadn't consciously told myself to do that.

But I was tired, in pain, exhausted and freaked out, and had just had a major problem dumped into my lap. I was actually going to have to act like a senator for once or threaten the war effort, and so what had I immediately done? Drawn blood on somebody who, no matter what he looked like, was probably important or he wouldn't be here.

Awesome.

Chapter Twenty

I looked up into startled, rheumy gray eyes and tried to think. Dragons liked strength and a show of force, but I doubted that they liked this much of one, considering how Steen had reacted last night. I had to get out of this without looking weak, which was hard when my arm was already starting to tremble, and without getting tossed the length of a soccer pitch, which I doubted I'd survive a second time.

Screw it, I didn't know how to do this! I was a *vote*, just another nod to my father's faction on the senate and whatever the hell they wanted to do. I wasn't supposed to be negotiating major shit like this. Or any shit!

"Are ye going to kill me, girlie, or watch me bleed to death?" the old, hippie-looking man rasped, and I noticed that my knife's blade was sheened with red.

I withdrew it.

"Sorry," I told him, a little unsteadily. "I didn't get the tip into the skin when I tried that with Steen, and he grew scales under the blade."

"And then threw ye the length of the room," he added, because the story seemed to have spread. "Nice to know ye can be taught, anyway."

I started to pull the weapons back under the blanket, along with my seriously burned and beat up arms, but he grabbed my wrists before I could. Not in a harsh way, this time; there was no attack. But not in the "she might break if we touch her" way the others had been doing, either.

He was looking at my arms, which were a mess of bloody, half-closed wounds, sticky green salve, burns, a few scars over the smaller cuts, and a mass of black bruises. And then there were my hands, which he examined after removing my weapons and tossing them lightly on the ground. He seemed surprised that I'd even managed to hold them, and frankly, so was I, because I basically had chewed up hamburger meat at the ends of my arms.

The scales I'd been clinging to had sliced open my palms repeatedly, leaving crisscrossing wounds that almost obliterated the skin, and that plus muscle strain from clinging on for dear life had blown my hands up like Minnie Mouse gloves. I'd had trouble just holding onto my spoon this morning, so that I could calm the gnawing hunger I'd woken up with. I was not a pretty sight.

He seemed agree, wrinkling up his nose at the stench of the salve, and then letting out a whistle between cracked and yellowed teeth.

"Flimsy!" he proclaimed, loudly enough that it echoed around the glade. "Puny even! With no armor or protection of any kind! Just meat, and a small, bony sack of it at that. And this is what we're supposed to ally with? To risk our necks for? To fight alongside?"

There was a murmuring around the glade, and it was clear that he'd just vocalized what a lot of people had been thinking. I glanced at Regin, but he was still looking impassive, as if we were discussing the weather instead of his lord's foreign policy, which was fast going down the drain. And the old hippie causing the ruckus had just gotten started.

"Look at her!" he raged, suddenly angry. "*Look at her!* Look at what the battle *did* to her!"

He jerked me forward, and it was so sudden and so unexpected that I didn't fight it. Or manage to keep hold of my fur, which dropped away, leaving me standing there in a ragged gown that was more tatters at this point than anything else, having been shredded on the dead dragon's scales. And that showed a lot more of my lacerations than I'd have liked.

I heard a few indrawn breaths, as the extent of the damage became apparent, but I didn't know what to do. They'd seen it now, and were seeing more as they crowded closer, seemingly intent on getting a good view. So, dragging the fur up again wasn't likely to help and might even hurt, especially if I couldn't keep hold of the heavy thing.

And my knees were already starting to buckle.

"She can barely stand!" the gray-haired hippie shouted. "She's swaying on her feet! Aye, look at her, poor, helpless creature that she is. Look. At. Her!"

And they were. Those who had met me, and those who had been staying on the edges of the glade, maybe members of the entourages of the leaders, were all surging forward now. And silently judging me, with the weight of their eyes almost a physical thing.

I'd have fallen, except that the hippie wasn't done yet, and his grip on my mostly undamaged upper arm was like iron. "That's right, come closer," he told them. "Get a good look, those of you who didn't see her before. Get a damned good look. And tell me, if ye can: if you were one such as this, soft, vulnerable, with no physical advantage save fangs so small as to practically not deserve the name—"

"They are," someone broke in to say, and laughed. "They're tiny!"

But to my surprise, the bastard gripping my arm didn't laugh with him. In fact, he glared into the crowd, peering about until he singled out the speaker. And then motioned him forward.

"Ah, Axsel son of Thorra, good son of a great mother. Come forward, lad, come on."

Axsel son of Thorra came and stood in front of me, a sapling maybe sixteen years old but already almost as tall as Regin if perhaps a third as wide. But a third was still intimidating and likely would be more so soon. He reminded me of Tanet from a year ago, right before he had a growth spurt and put on a hundred pounds of muscle practically overnight.

Not that this one needed it. He was wiry but could probably snap me in two without even feeling it. And it looked like he thought so, too, smirking down at me in a way that might have gotten him a little lesson on another day, in another world.

Come to New York, I thought evilly. And I'll see if I can't manage to wipe that smirk off your face. But we weren't in New York, and his expression wasn't going anywhere, except spreading to other members of the crowd.

And spreading fast.

I needed to do something to counter it, right freaking now, before I lost whatever respect I and my senate had left. I briefly thought of the consul, who headed up that august body, she of the snaky accessories and beautiful face. Beautiful until someone crossed her, that was, and was quickly shown the ruthlessness behind the façade.

She would never put up with this kind of treatment, but then, she wouldn't have to. She wouldn't have been dumb enough to come here in the first place! But I had been dumb enough, and that streak seemed to be continuing, because I was blanking on a response.

My brain appeared to be exerting all its focus on not letting me fall over, and even that was dubious. If it hadn't been for the hippie's iron grip, I'd have probably face planted already. And possibly taken the alliance along with me.

But then he spoke again, deceptively soft, although there was anger behind the words that I didn't understand. "Yes, yes, no fangs worth mentioning," he said. "Not like us, hm? Not like you, mighty Axsel, with your father's powerful physique just starting to show. You'll be a fine warrior someday, and someday soon no doubt—"

The boy puffed up with pride, as if he'd needed any more height. But the woman behind him, with long, gray-streaked blond hair and sharp gray eyes, started to look worried. She glanced from her son—I assumed—to the hippie and back again, and tightened her grip on the boy's arm.

But he, enjoying the public praise he was getting, didn't seem to notice.

"Yes, and a great maw of teeth, so many and so sharp," the hippie continued. "And perfect, unbroken armor, not shattered and damaged in places like mine—"

More people began to look worried at that comment, and I spared a thought as to how said armor had gotten shattered. Maybe the reason had something to do with why a group of people who looked like kings or very well-heeled nobility were listening respectfully to a guy who might have crawled out from under a bridge. And while there was some uneasy shifting in the crowd, no one interrupted again, although the hippie raised his voice anyway.

"—yes, not damaged like mine, shattered in battle for your lord. No, pristine and perfect, you are—and untried, untested, unproven. A good warrior you might be someday, *boy*, even a great one if ye're anything like your parents, but for now—"

It could be my imagination, but I thought I saw the crowd drawing back a little from poor Axsel, who was starting to look a little concerned himself. The smirk was still there, but his eyes, so blue, so confident, so assured a moment ago, were glancing about. He was smart enough to know that he'd somehow stepped in it, but not to see what was coming.

That made two of us.

"But for now," the hippie suddenly thundered, loudly enough to stagger me except that he wouldn't allow it, "ye're a child and a damned foolish one! Which is fair enough, as ye *are* still a child, but less forgivable in the elders among us who should know better!"

"Know better . . . about what?" Axsel asked, confused. And then yelped slightly in pain when his mother's nails stabbed into his bicep to shut him up.

"Know that weapons don't make a warrior. Or armor or magic or bloodlines, either! I've seen more battles than any of ye, and yes, perhaps it has rattled me brains some, wouldn't deny it. But it seems I still see sharper than some. I watched you, oh yes,

I did, filing over here with barely concealed contempt on your faces. Or anger—outright fury—that you had to show respect to one such as this."

He shook me a little. "One such as this," he repeated, his voice acid. "Who ripped apart the bastard who dared to swallow her, who carved her way out of his stomach through sheer bloody-minded determination. Who held onto his hide even as she was sliced to ribbons, then stared down the bastard of Vitharr himself before blowing half a dozen of his warriors out of the sky! And she did it *without* armor, *without* talons, *without* fangs. But I'd say she has bigger fangs than you, proud Axsel, bigger than any of you, whose blood I didn't see staining the sky last night alongside hers!"

"But you'd see it now," someone said, a grave looking older man with shoulder length dark hair. "You'd see us join an alliance that might get us killed—"

"Alliance?" the hippie looked at him blankly for a second, and then laughed. "What do I have to do with yer damned alliance?" I could care less about politics, and whether ye join Lord Rathen's war party or not. I will; I like a fight. And I like even better the idea of fighting beside warriors such as this," he shook me some more. I really wished he'd stop doing that. "Who is the only one I ever met who might be crazier than me. We'll savage the bastards together," he told me, grinning. "You could probably do more damage in your current state than half of them here anyway."

Yeah, I doubted that. And maybe he did, too, if he was telling the truth, instead of putting on whatever farce this was supposed to be. Because he plopped me back down on my log again as if suddenly losing interest in the conversation.

"Then what do you expect us to do?" the same man demanded, as people began looking at each other again, then at me, and then at the hippie, as if expecting guidance from one of us. But they weren't getting it from him.

"What?" he looked up from a low-voiced conversation he had started with Regin. "What are you saying? Stop mumbling, boy, I'm old!"

The "boy", who clearly wasn't one, scowled. "I said, what do you expect us to do, then?" he shouted.

"About what?"

"*About the war!*"

The hippie blinked at him. "Didn't I just say?" he asked irritably. "Do as you damned well like. Are you dragonkind or aren't you?" And then Regin got up and the two men walked off, still chatting.

Which was probably why everyone's gaze suddenly turned on me, since I was the only one left.

I gazed back, caught off guard, and without a speech prepared. Not that I'd ever had to give one, or ever expected to; again, that wasn't my job. Only they didn't know that, didn't realize that I was a fraud, a walking vote who now found herself the spokesperson for my entire senate.

And just when I thought my day couldn't get any worse.

I hesitated for a moment, but there was nothing else for it. I stood up again, climbing on top of the log this time, not that it helped much. But the people in front of the now-sizeable crowd hunched down slightly, with a few of the men even going down to one knee so that the ones in the back could see better.

And then they waited.

I fervently wished that my father was here, he of the eloquent speeches and perfect timing. Or Louis-Cesare, who fit in with these people a lot better than I did, and was tall enough not to need the log. Or Claire . . . alright, maybe not Claire, at least not now.

But there was only me, so I opened my mouth, hoping against hope that something eloquent was going to come out of it. What I got instead was Lord Rathen, his voice bellowing out of nowhere, and almost causing me to fall off my perch. And startling the crowd almost as much, who hadn't seemed to expect that, either.

"Can she see us?" Rathen demanded as the glade winked out, leaving me staring at a dark void. But a moment later, Louis-Cesare's vision cut in, dispelling the blackness and showing me—

"What the hell?" I murmured, and the crowd murmured with me.

I had the impression that they were seeing what I was, although how they were, I didn't know. I hadn't gotten my father's mental gifts in the genetic lottery, Dorina had. But the scene I was receiving—and somehow broadcasting—was as clear as crystal.

We were looking at a valley, a once pretty one judging by the ring of blue mountains in the distance and the undamaged pieces I saw here and there, when Louis-Cesare's eyes flicked from bit to bit. He didn't seem to know what to let them light on, although my partner was not squeamish. But what I saw at the center of the valley . . .

Was a nightmare.

"The *Turl uh Talat*," Lord Rathen said, looking at us as if at a camera. "Or so it was until last night, when Lord Steen's people descended upon it. They came out of nowhere, furious at their defeat at our hands, and determined to inflict the same on innocent people. We found a few locals who told us the tale, how they didn't pause to plunder, or to take prisoners, or for any reason at all, but simply came in fast and low and burnt everything they found.

"And everyone."

He said no more, but he didn't have to. Louis-Cesare's eyes had vampire vision, and kept zeroing in on pieces of the still-smoking carnage, giving us up close examples of Vitharr's fury. They were needed, as the whole valley was a blackened mess, a pit of smoking charcoal with only a few pieces still identifiable: a little carved horse, a child's toy, with a metal bridle winking in the sunlight; a banner on a leaning pole, red with some kind of flower on it, still snapping in the breeze that was blowing charcoal dust all around; a shiny copper pot.

There was even a gaily painted wagon, turned over and half burnt, with the other half showing a laughing troll girl with a mug of ale in her hand. It was an animated image, probably some sort of advertisement, but the damage was causing it to fritz. I saw her only intermittently as a result, with the smoking interior of the wagon visible in flashes, along with a skeleton still in place.

I wondered if it was hers.

I decided that I didn't want to know.

Whoever it was appeared to have been taken unawares, perhaps killed in the first pass, but others had fought back. I could see what remained of them, huddled with blackened swords, staves and spears in their hands, behind whatever shelter they could find, waiting for a chance to counterattack. And maybe some of them had, fighting a rear-guard action to allow others to escape. Sooty wheel tracks veered off from the blackened crater and headed for the woods in numerous places, and I assumed that some must have made it.

But others hadn't, as evidenced by the piles of burnt bones amidst the smoking ruins.

Lord Rathen stood up abruptly. He was in human guise at the moment, although he had partly transformed like Regin, with heavy, dull gold armor under a pure white tabard. He looked like a man out of time, a medieval knight surveying a blackened, smoking battlefield.

All he needed was a sword.

But then he started speaking and I decided that I'd been wrong; he didn't need anything. The usually mellow voice was harshened by emotion, and the blue eyes were liquid with tears for the fallen that he wouldn't shed. He wasn't wearing a crown or even a circlet, but in that moment, he looked every inch a king.

"These were our people," he said softly. "The so-called dark fey, the outcastes, the ones nobody wanted. I know that many of you don't see them that way, that you view them as beneath us, as rude, unsettled vagabonds with little to offer. But they were our brothers, made like us, discarded like us, and like us, seen as failures worthy of no renown. Yet resilient, strong, carrying on despite everything that the world—several worlds—could throw at them.

"Now they are here, murdered indiscriminately by a monster who would do the same to us, given the chance. Yes, I know you think we are different; we are better; we are stronger. But the creatures the chieftain of Vitharr serves, and who protect him no matter how foul his deeds, don't view us like that. They view us like this, like something to be used and discarded when no longer convenient, to be butchered like the animals they think us to be. Steen will find out about that in due time, should he live long enough, when they eventually turn on him as well, but I will not.

"I will not be a slave, not to him, who ignores all rules of conduct and invades my home, slaughtering my people within its very walls, not to the so-called gods he serves, not to anyone.

If you are willing to bow the neck, to accept the yoke until your strength is used up and your life is spent, you are free to do so. But I will stand, alongside our new allies and every other one I can find, and I will *fight*. I have made my choice.

"Make yours."

The images cut out, hard enough to leave me staggering. And then sitting abruptly and with no grace back on the log, which I had to catch the side of not to fall off. But nobody noticed. Everyone was too busy looking the way I felt, like they'd just been given a punch straight to the gut.

And that, I thought dizzily, is how you make a goddamned speech.

Chapter Twenty-One
Dorina

I awoke to a *sush-sush-sushing* noise that I couldn't place. It sounded like someone throwing sand against glass, or miniature hail stones striking a windshield. I did not open my eyes to see which.

I had long ago learned to gain information before alerting anyone that I was aware, especially in dangerous circumstances. And in Faerie, that was essentially everywhere. Luckily, there were things I could see without eyes.

My senses were more acute even than most vampires, but on Earth I didn't need them. I could throw my spirit outward, leaving my body and traveling partly in someone else's, using their connection to the world to tether me to this life while I rode them about like a horse. If they were weak minded, I could even take control, suggesting things, clouding their minds, steering them where I wanted to go.

All I had to do was to reach out and grab someone—

Like that, I thought, when I accidentally snared a body that had been passing by.

That shouldn't have been possible in Faerie, where my soul and body could not separate. That was why I, as a disembodied spirit, had manifested a corporeal form to begin with. Yet that seemed to be what had just happened.

It surprised me enough that I didn't conceal my presence as I normally do, and this person was definitely aware, immediately screaming and flailing and hitting a wall. Before scrambling up and pelting headlong down a corridor, leaving me behind. And without a tether to tie me to this world.

I felt the usual lurch of panic as I spun around, preparing to rush back into my body's embrace and save myself from dissolution, as I could not survive as merely a spirit for long. But I found myself hesitating, although not because another potential tether had come along. But because . . .

It felt different this time.

There was none of the usual sucking sensation, no pull of another realm that no living soul knew, no threat of dissolution. There was nothing except a dulling of the senses, as if something had been draped over my head, making everything slightly out of focus and indistinct. And leaving me with the disturbingly comical image of myself as a fake Halloween ghost bobbing about in her swishy sheet—

Was this what death felt like?

The thought rocked me, along with the possibility that I had sustained some wound in battle that I didn't recall that had drained me over time. Leaving me as nothing more than this . . . this thing, this disembodied remnant, who had no living form to go back to. Stuck forever as I had lived for so long, as a consciousness with no substance to it, no reality, no life.

The idea alarmed me to the point that I pelted headlong back through a wall and into the bedroom where my body lay, on an impressively sized, opulently draped bed.

It took me a moment of panicked examination to realize that it was breathing, a fact that I had to bend close in order to see, as my vision was really quite bad like this. But it was alive—*I* was alive. I even placed an incorporeal hand on my chest to make sure, feeling it rise and fall under the fine nightgown that someone had dressed me in.

I shouldn't have been able to feel dizzy like this, yet I did, with the room spinning slightly around me. I clutched the bedpost for support, only to have my hand go right through it. And yet, I *had* a hand, right there on the bedcovers, with a little dried blood visible under the fingernails that whatever bath I had been given had failed to scrub off.

It was enough to stagger me, the overwhelming relief that I had survived. I was not accustomed to such thoughts.

I had no fear of death, had not had in as long as I could remember, with my life never having seemed all that real to begin with.

Dory had caused me a few palpitations through the years, but when I fought, I fought for her, to keep her alive. To give her time to find a place in a world that would never have one for me. So, the fact that I could look down on myself and feel such concern, such emotion, such *fear* . . .

Was new.

And then someone spoke behind me, causing me to jump again and clutch at my chest, for I was not myself today.

Not at all!

"Yeah, that's not gonna work. Like not even close, okay?"

It was Ray, I realized, and he was sounding crabby.

A tiny voice answered him, but I did not understand it, and neither, it seemed, did Ray. Because he sighed in that frustrated way I had come to know so well since we came to Faerie, where the merchants' cant he spoke only got us so far. Faerie was like Earth, with a multitude of languages, and we knew almost none of them.

I turned to see him standing at the door, which was now open and framing a small pixie. She was hovering in the air, her tiny wings going a mile a minute, while four more were just visible in the hallway behind her holding up a large, silver tray. It had a dome over it, so I could not see the contents, and with my limited senses at the moment, I could not smell it.

But my body could, and I saw its nose twitch on the bed beside me.

"Look, I don't know what you just said, but this," Ray waved a hand contemptuously at the tray the pixies were straining to support, "is not gonna cut it. You ever see a dhampir eat? Specially after a fight, much less a fight like that? This ain't even an appetizer."

The pixies did not appear to understand him, and the one in charge—at least, I assumed so since she wasn't carrying anything—gestured with her tiny arms for him to move out of the way.

Ray did not move. "Bigger," he said, putting his hands together at the approximate size of the tray and then spreading them wide. "Much bigger. Do you get me? You're gonna need a lot more."

The pixie, who was a brunette with snapping lavender eyes, seemed to understand that, but she didn't like it. She began chattering away and gesticulating at me, somehow conveying the message that I was not really very big for a human, and that she had brought enough for a platoon. Which was not true, but probably felt like it to her, considering that many pixies could have fit into the space under that dome.

"Yeah, I don't care what she looks like," Ray said. "She hasn't eaten in two days and has had to heal besides. I'm gonna need—" He paused and held up a hand with the fingers spread wide. "Five, you get it? At least five times this much, and that's assuming that plate is loaded for bear."

The pixie stared from his hand, which he was waggling the fingers of to drive home his point, to me, to the tray. And then her tiny face flushed with outrage, and she began chattering even faster and at a much higher pitch. Meanwhile, Ray reached for the dome, lifting the silver cover to see if his estimate was accurate or needed to be enlarged even more and—

And I smelled *that*, I thought, as the wonderful aroma of spices and herbs and meat reached my nose, so wonderful, so heady, and so immediately overwhelming that, for a moment, it was all I could think about. And the next thing I knew, I was there, ripping a roasted bird's leg off a carcass and stuffing it into my mouth.

And I *had* a mouth suddenly, although how I did, I didn't know, as I did not recall rejoining my body. Nor was I entirely sure that I even knew how to do so as I still didn't understand what was going on. But I didn't need to.

I only needed this.

"Yeah, okay, we'll take this as a start, but I still need five more," Ray said, holding his hand up to the outraged pixie's face, which was fast losing its expression as she saw how quickly the food was disappearing.

The tray *was* loaded for bear, but I was starving, so hungry that its contents seemed to vanish before my eyes. There was roast duck in some kind of sticky sauce, venison or some near equivalent, sausages of an indeterminant kind, several types of cheese, and on the tray alongside the covered dish was a whole loaf of bread glistening with butter and still warm from the oven. Not to mention a good-sized tureen of stew that I knew on some level was tasty, but that I drank down so fast, grabbing it up and gulping it in a moment, that I couldn't truly appreciate it.

Then I stood there, in the midst of the carnage of a different kind of battle, with buttery fingers and greasy lips, and five shocked pixie faces staring at me.

My stomach rumbled plaintively.

"See?" Ray said, and held up his hand again. "Five, okay?"

The lead pixie nodded; her eyes huge. They took the empty tray away, tiny wings whirring, and Ray led me back inside. He was saying something, but I was finding it hard to concentrate with my appetite now awakened but not satisfied, and the fuzzy brained feeling I had had as a spirit now completely absent.

In its place were pains and strains and throbbing insistence from several wounds that distracted me, making it hard to grasp hold of his words. They seemed to slip away as meaninglessly as the pixie's chatter. All I could think about was my stomach, that it *hurt*, that it wanted, that it *roared*—

"Okay, okay, I was afraid of this," Ray said, and I heard him that time, because he was holding something in front of my face. Something tasty. Something—

I grabbed it and stuffed it into my seemingly insatiable mouth.

"Is—is she alright?" someone asked, sounding worried.

"No, keep 'em coming," Ray said, and more little cakes appeared, every time I finished swallowing the last one. Ray did his best to keep pace with me, stripping the small items out of their cellophane covers almost as fast as I could eat them.

Almost.

I do not know how many I consumed, but judging by the scattered boxes and mountain of wrappers around my feet when I came back to myself, it was a lot. I stared at them numbly, feeling crumbs on my face that I was not currently strong enough to wipe away. If felt as if my stomach had commandeered all of the blood in my body and was not giving me access to any of it.

I did not understand why I was so hungry. If my memory was correct, I'd eaten a large part of several dragons, ripping through layers of fat and meat and bone, crushing it all under the force of my bite, and having the hot, rich blood run down my throat. It had felt delicious and satisfying at the time, like sweet, sweet victory.

Now, it made me want to throw up everything I had managed to get down.

They had been sapient and I had savaged them, and yes, eaten some of them, maybe a good deal of them; I couldn't entirely remember. It had been like being in an animal's mind, yet not. I had possessed a few of those in the past, and understood the simple, linear way they thought, but these weren't animals and enough of their higher mind had remained that—

I was going to throw up.

"Okay, okay, over here," Ray said, putting an arm around me before I collapsed and leading me somewhere. It was to a chair, a comfortable one that I hadn't noticed before, perhaps because it was located on a small balcony. But not like any balcony I had ever seen, although not because of the space itself, but because—

"What is *that*?" I croaked, distracted by what appeared to be a furious sandstorm raging only a few yards away.

It was the reason for the shushing sound I'd been hearing, which was louder out here, but still strangely muffled, and none of it was touching us. I reached thoughtlessly toward it, despite knowing that there must be some kind of ward there keeping it back, because the glittering, golden bands were almost hypnotizing. But Ray grabbed my hand, pushing me gently but firmly back into the chair.

"Nope, nope, nope, let's not do that," he said, and then looked at someone behind us, back in the bedroom. "Where are those damned pixies? I'm almost outta oatmeal pies!"

"I'll go get 'em, boss," somebody said, and I heard a door opening and closing, but didn't feel well enough to wonder what that was all about.

"Yeah, I was afraid of this, too," Ray said, as I started to shiver uncontrollably, and something touched my lips. I opened my eyes to see a glass with some water in it, and I obediently drank.

It seemed to help slightly.

"What is happening?" I croaked, as Ray settled into a chair beside me. He must have been out here before, because there were butts from the type of cigarettes he liked all over the small wooden table, and spilling out of a little glass bowl he was using as an ashtray.

I did not know where he'd gotten them, as we'd had none before this, but I was probably to blame for the mess. I vaguely remembered bumping the table when I sat down, and moved to help him pick up the butts with trembling hands, but he shooed me away. And did it himself, faster and more efficiently than I could have.

"You want more Little Debbies?" Someone asked, and I looked up to see one of Ray's boys standing in the doorway to the bedroom, a box of fudge cakes in hand.

"No, damn it! I want those goddamned pixies to do their job and bring her something nutritious. She's shaking from all the sugar already. Go help Dan hurry them up," he added, naming another member of his family. This one was a handsome, Korean-looking man whose face I knew but whose name I didn't recall, but he ran to obey.

"Why . . . are they here?" I asked, watching him go. "I thought you didn't have family in Faerie."

"I'm not supposed to," Ray said sourly, wiping my lips with a handkerchief. His beard was gone, I noticed, and he had on new clothes. I must have been out for a while. "If I'd known the bastards were here, it would have saved me a lot of trouble," he added. "The same amount I'm gonna cause them, soon as I get 'em home."

"I don't understand."

He sighed and sat down in the other chair. "You know I parked them at the senate, right?"

I shook my head. Then thought about it some more and nodded, because I seemed to remember something about Dory having to find a home for Ray's family, once he became her Second. That made them part of her family as well, something that every other senator had, but that she had never before had to worry about as a dhampir.

Dhampirs couldn't have children, neither of the body like humans nor of the blood like vampires. We were the end of a line, genetically speaking, something that sent a pang through my heart whenever I thought about it. So, I tried not to, and between that and the confusion of sharing a single body with a second consciousness, I had had little incentive to get to know Ray's boys.

I recalled them vaguely, however, as a rag-tag bunch of sometime smugglers, sometime nightclub attendants who had been rather overwhelmed at the idea of joining the illustrious Basarab family.

"Good," Ray said, watching me. "I'm not sure what you remember from the times Dory is in charge—it gets confusing. But as a senator, she has rooms at the consul's place in New York, so I left 'em there while I figured a few things out. They shoulda been happy—no real work to do, cushy surroundings, and no one is tapping them for the war. They had the life of Riley, right?"

I nodded. I found myself calming down somewhat the longer I sat. I usually found Ray's presence soothing, even when he was yelling at me, and could listen to him tell stories like this all day long. It didn't even seem to matter what he said; just the lilt and fall of his voice, and knowing that he was watching out for me were enough.

"Well, tell them that!" he said crabbily. "Instead of staying there and learning some damned manners so they don't embarrass themselves, getting fitted for some nice clothes, and just freaking relaxing for a while, what do you think they did? Go on, guess. What do you think those bastards have been up to?"

"Going into Faerie?" I asked, because obviously.

"Going into Faerie!" he agreed, slapping the table. "In the middle of a *war!* And do you want to know why?"

I looked from him to the pile of colorful boxes scattered about the bedroom. They looked strange, lying there on a medieval looking plank floor, with the hand saw marks still visible. An undyed sheepskin had been draped across the boards as a rug, to keep away the chill, and the whole was surrounded by a bunch of timber and stone walls, and old fashioned, four poster bed, and a metal banded chest for clothing.

Next to all that, the garishly cheerful modern boxes were . . . jolting.

"Something to do with snack cakes?" I guessed.

Ray shook his head. "Oh, no. Those were just the sweetener, the stuff I found out the fey liked 'cause sugar is almost unknown here and honey is pricey. So, like I told you before, I used a few boxes to help seal deals, back when I worked for Cheung and he had me smuggling stuff in and outta here, right?"

I nodded some more.

"Well. My genius boys decided that living in the consul's own house was the perfect cover for a little more smuggling. The court is crammed with vamps from all over the world right now cause of the war, and being away from home, they're also away from their usual sources of supply for all kinds of things. That includes fey wine, which means they can't get a buzz on unless they suck the blood of a human who is high as a kite, and the consul frowns on that seeing as how we need the Circle for the war right now—"

"Ray."

"Right. Well, my guys overheard some people saying what they wouldn't give for a little something-something from Faerie, only the war has interrupted the trade routes."

"So they decided to arrange a supply."

"Yes! Without telling me, 'cause I was away on war business, or so they said." He cocked his head at me. "You doing better?"

It was times like these that I wondered whether Ray understood what he was doing when he prattled on about random things, and knew that it helped. I'd had a succession of shocks in close order, and had been close to some kind of break down. But now . . .

"Yes," I told him. "Better."

"Good. 'Cause I got enough trouble with two assholes who *can't be left unsupervised* for more than *five goddamned minutes!*"

I didn't know why he was suddenly shouting as I was sitting right beside him. But then I saw the two vampires cowering in the doorway, looking as if they wished the floor would open up and swallow them whole. And in the dimness behind them—

"Oh," I said, as an entire army of pixies descended onto the balcony, with five large, silver covered salvers. The lead pixie was back, her lavender eyes snapping, and clearly intending to make a point about her people's hospitality.

I hadn't thought I could eat anything else, with my stomach as jumbled up and confused as my mind. But the smells coming off all that food had my insides rumbling and my mouth watering and my eyes widening as I stared around at the floating feast. And a bunch of eager little faces determined to see me fail to finish the repast they had prepared, which they probably thought of as a meal for a hundred.

But that was a hundred pixies, not a hungry dhampir.

I looked up at Ray to find him smiling, a knowing glint in his eye. "Do the family proud," he told me softly.

And I did.

Chapter Twenty-Two

Ray bumped into the wall of the hugely oversized corridor we found ourselves in, before staggering off clutching his nose. Some spicy language followed, perhaps because it was not the first time he had done that, or even the fourth. His face was moving oddly under the hand I raised to the damaged area, with vampire healing abilities causing it to swell and then deflate in rapid succession.

"You said for me to drive," I reminded him.

"Only because we weren't getting anywhere with both of us doing it!" he hissed back. But he hissed quietly, because we were approaching the Great Hall. Of course, we had been approaching it for some time without actually reaching it, and that did not seem likely to change.

"Perhaps you should take over," I offered, as the body we were sharing veered drunkenly toward the other wall.

It was a good distance away, as this part of the palace complex had been built originally by giants and looked it. The ceiling was so high that it disappeared into darkness, with the lanterns that somebody had placed considerably higher than my head failing to illuminate that far. And the width could have accommodated a whole chorus line.

"Or I could try again," I offered, only to have Ray growl at me. And then send us staggering backward through a doorway because his eyes were still crossing.

It was not the door to the hall, fortunately, but to a small, dark room with a large, bright balcony. Like my bedroom, it looked as if it had wondered in from somewhere else, as I couldn't imagine a giant squeezing in here. I guessed they had made accommodations for their smaller guests, who might feel somewhat uncomfortable in a bedroom the size of a football field, but this one gave the impression that it hadn't been used for anything in a while.

Except as a depository for ravens. Not live ones, but décor items, a huge number of them stacked almost ceiling high in places, with some looking quite old. Like the two stone carvings that flanked the fireplace, which had been painted at one time, but were now mostly bare stone with just a little black paint in the creases of the feathers.

There were also raven sconces, raven candleholders, raven lamps and raven covered tapestries, although those were fairly motheaten and faded to the point that I could barely make them out. They contrasted with the banners stacked in bunches that looked fairly new, with green silk backgrounds that gleamed in the light from the hall, and a large black bird in the center. There was even a stack of shields with a raven painted on them, and they looked new, too.

"Hrafnavirki," Ray said, noticing my interest.

"What?"

"Raven Fortress. It's what this place is called. It started out as a giant settlement a long time ago, someplace with a crap ton of ravens. They still got an aviary of them somewhere out front, for old times' sake, I guess. I was talking to one of the guards about it, while you were out."

"Someone seems to be thinking about changing the name."

"That would be the new queen, although I doubt she'll go through with it. It's tradition, and anyway, the king's not dead, just missing."

"Missing?"

Ray nodded. "The Svarestri grabbed him, or so some say. Others think he really is dead. Course, those two things aren't mutually exclusive."

"No," I agreed, thinking about what I knew of the silver haired fey, who looked so pretty and yet were so deadly.

"Anyway, she's placeholding until they get him back, assuming they ever do."

Placeholding. I glanced around. I wondered if she knew that, considering that she was already redecorating.

But the little storage room provided a welcome respite, and a place to gather our thoughts. Together, we stared at the sandstorm still raging outside and attempted to sort things out. Or Ray did; I had already shown how useful I was likely to be at that.

The storm was ferocious enough to have scoured the skin right off of our bones had a ward not protected us. But there was a usefulness in its savagery, as it would also scour anyone else who came close enough to have a look. Although that seemed unlikely as we were no longer in the lovely valley.

If we could see anything besides blowing sand, it would be a vast, snow-dusted desert, one of the areas stolen from the dark fey by the Svarestri for the ore that lay under the ground. Most of the former residents had been run out years ago, or turned into slaves to mine the land that had once been theirs. But the pixies were the exception.

Their small size and the fact that they had learned to build cities underground had made them difficult to find, as did the sandstorms. The area was naturally prone to them, Ray had said, and whenever the pixies didn't want to be seen going from place to place, they conjured one up to use as moving camouflage. And sometimes, as in this case, they took a whole city along for the ride.

That wasn't hard, as it fit neatly into a satchel.

Dory used a similar rig for her armory, only the pixies' version of a pocket reality was even stranger. Ray had said that they'd learned to coax a bit of non-space out of the mouth of a portal, causing it to protrude into Faerie. They then continued to pull it further and further until it completely engulfed something they wanted to transport, before folding it over and sending it back where it belonged, dragging whatever it had captured into the pocket dimension that they had created.

It sounded to me like a tongue sticking out of a mouth long enough to snare a sweet, then slurping it back inside. Except that the tongue was another universe and the sweet wasn't a single person or house, but palaces, cities, even whole armies. And the pixies could apparently accomplish this feat whether there was room for said items within the span of the portal or not, because non-space paid no attention to the limitations of our universe.

Its physics were not our physics, its laws not our laws.

Then they packed the whole thing away like a piece of luggage and flew off with it.

Considering how much energy Dory's small armory took, that must have required an insane amount of power, to the point that I had no idea how they did it. I would have said a ley line sink, where two or more of the rivers of power that connected worlds crossed and pooled their energy, but they were not portable. Yet there *was* magic here, I thought, staring at the ever-changing golden whirls and ripples outside the balcony.

I could trace the patterns it made, enveloping the roaring storm and plaiting the winds together like a braid. Not one strand of power, but many, each unique, each a delight, each like an unknown spice on my tongue. Amazing.

"Okay, that works," Ray said, lifting an arm and then putting it back down again. "That's better."

"What is better?" I asked, distracted, but following the movement with my eyes. And hearing him curse when his arm suddenly shot out and began punching the wall repeatedly, hard enough to crack it.

"Fuck, fuck, fuck!" he said, as his boys came running through the door and pulled us back. Only to get almost decked by the wildly swinging arm for their trouble.

The scrawny one named Dan ducked just in time, but the handsome one got clocked in the throat and went down. Only to jump right back up again, because the last thing a vamp who was already in trouble wanted was to further piss off his master. And his master *was* pissed.

"What are you doing in here?" Ray yelled as he was grabbed again, less than helpfully. "Get off me!"

They got off.

"Sorry, boss," Dan said. "But they, uh, started serving."

"And I care about that because?"

"The Great Hall eats after the queen. So, she and her guests musta already got theirs."

"That means they'll be talking soon," the handsome vamp added helpfully.

He was tall, with a haircut that would have done a K-pop star proud, and either perfect golden skin or an expensive glamourie to make it appear so. He was also dressed better than his counterpart, who had opted for a troll-like outfit of worn leather and old furs. This one preferred turquoise silk for his shirt, suede in a slightly darker but complimentary shade for his trousers, a scarlet sash around his waist, and shiny, thigh high boots.

He looked more like a pirate than Ray had ever done.

"Although probably not until after dessert," he added, "as they don't seem to like discussing business at table. But that might not take long. They all eat like they're afraid somebody'll take it away from them."

Ray shot him a stink eye. I couldn't see it, but felt it radiating all over his face. "Maybe somebody did in the past."

"Yeah, but the point is that they'll be having that talk you wanted to hear soon."

The stink eye increased. "Thank you, Bonhwa. I would have never gotten the point without you."

"You're welcome." Bonhwa seemed pleased that he had managed to help his master. Dan sighed and shook his head, and didn't even flinch when Ray exploded.

"Get back in there! I'll be in soon enough, and you two better be ready!" They ran off like frightened chickens and one of Ray's knees buckled. And despite what I'd just seen, I made the mistake of trying to help him back up. "No, no, no, goddamn it! That's not helping. I need you distracted!"

I went back to watching sand.

I had an excellent view, because our hosts had made the receptacle containing us transparent. That was likely for security reasons, to allow their warriors to look for signs of trouble from all directions. But it also provided a view of the wildly whipping storm from any balcony or window, giving the palace a strange, otherworldly feel.

Of course, it was *in* another world, but you really felt it here: a frisson over the skin, a tingle down the spine, a lifting of the little hairs on the back of my borrowed neck. Or perhaps I was imagining it, as I was not accustomed to what Ray and I were attempting. It felt somewhat similar to what I did on Earth, detaching my soul from Dory's and throwing it out into the world to mingle with others.

Except that I hadn't this time.

My body and soul were right where they should be, namely back in bed sleeping off my feast, but part of my consciousness was here, in some sort of mental symbiosis with Ray. My powers seemed to manifest differently in this world—very differently, I thought, thinking back to the arena—and it took some getting used to. I decided to work on that.

It was surprisingly difficult. Ray was larger and more solid than me, with a rugged hardness to him that I did not know whether to attribute to his vampire-ness or his maleness, but which kept throwing me off. He felt like trying to wear a coat that was too long and had rocks in the pockets, with his frame being more substantial than I was used to.

It kept tripping me up when I tried to walk, because his legs were longer than I expected and threw off my stride. I kept missing when reaching for door pulls, because his hands were farther away from my shoulders than they were supposed to be. His center of gravity was also strange, being considerably higher than mine, which was why I'd had trouble staying balanced when he gave me control.

Well, that and the fact that his mind kept trying to take it back. But now that I wasn't distracted by all that, I could appreciate things I hadn't noticed before. Like how well put together he was.

He was shorter than usual for a man in the modern era, but not by as much as you'd expect. The Dutch were some of the tallest people on the planet, and he must have gotten a boost from his terrible father in that way, at least. He also had a wiry, compact strength that had probably made him more formidable than he appeared even before his transition.

I could see him scrambling up the rigging on his old master's pirate ship, scanning the horizon with vampire vision, looking for threats. Or for one of the heavily laden merchant ships that were his old family's favorite prey. He had always been a good climber, scaling the palm trees of his homeland as a boy for food or to escape the near-constant bullying, and he hadn't forgotten how.

And for a moment, I *could* actually see it, perhaps because I was currently in his mind: Ray, shirtless and sweating, with straining muscles glistening under a full moon, his once long, black hair whipping around his face courtesy of the high winds off the ocean, and his loose fitting, wide legged trousers blowing back against a surprisingly impressive—

"Auggghhhh!" he yelled suddenly, and for a moment, I didn't know if that had been memory-Ray or the current one.

The current one, I decided, snapping back to myself to find his whole body vibrating. For a moment, there was a great deal more cursing going on. And then he found a mirror on the wall and used it to glare at me.

"I am *trying* to *concentrate!*"

"Sorry," I said meekly, and he snarled out something incoherent in reply.

That was fair, as he was doing me a favor, but I kept making it more challenging. I tried focusing on the storm again, but found that challenging, too. I kept wanting to touch him, to learn this new body by feel, but he didn't seem to like that.

I ran a hand down his chest, enjoying the sensation of hard muscle under soft suede, and got growled at in reply. So, I pretended that I had just been admiring his clothes, which were very nice, although they weren't the ones we'd bought in the marketplace. The new shirt felt like raw silk, with a nubby, homespun nap, and both it and the buttery suede vest and trousers he had paired it with were a burnt sienna that went well with his coloring.

The only problem was that they were too small in places.

The pixies weren't built the same as humans, so just sizing up their usual attire to replace the stuff that the arena had ruined hadn't completely worked. The fabric stretched taught over his thighs and biceps, and the breadth of his shoulders made the shirt pull a bit. His muscles in general were well proportioned from years of hard work before his change, and while he was no bodybuilder, they were larger than any I'd ever had.

I found them oddly fascinating.

My fingers traced an old tattoo I couldn't see, but which had left a textural change on his otherwise smooth skin. I tried to follow it to discover what it was, because I did not want to interrupt again to ask. But little goosebumps followed my fingers despite the gentleness of the touch, as I attempted to discern the pattern through the roughness of his sleeve.

It was a strange game, and a difficult one, trying to tell the difference between goosebumps and little silk nubs, and between old ink and firm flesh . . .

I was disturbing him again, I realized unhappily, and tried to stop it. I tried to stop everything and just sit quietly in his head for a while. But that did not appear to be working, either.

Sweat was dripping down his face although it wasn't hot in here. A drop plunked onto our shirt and he flinched, while I found myself wanting to taste it. It was bizarre; I knew so much about vampires, was practically a walking encyclopedia of information about them, and yet did not know if their sweat was salty like a human's or—

I decided that perhaps I should concentrate on my own body for a while.

I could still sense it if I tried, could feel the softness of the sheets, smell the faint sent of the soap they'd been washed in, hear the soft conversation of a guard outside my door, the same one I had briefly hijacked, talking with the friend he had brought along for moral support. I could even drag my sleeping hand along the undulations of my body underneath the covers, the swell and peak of a breast, the dip of my naval, the rise of the flesh below. And experience myself stretching luxuriously from this far away, under the warm cocoon that the blankets had made of my heat.

It was all distant, like an echo after a spoken word, or the faint roar of the winds there, which varied slightly in pitch and tone from the ones here. But it was very real, and might be another reason why I could not steer us about. It was difficult to walk when lying down, or to turn a corner when in danger of falling off a bed.

You'd think I'd be better at this, I thought, frustrated, considering how long Dory and I had had to share. But I had been controlling my own body then, not someone else's, and we were rarely awake at the same time. But this . . .

I did not know how to do this.

And Ray didn't either, because he sighed a second later and gave up.

I could feel when he let go, when I started to drift away from him, because I was much weaker in this form and could not force the issue. He'd had to grasp my hand when we first tried this to allow the mental intrusion. And right before I lost contact, I felt him do so again, which was frankly ridiculous as I didn't have a hand!

But he gripped it anyway, and when I opened my eyes, they were fuzzier than they had been a moment ago. But clearer than when I'd been floating about on my own in the hallway. It was rather like being a human who had forgotten her glasses, but could still see.

And what I could see was Ray, since I was now separate from him, if only slightly. He was handsome, I thought, examining him from inches away as I rarely had reason to do. Why had I not seen that before?

Perhaps being someone else for a time gives a new perspective.

"I got hair on my butt," Ray said abruptly.

"What?"

"I have to shave it off, okay? If I don't, I got a hairy ass. Something else to thank my dickhead father for."

I felt around behind him, using his spare hand. And slipped it below the waistband of the trousers, which was loose thanks to a draw tie closure. I encountered smooth flesh and hard muscle, but no discernable hair.

"I shaved it already," Ray snarled. "And stop that!"

I stopped it, but failed to understand this conversation.

"I can't even grow a beard properly," he added, in an aggrieved voice. "Unless I'm on some weird fey enchantment. But I got hair on my ass, and I don't need this, okay? I know who I am; I know where I rank; and I. Don't. Need. This. Do you get it?"

No, I thought, confused, and he sighed deeply. And then pushed off of the wall that I had the vague idea he had been softly beating his head against and stood tall. Because he could move!

He realized it the same moment that I did, and froze. Then slowly, carefully, tried out first one foot and then the other, waggling them around as if wearing a pair of new shoes that didn't quite feel right. But he could walk in them, oh yes, he could!

He took a small turn around the room, and did not run into anything. Of course, there wasn't much to run into, there being no furniture, but that had not stopped us in the hall. And then he did it again, just for fun, speeding up slightly.

"Are we doing this?" I whispered, despite the fact that no one could hear me.

But he could, and the smile that lit up his face suddenly echoed the one on mine. "Yeah. Yeah, I think so. Okay, distance seems to be the thing we gotta balance. Too far and you drift away; too close and I can't think straight or even move. But this . . . seems to work, right?"

I nodded. I wanted to throw my arms around him and say thank you, but . . . distance. "Yes. I think it works."

"Good. Then let's go find out what that bastard of a father of yours is hiding."

Chapter Twenty-Three

The dining hall was both familiar and very much not. The bones of it were pretty standard, if one's standard was a massive medieval hall. Heavy old timbers separated stretches of stone reaching up to another ceiling that disappeared into darkness; colossal wooden beams spanned the space from perhaps three floors up, supporting huge iron candelabras that nonetheless did little to displace the dark; flagstone flooring with a few withered rushes were scattered about, along with some old bones that a few dogs were gnawing in the corners; and a greatly oversized fireplace occupied the right hand wall, with more carved stone ravens framing the lintel, which was burning what appeared to be an entire tree. But it was the people who really caught the eye.

The tables for the pixie contingent were essentially small wooden planks coming out of the walls on either side of the room, complete with attached benches. They were off the ground to keep them out of the way of heavy boots and inconsiderate elbows, some at troll height, others even higher. This, of course, did not inconvenience the diners, who could fly.

There were boughs of greenery, mostly pine from the scent, either growing out of the walls along with the tables or secured around them somehow, creating a sort of floor on which the diners could walk to visit friends at neighboring tables. And forming islands of floating greenery along the walls that helped to perfume the space.

There were also small lanterns set amongst the branches and drooping down from the ones above, and glimmering softly. And showing me hundreds of small, animated faces enjoying their meal. I wanted to go see what they were eating, as I found pixies fascinating, but had the vague idea that that might be considered rude.

The big slabs of what looked like oak in the middle of the floor, on the other hand, that were masquerading as tables, were occupied by trolls, their size straining even the thick bench seats. Ogres, shorter and stockier but no less solid, were also there in numbers, eating around their massive tusks. As were duergars, a type of dwarf.

I knew little about them as they were a secretive bunch, half the size of a man but twice as strong, with large noses and bright eyes, the latter visible as they peered distrustfully out of the hoods they had not bothered to pull down. The rest of the crowd seemed to be primarily human and part-human hybrids, except for a group of brownies at a few tables to the left. They looked like short, stick-thin humans with dark skins and oversized heads, or essentially anything else they liked since they were shapeshifters. That might explain why a few satyrs were dancing a jig by the fire, or perhaps they were really there.

I didn't know anymore.

But they fit right in, as it was a rowdy crowd, something only added to by the swarms of pixie waiters flying about, trying to keep everyone satisfied. And carrying more of the tiny lanterns under their trays, I supposed to keep anyone from stumbling into them. Or hitting them when the diners slammed their tankards down onto the tables rhythmically, in time to the band that was playing to the left of the fire.

They were out of tune and had a mishmash of instruments that didn't necessarily complement one another, but nobody seemed to mind. And I found that I didn't, either. The tiny lanterns whizzing by and the scents of food and pine reminded me of a feast in a forest surrounded by fireflies. It was even more amazing when you considered what was happening outside, where the cold, conjured winds howled as we were blown across the sky.

Yet, in here, it was warm and cozy and loud and happy, and suddenly, I was, too. If I'd been in my body, I'd have wanted to dance right along with the satyrs. The band's artistry might be suspect, but its rhythm was infectious.

But I wasn't in my body, and we had a job to do.

Ray thought the same, and tugged on my mental hand a little. "Okay. Nice and subtle. Remember, we're just looking for a table."

I nodded even though he couldn't see it, and we started forward. I spotted his boys on the other side of the room, where a couple of doors had been set into the patchwork of wood and stone that made up the walls. The smaller of the two, on the left at perhaps troll height, led to the kitchen, which was somehow keeping up with the preferences of so many different creatures. The other was our target, although I wasn't sure that "door" was the right word there.

It was a huge thing composed of planks of wood three times as wide as me and with the biggest hinges I had ever seen. They were the strap type in some kind of dark metal, hand hammered and full of scrollwork that scrawled across much of the surface of the wood. They were also easily twelve feet across, which wasn't surprising as the door itself was almost as tall as the cavernous ceiling.

They were a bit intimidating, and I wondered whether they were opened much. Maybe not as there was a smaller door set into them, which was more practical for the staff, who had to fly in and out with every course. For those doors led to the royal dining room, as the queen did not partake among her court except on special occasions.

Otherwise, she dined with her senior advisors or favored guests. Like tonight, when father, the Pythia and Senator Marlowe were joining her. I knew that because Ray had entertained a guest of his own while I was sleeping.

If I had been more myself, I would have scented our caller as soon as I awoke, or noticed that the cigarettes in the little bowl on the balcony table weren't all Ray's. Most were the ones he favored, but others were small, slim, dark things, cigarillos rather than true cigarettes, hand rolled and slightly lumpy, and made in one particular factory in Spain. I knew of only one person who used them, especially here in Faerie.

My father had dropped by for a visit.

Ray said that they'd talked for a while, because Mircea was a diplomat these days and liked the pleasantries. There had been a lot of those, and a lot of catching up on how we came to be here. But he was also a warrior and his direct nature had never been entirely eclipsed by the demands of his office.

It hadn't taken him long to get to the point.

He wanted Ray to get me out of this world, along a route that he had thoughtfully marked on a map. It was supposed to be the safest way and ended at a trusted portal, possibly the one that he and Marlowe had used because it was senate controlled. Or perhaps they had more than one; I didn't know.

I wasn't sure why he was so insistent; he knew who I was now, after that display in the arena. There simply couldn't be any confusion. And if there had been, Ray had cleared it up.

But perhaps he was worried about Dory without me there to protect her.

He really should know her better.

Or perhaps he was concerned that our senate seat would be revoked, should she try to hold it on her own. The senate kept making the mistake of thinking that I was Dory's vampire half, and that she was the more human part of us. And treated us accordingly.

I could not really fault them, for even she and I had long thought that way. But in truth, she was the dhampir—I was something very different. But they did not understand that, and I couldn't explain it since I didn't completely understand it myself.

But whatever his motivation, Ray said that he had been insistent. And Ray hadn't argued, since getting me out of here was also his goal and I believe he felt conflicted. But he had pointed out that I might not be entirely in favor of father's plan.

Mircea had then asked if he would like some help, which Ray had taken to mean help knocking me out and "stuffing my ass through a portal," as he had colorfully described it. And he was likely right. Father looked and talked like a diplomat, but he acted like a prince, and one used to being obeyed.

And in Ray's case, he had every right to expect compliance. Mircea was head of House Basarab, which Ray was now part of as my and Dory's Second. But father had underestimated him, as people so often did.

And Ray was loyal to me.

It made me feel strangely warm as we threaded our way across the raucous scene. I had never had anyone loyal to me before and still had trouble grasping it at times. But Ray's hand was steady in mine, and he'd kept his face blank when answering Mircea. And his mind, too, I supposed, as Mircea was an expert mentalist.

And had merely said that that wouldn't be necessary.

"We'll go home when you're ready," Ray had told me afterwards. "And not before."

I had blinked at him. "When did you decide that?"

"When I realized that you don't need to be worried about Faerie. It needs to be worried about you."

"But you said—"

"Yeah, I said a lot of things, most of them stupid." He had taken my hand. "Look, I'm out of my depth here. I want you back home; I do. Faerie scares the shit out of me, especially now, and having you here . . .

"But I get it now, why you don't wanna go back yet."

"You do?" I wasn't sure that I entirely understood that myself.

He'd nodded. "You know who you are there, and what you can expect. You have half a life, trying to share one with your sister, only that isn't really working for either of you, is it?"

I had numbly shaken my head.

"Yeah, I didn't think so. Nobody should have to live like that, and you've done it long enough. The riddle to what you are is here, and only here. You gotta be the one to decide if you want to find it. Not me, not Mircea, not anybody else."

I had blinked again when he said that, and might have done more if I hadn't been in too much of a food haze. And not just because it was almost unheard of for anyone to take my side. But because people did not tell Mircea no.

They nodded and bowed and were grateful that he had deigned to notice them. That was especially true for people like Ray, whose rank as a master might be impressive in some areas, but at the senate wouldn't even get him a servant's job. And whose own master had cast him off for being troublesome and not powerful enough, leaving him alone until Dory took him in.

Was that why he was so loyal to us? I wondered. And why he had stared his head of house down as far more senior masters would have trembled to do? The thought should have made me happy, even elated, but it did not.

Gratitude wasn't what I wanted from him.

The thought surprised me, having come out of nowhere, and seemed to surprise him, too. For he stumbled a little and almost connected with the swinging arm of a large troll. He managed to miss it at the last second, only to run straight into another troll coming this way, carrying a dozen huge tankards in each burly fist.

Beer sloshed, the troll cursed, and Ray and I found ourselves snagged on one of the creature's meaty fingers, which I supposed was all he could spare without dropping the rest of his burden. But one was enough. They truly were amazingly strong, I thought, as we were jerked closer, and had something that neither Ray nor I understood growled in our faces.

The troll looked like a waiter, with a full-length apron now splashed with beer, perhaps having been co-opted by the pixies to help keep up with the needs of tables full of his kind, who could drain the enormous tankards in a few hearty gulps. They were thirsty, it seemed, for we were quickly surrounded, or perhaps they just wanted to witness what the waiter would do to us. The trolls I had met at Claire's house had liked mayhem only slightly less than food and drink, and now they could have both.

We were backed into a wall of flesh that felt only slightly more yielding than stone, while being peered at by a ring of fascinatingly ugly faces. I didn't know whether the trolls I had met on Earth were simply more attractive than normal, the movie star version of their kind, or whether these were just particularly ill-favored. But I had never seen faces quite like them on anyone else.

It sent a shiver of excitement up my spine, as it did every time this world showed me something new. There were noses of every size and shape imaginable—cauliflower, bulbous, elephantine, long and beaky, short and piggy, twisted in such a way that made it difficult to imagine how the owner could possibly breathe, and full-on Cyrano de Bergerac. They were matched by tiny, beady eyes ranging in color from mud-brown and bruise-purple to vomit yellow, and hair that was mostly too clumped with mud, forest trash and bird droppings for me to really discern the color. And their skin was every shade from old bronze crusted over by brownish rust to a brilliant green that had been deliberately scarified, with the wounds making elaborate ruddy swirls across the features.

There was even a dark blue, a color I had never seen on Earth, and that must be rare here, too, as there was only one. He had had most of one cheek blasted away at some point, but instead of hiding it as most people would have done, he had seized the opportunity. And set the teeth that had been revealed in his cheek with precious stones, highlighting the injury and turning it into something strangely beautiful.

At least, I found it beautiful. Ray seemed to be having a different reaction. Ray had begun making small hurking noises, which I had not heard from him before, and which I was at first somewhat worried about.

"What are you doing?" I asked.

"Trying to look like I'm sick," he whispered back. "Plagues are a problem here. It's the best way out of something like this."

"Yes, but I don't think they heard you," I pointed out. Because the room was very loud, and while trolls usually have good hearing, discerning Ray's subtle sick sounds in all this would be unlikely. Particularly as the band had just started another song.

"Hurk!" Ray said in reply, elevating the decibel level beyond that which what was really believable, but the trolls didn't seem to notice. In fact, a few of them leaned closer as if under the impression that he was speaking some kind of strange, off-world language.

And then we were grabbed by the back of our tunic.

"Hurk! Hurk! Hurk!" Ray yelled frantically.

That did not help, either, but something else did. One of the trolls, a younger specimen with a round, boyish face, a shaggy tunic made out of something's hide, and a bright piece of silk wrapped around his wrist suddenly bellowed a few words at ear-splitting decibels. There was an abrupt silence, with the bow of someone's fiddle sliding discordantly off the strings, all conversation ceasing, and every eye in the place turning—

On us.

The silence persisted, echoing in my ears, for a moment, while several other nearby trolls checked us out more thoroughly. I didn't currently have a face, at least not with me, but Ray did and it was immediately full of trolls. Others tested out his limbs in a way that was probably meant to be a weak tug but which would have ripped a human's right off.

An older troll said something, with a gold tooth winking at us in what I belatedly realized was a grin. And then we were airborne, hefted onto burly shoulders and carried around the room, not to silence anymore, or even to noise. But to utter pandemonium.

"I do not think we are succeeding at being subtle," I told Ray, but doubt he heard me.

We were eventually plonked down at a table near the band, which seemed to be considered prime seating, and plied with food, drink and laughing, happy company, none of whom could understand a thing we said and vice versa. But all wanted to talk a mile a minute nonetheless.

That was extremely odd for trolls, who usually took taciturn to new heights, but not tonight. They talked and bellowed and laughed and drank, and we were pulled into all of it. I found myself getting my dance, after all, being swung from massive hand to massive hand, to the point that I wasn't sure it counted as dancing as my feet rarely hit the floor.

Which was just as well, because in Faerie, the term "rivers of wine," or in this case beer, was not a metaphor.

It seemed that we'd stumbled into a celebration. And slowly, over the next few minutes, we understood why. Because somebody came running with a torch and one of the older trolls made the flames dance, too.

"Oh," I said in wonder, as a plume of fire billowed outward, slicing across half of the room before forming itself into an unmistakable shape.

Several pixies chattered angrily, having barely dodged out of the way in time, and then had to continue doing so as the fire-creature chased them about the great space. It was a dragon, and it was flying on wings that shed sparks everywhere it went. They fizzled out on the cold stones of the floor, but occasionally some dried rushes went up before being crushed under the rock-hard heel of a troll before they could do any damage.

I barely noticed; my eyes were filled with fire. And it wasn't just red, orange or yellow. There were flickers of purple in there, too, and I thought perhaps an occasional flash of green, and the eyes of the great beast—

Were liquid gold, and almost as spellbinding as the real thing. I could see them well, as it had paused right in front of us, shedding sparks that Ray had scrambled to back away from, only there was nowhere to go. Trolls were all around us, hemming us in, sitting on the table on all sides and spilling into the floor, and hugging us as closely as if they would keep us with them permanently.

And maybe they wanted to, because yes, this was a celebration, I realized—of us. Or at least, of what we'd done in the arena. "They want to say thank you!" I told Ray, finally understanding. "I don't think they like dragons here!"

"I don't like 'em, either! Not when they're about to set me alight!"

But they didn't. The sparks from the great wings fell just short, mostly raining down onto the stones a yard or so in front of us, reflecting in all the spilt beer. And in Ray's eyes and splashing his face with color as he stared up at the creature in fear and awe.

Not being inside his head anymore, I could see him clearly, and he was amazing, too. The light limned his hair with red, turned his eyes to fire, and played off the lines of his face. Ray might not be conventionally handsome, and certainly didn't see himself that way. But there was beauty there, nonetheless, and generosity of spirit, and a good soul—just as there was in the trolls, if someone cared to see it.

I suddenly wished that I could dance again, and with him this time. I wished for it so much that I was hardly surprised when my body appeared beside me. But not the one sleeping in my room, lulled to sleep by the sounds of sand against the ward, happy and warm.

But another one, right here, right now, that was merging with me.

I took Ray by the hand this time, and pulled him up.

"What the—oh shit, oh no," he said, his eyes huge, because my hand was fire.

I noticed an old female troll, with heaps of beaded strings around her neck—along with little bird bodies impaled on pins, dried toads, and herbs in bunches—off to one side, watching me and cackling delightedly. And I remembered something Dory had said about the dark feys' magic being fire. And then I laughed along with her, because I had another body now, if one as ephemeral as the substance that had created it.

But I had it, and I wasn't going to waste this chance.

"Dance with me!" I said to Ray, who stared from me to his hand, which had yet to go up in flames, and back again.

"You really are mad."

But I guessed he was, too; it was that kind of night. Because the next moment, he was up and we were whirling around the floor, feet flashing and people clapping. And stomping and yelling and laughing and trying to grab us as we whirled past, because this was Faerie and there were no true spectator sports.

I'd no sooner had the thought than everyone was dancing, the whole room caught up in the spell of the moment. In the fire flashing in a hundred eyes, winking off metal hilts and jeweled teeth, and sparkling in the air like rubies as we showed them what vampire speed could do. And dared them to keep up.

All while shedding sparks wherever we went and yet emerging unscathed.

"Only in Faerie is it this exciting to walk across a room!" I told Ray, laughing.

"Exciting. Yeah. Fuck!" he said in return.

And then he danced even faster, whirling me around until the fire all flowed together and I could see nothing else.

Chapter Twenty-Four

"Come in here before you set the trees on fire," someone said, almost as soon as we made it through the door.

We'd used the smaller one that was inset into the massive one, slipping through once Ray's boys provided a distraction by spilling drinks on the guards protecting it and then running like hell. The guards had chased them and we'd passed on through, with no one else seeming to care. It helped that the party had reached the sloppy drunk stage and I doubted that anyone could still see well enough to notice.

The only problem was that my light hadn't faded entirely. It was dimmer than it had been earlier, more of a vague flicker around my form, but still bright enough to cast moving shadows on the forest of trees growing out of the floor in the next room.

I stopped to look at them in surprise.

The large space had the same construction as the room outside, or rather, it had started out that way. But mature oak and ash trees had scrawled their roots everywhere, not only underfoot, but also climbing up the walls like bark-covered vines. Creating a wooden obstacle course and giving the whole place the ambiance of an ancient temple lost in the jungle.

"How?" Ray called, answering back. "All I see is a forest!"

"There's a path around to the left," the voice said. "Look for the curtains."

We gazed around, but the room was quite dim, with the only light coming from me and a scattering of tiny lanterns in the tree limbs. And the occasional miniature doorway or window that had been set into their trunks. I blinked at that realization and looked closer, but no, I wasn't imagining things.

The nearest little door on the trunk of a fat oak was closed, although painted a pretty blue with white scrollwork. But the nearby window was open and it was the most exquisite thing, with bits of flattened horn for the panes, scraped thin to let in light when there was any, and a window box planted with flowers. The flowers were the product of a tiny weed that the dark fey called forest snow, because from any distance at all, the multitude of miniscule blossoms just looked like frost. But here, they seemed huge, as big as a pixie's two fists put together, and spilling in riotous profusion down to the trunk below.

Inside the small dwelling was something even more delightful: a woven rug, in reds and blues and green. It was the kind known as a rag rug on Earth, which utilized scraps of old material to make a new creation in a multitude of colors. It couldn't have been much bigger than the size of my palm, but it covered a good deal of the floor.

The rest was taken up by a table and two chairs, which would have struggled to accommodate a Barbie doll; a tiny candle in a wooden base with a flame kept equally small by the size of its diminutive wick; a wooden bench seat covered with several cushions embroidered with tiny scenes; a portrait on the wall, which was too small for me to make out many details; a kitchen off to the right with a bunch of bright copper cookware; and an archway that had some stairs inside it, leading further inside the trunk.

And an outraged pixie face, staring out at me, and all but shooting daggers from his eyes.

The trees must be where they slept, I realized. And in my fascination, I had bent so close that my eye must have been taking up most of the space in his window. Before I could apologize for disturbing him, tiny shutters slammed closed in my face, cutting off my view, and leaving me feeling like a gigantic Peeping Tom.

I looked back at Ray. "I didn't—I wasn't trying to—"

He took my hand. "Come on. We've been summoned."

We made our way through the trees with me refusing to so much as glance at any more of the interesting views offered by tiny balconies and open windows. That was despite some miniscule faces peering out at me, because my light was enough to paint shadows on the trunks as we passed. Finally, we found a route that hugged the wall, cutting a path through the mass of roots and giving us space to walk.

"Do you think the witch lit me up on purpose?" I asked Ray quietly. "So that I couldn't skulk about?"

"I don't care," he said, a thread of defiance in his voice. "And why should we have to skulk? They kidnapped us, tried to have their champion squash us, and didn't even invite us to dinner!"

"I didn't have anything I thought you might like," the voice rang out again. "Not for a vampire, that is. Although I've heard that the dhampir eats like a troll!"

"Thank you," I said, and the voice laughed. It was a woman's, and it tinkled like bells.

"Come, come. Join us for dessert. It's one thing both our cultures can agree on."

There were curtains at the end of the path, filmy things in dark green that blended in with the trees and were barely visible in the shadows. They cut the pixie's sleeping quarters off from whatever lay beyond and should have muffled the voice, only I was fairly sure that it was being magically enhanced. Ray held the curtains out of the way for me, so I wouldn't set something ablaze and get us into even more trouble.

The other side was more of the same, but I didn't see any dwellings among the branches of the much sparser number of trees. The walls were also the same, although the ceiling was even higher than the one outside, and the place was vast, instead of smaller and more intimate as I had expected. I decided that I should stop expecting things in Faerie, and we moved forward.

The trees cut down the echoing void somewhat, but it was still a very large space with very little in it. Except for four huge banners hanging on the wall at the far end of the room, made of crimson silk and bright enough to cut through the gloom. They each had a large, gold and white flower in the center that flashed in what little light there was, beckoning to us like a beacon.

There was also something under them, at the far end of the space, where dim light flickered at us from among the trees. It finally resolved itself into a long table on a dais lit by standing candelabras on either end and smaller lights that were nestled into patches of greenery in between. So much for lurking about, hoping to overhear something, I thought.

When we'd started this excursion, I had had some vague idea of a situation like the one at the consul's court, where there was always a crowd and some of them weren't as discrete as they might have been. Lurking about there was often an education, drifting from group to group in the noisy mass, following tidbits about the room like a detective trying to put things together. Which was especially easy when the detective was an invisible spirit.

Ray had come along as my base, a familiar body that I could go back to if I needed to rest, or if I was summarily excised as I had been by the guard earlier. But that idea was out of the window now, and Ray must have been thinking the same. Because he sighed and headed into the echoing cavern of a dining room.

I followed, splashing the floor with light.

"Ha!" The voice laughed. "I like this new form, although not as much as the other."

The speaker was hard to find, despite sitting on a throne large enough for a giant. Which must have been who it had been made for, as it was plush and padded and easily twelve feet across, leaving its occupant to dine in solitary splendor even among guests. But she was still hard to see, and not just because her crimson robes were the same color as the velvet seat cushions.

But because she was all of eight inches tall.

"Pixie," I said, in surprise, and she smirked at me.

"You were expecting something else?"

"I . . . wasn't sure what to expect," I said truthfully, and only after I spoke did I realize that the voice was coming out of Ray.

I wondered if he had been talking to himself this whole time, and couldn't remember.

But the pixie only clapped her hands again, and laughed some more. "Oh, this is too fun. That was you, wasn't it, who scared off my guard?"

"What guard?" Ray asked.

"The one I put on your room. Not to keep you two in, of course; I don't think any of my people are up to that. But to keep others out. Everyone here was so curious and you were exhausted and needed to rest.

"But a few hours later he comes tearing in here, half crazed, and babbling about some foul miasma trying to leech into his bones. I did wonder . . ." She eyed me up and down.

I attempted to look entirely unlike a foul miasma. And returned the scrutiny, although she appeared almost identical to the small creature who had served my lunch, except that she was a redhead. And unlike the other, whose locks had been close cropped, she appeared to have a great deal of hair.

It was piled on her head in coils of fat braids and in little curls that hung down around her face. She also had huge, lavender eyes and the prettiest, delicate green wings that were currently folded downward as they were not in use, giving her the appearance of wearing an iridescent cape about her shoulders. I could see them because she was sitting on a tower of cushions to get her above the slab of beautifully polished wood serving as a table top.

There was no crown nestled in all that shining abundance, but she didn't need it. There was no doubt whatsoever who was in charge. Something that was impressive considering who else was at the table.

But before I could properly acknowledge them, something stirred in the pixie's lap, under the tiniest of blankets. Forgetting my previous lesson, I moved closer, surmounting the few steps leading up to the dais to get a better view. And what I saw . . .

Drove everything else from my mind.

It was . . . it was . . . it was *precious*, so much so that I gasped in wonder and put out a hand, before remembering my current state and snatching it back. Ray hadn't gone up in flames when I touched him because we were linked, with the witch's spell seeming to view us as one and the same. But this beautiful creature did not have that protection, and I wouldn't have hurt it for the world.

On the contrary, I felt a surge of overwhelming protectiveness sweep over me, something that the pixie seemed to sense. For she sat the tiny bundle up a bit more, and pulled back the blanket that was partially covering the face. And let me see. "My son," she told me proudly. "Is he not perfect?"

"Oh," I breathed. "He is. He is utterly perfect."

It was true. He must have been a new born, for he wasn't even the size of my pinkie, with an exquisite little face smaller than a fingernail. He had no hair yet, at least not to speak of, although there was a bit of downy fuzz on his head so fine that I was not even sure that it was there.

He looked like a doll, something a master carver had made out of alabaster with the tiniest opalescent wings just visible in flashes as she adjusted him. But he wasn't a doll. I could see that clearly when I got closer, moving around the long table and up to the throne, where the queen allowed me to get nearer, waving off the group of winged, leather clad guards that had descended on me like a cloud of locusts.

I barely noticed them; I was too busy bending over the bundle, being careful not to get too close. But he must have sensed something, because he moved, pushing an arm out of the softness of his blanket and waving the tiniest of fists about. As if to say, what is this huge, bad-mannered person who dares to breathe on me?

And then he yawned, a ridiculously big, open mouthed expression of displeasure and sleepiness that made me fall in love immediately.

I would have died for him.

"He likes you," the queen said, her lavender eyes sharp. "He tends to scream at everyone else."

"He is perfect," I breathed. It was all I could think to say. But it seemed to be the right response, because she patted the seat beside her.

"Come, sit by me. I think he finds your presence soothing."

"I—I can't. I might scorch the seat, or—or hurt him." It was unthinkable.

"Don't worry about that," she assured me. "The flames won't get through my magic."

"'Scuse me," Ray said to someone from behind me. Because he must have moved when I did.

I turned to see him surrounded by the pissed off guards, who he was batting away like annoying gnats. And then noticed the woman in the seat of honor on the queen's right. It was the Pythia, looking uncomfortable, perhaps because my butt was in her face.

I moved it slightly, and she flashed me a look out of pale blue eyes that I couldn't read. That was probably just as well, as the last time we'd met, I had tried to kill her. I had been laboring under a misapprehension caused by the North American consul, who had wanted to drive a rift between her and my father, and had used me to do it.

And yet, she limited her reaction to seeing me again to a stern look? I remembered the wide-eyed, frightened woman she had been that night, and did not understand what had changed. But something had.

I looked from her to Mircea on the queen's other side, who was looking quite at home, and as perfect as if the fight in the arena had never happened. His daywear had been exchanged for dark blue velvet robes with silver embroidery at the neck and the cuffs of the tight-fitting sleeves. His hair was dark and shining, as were his eyes, which reflected my flames as he looked at me.

His expression was neutral, and as usual gave nothing away unless he wanted it to. But his gaze was strangely intense. I didn't understand it for a moment, as he had seen me in many guises through the years, with this far from being the strangest of them. But then I realized: yes, he had seen guises, but he hadn't seen *me*, not without Dory being present.

He had never seen me just on my own, with nothing else in the way. Not before today in the arena, where there had been no time for scrutiny. In a real sense, then, my father and I were meeting face to face for the first time.

I suddenly felt flustered and looked away, not wanting to know whether he approved of what he saw.

And met another pair of eyes, only these were easier to hold, despite not looking any happier. If anything, the opposite was true. Marlowe was on the other side of father, leaning forward so that he could see past him, and looking as fierce as he had when faced by an army of fey.

He had cleaned up nicely, however, with his goatee well-trimmed and his own robes, deep green and without ornament, being attractive enough. But his hair was a riot of dark curls that it appeared no comb had ever touched. I blinked at them, wondering if he had merely forgotten to brush them, or if this was supposed to be a fashion statement.

I did not know.

"What is this?" he demanded furiously, as if he didn't know what to make of me, either. "What fresh hell are you up to now?"

I gazed back at him, unsure how to respond to that. I looked at Ray, who was now flanked by a whole bevy of pixies with knives on their belts and swords slung over their backs. They looked rather fierce, possibly because of the previous batting, but Ray was snubbing them with the aplomb of a man who had recently stared down a giant, a dragon and a vampire senator.

"Ignore him," Ray advised. "He's just being a bitch."

"Sit, sit," the queen said impatiently, and I sat.

"I have a problem," she began, before Marlowe cut her off.

"Haven't you been listening?" His hand hit the table. "She'll only make it worse! She's a time bomb waiting to go off! Impossible to predict, and we don't even know—"

He stopped talking rather abruptly, I assumed because father had silenced him. Outbursts were rarely useful and not his style. But when I leaned forward a little to look around Mircea, I found Marlowe with two tiny, leather clad guards in his face, small spears out and almost touching his nose.

Their expressions were eloquent, and I didn't need to know the language to read the message: "Don't try it."

"Our apologies," Mircea said, smiling ruefully. "Kit is still ruffled by our experiences in the arena. He doesn't usually speak out of turn."

"I should hope not," the queen said, waving a small hand. The guards broke off and went back to their positions by the wall, but not without a few more spear flourishes in Marlowe's direction.

"However," Mircea said, and she scowled. "He has a point. Fairie appears to have brought out new abilities in Dorina, ones that she has had no chance to learn how to control. Employing them on any kind of a—"

"Bored now," the queen said, and turned to the Pythia. "Are you going to try it, too?"

The pretty blonde, who was wearing a lovely gown of tissue of silver that clashed terribly with an ugly gold and ruby necklace, just sighed. And rolled her eyes, shook her head and drank wine, all at the same time, the latter rather aggressively. The queen smiled briefly at her and then switched it to me.

"As I was saying, I have a problem that we should discuss, but perhaps I should put the little one to sleep first, before we are interrupted. He gets fussy when he's tired."

"Oh." I tried to hide my disappointment. "Do you have to?"

Her smile broadened, from smug satisfaction to something more genuine. "You can come with me, if you like."

I nodded and got up.

"I gotta go, too," Ray said, somewhat aggressively for one addressing a queen. "She can't talk without me and I—"

He broke off, but the queen wasn't fooled. "You don't trust us?"

He didn't answer, but she didn't look offended. "She is perfectly safe here."

"It's Faerie," Ray said, the words bursting out of him as if a dam had broken. "No where is safe."

"Some places are." Shrewd eyes slid to me and then back to him, as if evaluating something. "And if I wanted to hurt her, I'd go after the body lying alone and unprotected in your room, wouldn't I? Save for the guards I had to bribe to go back there."

"What?" Ray looked suddenly alarmed, as if he hadn't thought of that. And started for the door, only to find a cloud of pixies in his way. He whirled on the queen. "Tell 'em to move—now."

"Or what?" she asked curiously.

"I'll move 'em!"

She laughed, and once more, I was reminded of bells. "I think you would try," she agreed, sizing him up. "But it isn't necessary. My guards are there to protect the body whilst the mind is elsewhere. And you can come along," she added, before he could speak again. "You are linked, and she might vanish if you get too far away."

"I, too, should like to see the nursery," Mircea said, only to have the Pythia snort into her wine.

The queen shot her an amused look. "Another time," she said, and glanced at her guards, "Keep them here."

And then she flew off into the darkness, with Ray and I scrambling to keep up.

Chapter Twenty-Five

I expected her to head to the forest in the next room, but instead she flew the other way, across a considerable space of uninterrupted flagstone to a hallway hiding in the gloom to the right of the table.

A bevy of tiny bodyguards swarmed through the air after her, but a glance over my shoulder showed that some had stayed behind, I supposed to guard her guests—or to watch them.

The Pythia didn't seem to care, having already gone back to eating, using bread to sop up the juices on her plate and calling for more wine from a tiny steward. She had seemed the most unbothered by my presence, and appeared equally so by my absence.

But she was the only one.

Marlowe was talking urgently to Mircea—I could tell from his expression and the way he leaned in, although his lips weren't moving. The two were speaking mind to mind, probably to avoid being overheard, and thus his words were likely important. But I wasn't sure that father noticed.

His eyes were on me and nowhere else as we disappeared into the hall and I lost him from view.

The queen did not speak as we made our way past numerous darkened doorways, some of which had loud snores emanating from them that could only belong to trolls. I had learned that music well enough on the road with the Wanderers, where I'd questioned why they bothered with stealth when they brought thunder with them wherever they went. Those rooms often had cracked or open doors, as if the occupants were unconcerned about being attacked here.

But others were tightly closed and slightly ominous, with misty, neon-colored wards gleaming in the air outside them.

We went to one of the latter, where three of the queen's guards muscled past us to break through the ward. And then flying inside to check the place out, zipping about the small room as if determined to examine every square inch. I did not know what danger there could be in a magical castle hidden in another realm and disguised as a sandstorm, but they were taking no chances.

They finally allowed us inside and there was a forest in there, too, although not a real one. But it looked almost lifelike, with painted boughs and pinecones that almost sprang off the walls they had been so cleverly done, and then enchanted to sway slightly as if in a small breeze. A riot of spring flowers likewise decorated the bases of the trees, and I swore that I could smell them with the aid of Ray's excellent nose, shedding a subtle but sweet perfume.

It was an enchanted glade at nighttime, I realized, staring about at the walls and ceiling and floor, with glistening mushroom caps pushing up through the rich soil and shimmering dewdrops on delicate insect wings. There was no sky, with the boughs closing overhead like a protective embrace, and no windows. The room looked as if it might have been a converted closet, something that probably seemed enormous to pixies, yet would be of little use to anyone else.

So, they had made it into a perfect nursery designed to encourage slumber, and it did its job well.

I felt a yawn coming over me, despite the fact that my body was already sleeping.

The pixie flew over to a small crib shaped like a flower among the colorful profusion under a tree. And snuggled her little one in downy comfort amid a mass of soft blankets in the center of it. He quieted down immediately and drifted off to sleep, while the queen took a seat nearby, on a small mushroom protruding from the wall.

It wasn't the only piece that was three dimensional, I realized, with elements of the mural extending into the room and forming the necessary furniture. There were small tables masked as mossy tree stumps, a mobile above the crib of fluttering butterflies, and a wardrobe hidden inside a painted waterfall, the slowly moving splash sending pale, rippling shadows across the room.

There was no furniture suitable for Ray and I, as I doubted any non-pixies were ever let in here. But we settled well enough onto the floor. Where areas of grasses and tiny flowers had leeched off of the walls like paint spills to decorate the old boards.

"We come from the desert, but learned to love the forest where many of us took refuge for a while," the queen told me, glancing about, as if seeing it through my eyes. "I find I miss it these days, when I'm not there, although it isn't home."

"It's beautiful," I said, because it was. "And . . . cozy."

She seemed to find that amusing. "I'm glad you're comfortable here. You should try being one of my people. This whole place feels ridiculously huge to us."

"Because giants built it," I said, remembering what Ray mentioned.

She nodded. "Yes, long ago. Or they started it, at least. But a terrible toll has been taken on their kind in recent years. They cannot hide as well as we can."

No, I didn't suppose so.

"The king was a giant, wasn't he?" Ray asked, and the queen nodded.

"Yes. I was the captain of his guard. After he was taken from us, I assumed the throne as he had no children, and everything was in chaos. That is what I wanted to talk to you about, in fact."

She got up to check on her child, wings whirring and tiny forehead wrinkled. Her son was sleeping soundly, making occasional happy gurgling noises, but that didn't seem to reassure her. She fussed over him for a moment, then came and sat back down.

"They say a crown weighs heavily on the brow," she told us. "I didn't understand that at first; it was just a job that needed to be done and I did it. But now . . ."

"Being a mother changes a person," Ray guessed, and she glanced at him in surprise.

"How would you know that?"

He shrugged. "Well, I wouldn't know about being a mom, and my own was . . . not real motherly. But I found out after I became a master, and started getting a family, what being a father is like. And I suppose it's not so different.

"There's always someone relying on you, somebody looking to you. And they have to, 'cause they can't protect themselves. You're all they got, and you gotta come through, even when it seems hopeless. You gotta find a way.

"There isn't anybody else."

She stared at him for a moment, as if reevaluating him. Or as if she hadn't bothered to evaluate him at all before now. Then slowly nodded.

"Yes, that's it. That is what I am trying to do now—find a way. But it is not easy.

"It wasn't for him, either. Kaliphranges, our old king, was a bastard, of course; monarchy practically requires it. I don't know if it's possible to be a good king and a good person at the same time. So often you are forced to make hard decisions, to do hard things, to survive and to make sure your people do, too.

"It can turn you into a monster, if you're not careful."

"Was he a monster?" I asked, wondering where I stood with her. I had killed her champion, who had been another giant. If they were already vanishing . . .

She glanced at me, as if hearing my thoughts. "No, although the one you killed could be called such. I gave him a choice: execution for his crimes or the arena. He chose the latter. He stayed alive as long as he won, and would gain his release after fifty matches.

"I would have preferred him dead, but alienating his clan wasn't smart. It is fortunate for us that you ended him when you did."

"Fortunate?"

She smiled slightly. "He had less than a dozen fights left."

"Was that why the dragons showed up?" Ray asked. "Did you call them to end him, before you knew Dorina would?"

"Call them?" she almost choked. "No, I didn't call them! The bastards have been harassing my people ever since they joined the Svarestri in this stupid war! I suppose Aeslinn was afraid we might join the other side and wanted to keep us busy.

"But we're not without teeth, either," she added, baring her own, which were pointier than I'd expected. "They well know it, too. Which is why they usually pass high overhead, start a fire or two, and maybe roast a few people who don't get to cover soon enough. To remind us that they're there and what they can do, as if we're likely to forget."

"But that's not what happened this time," Ray pointed out. "They targeted Dorina. They went straight for her."

The queen nodded. "Yes, and they came in force. Usually, one or two is enough to keep us in our place, but this wasn't a mere raid, a show of force at the opening of the faire. This was . . . something else."

She couldn't seem to sit still and got up again, flitting about the room as if agitated. But Ray didn't care about that. Ray wanted answers.

"What else? Because they tried their best to kill her. And came damned close to succeeding!"

I stared at him, as that once again wasn't the voice one used to a queen. The rippling effect of the waterfall over his face made it seem to morph and change, almost to the point that I didn't know him anymore. And maybe I didn't.

When Dory first met him, he was a beaten down nightclub owner still working for his old master, and going nowhere in an organization that valued strength above all things. Ray didn't have a lot of strength, and struggled even to protect his family. But he did have cunning, bravery and determination.

And now, it seemed, he had something else, some quality I couldn't quite define, but it was different. He was different. Faerie was changing him, too, I thought, watching him square up to the queen who hadn't liked his tone, either, and this time, she was in his face.

But she deflated quickly; I didn't think she wanted to fight tonight. But she did want something. It was in every line of her body.

"We have a common problem," she said, perching on a tree limb that protruded slightly from the wall, bringing her to my eye level. "The Svarestri are after you; it's the only explanation. Steen works for them, and it was his dragons who came for you—"

"Steen?" Ray asked sharply.

"Lord Steen of Vitharr. One of the Dragonlords of the Northern marches. I don't know any reason he would want you for himself, and anyway, he's their errand boy. Although whether he planned to kill you or take you, I couldn't say—"

"Take her where?" Ray asked.

"The Svarestri have been using Steen's thugs to kidnap our people. Not many, and not often, but when they come for someone, they come in force, like they did today. And they get what they want. They took our king that way."

She fluttered up again, flying in a little circle in the air, which reminded me of a human pacing in agitation. And began speaking a mile a minute, to the point that it was hard to understand her. But I didn't ask her to slow down; I was fairly sure she couldn't.

"They knew that a lot of our people had fled the war, going into Earth through illegal portals and setting up colonies there. And that Kaliphranges had contacts among them. They wanted him to find a book of spells, for which they would guarantee him his life and that of his remaining people. But the Pythia was looking for it, too, and she obtained it first and burnt it, as it was supremely dangerous. It contained a spell that could drop the barrier between worlds and allow the gods to return and—anyway, she destroyed it.

"This was some time ago, a few months for her and a few years for us. He managed to fob Steen off for a while, citing the strangeness of Earth and the difficulty of working there. But when the Svarestri heard rumors that the book had been destroyed, and he couldn't produce it . . . they took him.

"And that's a problem for me," she added, whirling on me suddenly. "For all of us! If they had just killed him, it would have been bad, but nothing we couldn't come back from. But instead, they *took* him, and he knows it all—where our cities are hidden, how many of us there are, the routes we take when threatened, our favorite hiding places, spells and incantations to get through our wards—it just goes on and on!

"I need to find him—quickly. I know him; he'll hold out for a while, but he'll break sooner or later. Anyone would! I need him back or I need him dead, but I don't know where he is—"

"You didn't follow him?" Ray demanded. "He was your king!"

"Yes, of course we did," she said, shooting him a look. "All the way to the warded area around their base, where one of my guards almost had his wings burnt off! But he's not there anymore—"

"They took him somewhere else?"

"No, they took *it* somewhere else. The base is like this one, it moves around—"

"It moves? Is everybody flying about Faerie in dust storms these days?"

Her wings fluttered agitatedly. "It moves through a network of portals that Aeslinn established years ago, and will you *shut up?*"

Ray wisely shut up.

"I have people searching for it," the queen told me. "It's elusive, but we'll catch up to it again; we always do. But even if we find it, we can't get in there. We've tried everything, but the defenses are formidable, and anyway, whenever we attack, it just takes off again!

"I've been trying to act normal, to keep my people from finding out how much trouble we're in, but it won't matter when the Svarestri show up in force. They don't trust us, and think us as little more than vermin. They won't even offer us a chance to ally with them to save our lives; they'll just kill us and I'm queen, I'm supposed to prevent that, but no matter what I try—"

She suddenly grasped a bit of my arm, and she must have been right about her magic, because she wasn't burned. Even odder, I could almost feel the touch, as if on my actual skin. She was powerful, this one.

"But you," she said, staring at me. "You're different. You can disguise yourself as one of their dragon allies and fly right in there. You can kill him for me—"

"What?" I asked, trying to keep up with the rapid-fire flood of information.

"—or rescue him, if possible. But kill will suffice, just so long as he doesn't talk—"

"And why the hell would she do that?" Ray demanded. "If the goddamned Svarestri are after her, we need to get her out of here! Not head straight into their hands!"

"That does seem like a better plan," I pointed out.

But the queen suddenly stilled, settling onto the tree limb again with her small wings folding up calmly against her back. And, immediately, I knew why. I had seen father gain this same stillness many times, when the social niceties were out of the way and it was finally time to negotiate.

"Yes, that was what your father thought," she said idly. "That it was best to get you away. But I decided to try to persuade you—or bribe you; I'm not above that."

"Ha!" Ray said. "There's not enough money in the world to make us take on those things again. We're lucky we survived the last time!"

"Just as well I'm not offering money, then, isn't it?" she said to him, although her eyes never left me.

"What are you offering?" I asked, only to have Ray get up and head for the door.

"Doesn't matter. Nothing's worth your life, and we're outta here. Never thought I'd agree with Mircea about something but—"

He cut off, but not because he was finished. But because the tiny guards I had almost forgotten about all but shoved him out the door and slammed it in his face. They must have warded it, too, because he did not immediately rip the whole affair off its hinges.

I could hear him faintly on the other side, beating against the heavy ward, and then throwing his body against it, cursing all the while. But he did not get in, which didn't surprise me. These wards protected the queen's greatest treasure, and were likely the very best they had.

I glanced at the beautiful boy in his flower crib, and despite everything, I smiled.

No, Ray would not get in here.

I looked back to find the queen watching me.

"I know that look," she said softly. "I know that hunger. I've seen it on my own face often enough, and on those of minister after minister at my court."

"But I'm not hungry," I said, confused, and this time, I heard the words in my own voice.

It was distant, a sleepy mumble from far away in my room. Yet it somehow echoed here, as her voice had done in the outer room of the Great Hall. It seemed that she did not need Ray, after all.

She smiled slyly at me. "Do you know how I became queen?"

I shook my head.

"It wasn't because of my charming personality. It was this," she made a gesture and pulled something out of thin air.

It was maybe an inch tall and appeared to be carved out of an old piece of bone. It had a small hole in the top through which a slim, golden chain had been passed, I suppose so that someone could wear it. Someone who was not a pixie, presumably.

But the chain looked rather strange on such a weathered piece. An old scrap of leather would have suited it better, as it reminded me of something a cave man might have used as an ornament. Or a talisman, as the queen was staring at it as if at the face of God.

"What is it?" I asked, intrigued.

"The greatest gift a dying people could be offered. It is Jera, an ancient rune of unspeakable power. Not to mow down armies or to siege cities, but to do something far more precious."

She looked back at her child, and her face grew fierce and possessive and vulnerable and a thousand other things I couldn't name. "Before I obtained it, I was barren, as are many of my people. Now, I have a *son*." She looked back at me, and the huge lavender eyes were wet. "And it can be used more than once, do you understand? It needs to charge up for a month after each casting, yes, but it can be used over and over. I've a list, longer than my arm, longer than yours, of favors already promised to members of my court, but it's up to me who goes next. And for the right person . . ."

"Well, I could make an exception. Couldn't I?"

I felt strange suddenly, light headed and overly warm, and my heart was thudding in my chest. I could feel it, even this far away, beating like a wild thing. And felt my body move restlessly on my bed, as if in the throes of a nightmare.

But this was no nightmare.

This was . . .

"I don't understand," I heard myself say hoarsely.

But the queen didn't believe me. Her eyes were still wet with emotion, but her smile was back, and it was *that* smile. Knowing and sly and triumphant as it curved her lips.

"Oh, I think you do. Didn't I say I saw your eyes? And I can give it to you, what you've always fiercely desired but never thought to obtain. I can put you at the front of the line. I can give you a *child*.

"As long as you do a little something for me."

Chapter Twenty-Six

I sat up in bed abruptly, the room dark and quiet around me. I was back in my body and feeling it, with my heart thudding almost painfully in my chest, my head jumbled, and my fists grabbing the covers below me as if I would tear them to pieces. For a moment, I thought it had all been a dream.

But no. That had been real; I knew it had. I could still taste the fey ale on my tongue, rich and heady and burning. Could see the sparks flying as Ray and I danced, fast, fast, so very fast, a jubilant expression of life and joy and wonder that had made our heels sound like castanets on the flagstones. Could still see the tiny face of the queen's child, and the downy fuzz on his little head . . .

I got up and threw the covers back.

I did not feel well. Part of it was too much food, as I had rarely eaten that much at one time and suspected that it wasn't healthy, even for a dhampir. But that wasn't why I was swaying on my feet, and stumbled when I took a step forward.

There was a good chance that I would have face planted, but someone was there beside me, someone who had had no trouble getting past the queen's guards, someone who caught me before I hit the floor.

And took me out to the same chairs on the balcony where Ray and I had sat and I had consumed my floating feast. And where my visitor had talked with Ray and plotted to get me out of Faerie, whether I liked it or not. And where he now intended to convince me of the same, I was sure of it.

"No!" I pulled away.

"No?" One of my father's expressive, dark eyebrows went up. "You do not wish to sit out here?"

"That's . . . not what I meant," I gasped, out of breath although I didn't know why.

He gave me some water, pushed my hair back off my face and brought me a blanket from the next room. His hands were warm and gentle as he tucked it around me, and his voice, murmuring reassurances, was soothing. Or, at least, it was supposed to be.

But for some reason it had the opposite effect. I didn't want him tending me as if I were his child, when we both knew I never was! I didn't want him touching me at all!

"Get away! Get away from me!" I lashed out with a hand and the water glass flew into the ward beyond the balcony, shattering into a hundred pieces before dropping out of sight.

Mircea did not go away, but he did release me. I sat there, doubled over the arm of my chair and staring at the floor. And at the few shards of glass that had ricocheted back onto the tiles, one of which was still spinning.

They didn't look like anything anymore. Not the drinking glass they'd once been, not something else. Just formless, useless, broken.

I stared at them for a long time.

"Dory will be alright," I finally said, my voice hoarse. "She's stronger than you know. You don't have to worry about her."

"I am not worried about her," he said quietly. "I am worried about you."

And for some reason, that also enraged me. I sat up and whirled to face him, and for an instant, there was fear in his eyes and he moved backward slightly. I was pleased to see it.

I wanted him to be afraid of me, as much as I'd once wanted him to love me. Wanted him to understand that he could no longer control me. Not where I went, not what I did, not who I was.

I hadn't felt it until now, the absolute certainty that I wasn't mere shards on a floor. I wasn't something useless to be thrown out. I wasn't *wrong*.

And I wasn't going back.

The words weren't spoken aloud, but Mircea didn't need them to be. I had practically yelled them mentally, and they echoed in both of our minds. Loudly enough that he flinched, but did not turn away.

"Faerie is dangerous," he told me, after a moment. "Particularly in the service of the queen—"

"Life is dangerous," I cut him off, as I once would have never thought to do. "And messy and uncertain and sometimes tragic. But it is *life*, nonetheless.

"And I want it."

I wanted it more than anything.

And for a second—no, not even that; for an instant, the surge of emotion I felt caused my control to slip and he saw what was in my mind.

"A child." There was wonder in his voice. "This is what she offered you?"

"You sound surprised." I got up, because I could not sit still, no matter that there was nowhere to go.

"I did not know that you desired such so badly."

"Of course not!" I laughed and it was ugly, but I didn't turn to face him; I didn't know what I would do if I did. I hadn't expected this . . . this rage . . . that had come out of nowhere. But suddenly, it was all I could feel.

"Dorina . . . I am sorry—"

I was in his face in an instant, for it was the worst thing he could have said. Once, I would have given anything for an apology, some understanding, a look, a glance, any scrap of affection that was just for me. Would have begged—did beg—for him to acknowledge that I wasn't the problem, that I wasn't the monster he thought me to be, that I didn't want to hurt his child.

That I *was* his child.

But he had *never* understood that, had only sought to contain the creature who was threatening the only daughter he had ever acknowledged or cared for.

The only one that he still did.

"That isn't true," he said sharply, and for a moment, there was real emotion there, not the cultivated calm he showed everyone else.

Did I scratch him? Did he bleed? No, I thought, searching his face.

No, not for me.

For wounded pride, perhaps—

And there it was again, and still, I couldn't read it. A flash of something in his eyes gone too quick. But it didn't matter.

Not anymore.

"It does matter," he grasped my upper arm when I started to turn away, and I liked that we both knew that his hand only remained there because I allowed it. For my whole life, he had been the stronger, the one who made the rules, the one whose stubborn refusal to listen had left me crying in the dark.

But he couldn't control me anymore. Not here in Faerie, and maybe not anywhere. I was growing, changing, and he didn't like it.

"I don't like the fact that we know nothing about this," he said sharply. "Kit put it badly but he wasn't wrong. So much happened today, and we understand very little of it. Do not make a hasty decision you may regret—"

"Regret?" I turned on him again, and pushed off his hold without effort. "What do you think I am likely to regret? Not being a slave anymore? Not that Dory made me that, but you did. I was *nothing*; I was her servant, her lackey, her protector, and I thought I deserved it because I had hurt her! I had been the monster growing under her skin like some kind of cancer. I had deprived her of a normal life, of friends, of her rightful place in our society. She should have been a little princess, petted and pampered, but instead, she was shivering with cold, half starved, eating dogs' leavings and glad to get them and it was all because of me!

"Only it wasn't because of me.

"I didn't do that, not any of it." I heard the wonder in my own voice, because it only now hit me, the implication of what Nimue had said, that dying queen of the fey who had finally told me the truth. "I'm not a dhampir. Her struggles were not because of me. I don't know what I am, but it wasn't my *fault*—"

"It was," Mircea said, surprising me. And enraging, because this was the part where he groveled. This was the part where he *begged*. And apologized and meant it, and despite the fact that I had just thought that I didn't want one, I realized that I did. I craved an apology, a real one, and more than that, I deserved it!

"You do, but not from me," he said, effortlessly reading my thoughts, and grasping both of my arms now as though he would make me listen. "From whoever did those experiments on your mother, from whoever made you like this—"

"Like what?" I stared at him, uncomprehending. "What is so wrong with me? I am not vampire; I am not human; I am not even dhampir. But I am not trash!"

"I never said you were."

"Not said, no, but treated me as that and worse than that—"

"You were ripping your sister apart!" The dark eyes flashed. "I didn't know what else to do—"

"And didn't ask! Didn't listen—"

"You may hate me for what I did if you like, but it saved you both—yes, you, too! Had she died, you would have died with her. I would have lost both of you—"

"So, you sacrificed one."

Mircea's face changed, and yes, there was pride there, and pain, and disbelief that I still didn't understand.

When I did, and better than him.

"I did what I had to do," he told me stiffly. "The only thing I knew to do. Should I have let you die?"

I thought back to the long years of what I wouldn't call a life, wouldn't know what to call it.

And didn't know the answer to that. I just didn't know.

Some of my thoughts must have leeched through, because the dark eyes softened as he watched me. "I will say this," he said. "And mean it. I am sorry for the life you've lived, or have not been allowed to live. I am sorry for fearing you instead of trying harder to understand you. I am sorry for prioritizing one child over the other, for not even realizing for a long time that I had another.

"I am truly sorry for all of it.

"And you are right; you are not dhampir. But that is the point. We do not fully understand what you are, merely what Nimue told you. But even if she spoke truly, we do not know the extent of your abilities or their weaknesses. And a lack of knowledge has caused misunderstandings and hardship in the past. Before you decide anything, we must first—"

"*Goddamn*, you suck at this."

My head jerked up, because that had not been me, nor Mircea, either. Ray stood in the doorway to the bedroom, looking the worse for the wear, to the point that I thought it entirely possible that he *had* gotten into it with some pixies. Possibly a lot of them.

But he must have won. For he was here, and despite a few torn areas on his clothes and tiny burn marks that were already melting back into his skin, he looked fairly normal. Except for the rage on his face, which almost matched mine.

"This doesn't concern you," Mircea told him tightly.

"Oh. Oh, excuse me, massa, I didn't understand that. I'll just tug my forelock and go stand in the hall with the rest of the servants. Is there anything I can get you while I'm out there? Some brandy or—"

"Have a care," Mircea said, in a voice that would have sent sensible vampires running.

But Ray was not sensible, never had been, and in Faerie, he was acting even less so than normal. In Faerie, he was acting insane. "Oh, don't beat me, massa!" he said, falling theatrically to his knees with his hands held up and gripped prayerfully in front of him. "Your slave is just a poor nothing of a creature, too dumb to know what he's saying . . ." the arms fell. "Kind of like you."

"I tire of this!" Mircea said, and waved a hand. Which must have had a suggestion behind it, because Ray's face went blank and he got up and walked calmly off the balcony and into the bedroom.

Only to return almost immediately with a tray on which a bottle of something sat, along with two glasses. "We don't have any brandy," he said, in that same, mock servile tone. "But maybe this will do?"

"What is wrong with you?" Mircea demanded, looking as if he thought Ray might be as mad as he was acting.

"Funny. I was about to ask you the same thing." Ray sloshed some of whatever was in the bottle into a glass and gave it to me. For a moment, I thought it was another test, like the one on the road, to see if I would drink it just because he indicated that I should. But a moment later, common sense returned.

We were way past that.

I drank it because I wanted it, belting it back although it tasted like fire and burned all the way down.

"A couple days ago, she wouldn't have hesitated," Ray said, as if reading my mind, which maybe he was. I seemed to be an open book tonight. "Wouldn't have asked herself if she wanted it. Would have just done what I said.

"But she learns fast. Faster than you."

"This isn't your concern," Mircea told him again. "Get out."

"Isn't it?" Ray looked thoughtful for a moment. "Let's find out. Dorina," he turned to me. "This is your room; you decide who stays and who goes. So, is it my concern? Or should I go find something else to do?"

He was trying to needle Mircea, but I knew, I *knew*, that if I asked him to go, he would. Not because he'd want to, as Mircea was well known for persuading people to do as he liked, and that was especially true for me. But because he respected my choice.

He believed that I should *have* a choice.

"It's your concern," I said briefly, and drank more of whatever it was.

But Mircea wasn't a fool, and he'd done deals with harder nuts than either Ray or I would ever be. He settled for ignoring him. "What do you want me to say?" he asked me, and would have gone on, probably into another pretty speech.

I cut him off. "If you have to ask, it would only be a lie."

"Go get him," Ray muttered, and Mircea turned on him.

"Yes, encourage her to spread her wings, and to use her newfound autonomy to involve herself in fey politics! But tell me, how are you going to feel when she lies bloody and lifeless at your feet, after dying uselessly in battle for a queen who will merely go on to her next target, her next *patsy*, before she's even cold? They do not value life here as we do; I sometimes wonder if they value it at all. And my daughter will not be—"

"Your daughter is back on Earth," I said, and reached for the bottle because my glass was empty. "She's fine. She has the senate seat, and if they try to take it from her, they'll find out what she's capable of. Your majority is in no danger. Just leave me alone."

Mircea stared at me, and for the first time, I thought that something I said might have gotten through. At least a little, at least in part. For all the color suddenly drained from his face, or maybe his glamourie failed him.

It didn't matter; he only used it to color his complexion anyway.

But it wasn't just the pallor. His eyes darkened and his face fell. He looked tragic, suddenly, and if it was an act, it was a good one.

Of course, it *would* be a good one, I thought cynically, and drank some more.

"Is that what you think of me? Is that why you think I'm here?" he asked. "To protect my majority?"

"Why else?"

"Why *else?* You are my daughter—"

"I am your *burden!*"

I had thought that I was done talking, and was content to have Ray take over. Had planned, insofar as I was able to plan anything currently, to drink enough to get drunk, and then to go back to bed. To try and forget all this.

But at his easy proclamation of the title that he had so long denied me, I snapped.

"I am the albatross you wear around your neck," I spat. "The one you could never be free of! I am the monster you would have killed to save her that you love, only we were inseparably linked and you could not!

"I am the one you never wanted; the one you feared; the one you thought might one day swamp your daughter's mind and take over, stealing her life away from her, away from you. I am the one you prayed to God about when you thought no one could hear, for him to excise me like the demon you thought me to be.

"I am the one you wanted gone, and when you couldn't get rid of me, you bound me, in chains worthy of a demon lord. But

I escaped them and my life is *mine*, do you hear? Mine, and I will not give it up! Not for you, not for anyone. And if I wish to throw it away, that is my right, too! So, get out!"

Vaguely, I realized that I'd gotten up in the midst of all that, sobbing and shrieking like a mad woman, and had backed him, the great Mircea Basarab, the father I loved even now, in spite of everything and more than anything, all the way off the balcony, through the bedroom and to the door to the hall. Which I opened and thrust him out, before he could say anything else, before I could lose my nerve and fall to my knees, and beg him to love me as he never had and never would.

And slammed the door in his beautiful face.

I fell to my knees afterward, dry eyed and shaking, and wondering if it had finally happened, if I had actually gone mad. It felt like it. And even more when I realized that he was still on the other side of the door.

I could hear him being questioned by the startled guards, whose minds he had overthrown to get in here, and who didn't understand how a man they'd never seen enter had suddenly stumbled out of the supposedly secured room. And shut up just as quickly, because he willed it so. I heard them go silent, heard him breathing hard, in anger or something else, heard him hesitate for a long moment.

And then I heard him walk away.

Chapter Twenty-Seven

I did cry then, sinking to my knees and sobbing hysterically in Ray's arms, because he was there, he was always there. I couldn't speak, and wouldn't have known what to say if I did. But I remembered—so many things.

Mircea laughing, the handsome face speckled with a multitude of colors in the front room of our little shack in Venice. He had been trying to teach me to paint, because I had begged him, curving my chubby hands around the end of his brush. He had shown me how to form the delicate petals of a flower, which I had made with his help, such a beautiful thing!

Then I tried it myself, only to find that my solo effort looked more like an old man with a huge nose, and which Mircea had quickly turned into one. Old Gurian the fruit seller, who everybody called Melanzane for his eggplant of a nose, lived down the street, and it was a perfect likeness. So perfect that we had laughed and laughed.

Or the time he had taken me to a bagatelle during Carnivale, where street performers of all types—jugglers, conjurers, and puppeteers—grouped together to entertain the crowd. He had swung me onto his shoulders so that I could see over the heads of the tall people, making me the tallest around. The puppeteer was performing at the time, and I was especially interested, as the only such shows I'd ever seen were the ones that the church put on as morality plays.

This one didn't look very moral, as the first thing I saw was the little man puppet beating his wife with a stick. Only to see her quickly take it away from him and return the favor. I remembered clapping my hands together and laughing delightedly, while the crowd booed.

Or the time we went shopping in the marketplace for mullet. I could still smell the sea, and see the way the sunlight flashed off the silver scales of the fish laid out on their tilted tables, on the glistening black mussels in their wicker baskets, and on the rough gray shells of the oysters. But we didn't buy any of those.

Father heard a rumor of a man selling cranes illegally off a boat by the Ponte della Carità and we went to see if it was true. The man turned out to be from Treviso and didn't want to pay the toll for selling in the marketplace, so was offering a good deal on a meat mostly reserved for nobility. It was caught by falcons, instead of more common methods, so I had never tried it before.

He also had some of the ducks with red feet that were common in the Lagoon. They were so fat and juicy that they were my favorite meat, as our old servant would roast them above a pan filled with vegetables and the fat would drip down and flavor them, too. But the seller was trying to get rid of the cranes, as they made him too visible, and promised me a story if we bought one.

I loved stories and wavered, and the man spotted his opportunity. And launched into the tale of an aristocrat named Gianfigliazzi, a notable man in Florence, who liked to hunt. He brought down a plump young crane with his falcon one day and was quick to send it to his Venetian cook, a man named Chichibio, to roast for supper, as he was entertaining a friend that night and wanted to impress.

As the bird was cooking, a pretty young local woman named Brunetta happened by, with whom Chichibio was enamored. She asked for one of the legs of the bird, as she had never tasted crane, but was refused as it would ruin the look of the dish when presented. For the master had requested that it be served whole.

Angered by this answer, she informed the love sick man that he would never get anywhere with her if she did not get the leg, at which point he finally agreed. The lopsided dish that subsequently made it to table did not please Gianfigliazzi, who angrily demanded an explanation from his cook. Chichibio replied that cranes only had one leg, and that he could prove this.

The two men went out riding the next day by a riverbank well known for its cranes, and Chichibio was the first to spot some. They were asleep, and as usual for sleeping cranes, they stood on one leg. Greatly relieved, he pointed out to his lord that cranes did indeed have only one leg, as he could see for himself.

His master was not satisfied with that answer, however, and rode at the cranes and shouted at them, flapping his hat. Startled, the flock dropped their other legs, ran a few paces and took flight. "Oh, ho! What do you think of that, you scoundrel?" Gianfigliazzi asked, turning back to his cook. "Do they or don't they have two legs now?"

Chichibio nodded nervously, but managed to say: "Yes, sir, but last night you did not shout, 'Hey! Hey!' at the crane that was served for dinner. If you had, it would have pushed its other leg down, just as these did."

Gianfigliazzi stared at his servant for a long moment, and then laughed so hard that afterward he forgave the man his lies, and they rode back home together in friendship.

"So, you bought the crane?" Ray asked, as the story ended, for he must have been following it in my mind.

"No, the duck. But father gave the man a coin for making me laugh." I found myself smiling at the memory, despite the tears still wet on my cheeks.

"You always do that," Ray said, watching me.

"Do what?"

"Every time you're sad, you go back to Venice. Even though it was so long ago, when you were just a girl."

I didn't deny it. "I've gone over each of those memories so many times, every day and hour and moment, that they are burned into my mind. They seem more real sometimes than anything else."

His brow knitted and he looked puzzled. "But isn't it painful?"

"No, it soothes me. Reminds me of . . . better days."

And there were no more memories after that worth keeping. For as soon as Dory and I were separated, my life effectively ended. And I began to realize that it hadn't been me that father had laughed with all those times, hadn't been me that he'd carried on his shoulders, hadn't been me that he had loved.

So, I'd clung to the illusion instead of the pain, and lived there, in those far off sunny days, with blue skies and laughter and a warm, loving touch that had never been for me.

"Maybe it *was* my fault," I said, hugging my knees. "Some of it, possibly all of it."

"What was?" Ray asked, his frown growing.

"What happened to Dory. I thought, if I was never dhampir, but something else, something created out of the gods' tinkering, then I couldn't have been the one to hurt her. Those night terrors weren't me. The dhampir madness wasn't because of me. And maybe it wasn't.

"Maybe it was worse than that, worse even than what dhampirs experience, because I was worse. Father fought me, and he was strong even then. Yet he battled with me mentally and barely won. That's why he feared me so much, feared what I could do to her."

"That's why he locked me away."

"Yeah." Ray got up, went to get the bottle from the balcony, and brought it back inside, settling onto the floor alongside me. "Or maybe that's bull crap."

I looked up at him as he passed me the liquor. He hadn't brought the glasses, but I didn't need them. I took a large swig and felt it burn terribly on the way down.

But it helped to ground me, the sensation pulling me back from the edge of grief so black that I didn't know how to deal with it.

Forced me out of my head and back into my body in a stunning, abrupt sort of way. I was beginning to understand what humans saw in this stuff.

"It isn't bull crap," I told him, while my tongue burned.

"How do you know?" he demanded. "How do you know that it wasn't the other way around?"

I looked at him blearily. The drink was having an outsized effect, or perhaps I was simply so vulnerable that it felt that way. But I suddenly wanted to burst into tears again, because he didn't understand.

"Listen to me," he said, taking my hand. "And think. You met a few dhampirs through the years, and heard about more. I heard about 'em, too, and you know what I heard?"

I shook my head and tried to pull myself together, but didn't manage it.

"I heard that they were crazy and therefore easy to kill, at least for a master. I heard that they picked off revenants and low-tier vamps who weren't paying attention, but weren't a real problem for anybody else. I heard that most of 'em died before they had a chance to grow up, 'cause they couldn't control themselves well enough to stick to revenantsmnants, and instead would run straight at a master and, well, that was it.

"Was that what you heard?"

I nodded. I had observed some older dhampirs, when Dory decided to seek them out, to learn more about her condition. But there had been so few of them!

And those that she did find could not tell her much, as they had only survived their fits by getting as far away from society as possible and living as hermits.

They didn't have any advice to give.

"Yeah," Ray said, following my thoughts. "So, you can imagine my surprise when a drop dead gorgeous dhampir shows up at my club and within about a minute has my goddamned head in a bag! Me, a master, and not a young one, either. And I ain't sayin' I'm the strongest around, but I'm not a weakling, either. I can hold my own in a fight."

"You can," I told him truthfully.

"Damned straight. Yet there I was, in a bag. Well, part of me. The rest was bumbling around, running into things, while that same dhampir took me in for her bounty. And she wasn't anything like the old stories. Sure, she had a few fits now and again, but she was smart, and she'd learned how to handle them, and she was *sane*, something I didn't think possible for her kind."

"She is mostly sane," I corrected, because neither of us would win any awards in that area.

But Ray was shaking his head. "She's okay. I known masters who were battier. Anyway, you think I woulda signed on as her Second—and yours, too—if I didn't think I could trust you? And you can't trust a crazy person. They might mean what they tell you one minute, then change their minds the next, or forget what they said entirely and then where are you?

"Nope, she's not as nuts as she thinks. She's just traumatized as hell from the life she's lived, and if that's true for her, it's triple for you. But she does alright. That's why she's over five hundred years old, despite not being a hermit living in a cave somewhere. And that's why this is bull crap."

I blinked at him, having lost the thread of the conversation somewhere.

"What is bull crap?"

"What have we been talking about?"

"I'm . . . not sure."

"You and Dory! Okay, okay. Try this. As I understand it, your mom was supposed to be some kind of uber strong, god-killing, super weapon, right? Crafted by one group of gods to take on another, using every dangerous creature they could find whose traits were compatible."

"Supposed to be," I repeated. "She was a failed experiment."

"Yes, but she fled to Earth and hooked up with your dad, and the two of them made you and Dory. Only Mircea had already been cursed by then, and was halfway to turning into a vamp. So, Dory ended up as a dhampir, something that didn't happen with you 'cause I guess you were already so many things that it got lost in the wash.

"But nobody knew any of this, much less your dad, who was only told that you would eventually rip Dory apart. That that was what happened to dhampirs: they and their vampire half, which is what he thought you were, couldn't co-exist and the battle between them was usually fatal. Yet that didn't happen to her."

"Because he separated us," I reminded him, wondering what his point was. Both of us already knew all this. "He made sure that we were never awake at the same time, isolating my mind from doing further damage to her."

"Yeah, that's one possibility, and it's obviously what he thinks to this day. And was dumb enough to say to your face 'cause his diplomatic ability goes out the window where you two are concerned. But what if something different was going on? What if, instead of hurting Dory, you were actually helping her?"

"Helping her?" I felt my forehead wrinkle in confusion. "What—that doesn't make any sense."

But Ray seemed to think that it did, and he was enthusiastic about it. "Just think for a minute. You can do all kinds of stuff that a dhampir can't, that nobody can. Like mentally possessing people and riding them around, or transforming into a big ass dragon and eating—" he broke off, probably at whatever was on my face.

"Sorry. But my point is, you can do all kinds of things thanks to all of those different beings that went into making up your mom, maybe even including some god blood. That was one reason Mircea never listened to you, right? You told me that you tried to talk to him by possessing other people and using their voices, even following him around Venice all afternoon once, but it only weirded him out."

I nodded slowly, remembering. "It's one reason he thought I was some kind of demon who had possessed his daughter. It's why he never trusted me." Not that he had before, but that had cemented his feelings in stone.

"So, would it be so weird if there's something else unusual that you can do?" Ray asked. "Something that you employed instinctively when you felt threatened?"

"Like what?"

"Like those night terrors that Dory suffered. What if they were you, but instead of attacking her, you were attacking the dhampirism threatening you both? And ripping her brain apart in order to put it back together as something that *worked*? What if you attacked Mircea because you saw him as a threat to the job you were doing, and therefore to your and Dory's whole existence?

"What if, instead of being her cancer, you were more like . . . like her malaria?"

I stared at him blankly. "Malaria?"

"Yeah." Ray nodded. "Back in the day, they didn't have a cure for syphilis, which killed a ton of people and killed 'em hard. But some enterprising doc came up with the idea of fighting one disease with another. He'd give patients who had syphilis, a disease that nobody could cure, another disease—malaria—which they could. Cause they had quinine for that, right?"

"Ray, I don't—"

"Just listen. So, the doc gave his patients malaria, which causes really high fevers. Higher, as it turned out, than syphilis could handle. The malaria killed the syphilis, which couldn't survive the high temps, then the doc gave the patients quinine to kill the malaria. And they were fine!

"Well, those that survived, that is. Malaria did kill some of them, but they were gonna die a harder death from syphilis anyway, so what are you gonna do? But some survived who wouldn't have otherwise, 'cause malaria was less scary of a disease. And before antibiotics, it was their only real chance." He smiled at me triumphantly. "You get it now?"

"No."

He frowned and took my bottle away.

I didn't protest; it was mostly empty anyway.

"I'm saying," he continued, with the air of a man who is striving against overwhelming odds, "that Dory had an incurable disease—dhampirism. She was born with it, and it kills almost everybody who gets it, or wrecks their lives so bad that it may as well have done. And like syphilis all those years ago, there's no cure.

"At least, there isn't supposed to be. But Dory had an advantage. She had you. A second consciousness birthed alongside her from whatever weirdness the gods were doing, filtered through two very unusual parents and a pregnancy that wasn't supposed to be possible, 'cause dead sperm don't swim.

"But it was possible, 'cause Mircea wasn't totally Changed when he and your mom got busy. And she must have passed you most of the god-tinkered-with genes, because you were so strong that even dhampirism couldn't defeat you. You were Dory's malaria, the thing that would either kill her or save her, and ended up saving her."

I just sat there, staring at him blankly. I knew I should probably say something, but my mouth didn't seem to work. But Ray didn't appear to mind.

"I know it's a lot to take in," he said. "But I've thought about it plenty, 'cause I knew how much it bothered you, thinking that you were the one who hurt her. But I don't think you did, or if you did, it was like the syphilis sufferers getting a bad time from the malaria. Yeah, it sucked for a while, but it also saved them."

"Like you saved Dory."

"I saved her." I repeated the words, but they still didn't make sense. And I didn't have many memories to help me understand.

Unlike the days in Venice, the nights were... cloudy, indistinct, and filled with so much pain, so much terror, that I couldn't remember much about them. But what if, as Ray had said, I hadn't fought father except when he tried to interfere? What if I had been battling the disease instead? And changing it, from something deadly to both of us to something... inconvenient.

No, it wasn't possible.

"Why isn't it possible?" Ray asked. "Nothing about your birth was normal, and frankly, if this is true, it wouldn't be the weirdest thing about you."

I couldn't argue there.

"You think what you want," he added. "But I don't think it was Mircea who saved the two of you. I think he did the best he could with no real knowledge to go on and nobody to help him. But I think, if he hadn't done anything at all, it would have worked out just the same. Cause he wasn't battling the dhampirism, you were.

"And if there's one thing I know about you; you always win."

Chapter Twenty-Eight

I sat there for a long time when he finished speaking, staring at the floor. Ray didn't say anything else, just let me think. He knew me so well.

Better than I knew myself, it seemed. Because what he'd told me, which should have brought me relief, even joy, had only enraged me. I was glad that I was drunk, as I didn't know what I would do otherwise.

Or who I would do it to, as this wasn't father's fault. He had locked me away because he thought he had no choice, and there had been no one to tell him he was wrong. It wasn't Dory's fault, who hadn't known about me for most of her life, and when she found out, had tried her best to help me. And now I learned that it wasn't even mine.

It wasn't anyone's fault, it just was, and I couldn't seem to wrap my head around that. All those lost years, all that loneliness, all those tears with no one to wipe them away or even to hear my cries. All those days wanting so badly to kill myself, just for it all to end, but knowing I couldn't because I owed her for the pain I'd caused when I never had?

What the hell had it all been for?

The gods did this, I thought.

It was *their* fault.

But the gods were gone, so who did I blame now?

And yet, I wanted someone to *bleed* for this. It was all I knew and the only way I had ever been able to express myself. Such a good little monster, just as the gods had made me.

I wished I could kill them all. Wished I could show them exactly what their rivalry and lust for power and disinterest in who they hurt had wrought. I wished that so hard that I could feel my nails cutting into my palms, making little red wounds and then worse, as blood began to drip onto the floor.

"Hey," Ray said, alarmed, because if there was one thing that vampires didn't miss, it was blood.

"I'm alright," I told him, but he didn't believe me, and forced me to show him my hands. And then made a sucking sound in between his teeth and got up, fetching a spare sheet that he tore into bandages, after splashing the remaining alcohol onto my wounds.

The pain felt good, something to distract my mind, and being fussed over felt better. To have someone care that I was hurting and want to alleviate it was a strange new thing. And he tried; he really did.

He carefully wrapped up my hands, taking his time, murmuring words to soothe me all the while, for he had realized that I wasn't taking this well. He had thought to help by giving an alternate explanation for the wreck that was my life. But since it had done the opposite, he was trying to make it better.

I didn't deserve him.

"Maybe you just need some new memories," he was saying. "Venice was great and all, but that was a long time ago. And this isn't Earth. It's a new world, and you're a new person. You have a life now, and you can do whatever you want, make whatever memories you choose."

"After so long?" I met his eyes and let the uncertainty show in mine. "I don't know how to be normal. I never did."

He shrugged. "Who says you gotta be normal? I ain't normal, and I do okay. Dory sure ain't and she's a senator. And this is Faerie, which is weirder than either of us, you know what I mean?"

What I knew was that, when Ray was running on, giving me time for whatever reason he thought I needed it, his Brooklyn accent became more pronounced and his grammar worsened. I wondered why that was. Had it been easier, when he was with Cheung, if people underestimated him? Had it been safer?

He looked up at me suddenly, probably because he had heard that. I should learn to guard my thoughts better, but I was a sieve tonight. Everything was getting through.

Although he was so perceptive that he picked up much of my mental dialogue anyway. It was odd, after centuries of never being heard, even by those who had the ability to do so, to be around someone who could see every flicker across my brain. Most people would have found that disturbing.

I was strangely comforted.

"Good, 'cause I'm not gonna stop," he said, in a more normal voice. "And, yeah, sometimes I exaggerated the poor, dumb flunky routine; why not, if it got me out of a beating? Most people thought of me that way anyway."

"They were wrong," I said. "If you hadn't done what you did in the arena, I would be dead. We might all be. Mircea and Marlowe will never say thank you, as it would offend their dignity, but I will. Thank you."

He blushed—I saw it—a faint stain on his bronze skin. Then he went back to bandaging, although I was already wearing the equivalent of mittens. "Yeah, well, thank you for biting out that bastard's throat. I swear I peed my pants a little when he came at us."

"I think I did, too."

He laughed, and his blue eyes sparkled when he looked up at me. "Liar. You were as cool as a cucumber. I never even saw—"

I kissed him.

I hadn't planned on it, wasn't even thinking about it. Didn't fully realize that it had happened until our lips met. And I discovered that his were soft and strong and warm and sweet, and then harder and more demanding, more passionate.

He deepened the kiss, or maybe I did; I wasn't sure, couldn't think. Suddenly, the world had been reduced to sensation: silky hair and hard muscle under soft suede; sweet smelling tobacco mingled with the herbal soap the fey used and some cologne he must have gotten from his boys, as he had had none when we came here; the hungry sound he made deep in his throat as his hands gripped my arms and he pulled me close; the taste of fiery spirits on his tongue, or maybe they were on mine; couldn't tell, didn't care—

And then nothing, because he'd broken away, and was staring at me in shock, as if I had just plunged a knife into his ribs.

His hair was mussed, and it pleased me that I had done that, and his cheeks were flushed even more than before. That was not normal for a vampire, and I reached out and touched one. It was warm. And then it was gone, too, as Ray scrambled back.

It was just a couple feet, but it was clear that he was trying to put more than just physical distance between us. I sat there on the floor, unsure about what I'd done wrong, as I so often was. I hadn't interacted with people enough to understand even easy emotions, much less whatever this was.

And he knew that. He paused, having gotten to his feet, and stared at me some more. And then put a hand behind his neck as if it pained him. "Look," he said, the blue eyes dark with emotion.

Then he stopped, as if he had run out of words when he never did.

"Is something wrong?" I asked.

"No! I just—that is, you need—" he stopped again.

"You are upset?" I guessed, after another pause.

"No, you're upset! You've had a hell of a day, and it's no wonder you're a little—but I'm—and you're—this isn't—"

He seemed to be having trouble forming sentences, which was unprecedented. I got up, becoming worried about him, but that seemed to make things worse. Because I hadn't even made it to my feet before he was moving away from me again.

"I gotta go check on the guys," he said quickly. "You, uh, you get some sleep and—and you'll be fine. I just gotta go check on the, uh—"

He turned around and ran into the wall beside the door, course corrected and fled, there was no other word for it.

Or, at least, he tried. But I reached into the mind of one of the guards, and had him push Ray back into the room and close the door on him. Which . . . did not make my companion any happier.

He whirled on me. "That's cheating!"

"Then we are even." I sat on the end of the bed.

"What? I haven't cheated you out of a damned thing!"

"You think it fine, then, that you know all my secrets, every corner of my mind, yet I do not understand you at all? You take my thoughts but give nothing in return. How is that not cheating?"

Ray stared at me for a moment, as if he hadn't expected that. Just as I did not expect his answer. "You don't want my thoughts."

"And why not?"

"Because you won't like them!"

He turned to go again, but the door did not open. He put his back into it, and then his shoulder, pushing and shoving against it, but there were two ogres on the other side holding it shut, and then a third who I snared as he walked down the corridor. Ray finally gave up and turned on me, scowling.

"The queen won't like it much if I punch through her damned door!"

"You would prefer that to talking to me?"

"Yes!"

I couldn't help it; I felt hurt. And because I was unusually emotional tonight, my eyes welled up with tears. He saw, and his own face went through a paroxysm of emotions.

It finally settled on defeat.

He walked over and sat down beside me. "Don't do that," he said, and wiped my tears away with some of the left-over bandages.

"I don't want to defeat you," I whispered, because it was in his mind, too. "I just want to talk."

"Yeah, but you've had a day. It can wait."

"No, it can't." I wondered how to explain to him how many years I had spent waiting, having to be so patient. If I wanted to go somewhere, I had to hope that Dory wanted it, too. If I craved a particular food, I had to try to plant that thought in her mind. If I wanted to talk—

I gave up, because it was impossible to explain how little I had ever been able to talk to anyone. It had seemed so strange, so wonderfully and amazingly strange, to be able to vocalize my thoughts and have others actually hear me and answer back. I hadn't realized before how much speaking forced a person to focus on what they were saying, and to make vague ideas come together into coherent sentences.

You couldn't hide so easily when you had to put things into words. And an idea that seemed to make sense in your head was less so when spoken aloud. I was thinking more as a result than I ever had, and thinking clearer.

But it was still difficult sometimes to explain how I felt. Even though it was easier to express myself with Ray than with anyone else. He heard half of my thoughts anyway, and helped me to put my words together. And he liked to talk!

It was my favorite thing about him, and I had many favorite things.

"Don't do that," he repeated tightly.

"Why not?" I got up and faced him, wanting to understand. "You like me—"

He laughed, a sudden burst of sound.

"You do," I insisted.

"Yes."

"Then why?"

He stared up at me, and I couldn't claim that he was guarded now, with all the pain I felt mirrored in his eyes. "You know why. But you don't need to hear it now."

"I do. I want to understand—" I spread an arm and gestured around. "Something. Anything. But especially you."

This was absolutely true. Unlike Dory, I had never had a family. I never had anyone until Ray, and now he was rejecting me.

"I am not rejecting you!"

"Then what would you call this?"

He shook his head wildly, like a man possessed. And then he exploded, coming off of the bed so fast that I could barely track him, getting in my face. Reminding me of what he was.

"It's not what I am," he hissed. "It's what I'm *not*. You think I didn't hear you and that bitch ass pixie today? You want a kid. That's why you're doing this, but I can't give you one. I can't give you anything!

"You wanna understand me? It's easy. I'm nothing. Nobody. Never was, never will be. There's no senate seat in my future. There's not even another step up in power. They say you don't know when you're finished as a vamp; I say you do—*I* do! I feel it here," he smacked a fist against his chest. "This is as far as I will ever go, as powerful as I'll ever be.

"And, babe, you are out of my fucking league."

He started for the door again, determined this time, but so was I. I caught his arm; he shrugged off my hold. So, I caught it again, which only enraged him further.

"See?" he said, turning on me. "I can't even leave!"

"I don't understand why you want to," I said, in genuine bewilderment. "Do you think I care about how strong you are?

Strength never helped me—it imprisoned me! It isn't everything—"

"Then let's talk family. You're a Basarab—and before you tell me that don't matter, it isn't up to you! It matters to everyone else! You know why nobody raised a fuss when Louis-Cesare married a dhampir? A senator and a dueling champion, the one-time golden boy of the European Senate, teaming up with an outcaste who isn't even supposed to exist? But did you hear a peep out of anybody?

"No, 'cause she wasn't just a dhampir. She was a *Basarab*. And they do whatever the hell they want!"

"Good, then I want you." I reached for him, but he danced back out of the way.

"No! Goddamn it! This isn't love, it's trauma bonding! We've been through hell together, but I am not a freaking teddy bear!"

"I never said you were—"

"You didn't have to say it. I can feel it radiating off you, see it in your mind, taste it on your lips. You want comfort, security, somebody familiar, and who can blame you? You're scared—"

"Scared of what?" I demanded, bristling. "I'm not scared!"

"Like hell you're not." The blue eyes met mine head on. "Not scared of Faerie like most people would be, no, but scared of yourself. Of this new existence you suddenly have and don't know how to handle. Everything was simple before: wake up, kill a few enemies, prowl around a little, go back to sleep. It wasn't much of a life, but it was easy.

"This isn't. And in ain't gonna get any easier."

"You think I don't know that?" I glared at him.

"Yeah, I think you don't know that. I think you don't know anything, 'cause you might be five hundred years old, but in a real sense, you're a baby. A drunk baby who's scared and wants someone to cling to—"

"That isn't what this is!"

"—but you won't always feel like this and I *can't*—"

He stopped abruptly, swallowing, and then came closer to take me by the shoulders, breathing hard.

That was two master level vampires I had reduced to that in a single day. I should feel proud, I thought, and wanted to cry again.

"Look, I'm not leaving, okay?" Ray said. "I'm not going anywhere. I'm your Second, and I'm proud of that; I always will be. But you gotta understand: that's all I'm gonna be."

"Why?"

It was a simple question, but I still hadn't gotten an answer. He had danced all around it, but while everything he'd said were answers, they weren't *the* answer. And we both knew it.

Ray shook his head. "I never can get around you, can I?"

"Then maybe stop trying."

He took my face in his hands, and let our foreheads touch. "You're out of my league," he whispered again. "In basically every single way. And one of these days, you're gonna realize it. And I... can't do this. I can't have everything I ever wanted, then have it snatched away. Or worse, have you stay because you can't bear to hurt me, and end up in another trap you can't get out of. I won't imprison you like that. I *won't*."

I took a moment to absorb that.

I decided it was bull crap.

"Mircea always did this," I told him steadily. "Always made my decisions for me. I didn't think you'd do the same."

Ray reared back as if I'd slapped him. "That was a low blow."

"But it's true." I searched his features, and they were so dear to me. And so maddening. It was as well that he had joined the family; he was as stubborn as a Basarab when he wanted to be. "If I'm not adult enough to know what I want by now, when will I be?"

"When you figure out who you are, what you are. When you're comfortable in that new skin of yours. When you've met more people, better people—"

"There are no better people."

"Dorina! Stop this! I'm trying to help you."

"No, you're trying to help you." I walked back over to the bed and sat down, and began unwrapping the mittens. Or started to; there was a lot of fabric. "You're afraid, too."

"Hey, don't do that," Ray said, following me over. And was pushed onto the bed with me straddling him, because I was done being coy. "Hey!"

"You're afraid," I repeated, taking my time unwinding the bandages I didn't need, as my wounds had already closed up, while keeping him imprisoned with my thighs.

"Of you getting an infection maybe!"

"Dhampirs don't get infections. And that's not what you're afraid of. You're afraid because this is a new world for you, too. Here you're not Ray, the unwanted, bullied child cast out into the world too soon, with no one to help you. You're not Ray, the sometime nightclub owner and Cheung's favorite whipping boy. You're not Ray, bound by vampire customs and limits, with a set place in their society and that near the bottom. You used to be all of those things, just as I was a hated monster instead of a daughter. But you said it yourself: this is a new world where none of that matters anymore.

"If I can be anything here, so can you. But that's the problem, isn't it? You may not have liked your old life, but you knew who you were, what you could and couldn't do, who you could and couldn't be.

"Now you don't, and it terrifies you—"

"You're the only thing that terrifies me," he muttered, trying to get away, but not trying very hard.

"—now you're just Ray, a new man in a new world who can have whatever he wants. Or whatever he's willing to reach out and take. I imagine after hundreds of years of being told where you fit, and what your limits are, that that could be . . . panic-inducing."

"I'm not panicked!" he snarled, and flipped me.

I looked up at him, and his expression was angry and flustered and hopeful and terrified, as if he couldn't settle on just one. "You're only thinking of me," I said wryly.

"Yes!"

"Good. You keep telling me that I have to learn to think for myself, to make my own choices, and now I have. I choose you." I smiled up at him. "What are you going to do about it?"

Chapter Twenty-Nine

"Leave," I thought he'd say. And get up and walk away again. Because he *was* afraid, whether he admitted it or not.

I could feel it in his hands, trembling on my skin. I could see it in his gaze, flickering around the room. He wasn't into this; he wasn't into anything.

"It's okay," I told him, after a moment, my heart dropping. "We don't have to do this. I don't want you to be—"

"But *I* want!" Ray said, his eyes suddenly blazing as they came back to me. "And yet I'm—why am I like this?"

"Maybe we *are* broken," I whispered, wondering if it was possible for two people like us to really make a new life, or if we were only kidding ourselves. All of that had sounded good, but what did it mean in practice? If it meant anything at all.

Perhaps the scars of the old world were just too great.

But he shook his head again savagely. "No! We're not broken. *They* are. They always were." And he kissed me.

And there it is, I thought, my arms going around his neck. The courage and passion and joy that I had always associated with him. There it is!

I found myself laughing in relief, and then so was he. "Don't laugh yet," he told me gasping. "Not yet. You haven't even seen my dick."

Which set us both off.

Is it supposed to be like this, I marveled as we rolled across the oversized bed. It never had been with Dory's lovers. Except for possibly Louis-Cesare, but I had made myself scarce whenever they were together, trying to give them privacy.

So, I didn't know in his case. But the others . . . there had been no joy there. Just fast, desperate couplings in order not to feel alone for a few minutes, often followed by regret. No laughter, no friendship, no love.

And I'd had to watch it all, because I didn't trust them not to hurt her.

"Sons of bitches," Ray muttered, because he would never hurt me. In fact, he was treating me like spun glass, as if he was afraid that I'd break, which was not what I wanted, either. So, I threw off the rest of the damn mittens and kissed him back.

And yes, that had been a good idea, I decided, as the shaking in his hands went away, and the delicacy of his touch followed suit, and—

And I might have been wrong about him not being into it, I thought, as my nightgown hit the floor and he began kissing me all over. Which was nice, which was very nice, because he was warm and he smelled good and his hands were rough with calluses but his hair was soft as silk. And his mouth—

He had a very talented mouth.

But being naked when he was not left me at a disadvantage. I decided to fix that.

"I'm not much compared to Louis-Cesare," he said, catching my wrist as I started to strip off his vest.

"Louis-Cesare doesn't interest me."

"But Dory—"

"I am not Dory."

Ray regarded me strangely. "So, what does interest you? What the hell could someone like you see in someone like me?"

This time, it wasn't said in anger, but more like bewilderment, so I answered him while helping him out of the vest. "Someone curious enough to want to know what lay beyond the confines of our world and brave enough to risk finding out. Someone clever enough to make contacts in a wholly different place, and kind enough to see the good in the dark fey that everyone else seems to despise. Someone selfless enough to put his life on the line for me, over and over, when he didn't have to."

"So, you love me for my personality," he said wryly.

I tilted my head. "Is that a problem?"

"No, I'd just kinda prefer that you were lusting after the bod."

"I have not yet seen it," I pointed out.

He sighed. "That's not gonna make a difference."

Sometimes, I couldn't tell with Ray what was self-deprecating humor and what he really believed. He was not a six-foot-four Frenchman, but I already knew that. And what he was, was quite pleasing.

I pulled off the shirt and discovered what I already suspected, that he was slender but had muscle, although not the kind made in a gym.

"The kind made by running for my life," he said, his hand smoothing up my outer thigh.

He also had a lot of hair, merely a fine dusting on his chest but more on his head, which was silky and dark and fine but poufy because there was so much of it. I let my hands run through it, smoothing it down, only to have it spring back up immediately. I did it again and laughed delightedly. His boys must not have had any of the gel he used back home to try to flatten it down, and nothing else seemed to work.

"Got the type from mom and the amount from the sperm donor," he breathed, and tried to roll me, but I wasn't done yet.

I flipped him over and pulled off his trousers, and found a very fine butt, as butts went. I did not have the same appreciation for them that Dory seemed to, but there was literally nothing wrong with it. Or with the rest of him.

In fact, I thought he was rather handsome.

"What is wrong with you?" I asked, puzzled.

"Do you want a list?" he muttered into the mattress, sounding a bit out of breath.

"No." I didn't need one. His life was all there, if anyone cared to see it. Calluses and small scars from early years lived mostly outside. A stab wound in his shoulder, stretched out of shape like perhaps he had still been growing at the time he received it. Whip marks on his back, old and faded now, but not erased because he'd acquired them before the Change.

I traced them with a finger and saw him shiver.

Nothing at all wrong, I thought, turning him back over and finding out that my initial impression from that old memory of his had been valid.

"You are very pleasing," I told him happily.

"I'm gonna lose my shit," he answered fervently, which I thought was a strange response. But then he grabbed me and kissed me again, and I forgot to care.

It was different this time, more urgent, as were the hands exploring my body. He seemed to find it pleasing, too, and was very thorough. Extremely thorough, I though, as several fingers slipped between my legs and—

"Oh," I said in surprise, my eyes widening. "That was—that was very—what was that? Do that again!"

But Ray did not do that again. Instead, his whole body stilled, and the magic fingers were slowly withdrawn.

"What is it?" I asked again. And found him staring at me in shock and something else that I couldn't define in those blue eyes.

He licked his lips, and when he spoke this time, it was very deliberate. "You've done this before, right?"

It took me a moment to focus on what he was saying, and even then, it didn't make much sense. "What?"

"You've done this. You've . . . been with someone before. Right?"

He sounded like it was important, when it didn't feel that way to me. "Yes, of course."

I tried to pull his hand back, but he wouldn't let me. "When?"

"What?"

"When was that?" he persisted.

I huffed in frustration. "I told you. Dory had encounters from time to time—"

"I wasn't asking about Dory. I was asking about you."

He seemed strangely intent, which was maddening under the circumstances. But I knew Ray. He wasn't going to budge unless I took the time to answer this.

"Well, not me, of course. I mean, not as myself—"

"Of course?" It was his turn to look like something didn't compute.

"It was her body," I explained, as patiently as I could manage. "Even had I met someone during the rare times I was in control, it would have been . . . wrong . . . to act on it."

"How? How would it have been wrong?" he demanded, looking at me a bit wildly.

"It never felt like my body. It wasn't my body. I was just the parasite—"

"That isn't what you were!"

"But it felt that way!" I was the one staring at him now. Why was he doing this? "You are ruining the mood," I pointed out.

"I am? *I* am? You're telling me you're basically a virgin, and I—what the hell am I supposed to do now?"

I took his hand. "You were doing quite well before—"

He snatched it back. "I can't perform like this!"

"You just were—"

"That's before I knew!"

"Knew what?" I was starting to get really frustrated. "I have known many men—"

"No! No, you have not! *Dory* has known many men. You were an unwilling participant and I am seriously not okay with that—"

"I did not enjoy watching them," I agreed. "But..."

"But what?"

"But I was enjoying what you were doing before."

He stared at me some more; he was doing that a lot.

"I enjoyed it very much," I added, in case I had not been clear.

"I—you—this—auugghhhh!" He threw a pillow across the room. And then just sat there, looking at me and panting.

"Can I ... do anything?" I asked, somewhat at a loss.

"You—" he grabbed me. "You deserve better," he grated out. "For your first time, for every goddamned time. But if this is what you want—"

"It is." I hesitated, but I needed to know. Because I wasn't sure anymore. "Is it what *you* want?"

"Oh, God," he groaned, and kissed me. And simultaneously went back to doing the thing, so I assumed that the answer was yes. It would have been nice to hear him say it, however—"

"Yes," he kissed my lips, my chin, my neck. "Yes," he nuzzled my collarbone. "Yes," he found my breast, and oh, that was nice, too. It was all so nice!

"Just 'nice', huh," Ray growled, and seemed to take that as a challenge.

I laughed; I had not meant it as one, but I was not averse to finding out what he intended to—

Oh!

His tongue replaced his fingers, and it was ... it was very ... oh, yes, it was *very* ...

I gave up trying to form sentences, as they required concentration and all my attention was on something else. His hair was like silk between my thighs, except for the occasional scrape of stubble, which was a different kind of pleasure. And his tongue was warm, warmer than his fingers had been, and our scents mingled together was quite . . . intoxicating . . . and—and—and—

I lost my train of thought again, and my eyes kept wanting to roll up into my head and I couldn't seem to make them come down. Because he had learned a few things over the years, hadn't he? A great many things, I thought, as hard hands grabbed my hips, adjusting my position, and that talented, evil tongue had me thrashing and laughing and groaning and—

Was the term coming?

"That's the goddamned term," Ray said, grinning at me as stars exploded behind my vision, spangling the room.

I did not grin back. What should have sated me appeared to have done the opposite, and my hunger ignited. That had been an appetizer and only served to make me want more, to make me want everything. I growled and pulled him up to me.

"Oh, *shit*," Ray said, and then said nothing more as I devoured his mouth, grasped the evidence of his own, unfulfilled, and rather substantial excitement—

"*Oh, shit!*"

—and guided it into me.

"Oh, shit!" Ray said, as I jerked our bodies together, as I savaged his earlobe and grabbed his very serviceable butt. And snarled into his ear. "Move!"

He moved. And he seemed to know a lot of them and he used them all, and I kept pace with him because I was discovering that this was a new way to fight and a much more pleasurable one. We rolled off the bed and onto the floor, wrestling about, and Ray had a look of a man who wasn't sure that he was enjoying this, but wasn't sure that he wasn't.

I decided to help him out with that, but didn't get a chance. Because his expression suddenly turned determined, and he showed me that he did know this fight, this dance, this... I wasn't sure what it was. But he was good at it!

"You sound surprised," he growled.

I laughed. I was not surprised. But I was delighted.

And greedy and needy and hungry all over again. "Faster," I told him. "Harder!"

"I don't wanna hurt you," Ray said, gasping.

"Dhampir," I reminded him, as we hit a wall. "You won't."

"Oh, yeah," he said. And then, "Oh, *yeah!*"

And the next thing I knew, we were back on our feet, or rather, Ray was, supporting me as I twined my legs around his body, my back to the wall, and a much more enthusiastic partner teaching me a new move.

It felt good, it felt very good! He was girthy, and the feel of his body moving through mine was... was... I went back to savaging his earlobe again, biting it hard and feeling him jump within me. I laughed again and found other things that made him jump, learned what he liked and what he *really* liked, and he snarled and picked up the pace, driving into me now and *yes, yes, yes!*

But it was also a little worrying, as the wall behind us seemed about to give way. I finally managed to notice through the haze of pleasure that we had not hit the wall but rather the door, which the three ogres were still valiantly trying to hold shut since I had forgotten to call them off.

I couldn't manage it now, couldn't focus well enough with more fireworks starting to go off in front of my eyes and my breath catching in my throat, and my body shuddering with every movement.

The ogres held somehow, although not entirely. Not enough to keep the door from briefly opening a couple of times, allowing me to see one of them giving us a thumbs up. I wondered what that meant in their culture.

Probably the same as in ours, I thought, right before the fireworks obliterated everything else from my mind.

Ray must have been experiencing the same thing, because he trembled against me for a moment before stilling and groaning and—

"Coming?" I guessed, but he didn't answer this time. He didn't do anything but sink to the floor, cradling me against him and murmuring softly in a language I didn't know.

It was very peaceful suddenly, with my body embracing him and his breath warm on my neck. The terrible hunger was still there, but it was satisfied for the moment. Very satisfied, I thought, giggling.

Ray chuckled back, until he noticed the three pairs of eyes peering in through a crack in the door, and slammed it in their faces. He picked me up, carried me to the bed, and deposited me on it before climbing up alongside. Then he lay there on his back, breathing hard and staring at the ceiling.

After a moment, he raised my hand to his lips and pressed a fervent kiss upon it. "Thank you."

I thought that it should be me thanking him, but was willing to share the sentiment.

"We do sex well," I said, and he huffed out a laugh.

"Yeah." Blue eyes met mine. "Only nobody, and I mean nobody, are gonna be happy about this."

I let my fingers stroke his chest, because they seemed to like stroking his chest. "Why?"

"I already told you. A daughter of a house like yours is . . . important. Your marriage could ally houses, buy support in the senate, all kinds of things."

"Or do nothing, if I simply disappear when I step back through a portal," I reminded him.

"But you might not, and in that case—"

"In that case nothing. Basarab never claimed me. Now I don't claim it."

"It might not be that easy."

"And I am never going back. The question is, are you staying with me?"

I didn't intend to just come out with it like that, but the emotions flooding my system seemed to be playing havoc with my brain. And once it was said, it couldn't be unsaid. It hung in the air between us, threatening to turn a wonderful moment sour.

Until Ray turned to face me, and his hand came up and cupped my cheek. "I already told you; I'm not going anywhere."

"You also said we were only going to be friends."

He huffed out a laugh and shook his head. "A man can only take so much. And you'd tempt the devil himself."

"I'm serious." I searched his eyes. "It's a big step. I'll understand if you say no."

"Yeah, but I won't. I have nothing back there."

"Your boys—"

"Are Basarabs now. They'll be fine. Dory will take care of 'em, and probably better than I ever did."

"But you're her Second—"

"And yours." His eyes searched my face. "You may as well just accept it. You're not getting rid of me."

I smiled tentatively at him, then broke into a grin after a few seconds. I couldn't help myself. We were both crazy, but at least we could be crazy together.

"I couldn't have put it better myself," Ray whispered.

I relaxed back against the bed, a huge load off of my mind, even more than I'd expected. A wave of pure happiness coursed through me suddenly. Ray was staying!

"Did you really think I'd leave?" he asked, more seriously.

"Everybody leaves when you're a dhampir."

"I don't." He cupped my face again, which seemed to be a favorite move, and I leaned into it, enjoying the calluses on his palm, the warmth of his skin, and the concern in his eyes.

I put my hand over his, a question trembling on my lips. I almost swallowed it back down, but tonight was about telling the truth. And asking for it.

"What is it?" he said, his eyes darkening.

I looked at him seriously. "You're not just saying that because I'm good at sex, are you?"

He stared at me, and then he pulled me close, rocking us together while his whole body shook. "Well, that might be part of it," he said, his voice choked. "A man has needs, you know."

I considered that, even though I was pretty sure that he was joking. A thought occurred. "You're a vampire."

"Guilty as charged."

"And vampires have perfect control over their blood pressure, do they not?"

Ray pulled back to look at me, and started to appear a little worried. "Uh. Yes?"

"So," I smiled at him. "You don't really need a refractory period. Do you?"

Chapter Thirty
Dory

"You need sleep," Louis-Cesare murmured, pulling the gigantic brown fur we were using as a bedspread closer about my chin.

I wasn't cold, even though my breath frosted the air whenever I exhaled. It probably would have at the castle, too, as open to the elements as that place was, but we weren't back there. We were still in the war camp that Lord Rathen was assembling from a dozen clans.

We couldn't go back to court because that wasn't neutral ground and Rathen wasn't leading this group—technically. Of course, he was in reality, but dragons were prickly so he couldn't look like it. This was just a group of like-minded people, friends in the human term, teaming up in a forest to go crack a few skulls.

More and more had been flying in all day, and I had been paraded about to meet them over and over. I was apparently some kind of trump card for Rathen's side, a human who could fight well enough to kill a dragon, even if it had left me looking half dead. But that very fact, and sight of my flimsy, battered body, seemed to shame creatures who were, without any doubt at all, far stronger and tougher than I was.

If I could fight, the implication was clear, why couldn't they?

It had been exhausting and nerve wracking, and I had been relieved beyond measure when better tents arrived and I had had somewhere to escape to.

This one was much more spacious than the cloak-on-a-stick set up I'd had before, and was furnished with all the comforts of home. Including reed mats to cushion the somewhat rocky soil, a woolen mattress on top of that, and the fur. I didn't know what animal it had been taken off of, and frankly was afraid to ask.

But it was huge.

Like my husband, who felt bigger than usual beside me, perhaps because I felt smaller.

No, I wasn't cold, but I wasn't sleeping, either.

Louis-Cesare drew me close, but it didn't help. He had been quiet since he returned from the faire-turned-graveyard, which was understandable; Lord Rathen's people had been, too. That sort of thing stayed with a person, clogging the throat when they tried to speak and tasted ashes, ashes that might have been someone they knew not so long ago. The exploratory party had eaten their evening meal in silence and gone to bed early. As had I, to give the ointments Claire had been bathing me in all day a better chance to work.

They seemed to be helping, but probably not quickly enough.

Nothing was quick enough here.

Louis-Cesare's arms tightened, and I wondered what he was thinking. Probably that I should go home. That I was as useless here as I felt, a puny human out of weapons and way out of her depth, in an alien world that seemed determined to destroy us.

And if he was thinking that, he was right.

The feelings had been growing all day, as I was scrutinized by dragon lord after dragon lord, and realized that my main use to the cause was how pathetic I looked. It didn't help that, in between 'diplomatic' sessions, I sat around with nothing to do but think. I had tried to help around camp, but everyone else could do it better and faster, and anyway, I was injured. I had been shooed away, back to my thoughts, which had gotten progressively darker as the day passed.

With Louis-Cesare gone for hours and Claire so different suddenly, and away much of the day gathering, chopping and mixing who-knew-what, I hadn't even had anyone to talk to. Or anything to do but toss and turn in my tent once it got set up and pretend that I wasn't panicking. I'd kept my weapons near even though I didn't need them. They seemed paltry and almost as useless as a child's slingshot, now that I knew what we were up against, and no one else had anything better to offer.

Everybody here was a weapon; they didn't need to carry them. That dusty collection at the castle were trophies, I had learned, taken in ancient wars and likely to crumble in my hands as soon as I looked at them. I had nothing.

We should leave.

"What?"

I hadn't realized that I'd said that last part out loud until Louis-Cesare spoke. I would have preferred to keep facing the door, where one of the ties on the tent flap had come loose and left the panel ruffling in the wind.

I could see the fire outside in flashes, which had burned down to embers now, and the stunning scarves of aurora borealis veiling the stars above.

It was beautiful, as Faerie always was.

It didn't make me feel any better.

I decided to stop being a coward and rolled over to face him. "I don't belong here," I whispered.

"Neither of us do." He glanced at the tent flap, too, and I thought about all that he had seen today. I didn't know most of it, as I'd only caught glimpses occasionally through his eyes when he forgot to shield, but it hadn't been pretty.

"This isn't our world," he said, as if reading my thoughts. "I feel it much as you do."

I shook my head. "No, I mean I don't belong here, pretending that I have a chance in hell of finding Dorina. Tanet was right. I'm going to get people killed."

Possibly a lot of people.

Possibly the man I was talking to.

My hand tightened on his arm. "We should go."

Louis-Cesare looked at me, his eyes tinted green in the reflected light from outside. "You don't mean that."

"I do!"

"You don't, though." He brushed a strand of hair off my forehead, his touch gentle. "I know you too well to believe that. It's the fear talking, the pain, the uncertainty—"

"It's all of those, but that doesn't mean it's wrong!" I hissed. "I was a fool to come here, a fool to think I could handle this! You were right. Without Dorina . . . I'm nothing."

His fingers froze in place, halfway through tucking an errant strand behind my ear. "I never said that."

"But you thought it. And you were right."

"I never thought it, either." He abruptly sat up, disturbing the warm cocoon that our body heat had made and letting in a great billow of cold air. It was like a slap in the face, but I didn't mind. I deserved it.

"I endangered you, all of you, by bringing you here," I told him steadily. "I'd heard of Faerie, but I didn't *understand*. No one can until they come here—how vast it is, how deadly, how *strange*.

"Rathen's people went to get our guards, but they'd be better off taking them to the nearest portal. I can't protect them if they come here. I can't even protect myself!"

Louis-Cesare looked at me as if he thought I might be more ill than he'd realized, specifically in the head. "You killed a dragon—more than one—all on your own—"

I sat up, too, finding it impossible suddenly to just lie there. "*I* didn't kill it. My weapons did. And my arsenal is now gone. So, what happens next time?"

"The next time you fight a dragon?" he lifted an eyebrow. "Are you planning on another?"

I glared at him. "I'm being serious! And how the hell should I know? I don't know anything about what to expect here. But Steen is still out there, and apparently after Dorina. So, if we do find her, then yes, I might end up doing an encore.

"And without anything to save me this time—or anyone else!"

"We'll find a way—"

"Don't tell me that!" I wrapped my arms around myself, my naked skin breaking out in gooseflesh for more reason than just the cold. "I tried to tell myself I was fine without Dorina," I said. "I told you that, every time you got a little too overprotective—and in our world, I was right. I can handle things there; I know how it works. But here..."

"Here, you are still Dory," he said, pulling the fur back up around me. "Nothing has changed—"

"Everything has changed!" I stared at him, and to my horror, felt my eyes getting wet. "What if I can't get her back? What if I'm not strong enough?" It was the only thing I could think of anymore, despite what Claire had said. But look what had happened to Claire! "What if she's already dead? What if I somehow survive this only to find her corpse? What am I supposed to do then?"

He didn't answer this time. Just gathered me into his arms, gently in concession to my bruises, and then tighter when I fought him, even though I didn't know why I was fighting him. Or what I was talking about, because we both knew I wouldn't leave. I couldn't just let her die, but I didn't know what to do, or if there was anything I *could* do, and the events of last night were starting to hit hard.

My skin was a rainbow of vivid hues, and my cuts had been stitched up with some kind of black thread that left me looking like a rag doll sewn together from spare parts, a lady Frankenstein. My skin was cold even when I was properly dressed, and just about everything on my body ached. But none of those things were the problem.

This was the problem. The growing certainty that the best part of me had gone with Dorina, and that there wasn't enough left to find her, or protect her if she was hurt. Not in this hellish place where even the flora was lethal!

I grabbed a knife off my pack and slammed it through a stalk of something that Claire had brought back from the forest, something that had crawled out of its basket and headed in our direction, slinking across the floor like a leafy snake.

It writhed like one, too, after I impaled it, and was either stronger than any plant had a right to be or else I was weaker. But I kept up the pressure and twisted the blade, and it abruptly dissolved in a haze of black smoke and a few withered scraps on the reeds.

"What was that?" Louis-Cesare asked, sounding slightly weirded out.

Although whether that was because of the not-snake or the fact that I was systematically beating the remains with a shoe, I didn't know.

"Dory," he grabbed my shoulder.

"I don't want to risk taking the knife out," I panted, smacking it some more.

It looked dead, but around here, you just never knew.

"Dory!" he took my shoe.

I took it back.

"What?" I looked up at him through tangled hair, flushed cheeks and crazy eyes, which I could see for an instant when my vision switched over to his. I wondered if that had been on purpose, this time. If he'd wanted me to see how insane I looked.

Like that was anything new.

I abruptly got up, only to have him immediately pull me back down again. "Talk to me," he said, and that was the wrong phrase since there was nothing to say. Not for him, not for me. My sister was gone, I was scared out of my mind, and for once in my life, I couldn't seem to tamp it back down.

It felt like someone had a hand around my throat, and with every hour, it squeezed a little tighter.

Words were useless.

I needed to move, to walk, to hunt, assuming I could find anything to hunt with. I'd go round up breakfast for everyone, assuming they'd eat it cooked instead of raw and on the hoof.

I couldn't just lay here with my thoughts another minute or I really would go mad!

But Louis-Cesare wasn't having it.

Louis-Cesare was putting his foot down.

Unfortunately for him, so was I, and a brief tussle ended with me socking him on the jaw. And immediately getting teary again, because I hadn't meant to do that! I hadn't meant to hurt him.

I hadn't meant a lot of things, lately.

"I'm sorry," I whispered, panting slightly and staring at him. "That wasn't—I'm sorry for all of it."

I started to go again, and again, his grip was iron. And this time, so was the expression in his eyes. It wasn't pleased and I couldn't blame him.

He took a hit well, but that didn't mean he enjoyed it. And I had never done that before, never crossed that line unless we were sparring and we'd both agreed to it. And now I had something else to be ashamed of.

"You have nothing to be ashamed of," he told me, pulling me in, comforting me when that was the last thing I wanted.

"Stop listening to my thoughts!"

"You were projecting."

"Yeah, I bet!" I was a wreck tonight.

I was a wreck every night.

"Why do you do that?" he demanded angrily. "You have done nothing wrong since we came here—"

"I've done nothing right or we'd have her back!" I struggled against his hold and went nowhere. It was maddening! "And in case you forgot, I'm the dumbass who charged Steen. I should have died for that alone!"

"But you didn't." The touch was gentle but the voice was sharp. "You got a knife in him instead, outplaying him on his own turf, and then killed his subordinate who attacked you. And since then, you have shored up the very shaky alliance of the senate with the dragon lords, and indeed have expanded it.

"I'd say that was rather good for a 'dumbass'."

"Because I got lucky! I don't know what I'm doing—"

"And you think the rest of us do?" He pulled back so that he could look at me, and after a moment of searching my face, his head tilted as if he'd figured something out. "But that's the problem, isn't it?"

"What are you talking about?"

"I'm talking about the life the rest of us lead. You have never done that, have you? Never been forced to rely on your wits—"

"I've done nothing but rely on my wits!"

"—with no one to back you up if you were wrong. You've never had to live knowing that any wrong move could be the end. Dorina was always there to pick up the slack—is that the term?"

It was the term, and it was also bullshit!

"I didn't know about her for years!" I reminded him, stung. "I thought I was crazy when she came out, thought I was more vulnerable than everyone else as a result, had to arm myself to the teeth and take all kinds of added precautions in case I went nuts in a fight! But I did okay—"

"Did you?" he looked skeptical, maybe because the bruise on his cheek was swelling slightly, and changing color.

We matched now, I thought, which only made me feel worse. And then angrier, although who I was mad at, I couldn't have said. Me, him, or the whole damned miserable excuse for a world that was Faerie!

"You're damned right I did!" I snapped. "I learned to buy the magic I couldn't make and to fight with human as well as magical weapons. The senate is talking about making me weapons master now that that idiot Geminus is dead, because I know so much more about them than anybody else ever bothered to learn. Because they didn't need them, but I did, and I made sure—"

I stopped, because he was smirking at me.

And I belatedly realized that I'd been played.

"That's on Earth," I reminded him, scowling. "And in case you didn't notice, I'm out of weapons! I have nothing here!"

"You have you," he said, hugging me again. "You are a weapon, and a better one than you know. And you are forgetting one other very important thing."

"And what the hell is that?"

"You have me." It was said with a simple dignity that stopped me, as nothing else had. "Dorina is currently missing, yes, but I am not. And we are a team, *non*?"

"Yes, but—"

"And I thought a fairly good one." He pulled back again to regard me soberly. "I am not Dorina. She has abilities that I do not and will never understand. But what I do possess, so do you. I will never leave you, Dory. I will always be here, as she was. And together, we *will* find her."

I stared at him for a moment, my eyes flooding with tears that, this time, I didn't even try to stop. I hugged him, clinging on harder than was smart in my current state, but I couldn't seem to let go. I didn't know what god I had pleased to bring him into my life, but I knew one thing.

I didn't deserve him.

The thought rang strangely in my mind for a second, almost an echo. But when I went to grasp it, it slipped through my fingers like wind. Leaving me holding nothing.

"What is it?" Louis-Cesare asked, his body tensing as that sharp gaze went around the room, following mine.

But there was nothing to see, not with the eyes, anyway.

"I don't know. Just..." *Dorina?* I reached out mentally. *Are you there?*

There was no answer, not even an echo this time. But something had brushed my mind, if only for an instant. I knew it had!

And, suddenly, I felt lighter. Suddenly, absurdly, I felt like laughing. "I think she's alive," I whispered. "I think she is!"

"*Sans doute.*"

I didn't know how he could be so sure, or if he was only saying that to comfort me. But right now, I'd take it. Right now—

The tent flap was jerked back before I could finish the thought, and a familiar head stuck in. It was Tanet, invading our privacy without even attempting a warning. But for once, he wasn't sneering at me.

"What is it?" Louis-Cesare asked, drawing the fur closer around me.

"Get dressed," Claire's brother said simply. "The traitor has been found and you're wanted."

Chapter Thirty-One

A powerfully built brunet man was on his knees in a small clearing, naked and bleeding and surrounded by members of Lord Rathen's court. We were a good distance from camp, out of what should have been hearing range, but somebody had put up a silence spell anyway. I could feel it close about us as we passed through, like stepping into a pool of cold water when not expecting it.

It rang in my teeth like biting an icicle, something less than pleasant on a night that already felt like the air was half frozen and crunching in my lungs like our footsteps on the forest floor. But we'd bundled up in the clothes we'd arrived in, which some of Lord Rathen's people had been kind enough to launder and bring out to us, as everything else had gone up in the fireworks display. The feel of denim, leather, and a fur lined parka was weirdly reassuring in a world where nothing else was familiar.

Louis-Cesare was dressed similarly, in blues to my blacks, although he didn't need protection from the cold. But the clothes made us a set and caused us to stand apart from everyone else. And I was fine with that.

Mircea could handle the pretty speeches and dress to fit in. Today had taught me one thing, at least: I wasn't a diplomat and I never would be. I was a warrior and was ready to get back to killing things.

Specifically, things that had ratted me out almost before I arrived.

There were a lot of people in the glade clustered about the bleeding man. I didn't recognize them all, but Regin was there, with the salt and pepper hair and closely trimmed beard shining in the moonlight. As well as Lord Rathen himself, his red hair somewhat dimmed by the night, but his eyes extra green in the reflected aurora.

No one spoke as we joined them except for the prisoner, who snarled as soon as he saw us. And despite the fact that everyone here was in human form, the sound was so bestial that it almost caused me to break stride. I managed to avoid stumbling, but it was a close thing.

Louis-Cesare, who'd also had enough of pretending to be a diplomat, drew his weapon, causing an even bigger reaction from the captive man.

And suddenly, I knew who I was looking at.

"Antem," I said, remembering the name that Claire had given me, which belonged to the black and yellow bastard who'd touched me on the balcony shortly after we arrived. It had been seeing the sword that had caused him to have a fit then, too, and he didn't look any happier this time.

He lunged at Louis-Cesare, who stood his ground with a small smile on his face, as if his calm and collected act in the tent had been just that. He looked like a man who would welcome a fight, but I wanted to hear what was going on first. And I guessed that Lord Rathen did, too, because he made a small gesture and the furious man was dragged back by two large guards.

"Perceptive," Rathen said to me. He was in dark green tonight, the material rich but unadorned, and blending in so well with the forest that it was hard to see him until he moved. "Yes, it seems that our Antem has been spying for Vitharr. He was the one who told Lord Steen about your arrival. He's been using trips to visit his mother to relay information without us suspecting anything."

"And they sent him back to try for more," Regin added. "We caught him spying on the war council not half an hour ago."

I guessed they'd already gotten past the proclamations of innocence phase, because Antem didn't even try to deny it. He did, however, lunge for me and Louis-Cesare again, which I thought a bit excessive. I also thought it was suspicious.

"He wants you to kill him," I said to Louis-Cesare, putting an arm in front of my impulsive husband. "He doesn't want us to learn anything from him."

"He'll not get that wish," Regin said, placing a hand on the man's shoulder. "Not yet."

And for the first time, I saw Antem's defiant air falter. For a moment, he looked like what he was, a young man—possibly very young by their standards—who had been trying to prove himself and was in over his head. Way over.

I saw the realization of that settle into him, and it took a lot of the fight along with it.

Rathen saw it, too, and crouched down in front of his captive, his face more sad than angry. "I noticed that one of my family was absent from the fight," he said heavily. "One who is usually in the thick of things, enjoying demonstrating his prowess. But not last night.

"I feared the worst, but hoped I was wrong."

Antem looked up at him, but couldn't seem to hold that piercing gaze. He looked away. Rathen sighed.

"What do we know?" the lord of Eddred asked Regin.

"Not much. Only that Lord Steen mistook Lady Basarab for her sister, Dorina, whom he wished revenge on for attacking and killing some of his people in the arena two days ago. The queen held the usual games at the faire, and they apparently became a bit . . . spicier . . . than usual."

I started at that, and clenched Louis-Cesare's hand tightly. Dorina had been at that faire? I saw again the blackened corpses, the piles of the dead, and all my newfound confidence fled into horror.

Louis-Cesare squeezed back, and some of his strength seemed to flow into me, enough that I stayed on my feet. I didn't know what I looked like, but Regin shot me a glance and then shook his head. "Apologies, my lady. I should have mentioned that the queen and her court departed shortly after the games, and your sister appears to have gone with them, for Steen lost track of her. By the time word reached him, she was nowhere to be found. That was why, when his spies brought him news of you, he assumed that she was here, at Lord Rathen's court, and came after her.

"Only to find out that fierceness runs in the family."

I nodded my thanks, feeling a vast surge of relief flow through me, followed immediately by more gnawing anxiety. Because that still didn't tell me where she was, or what the bastard of Vitharr wanted with her. Or anything at all!

"And the court?" I asked. "Do we know where that is now?"

"Not . . . precisely. I have dispatched scouts to look for it, but it can be . . . elusive. But we will find it, never fear."

Eventually floated on the air, but went unsaid.

"So, the second attack was spleen on Steen's part," Lord Rathen said. "Fury at losing to us in battle and—or so he believed—missing Lady Basarab's sister yet again."

Regin nodded, but Lord Rathen still looked puzzled. "And he is upset at her sister for . . . attacking a number of his people in the arena? Do we believe this?"

"No. The boy lies."

"I should hope so," Lord Rathen murmured. "Or else the sister is even more fearsome than our own lady." He smiled at me.

"I meant that he lied about who was at fault," Regin clarified. "We have a witness that said Steen's people attacked her, not the other way around, and that it looked as if they had come there specifically for that purpose."

Lord Rathen frowned, as if trying to parse that, but I didn't give him time. "Was she hurt?" I asked, my stomach muscles tense. Because I doubted that even Dorina could come through something like that with a whole skin.

But Regin was already shaking his head. "Not seriously. She seems to have emerged unscathed for the most part, after . . ." he hesitated.

"After what?" Rathen said.

"After stealing the form of Lord Steen's cousin and the commander of his guards, and . . . eating him."

There was a sudden silence all round, and I didn't break it. My head was spinning too fast from the rollercoaster of emotion, to the point that I couldn't do much except hold on to Louis-Cesare. And concentrate on the take away here: Dorina was alive! She had been alive and well just two days ago!

And then the rest of what Regin had said registered.

But I still didn't speak, because Rathen beat me to it. "What?" he asked politely.

"I know how it sounds," Regin said heavily. "But that was the story I heard from one of the guards we left behind. He found a witness—the one I was about to tell you about, before we were interrupted."

"What witness?" Louis-Cesare demanded. "When was this?"

Several nearby men looked at Regin, who in turn looked at his lord.

"I think we should all like to hear it," Lord Rathen said.

Regin made a gesture and one of his men came forward, a tall, powerfully built blond. He was clothed in green like his lord and the chief of the guards, only in his case that meant a long, loose-fitting tunic with open sides and nothing on underneath. He had the air of a dragon who'd just turned, a musky, teeth clenching sharpness that I was beginning to know well, and his eyes were still a little wild, as if he'd been in his altered state just minutes ago, and hadn't quite settled back into his human brain.

"While you were searching the village, we found a man cowering in the forest," he informed Louis-Cesare, before turning those disturbing eyes on his lord. "He'd stayed when others ran, to strip the dead most like.

But he said he'd been in the arena, that he saw it all."

"Saw what, exactly?" Rathen said, as if he still didn't understand. I wasn't sure that I did, either, although I was starting to have a glimmer of an idea.

"What Lord Regin said. That the woman was introduced as part of a match, during which she defeated a giant—"

"A giant?" Rathen repeated, his brow knitting.

"Yes. Or so the witness said," the blond added, as if he wasn't sure that he believed it, either. "It was the queen's current champion, or former champion now, I suppose. The crowd reacted . . . badly . . . to the loss—"

"Likely cost some a lot of money," another man, this one a redhead, said. The little ties on his tunic were also undone, and he had that same wild, musky odor. They must have been some of those who fought Antem in his dragon form, after he'd been found spying, and tried to get away.

He'd failed, as the blood on his body attested, some of which had splattered the redhead's muscular thigh, like extra-large freckles.

"If it's the bastard I'm thinking of, that is," the redhead added. "Most of the recent betting has been on how long any opponent will last against him, not whether or not he wins. He was a bruiser, even by their standards."

Lord Rathen nodded, but his focus remained on the blond. "She killed a giant, then, not Lord Steen's men?"

"No, she killed both," the blond said. "Lord Steen's people showed up afterward—"

"How many?" Rathen demanded.

"Half a dozen, possibly more. The witness wasn't sure; I believe he was cowering out of sight for most of it."

"Wise man," somebody quipped.

"But he managed to see some of the action, and from what he told us, the human woman transformed into a duplicate of Lord Lissan-Dor and, well, ate him."

"No, she ate the others," the redhead piped up, who I guessed must have been part of the same scouting party. "She just broke his neck and took a few . . . bites . . ." He suddenly noticed the expression on his lord's face and trailed off.

"Why was I not informed of this?" Louis-Cesare demanded, ignoring the tension in the air with aristocratic disdain. "You had plenty of time after my party returned from the village that you were so intent on having searched, a village which yielded exactly nothing!"

Regin didn't bother trying to deny the implication, but answered with his usual calm placidity. "My men wished to report to their lord first, as well they might. But he had already left to return here, to greet some important guests."

"And yet we have been back for hours!"

Regin regarded him cooly, aristocrat to aristocrat. "He was still greeting them."

Louis-Cesare did not like that answer, but Rathen interrupted. "We know about it now," he said, the green eyes intense, and this time, they were on me. "Can your sister do as they say?"

"I—maybe."

"Maybe?" It was polite, and he hadn't raised his voice. So why did all the hair on my body suddenly stand on end?

"It . . . might be possible, under certain circumstances," I admitted. "There was this . . . incident . . . with a demon lord a while ago—"

"A demon lord cursed her?"

"Uh, no. She, that is we, killed him—"

"You killed a demon lord?" Rathen still did not change expression, and his voice hadn't shifted tone. Yet his complete skepticism couldn't have been any clearer.

I really needed to learn how to do that.

"Are you speaking of Hong Kong?" Louis-Cesare asked. He had missed the incident in question, arriving only after the fighting was done, much to his displeasure. He had been filled in later.

"Yeah. The first trip, not the second—"

"You killed *two* demon lords?" Rathen asked, still polite.

I wondered how much longer that would last.

Hopefully not long, as it was getting creepy.

"No. Just the one. It was on the first trip. We, uh, we stay . . . busy."

"So it would seem. Leave us."

For a moment, I thought he was talking to Louis-Cesare and me, until everyone melted away except for him, Regin, Tanet and Antem, who Regin took over guarding, holding him by the back of the neck like a misbehaving puppy. "If you wish, I can go as well," Regin offered.

"You know damned well I didn't mean you," Rathen said, and yeah, the forced politeness part of this conversation had just ended, I thought, checking out his new expression. He looked back at me, and for once, he was every inch a king. "Explain yourself."

Yeah, I thought. That would be a good trick. But I tried, and thankfully, the properties of the little flower known as Dragon's Claw were well known to them.

Unfortunately, that didn't help with the whole disbelief thing.

"It doesn't do what you describe," Tanet said, when my account of the time Dorina and I assumed the form of an angel to defeat a demon was finished. "It is a children's toy! An amusement sold at faires—"

"That would explain how Dorina obtained it," Louis-Cesare said.

"It explains nothing!" Tanet snapped. "Dragon's Claw is far too weak to do anything but make cosmetic changes! It is used in glamouries, nothing more! I've never heard—"

His father made a small gesture, cutting him off. Lord Rathen was still staring at me, which was unnerving. The eyes were human but there was enough of the dragon behind them to shine though, especially when he was thrown off kilter, which had obviously happened here.

I just didn't know why.

"My lord?" Regin said, clearly as concerned as I was.

I gathered that Lord Rathen wasn't flummoxed often, but it was kind of looking like it now. And then it was looking like something else, when he suddenly grabbed me and started looking me over with a frown on his face. One that changed to a scowl when Louis-Cesare knocked his hand away.

But instead of starting a fight, the gesture barely seemed to register. Rathen looked at his subordinate, who was frowning now, too. "Fortune's Blade?"

Regin's eyes widened slightly, which from him was quite a reaction, but he said nothing.

"What?" Tanet asked, looking between the two men, neither of whom spoke. But at least they weren't focused on me anymore.

Instead, Rathen crouched in front of the prisoner again, his loose velvet robes puddling on the ground around him.

"You know that term, don't you?" he asked. "You flinched just now; I saw it."

"I did nothing of the kind!"

"Don't lie, boy," Regin said, his hand tightening around the back of the man's throat. "It will go ill for you."

"*Ill?*" Antem spat. "Worse than this, you mean? I know the fate that awaits me. Why the hell should I tell you anything?"

"There's death and then there's death. You would prefer the former."

"I'm no coward! Tear me to pieces and I'll still tell you nothing!"

"But I will."

The voice made everyone jump, ringing out crystal clear in the cold mountain air and coming from behind us. Louis-Cesare whirled, sword up and eyes startled, because there weren't a lot of things that could sneak up on a vampire. Or break through a silence spell that had been laid by another.

Or, for that matter, slip unnoticed by the guards that had been posted around the glade, and who were only now realizing that someone had gotten past them.

I saw them turn, shaking their heads and acting almost as if they were waking from a dream. But they barely registered, because my eyes were on the woman who had spoken, and who was standing there calmly, a tall column of blue velvet, as if she'd appeared out of nothing. Louis-Cesare pulled me back and got in between us, but I had the strangest feeling that it didn't matter.

If she'd wanted to get to me, she'd have done it. She would even now, with a first level master protecting me.

I didn't know how I knew; I just did.

And the strangest thing was that she didn't look like much. I was used to vampires, who believed in ostentatious everything, the bunch of peacocks, constantly trying to advertise how old and powerful they were by what they wore. It was practically a coded language, but it was not one this woman spoke.

Her gown was rich in material, but no more adorned than Lord Rathen's. She had brown hair, piled on top of her head in a crown of elaborate braids, with enough left over to tumble loosely down her back, and brown eyes. Not hazel or amber or anything exotic; just brown. She was handsome, as dragonkind tended to be, and would have been remarkable anywhere else.

Here, she was honestly kind of ordinary.

Yet she *was* powerful and I didn't need the feel of magic brushing over my skin to know it.

Tanet was shouting something at the guards, but he had passed through the silence spell and I couldn't hear him. But Rathen hadn't moved, nor had Regin, except to pull his prisoner a few inches closer to his body. The woman saw the gesture and smiled slightly.

Then her eyes turned to me.

"Such a small, unassuming package. So easily overlooked. But that would be a mistake, would it not?"

I didn't know what was going on here, so said nothing. But Rathen did, while very slowly getting to his feet. "That is Dory. The one your lord seeks is Dorina. They are not the same."

"Yes, so I understand. There are two. Why did it never occur to us that there might be two?

"Another trick; another deception. But the gods were always thus. They hid the one behind the other, so that we could not find her."

Her eyes finally drifted to the man kneeling in the dirt and slush, who was staring at her with an expression caught between hope and fear. "But that is Lord Steen's problem," she added. "I came for my son. I will trade the information you seek for his life, then we will go and trouble you no more."

Regin started to say something, but Lord Rathen held up a hand.

"Speak, then. If your information is worth a life, you shall have it—of me. But House Ondar may not agree. Their daughter died in the fight your son caused."

The woman bowed her head slightly, and her eyes were somber. "I am truly sorry for the girl, and will speak to her family," she said, moving forward.

Only to have Regin's hand around her son's throat become a mass of scales and claws.

She stopped as if surprised, and spread her hands. "I have come to talk, Lord Regin. Or do you think I plan to take on all of you?"

"You don't want to know what I think, witch!" He glanced at his lord. "Don't believe her lies. Vitharr is likely here in force; we need to get back to camp—"

"In force," the woman, or the witch I guessed, laughed as if he'd said something funny. "Yes, that will do."

And before I could even try to figure out what she meant, Tanet ran back out of the woods, on fire and screaming. He crashed into the silence spell, scrabbling against it as if it was a wall of glass, his face terrible and half burnt away, and unholy sounds emanating from his lips. I didn't know why we could hear them, or why he wasn't changing into a form that the fire couldn't hurt, or how a silence spell had suddenly become a shield.

I didn't understand anything, until I looked back at the prisoner. Who had been staring at what I belatedly realized was an illusion, just like the rest of us. Right up until his mother shoved a knife between his ribs.

Chapter Thirty-Two

There was a lot of screaming going on, half in human voices, half in shrieking dragon speech, to the point that it hurt my ears to hear it. And I wasn't even that close anymore. I wasn't in the little glade, or inside Lord Rathen's tent, where the uproar was taking place.

I was in another tent nearby, where Claire was fighting fate and fighting hard.

"I'm losing him," she told me, looking up, her strange eyes huge in that unbelievable face.

And despite the scales sparkling on her cheekbones like glitter in a nightclub, and the otherworldly crown of horns disturbing the riotous red hair, and the all-encompassing dragon skin making her look like she was wearing a couture jumpsuit, she was suddenly Claire again. Her dragon half seemed to have retreated and it was just her, looking lost and frightened, because she couldn't save him. Antem was dying.

"Her blade pierced the heart, and I don't—I can slow it down, but I can't stop it. I can't stop it!"

"Slow it down, then," Louis-Cesare said harshly. "We need answers!"

"I'll tell you nothing," the man—the boy—said, laboring with every breath. "Nothing!"

And he wouldn't. I could see it in his face, his eyes, the clamp of his jaw. After all, when you're so close to death, what is there for anyone to hold over you?

I wouldn't have talked, either.

"Don't yell at my patient!" Claire snapped. "Or I'll have you removed."

Louis-Cesare looked slightly taken aback by that, as people did not have first-level masters removed. First-level masters went wherever the hell they wanted and stayed for as long as they chose. But this wasn't Kansas anymore, and I wasn't sure that she couldn't do it.

I also wasn't sure that it was such a bad idea. Louis-Cesare and Claire were like oil and water at the best of times, which these weren't. Anything to lower the tension in here would probably be a good thing.

"Can you check next door; see how it's going?" I asked him, despite the fact that we could all hear quite well how it was going.

An auburn eyebrow raised. "Could I search the village?" he murmured sarcastically. But he went.

He was a good man.

And he knew we weren't going to get anything, anyway.

"Why don't you . . . go with him?" Antem panted at me. "Or do you want . . . to witness your revenge?"

"I'm not here for revenge." Seeing him stabbed by his own mother had been . . . illuminating. I wondered what kind of life he'd lived, trying to prove himself to a bitch like that. Only to have her demonstrate exactly how much he meant to her, at the end.

His face changed suddenly, almost as if he'd heard me, the defiance melting into something else.

"I did hear you," he rasped. "I have . . . the gift. Better . . . than most. It's what made me . . . a good spy."

"I'm sorry." I turned to follow my husband out, not wanting to make this any worse for a dying man, but he caught my hand.

"No. Stay . . . for a while. I don't want . . . to be alone."

I looked at Claire, but she only grimaced and didn't point out that she was there, too. He hadn't so much as glanced at her while she'd tended to him. She seemed to make him uncomfortable.

I sat back down on the three-legged stool by his cot, a little gingerly. He was strapped down, the huge body half dead, and Claire was here. But he was still dangerous.

And we all knew it.

There had been two guards outside earlier and maybe more now; I hadn't been out to check since we came in here, with Regin carrying the prisoner who could no longer stand. But Antem's lack of mobility had reassured exactly nobody, so guards had been posted and would have been inside the tent only Claire wasn't having it. She'd shooed them out and staunched the terrible blood loss, but as she'd said, the knife had pierced the heart.

And even dragon healing abilities only went so far.

It was only a matter of time, but I wondered if the guards would be fast enough if Antem intended his last moments to include an attack on me. But he didn't seem to. His face, so angry and belligerent a moment ago, had shifted now that Louis-Cesare was gone, and there was only me and his strange attendant to hear.

Perhaps because we were both women, and he didn't have to keep up the macho pretense anymore? Or maybe he'd just realized how little time he had left. I didn't know, but he seemed to want something from me, and not just my presence.

His grip on my hand became more urgent. "Is she . . . really dead? What Lord Rathen said . . . was it true?"

"Is who dead?" I asked, a little distracted because the hand holding mine was slippery with blood and yet so incredibly strong that he could have snapped my wrist like a twig, if he'd wanted to. But then I saw her in my mind, as clearly as if she was standing there: Tamris, in her starry dress, laughing and looking like she had at the feast, and understood what he wanted.

It was the way he'd last seen her, I realized, because he didn't seem to know what had happened during the fight. Perhaps he'd already fled by then, back to Vitharr. Perhaps he had never returned from the initial trip, when he'd sold us out.

But he didn't know until he saw the truth in my mind, and his expression changed again. Yet he seemed to need to hear the words. "Tell me!"

"She died in the battle," I confirmed quietly. "I'm very sorry."

He let go of my hand and lay back against the cot, as if the rest of the fight had just gone out of him. I didn't have to ask if they'd been close. No one seeing his face would have.

"She should have stayed out of it," he whispered, after a moment. "But her father told her . . . to marry the lord's son . . .

whatever it took. I suppose she thought that meant . . . fighting at his side." He looked at me, the brown eyes huge and lost and tragic. "Did you see it?"

I shook my head. "I didn't see much of anything. I was . . . busy."

"Yes, I suppose so." We were quiet for a moment. "She was beautiful," he finally said. "But many are. She was also . . . good and kind and gentle. Her father was the . . . usual scheming courtier. So, of course . . . he used her. She didn't deserve that." He winced in pain.

"You don't need to talk," I said, but he seemed to want to, suddenly. To tell somebody about her. "We were to be married . . . before her father . . . decided to make his play. Times are . . . fraught. If Lord Rathen dies . . . Tanet will rule, but he is young . . . and would need . . . advisors . . ."

He broke off with a gasp.

"Her father hoped to be the real king," I said and he nodded.

"We hadn't told anyone . . . how we felt . . . but it wouldn't have mattered. He wouldn't . . . have cared."

"I'm sorry," I said again, and he huffed out a breath that might have been a laugh.

"I think you mean that. Strange, how the only . . . one with me at the end . . . is my enemy."

"I'm not your enemy."

"No? Perhaps not." He closed his eyes, and for a moment, I thought he was gone.

But then he spoke again. "Her father craves power. So, I thought . . . if I became prominent in Vitharr . . . it might change things. If Tanet rejected her . . ."

"You could be together?"

He nodded and labored on, despite the fact that each breath looked like it hurt. "Mother said . . . I could be a hero of Vitharr. She introduced me . . . to Steen. He promised—"

His eyes abruptly flew open and he leaned over, grasping my hand again, even though it was a loose grip now, his strength almost gone. "Fuck them. They just used me . . . didn't they? They used . . . both of us."

I nodded sadly.

"Fuck them," he whispered again. "And now I'm dead and so is she, but you . . . you can still save your sister. But you have to hurry."

"Where is she?" I asked, stunned, and grasped his hand with both of mine, as if I would hold him there with me.

"She's the key," he said, his eyes burning. "The one . . . they've been searching for. She can get through . . . was made to get through . . . the door—"

"What door?" I asked, somehow keeping my voice level when I wanted to scream.

"—Odin wants . . . it open, but the king does not . . . and he's searching for her . . . to kill her, before his god finds out . . . he told Steen to be quick—"

"Antem. Please. Just tell me where to find her!"

But that had taken the last of his strength, and his head lolled to the side, his eyes fixed and lifeless, and I felt a scream building in my throat that I had to swallow back down because it wouldn't have helped.

Only I didn't know what would.

I looked up at Claire, but she just shook her head, her eyes full of tears for a man she didn't even know, but whose story had touched her. I knew without asking that she'd done all she could. She wouldn't let anyone die if she could save them.

But she was out of options.

And now, so was I.

I nodded, unable to speak, and stumbled out of the tent. The cold night air hit me hard enough to throw my head back, to leave me looking at a moon that wasn't mine, the markings of which made no sense to my eyes. I stared at it anyway, as it shifted and blurred, and didn't know who I was crying for: Antem, the misguided boy, Tamris, his dead lover, or Dorina, just as lost as she'd ever been and in more danger than I could name.

Or me, because any moment now, I was going to do it, I was going to start screaming and just not stop. And there would go any semblance of dignity or respect I had left. I headed blindly off to my tent, eager to get inside before anyone saw me, and almost immediately slammed into Louis-Cesare coming back this way.

But instead of grasping me, of asking if I was all right, he threw me aside and barreled back into the tent without a word, leaving me confused and staring after him. The guards looked confused, too, but since he'd been let in before, they didn't try to stop him now. Or me, when I followed him back inside, to find Claire trying to pull him off of the dead man, while Louis-Cesare was—

I didn't know what he was doing.

I grabbed his arm.

"Mircea," he told me tersely.

"What?"

"Your father!" Blue eyes blazed into mine, while Louis-Cesare's hand splayed on Antem's unmoving chest. "He's here."

"What? Where?" I stared around, even though that didn't make any sense. Father was back home, probably with a champagne glass in his hand trying to shmooze somebody onto the consul's side. That's where he always was.

Only maybe not. Because when I looked back at Louis-Cesare, a hand separated from his own, a spectral thing like nothing I'd ever seen, and slid *into Antem's chest.*

"The *fuck*?"

"Dory!" Claire said, stumbling back.

"I'm channeling your father, or his healing abilities, at least," Louis-Cesare said, his face deathly pale and his body shaking from effort.

"How? He isn't here!"

"He is. He's in Faerie. I don't know how or why, but he is. I tried reaching out to him through the bond, but didn't expect anything. I was just desperate—we cannot stay here, in this place! You'll end up dead; these people are all insane!"

The screeches rending the air seemed to echo his words, and were probably why the guards weren't in here yet. The little noise we were making was nothing to whatever was going on next door. But he needed to keep his voice down, and I needed to understand.

"We cannot stay?" I repeated. "But earlier you said—"

"I know what I said! And I know you!" He stared at me again, and this time his eyes weren't blue, or even the silver they became when his power was surging.

They were amber.

They were Mircea's eyes.

"*I should have known you'd come after her,*" a voice that wasn't Louis-Cesare's emanated from his throat. "*As soon as I saw her, I should have known you would be here, too.*"

"Mircea . . ." I whispered, before trailing off and staring at him, speechless. Because first-level master or not, senate member or not, he didn't have this much power. Not to heal from a distance through the body of another, not to *take over* another, and a first level master at that!

No vampire did.

"*I am in a triumvirate with several others,*" he explained not at all. "*It gives me added strength, but this remains difficult. I do not know that it will work. But if it does, it comes at a price—for you.*"

Of course, it did, I thought, staring in shock at my father's eyes in my husband's face. And if that wasn't a mind-fuck, I didn't know what was. But the price thing.

Yeah, that was normal enough.

"What do you want?" I rasped.

"*Your word. I heal the boy, and you go back to Earth. I will return Dorina to you, but I cannot do what I must if I am worried about you as well. I cannot guard both of you!*"

"I haven't asked you—" I began, only to be cut off.

"*I don't have much time! Promise me, and I will do what I can to see that he lives. Fail to do so, and he* will *die.*"

"*Promise me!*"

"I . . . I promise."

The words came automatically, because that was what you did when Mircea Basarab ordered you to do something: you obeyed. I had been struggling against that habit my whole life, but had never managed to fully break it. And a moment later, I was committed, because—

"Auggghhhh!" Antem came off of the table screaming, and Claire moved to the door before I could, because I still couldn't think straight. Too much was happening too fast, and my body was injured, and it seemed that my brain might be, too. Because I hadn't even bothered to think—

What good would it do to heal him, only to have the guards kill him?

But Claire intercepted the suspicious soldier who was on his way in, and he didn't argue. He backed out, his eyes only on her, because everyone around here acted like she was some sort of monster. Which was freaking rich, all things considered!

But I was grateful for it now.

I'd been halfway to the door, too late but trying, and turned back to see Louis-Cesare with his own blue eyes again. Thank God! That whole thing was going to give me nightmares!

Although it would have to get in line after this trip.

He had his hand over Antem's mouth and the man was slumped against Louis-Cesare's chest, but he was alive. And looking about like you'd expect for someone just dragged back from the brink of death by a spectral vampire hand. His eyes darted around the room, slid over Claire with a shudder, and landed on me.

And clearly said "help me" without being able to utter a word.

"We have to get him out of here," I whispered, and Louis-Cesare nodded.

But Claire had heard my words, too, and she was scowling. Maybe because she was checking over her patient as Louis-Cesare slowly lowered him back down, with a stethoscope on his chest and a blue-powder-covered hand on his forehead. I didn't know what the latter was, but she'd used it when diagnosing me.

And she didn't seem to like what either was telling her.

"No," she mouthed back.

"No?" I whispered, glancing back at the tent flap. "Then what the hell would you suggest? If we leave him here, they'll just kill him anyway—"

"I know that!"

"Then what do you want me to do, Claire?" I was fucked if I had any ideas, except to try to get Dorina's whereabouts out of him—whenever he woke up again. *If* he woke up.

Because he'd just passed out again, which I couldn't blame him for, but he looked like a dead man and I'd seen a lot of dead men.

His skin was waxy it was so pale, and his eyelashes never even fluttered. The only way I knew that he was still clinging to life was the very shallow, very rapid rise and fall of his chest.

Maybe I wasn't going to owe Mircea anything, after all.

"The heart has been repaired," Claire confirmed. "I don't understand how, but that can wait. But he's in hemorrhagic shock—"

"Meaning?" I asked.

"Meaning he's lost too much blood and there's no way to replace it! And without it—"

"We don't need him well," Louis-Cesare said. "Just conscious enough to tell us where Dorina is."

"You did not just say that to me," Claire hissed back. "And you weren't here! His last words were trying to help Dory, to make up for some of what he'd done—"

"And that makes it all right? We almost—" He stopped when the rest of what she'd said registered. "Wait. Then we already know Dorina's whereabouts?"

"No, he didn't get that far," I said. "But he was about to. If he comes around again—"

"Then he can tell us, and after that, he's on his own," Louis-Cesare proclaimed, looking relieved. Because, yeah, that would make things simpler.

But then there was Claire, who had some things to say about that, all of which were profane. Including a few comments on Louis-Cesare's parentage that were frankly uncalled for. The two of them had never gotten along, but I thought they had mended things somewhat over the past few months.

Apparently not.

And then it got worse.

"Our instructions weren't to let anyone in, Lord Regin," one of the guards on the other side of the tent flap said, and the three of us froze.

"Get out of my way," Regin snarled and started to come in, only this time, my body was ahead of my alarmingly slow brain and I was there, sobbing.

And stumbling out into the night, drawing Regin along with me, those courtly manners overriding his upper brain functions much as whatever I was currently doing had done to mine.

Or maybe not.

Because the hand that grabbed my arm wasn't gentle. "How is he?"

"Dead." I started to move again, to push him along, to get us as far away from the tent as I could and buy Louis-Cesare and Claire time to . . . do something. Only one did not push a dragon. My arm never even moved.

"Dead?" he repeated, as if he didn't know the word. He looked so strange suddenly, so bewildered, that I wondered if the damned translation spell was acting up.

"Yes, dead, dead! He died a moment ago."

And once again, it looked like he did not understand my words. Then he staggered and went down to one knee, and I grabbed the huge shoulders as if that would do any good, while calling for Claire. But there was so much shouting from Rathen's tent that I wasn't sure she'd heard.

I was about to go get her when Regin spoke again, stopping me in my tracks. "I was going to speak to Lord Rathen. I was going to . . ." He looked up at me, and if anything, the bewilderment had increased. "I was going to save him, after he'd had a scare. He did a stupid, dangerous thing, and he had to learn, but I was going to save him!"

He grasped me by the shoulders, and if I'd felt like a twig before, it was worse now, as if I could be broken in half and he wouldn't even realize it, not with the terrible grief I saw on his face.

"Why would you save him?" I asked. "He was your enemy—"

"He wasn't my enemy." He looked up at me, those brilliant blue eyes haunted. "He was my *son*."

And then Louis-Cesare was there and pulling him off me, because the great body was sagging and threatening to crush mine.

CHAPTER THIRTY-THREE

So, that was how we ended up back in my tent, with Claire attempting a blood transfusion on a couple of dragons and cursing up a storm.

She and Louis-Cesare had snuck her patient out of the back of the tent while everyone was distracted, and hid him under the huge fur once they reached mine. Meanwhile, one of the guards had helped me to get Regin to the same spot, looking weirded out to see his commander so shaken. Which was good, because both of them followed my instructions meekly, like little baby lambs, despite me not acting remotely normal because it felt like I was about to come out of my skin.

"I'll look after him until he's better," I'd told the man, and sent him back to help guard an empty tent. Which, if he bothered to so much as glance inside, meant that all of our asses would very definitely be grass, and damned fast.

Yet, amazingly, that was the least of our problems.

Because, after kissing his son's unconscious face a dozen times once he discovered the truth, and hugging Louis-Cesare—which had my husband disappearing under a mountain of grateful dragon and staring at me helplessly from under one of the man's gigantic arms—and kissing my and Claire's hands repeatedly, which pissed her off as she was trying to help her patient, Regin had informed us that his old flame was fucking everything up.

Not only was she refusing to tell anybody anything, she was countering Rathen's attempted alliance, many of the potential members of which liked the concept of staying out of war. And that was exactly what she was offering, selling the idea of this being a spat between two dragon lords that didn't need to involve them. Or their blood.

And if Rathen lost the argument, there was a better than average chance that some of them might decide to take the off-worlders who were causing all this trouble to Lord Steen as a make-up gift, meaning that we needed to go. Now. But Claire wouldn't leave her patient, who was not well enough to travel, I wouldn't leave Claire, and Louis-Cesare wouldn't leave me.

Not to mention that Antem hadn't come around again, and I still didn't know where the hell Dorina was!

"I thought you told your father that you were going back to Earth," Louis-Cesare said, reading my thoughts while taking up a spot near the tent flap where he could see out.

Normally, having him on guard would have made me feel better, only around here . . .

Well, neither of us were looking all that butch.

"Dory!" Blue eyes flashed. "Are we staying or going? It matters if I am to make plans!"

"Staying." I took the fur that Claire had just ripped off her patient and threw it on the other side of the tent. "At least until we find Dorina."

"So, you lied to your father?"

"I didn't lie. I said I promised to go and I will—as soon as we find her."

Louis-Cesare raised an eyebrow at that.

"What?" I asked.

"Nothing. It is just... you remind me more of him every day."

I stared back at him. "You don't have to be rude."

"I'm not being rude. Do you think he started out the way he is now? He had to learn diplomacy; it did not come naturally. Unlike cunning, daring, and guile—"

"You can stop talking," I said, as Claire thrust some plastic tubing and an empty blood bag into my hands. "And you weren't there to hear what Antem said. There's something going on here, something bad involving Dorina, only I don't know what."

"And I need to. He said that Steen was trying to kill her on Aeslinn's command before she did something that would make Odin happy—"

"Odin?" Louis-Cesare repeated, frowning.

"Or Zeus, or whatever name he's going by these days. The bastard running this show."

"But aren't he and the king on the same side?"

"Yeah, maybe. I don't know. Do I look like I know anything?"

"Shit," Claire said, trying to tie a tourniquet onto Regin's massive upper arm to increase blood pressure and make it easier to find a vein. But the little blue straps that had come with her transfusion kit didn't fit. They were something like eighteen inches long, and Regin's arms . . . were not.

"Shit!" she said again, staring around.

"Here," I passed her the belt that Louis-Cesare whipped off, which worked—barely.

"You know how to do this, right?" I asked, because I'd never seen it. Claire was great with herbs, including the fey kind, and was better than average with first aide—on a number of different species. But this was not her usual bailiwick.

"In theory—"

"In theory?"

"Yes, Dory, in theory!" she said hotly, bending over the massive arm and focusing on the bend of the elbow. "I have the equipment, but I've never actually done it. You understand that, right?" she asked, looking up at Regin. "I'm not an expert, not to mention that you may not have the same blood type as your son, and I don't have any way to test for that here. And even if I did, our tests don't know the antigens for goddamned dragon blood!"

"It is alright," he told her, considerably more placid than he'd been before. Hope had done wonders, it seemed.

"It's not alright! If I get it wrong, it will kill him!"

"And if you do nothing?"

Claire looked at him miserably. "It will kill him."

"Then act. He wants to live, princess."

"I'm not a princess, as you damned well know!" she snapped. And inserted a fat needle into Regin's arm. It was connected to some tubing with a clamp on it, that in turn led to a blood collection bag that she placed on the floor. She then released the clamp and blood immediately started to flow into the bag.

I found myself letting out a nervous breath that I hadn't realized I'd been holding.

"How long will this take?" Louis-Cesare asked.

"Five to ten minutes to fill the bag; then I have a rapid infuser to speed up delivery of the blood, so . . . half an hour?"

"*Half an hour?*"

Claire shot him a stressed look. "That is assuming that he doesn't need a second transfusion—"

"You do realize that we can be discovered at any time?"

"And you realize that if I rush it, I risk damaging the red blood cells and all this is for nothing!"

"Then we can all die together," my hubby snapped, because this place was getting to him, too.

"You can leave anytime," Claire snapped back. "I'm not going without my patient."

"Calm yourselves," Regin murmured. "He does not need to recover fully or even mostly. Just enough to Change. It will do the rest."

"Even this far gone?" Claire looked dubious.

"Even this far gone. You have much to learn about us, princess."

"A smart man would stop calling me that while I have a needle in my hand," Claire warned, and looked like she meant it.

He shut up.

Red ichor continued to flow through the tubing and we all watched it while I said a little prayer under my breath. It was all I could do now. Except to distract everyone, because the tension in here was suffocating.

"How did you end up with . . . what was her name?" I asked Regin.

"The lady Tova-Rae." He grimaced, and I didn't think it was because of the blood. "She wanted to seduce someone among my lord's trusted advisors, to pick his brain for her master. We knew what she was doing, as several of her intended victims had come to us, but we did not know what to do about it. She is . . . not the sort of person one wishes to have as an enemy, and she had many friends at court who might not take her being ousted very well.

"Lord Rathen therefore suggested, if I was amenable, that I . . . allow her to succeed where I was concerned. And then do to her what she was attempting to do to us, whilst also feeding her and her master lies.

"It seemed a perfect solution to a thorny problem, and it was—for a while.

"Until she told me that she was with child."

"I thought that was a rarity among fey," I said. I couldn't remember any children running about the castle, although I hadn't exactly been there long.

"It is. Enough that I tried to make my relationship work with her. I failed, but I kept my son." He looked at Antem, and then reached over to brush the hair off his forehead. "But she is poisonous, and somehow found a way to turn him, after all."

"Tamris," I said, and didn't have to say more.

"Ah, yes." He looked sad. "That would do it."

"What could cause someone to kill her own child?" Claire said, looking bewildered. That was understandable, considering how many times she had risked her life to save her boy. "And to forfeit her own life in the process?"

"Forfeit?" Regin shook his head. "She is one of the rare dragonkind born with magic, considered a great gift to the clans, and has also born two children and may bear again. She will not die for this. That is likely why she was selected."

"That's outrageous!" Claire's face flushed almost as red as the blood bag. "What kind of place is this? What kind of people?"

"Survivors," Regin said simply. "Most do not remember, but I am older. I was but a child then, but I vividly recall when the gods decided that they did not need us anymore. We were a failed experiment, too powerful, too hard to control, too dangerous. They decided to wipe us out, and almost succeeded. Have you not noticed that most of the so-called dark fey who remain are the weak ones? Trolls, duergars, ogres?"

"I wouldn't call those weak," I protested.

He smiled slightly. "Compared to those who came before? I can assure you; they are. After us and a few other experiments became . . . troublesome . . . the gods switched tactics. To weaker armies who made up their lack of strength in numbers.

"They survived by being many; we by being . . . elsewhere. Those of us who survived their purge took to the skies, and for years we had no home. We could not stay anywhere for long, as whenever we were found, we were killed immediately. By the gods themselves, or by their favorite children, the so-called light fey.

"We only settled here once the gods were banished. But by then the habit of staying apart, of trusting only ourselves, of being wary . . . it was ingrained. Your father wants to change that; he sees this war as our best chance to banish the gods once and for all, and to be truly free."

"But not everyone agrees."

"No, some would like to join them," Claire said angrily.

"They think it to be the only way to survive. And we are survivors." He shrugged.

"It is just that some of us would prefer to die rather than to live in their chains again."

Claire didn't respond that time. She was too busy checking the blood bag, which she had been massaging for some reason until it got too fat for that, and she must have approved. Because she knotted the tubing in two places a few inches apart and cut between them to free the bag, then grabbed me to use as a human IV stand. "Hold this," she gave me the warm, fat bag of blood, which I held as gingerly as if it had been a bomb.

"Hold it *up*, Dory! I need a gravity assist!"

I held it up. There were a lot more tubes now, and things attached to tubes, and a larger bag that she held out so that I could put the smaller blood bag inside. The second bag had more tubing that ended in a little squeeze ball.

"Pressure infuser," she told me, as if I'd looked curious.

I didn't feel curious. I felt antsy as hell, which wasn't helped by Louis-Cesare tensing anytime someone came within eyesight. And vamps have damned good eyesight! We were all close to losing our shit, which gave me a sudden, much better glimpse into what regular old humans had to do when faced with danger.

It was easy to be brave when you were the biggest, baddest thing in the room, or so loaded for bear with weapons that you clinked when you walked. It was a lot harder like this, when you were outclassed and knew it, and your "weapons" were peashooters that I wasn't even sure a dragon would notice. A *lot* harder.

I exchanged a glance with my Hubby, and saw the realization settling into him, too.

How's it feel to be human again? I thought at him, and I guess he caught it.

Because he shook his head at me before going back on watch.

I looked back to find that Claire had gotten things set up to her satisfaction, because the blood was flowing again, this time downward into Antem's arm. She had the little squeeze ball in hand and after a moment or so of intense scrutiny of the line, began using it. Only not as fast as any of us would have liked.

"Lord Rathen talked about something called Fortune's Blade," I said, less to clear tension and more to keep from jumping at every sound from outside. "You seemed to know what he meant?"

He inclined his head. "Ah, yes. The greatest experiment of them all. An old legend."

"About Dorina?"

He shook his head, holding a little cotton bandage over the wound that the needle had left, even though I'd seen it close up already. But he wasn't going to argue with Claire. He was no fool.

"About Tyche," he said. "Also known as Fortuna, a minor goddess of luck who believed that the gods were harming the worlds they interacted with, and harming themselves in the process. They had become greedy, war like and cruel. Having unlimited power and the worship of millions was not enough. For them, nothing was ever enough.

"It is said that Fortuna wanted them to go back home, and dwell as they once had, in peace. But the greatest of them could not go, for they had grown so powerful that to return would be to starve. They were energy beings, and having unlimited power for so long had fundamentally altered them in a way that was not reversable. For her and the others, there was still time, but not for the rest.

"So, if any were to be saved, the greatest must die, or else all would eventually succumb to the lure of power, and shut the door behind them. Something that would ensure their doom, and ours. She therefore made, not an army like the greater gods were doing, but a single being, one that she hoped would be powerful enough to fight a god—and to kill him."

"How?" I asked. "How do you kill a god? I thought it took another god to do that."

"It does. And therein lay the beauty of her plan. She used a variety of strands in her creation, one of which was a rare demon trait to be able to take on the form of another, for a short while. It was fitting for her—she ruled fortune, the flip of a coin, an even chance for any contest. And that is what she gave her warrior.

"After all, if you are your opponent's equal, then the odds will always be even."

"Even doesn't guarantee success," I pointed out uncomfortably.

"No, but with a god, it's as good as you are ever going to get."

I thought about that, and about my mother, and couldn't take it in. Had she really been just another fey experiment, another failure? Because Fortuna's experiment hadn't worked. Not until the supposed uber assassin hooked up with Mircea, and then birthed something that maybe, just maybe . . .

But then what about Dorina? Was she the fullness of a goddess' wish, as Nimue had seemed to think, Fortune's Blade? And if she was, what did that mean for her, in the middle of a war against the gods?

Everyone would seek to use her, and few if any would care what price she paid for it. She would be merely another weapon, more powerful than the others, but just as disposable. And with that thought, everything in me rebelled, to the point that Claire had to speak to me sharply, as I had unconsciously lowered the bag.

I held it back up, but all I could think of was: No. Not my sister. Not Dorina. Not now, not ever.

I *had* to find her.

And as if on cue, Antem woke up.

But the one thing we hadn't counted on was that, after everything, he might be a little... disorientated. Okay, make that a lot disorientated, I thought, as he looked around at us wildly. There was no recognition in those eyes even for his father, assuming that he noticed him.

Because his gaze had quickly become fixed on the red line running into his arm, or as far as he was concerned, running out of it. I guessed that it could look like we were draining him, I realized belatedly. And that seemed to be where his mind had gone, because his eyes narrowed.

"Ah, shit," I said, right before Claire went flying.

She'd been bending over him, trying to reassure her patient, but Antem didn't need reassuring. Antem didn't need anything, because the next moment, a massive black and yellow dragon had destroyed my tent. And, goddamnit, I somehow always forgot how huge these things were!

"Shit!" I said again, and couldn't even hear myself, because I couldn't hear anything. Not over the enraged bellow that the crazy bastard was giving off, which pierced my ears like an ice pick. And there was no way that anyone else was missing it, either.

"Dory!" I somehow heard Louis-Cesare yell my name, possibly because he was right beside me. And then we were both bending backwards almost to the floor to avoid the enormous tail slamming through the air where we'd just been.

A second later, the tail's owner was airborne, taking off into the night sky. And I guessed that Regin had been right, because there was nothing wrong with his son now. But there was about to be.

But Regin had a head start on everybody else, and he scooped us up and deposited on his own broad, hoary old back, having changed in an instant. Before following Antem into the night sky, although why I didn't know. Because Rathen and company could kill him there just as easily as on the ground.

And it wasn't like anybody could miss us absconding with their prisoner.

I dared a glance behind, and saw the camp looking tiny and lost amid the vast forest, and a bunch of minuscule people streaming out of Lord Rathen's tent. They were pointing and running about, but in a weird sort of way. Darting a few yards ahead and then stopping, before doing it again and again.

And even weirder, none of them were transforming and following us.

"Why aren't they changing?" Louis-Cesare yelled.

I was about to say I didn't know, but suddenly, I did. "Claire! She's a null witch!"

"Can she stop all of them?"

"Guess so!"

But for how long, I didn't know. Claire had a gift from her mother, who had been a human witch, that allowed her to suck all of the magic out of an area. And despite Regin claiming that magic was rare among dragons, he meant Claire's kind. Because they were all magical beings who used their own version every single day.

Unless a null witch was clamping down on it, that was, and clamping hard.

Thank you, Claire, I thought fervently, and only hoped that she could keep it up long enough for us to get away and then follow us. Although the latter might be a problem. Because Antem had just noticed that he had someone on his tail and panicked, tearing across the sky like a shooting star.

I felt my eyes widen, my thighs clench and my throat dry out, because I damned well knew what came next—

And *oh, fuuuuuuckkkkkk!*

But Louis-Cesare had one arm around my waist, and Regin's mane in the opposite fist—or Lar's, I supposed, since his dragon was most definitely in charge now. And was headed after his son with the sinuous grace that I'd noted last night, which did nothing to make me feel less like I was clinging to the wing of a 747.

God, I hated flying!

But Louis-Cesare did not, and once he realized that no one was coming after us, he actually laughed. And started to make a whooping noise, which so help me God! I elbowed him in the stomach, and the joyful expression cut off to allow us to hear Regin's transformed voice, which was cutting through the wind as easily as his wings.

"We will secure my son," he told us. "And his information. Then, together we will go after your sister. Do you find this acceptable?"

I looked at Louis-Cesare, who looked back at me. And then we slowly grinned, although our lips were flapping back against our faces so much that you couldn't really tell. But I felt the arm around my waist tighten, and the sparkle return to a pair of blue eyes, even before he spoke.

"Now that sounds like a plan!"

"Good, then hold on," Regin said. "I am going to fly fast now."

"Fast?" I said. "W-what have you been doing?"

I didn't get an answer that time. I got a demonstration. And Louis-Cesare, goddamn him, was whooping up a storm the entire way.

Chapter Thirty-Four
Dorina

I did not sleep, but Raymond did, hugging me tightly from behind, utterly exhausted from the day we'd had. I tried to get up after I was sure that he was out, but he mumbled something and tightened his grip, pulling me further back against him. And I knew he would wake if I forced the issue.

And I did not want him to wake.

Raymond was loyal and good and often kind, but he had a temper, and it had been tested enough today. I needed information not a fight, and I did not think that I would get it if he came along. Of course, I wasn't sure that I would do any better myself, with my nerves every bit as frazzled as his.

Perhaps there was a better way.

I waited until he settled down again, then mentally snagged the ogre who was still helping the guards to hold the door shut. He did not run screaming like the first one I'd snared, perhaps because he was very drunk, and very focused on finding another flagon. I released the other two, who stood there, blinking in confusion, and peeled him away.

He would not be easy to control without a drink, so stop number one was the Great Hall, where the party was over except for a few unconscious types snoring under tables or slumped against walls. And the only ale to be had was dripping from spilled tankards and puddling on flagstones. But the ogre was crafty and he headed for the kitchens, where he grabbed a small barrel for the road when the pixies weren't looking.

Only that road wasn't headed to a pile of his brothers in a dark cubbyhole, where he had been planning to sleep. Instead, I steered him after the faint scent of Mircea's cologne, which his nose picked up as well as mine could have. We followed the trail like a bloodhound along intersecting corridors, up long flights of too high stairs and then down even more for this place was a maze.

It also reminded me of a patchwork cloak, looking as if it had been built by many different species over the centuries, with different needs. We left the rough, rock and timber construction and oversized everything of the giants' area and passed into a corridor with red brick walls and low archways lining a central hall, which gleamed with the light of many furnaces. My nose twitched from the familiar smells of a blacksmith's shop: coal, hot metal, leather, sweat and finishing oil, and the nose twitching reek of past fires that had soaked into the very walls.

I remembered the smell, but had forgotten the *heat*, so intense in places that the air shimmered in front of us. It was cooler where the walls blunted it and gave us brief moments of relief, and blazingly hot when we passed open arches and got hit by new blasts. I glimpsed anvils inside as we scurried by, so large that they were being worked by five or six blacksmiths at a time, their hammer blows striking rhythmically even this late into the night. They were manned by the duergars that populated this area and who stared at us, their faces closed and secretive under their ever-present hoods, as we passed.

They sent a slight shiver up my back despite the heat and the ogre noticed. He paused to scratch the itch that my reaction had caused on the brickwork by an archway, threatening to crumble it under his weight. Until a duergar came out and shouted something at him, and gave him a coin to go away.

He pocketed the coin and ambled on, passing into an area of mostly trolls. They wore the homespun, rough leathers and old furs that their kind seemed to prefer, with the exception of a dandy showing off a cape made out of scraps of velvet and satin. Most of their clothing was practical, and some was strangely beautiful, but none was what could be called elegant.

Unlike their surroundings.

I gazed up at soaring, arched passageways carved out of pale, sand-colored stone that were spacious but seemed slender because of their great height; at delicate lamps swinging on gossamer chains; at cooking fires laid in tall arches where statuary had probably once stood; at slabs of wood with crudely drawn pictures serving as shop signs and hanging outside of doorways with finely carved vines twining up the sides; and at lines of wet clothes flapping overhead like colorful flags, and cutting down the lofty ceilings to something cozier.

If troll height could be considered cozy.

The inhabitants didn't match their environment, an impression that was only heightened when we passed into a courtyard with an exquisite central fountain featuring marble cranes, where some troll women were doing their laundry. They had their sleeves rolled up and pipes dangling from their lips, while children gamboled about, the toddlers already almost as tall as me. One of the huge babies bumbled into the ogre and he grasped it by the head, causing me a moment of panic.

Only to see him turn it around and send it back to its mother with a light swat on the backside. It waddled off happily, looking for new adventures, and she raised a hand in thanks. And to my surprise, the ogre raised one back.

Unlike on Earth, where old grudges often died hard, here the two groups seemed to have reached a truce. To the point where a sole ogre in less than full command of his faculties could wander these halls without fear. And pass unmolested through to the entrance of a wide staircase going up.

It was as broad as the hallway, with large windows cut into the walls, following the slope of the stairs and allowing me to see out. And there was much to see, with a huge open area sprawling out below us that confused the brain, as it seemed too large to be inside anything, even a palace. Maybe because it was, I realized, looking back over my shoulder.

It seemed that we had left the palace when the stairs transitioned into what I now recognized as a bridge overlooking a city at night. But not like one I'd ever seen or even dreamt about. And which appeared to be built around an immense hole in the ground, the bottom of which disappeared into darkness, while the pale colored, strangely striated sides supported the buildings.

And there were plenty of them.

The palace sat atop one towering sweep of stone, right on the edge of the chasm, and hundreds of buildings were clustered around the entire extent of the rest. For as far as I could see at least, because the sides, too, were lost in the night. Or hidden behind other buildings, as the chasm was not a perfect circle, being stretched here and elongated there, like the banks of an irregular lake.

But everywhere I looked, were buildings and roads and people and *life*.

So much that it was impossible to take it all in at once, and left me feeling slightly overwhelmed. But one thing I couldn't ignore was directly in front of the castle, between it and the bridge. But its proximity wasn't the main thing that had caught my eye.

I felt the ogre's feet slowing as I stared in awe, but not because I had suggested it. But because no one could have passed by and not stared a little. If for no other reason that to figure out what, exactly, they were looking at.

There were islands of greenery atop slender, white columns spearing up out of the darkness below. Some were short enough for me to look down onto their tops, while others were taller than the bridge itself and partially hidden from view by its roof. They would have been pretty enough on their own, having the same deceptively delicate looking architecture of the troll area we'd just left, but these had an added feature.

A cluster of them had been designed to fall at varying heights, allowing a stream of water to cascade down them from some unseen source above, creating a waterfall in stages. I blinked my eyes at it, not sure what I was seeing, but yes, I'd gotten it right. It had been cleverly made so that the water hit, not the greenery itself, although that was doused with the spray, but stone platforms which were angled to send it flying onward to the next little island in the chain.

The result was that the water hopped from base to base, creating a silvery river untethered to anything but gravity. And it was visible despite the darkness as the islands had flowers and rock formations on them that provided illumination. The flowers glowed dimly, and were only bright where many of them clustered together, but the rocks had cracks in places, deep fissures showing off crystalline formations that blazed with light and lit up the whole fantastic structure.

I stared at it in surprised delight, the relative brightness allowing me to enjoy the strange floating river that the fey had made. The islands of greenery atop the towers served as its flower strewn banks and all of it appeared to float in midair. I knew that was an illusion, but it was a convincing and beautiful one, so much so that it took a moment for me to recognize that there was something else dotting the islands.

Something far more unsettling.

Ravens, what must have been hundreds of them, were everywhere. I hadn't immediately noticed them, as the bright, sparkling river drew the eye and their coloring allowed them to be almost invisible against the night when they stayed still. And most of the ones on the islands were motionless, having bedded down for the night, save for a few who were strutting about with their chests thrown out as if they owned the place.

But now that I'd noticed them, they were everywhere, swooping together overhead as if the darkness had grown wings and chose to fly. And it was a great deal of darkness, as these were not Earth birds. They had to top six feet, reminding me of the massive stone carvings about the fireplace in the Great Hall, which I had assumed were exaggerated in size.

But perhaps not.

But they were as mischievous as the smaller birds I knew, with some soaring and diving and chasing each other around the vast open space, while others were playing with some trinket they'd stolen from a guard. I couldn't see what it was, just that it flashed gold in the night, but the troll clearly wanted it back. He was yelling at them from a walkway a good distance off, clearly demanding the return of his possession, but the birds didn't appear impressed.

Several dove at his head, causing him to stumble backward and bat at them, while the one that currently possessed his property dropped it from a height as if meaning to return it. The troll somehow spied it through the flapping feathers and made an impressive leap, trying to grab it before it disappeared into the darkness below. And he almost had it, was just about to close his fist on it—

When another raven swooped in and snatched it away.

"Bastards," my ride murmured in his own language, but I saw the meaning in his mind.

Perhaps we should walk on, I thought, letting the suggestion glide lightly along the surface of his brain, and I didn't have to do it twice. He might get along with the trolls these days, but he clearly drew a line at huge, badly-behaved birds.

And, frankly, so did I. There was something uncanny about them, with their actions a little too alien, a little too . . . non-bird-like . . . although I couldn't have said just how. But it caused me to feel uneasy, and then there was the fact that there were so many.

We started climbing again, with the ogre staring about suspiciously and clutching his barrel to make sure that no rogue bird tried to steal it away. It gave me a chance to gaze about a bit more, including back at the palace, which had a strange mixture of almost Grecian columns and medieval arches. It stood out from brick, wood and darker-colored stone buildings surrounding it, glowing ghostly pale in the low light.

The waterfall helped with that, sending dancing light shadows to further highlight it, as did the two statues that framed the portico. This time, they weren't ravens, but a giant on the left, his shaggy beard reminding me of the one I'd fought in the arena, although his clothes were considerably finer. And on the other, was someone who looked like a member of the light fey.

I thought at first that it must be another giant, maybe a younger version as he had no beard. But the longer I looked, the less I believed that. The two statues were of a height, probably so that they would match or be seen as equals, but even so, they were clearly not the same.

The light fey was far less imposing, with none of the bulging muscles and stocky, square body of the giant. His facial features were also different, being more slender, almost delicate, with a thin nose and lips and high cheekbones. Even without the height difference to go on, one would never be confused for the other.

So, what were they doing there?

I chalked it up to one of the very many things I did not understand about Faerie, and moved on. Or rather, I tried. But the initial shock had worn off now, and I was taking more in.

Causing me to keep stopping to gaze around in awe and growing realization. Because it was a city spread out around us. An entire city of the dark fey.

Ray had spoken of their unusual use of portals, but I hadn't really understood until now. They really had just picked up a city and taken it with them, hadn't they? But *how*?

How could they possibly power something like this? A village, yes, that I could understand, although it would have been quite a feat. But this broke the brain to even contemplate, or at least, it broke mine.

And my ride wasn't any happier, although the view wasn't what had caused a low growl to emanate from between his lips.

He was staring at something farther up the bridge, near the arch where it started down the other side. For a moment, I squinted in puzzlement, not understanding what I was seeing. It looked rather like a beaver dam which had somehow ended up blocking most of the pathway, just a great mass of sticks and debris.

But then I glanced to the side and saw similar structures on the towers and dotting the roofs of surrounding buildings, and light dawned.

It's a nest, I thought, and felt the ogre nod slightly. He'd already known that, and didn't like it. Perhaps because the gigantic creation covered so much of the path that we were going to have to get a bit too close for comfort in order to edge around.

Or perhaps his distress was because there were sounds emanating from it.

Ripping, tearing, gobbling sounds.

He thought briefly about the battle ax slung across his back. But grabbing it might be taken for aggression, and anyway, it would require putting down the barrel and he was not putting down the barrel. He edged closer.

The nest was a testament to the ravens' strength, being formed of small trees instead of sticks and containing a worrying number of bones woven through the mix. Along with wool, some sizeable tufts of some unfortunate animal's fur, huge strips of bark, withered grasses, and even pieces of clothing, the latter probably stolen from the trolls' laundry lines. But those were just the supports; the decorations were even showier, including small mirrors, pretty bits of ribbon, seashells, someone's boot, which had been made of red leather and buffed to a high shine, even pieces of jewelry and coins stuck in patches of dried mud.

But despite the latter, no one had come to retrieve their items, and as I passed by using the scant open area of path left to us, I realized why. For there were two birds inside, still with the bald, prickly skin of the recently hatched, without a single feather. Yet they were already savaging the carcass that a loving parent must have left for them.

I did not know what creature the carcass had belonged to, as it was too mangled for identification, but it was the size of a stag, giving some ideas of the little one's appetites. They were tearing into it with glee, their beaks bloody and their faces gory, until they paused when we came too close, to watch us with bright black eyes. I strove to look as unthreatening as an ogre can although I wasn't worried about the babes, for neither was above a foot high and the blue speckled eggshells in the muddy bottom of the nest proved that my estimation of their age was correct.

But there were altogether too many of the massive adults about, so many in fact that none cared that one of their nests lay on a public thoroughfare. And had probably been there for years, as ravens on Earth tended to reuse nests, and this one did not look new. But then, who was going to disturb it?

Not us, we mutually decided, and assured that our feet did not linger.

But we weren't fast enough, for a massive shadow rippled across the bridge as we cleared the obstruction, covering us in its shade. And a rustle of wings caused the delicate lamps swinging overhead to sway as if in a stiff breeze. The ogre started and looked about wildly for a second—and then looked ahead again slowly, to find himself staring directly into the eyes of the biggest raven I'd ever seen.

It was taller than us by at least two feet, had huge claws, a truly savage-looking beak, and a great mass of iridescent, blue-black feathers with tints of green in them when the lantern light hit just right. But its size was not the strangest thing about it, no, not by half. Because I'd been wrong before; it wasn't staring into the ogre's eyes, whom it barely seemed to notice.

It was staring into mine.

Chapter Thirty-Five

I looked back in shock, not sure how it could see me, but being certain than it did. It tilted its head slightly, and that razor sharp bill came even closer as it looked me over, as if it had never seen anything like me. The feeling was entirely mutual.

There was intelligence there, I thought, gazing into those dark eyes. A great deal of it, and something else besides. Something like a distant mirror, through which I could see . . .

Was that me?

I realized with a start that I could see myself, my real self, as a blue tinged ghost crouched on the ogre's shoulders with my hand disappearing into his head, like a puppet master with his doll. The view was unsettling, and not just for me. The ogre started, as if seeing the same thing I was, and that left me with a dilemma.

His very inebriated state was causing him to question his eyes, but I didn't know how long that would last, and I didn't want to hold him against his will. Or risk having him hurt himself trying to get away. But we'd only just started and I needed him to help me find my father.

I had been too upset earlier to ask Mircea what he was doing here, not that I would have gotten a straightforward answer if I had. He would tell me only what he wanted me to know and I needed more than that. I needed a great deal more if I were to risk myself and Ray in whatever mystery required a senator and a Pythia to solve, which I did not believe was simply the kidnapping of a king.

Especially not one who had already been replaced and whom nobody appeared to miss very much in any case. And I didn't think that whatever this was involved the senate, either, as Marlowe had been sent by them to fetch Mircea back. I didn't know what was happening, and I wasn't going to if—

What was *that*?

I found myself leaning in, until the bird's beak and the ogre's tusks almost touched, yet I couldn't see what was now being reflected in that dark eye. But I wanted to; it felt like it might be important and I was supposed to be good at things like this. I was supposed to be very good!

I focused, concentrating everything I had on the latest tiny image, but it didn't make any difference. It remained miniscule, just a reflection that I couldn't . . . quite . . . grasp. Well, not and hold onto the ogre, who drunk or not was starting to squirm now, like a panicked horse fighting its rider.

Soon, I would exhaust myself and lose him. And with him, my only chance to find Mircea before his scent trail disappeared.

I had almost reached the point of giving up, not understanding why I was engaging in a stare off with a giant raven when I should be heading—

"Augghhh!" the ogre and I both yelled, because suddenly, what had been merely a glint in the raven's eyes was zooming at us like an oncoming train. My ride staggered back, crashing into the nest and getting pecked at by the two menacing babies in the process, who did not appreciate the intrusion. He tore away and started to run, leaving the hatchlings and their guardian behind, but it didn't help.

We might be pelting along the bridge, but I could no longer see it. And I had the idea that the ogre couldn't, either, because when we topped the arch and started down the other side, he skidded and flailed and went down, sliding across the stone floor and shrieking. We were kept from falling off the edge only by the raised side of the bridge, but it wasn't very tall as guard rails did not appear to be a fey concept.

Leaving us hanging over the side and staring into darkness, something that I saw in flashes in between the image I had grabbed hold of and refused to let go. And then it broke over my head, swallowing me into another place like stepping through a door. But this wasn't anywhere I knew.

I was flying over a vast range of snowy mountains that seemed to go on forever. There was a river flowing through a cavernous valley far below, but it looked miniscule as we were very high up with clouds all around. And ravens, so many ravens!

They filled the sky to the point that there was a matching river up here, a black one frothing the air in the hundreds, perhaps in the thousands, while swirling about a castle in the sky.

It was bulbous and huge, more like a city than a single building. I could not tell the exact size because the clouds obscured much of it, and because I did not get to look at it for long. For my family and I were diving, tucking our wings close to our bodies and heading straight down until suddenly cutting hard to the left.

And flowing into a gigantic cavern where clusters of the light fey stood, clumped around the strange wooden vessels with which they tried to keep pace with us, but always failed. A golden god stood in the middle of them, shining like a star, no longer trying to fit in or to pretend to be anything but what he was. And the one they called king was beside him, arguing in their strange language, which grated in my ears as we curved about.

He was angry and trying not to show it, but he did not want the All-Father to use his Svarestri to hunt down some myth. They were at war, he said, barely containing his temper. He needed his army here! Caedmon had been driven off by the great storm he had conjured, but would be back and in force, and his magic was depleted—

"Spare me your cowardice," the All-Father said, as I landed in front of him, sliding a little on the slick stone floor even with my claws to catch me. "Ah, my scouts have returned. Show me; what did you see?"

He took my head in his hands, pulling me close and looking deep into my mind, drawing out images from the day. He saw the arena, far below, and the towering giant, large even at this distance. He saw the tiny creature beside him, small and dark haired and utterly insignificant, easy to miss in the churning dust—

Until she felled the beast, almost without effort, and laid him to waste in a puddle of his own blood.

He also saw what followed, and as he saw, he started to smile. "Your queen had the right of it," he said to the king. "She had the right! And now we have the key."

"Unless her guard lied," the king spat. "I would not put it past him; he was stupidly loyal—"

"He didn't lie. Just as my scouts do not. I see what they see, and I have seen enough." He turned back to me. *"Fly! Follow the woman wherever she goes, and come back and show me. Show me where to find her!"*

The world shattered around my head, and I came back to myself only to see the city passing quickly around me. The ogre had regained control and was galloping down the bridge as fast as his stocky legs could carry him. I twisted my neck, trying to find the raven who had shared the vision with me—or the warning, as it had felt more like the latter.

But I couldn't see her. And it had been a her; I could still see the connection she had to her hatchlings, the way she had swooped down to find out what this strange, double headed creature was that had come too close, and feel her shock at recognizing me. For her eyes were as good as a master vampire's, and she had seen me down there, in the arena, seen me close up and knew my face.

But I could not see her; I could not see anything behind us but swaying lantern light, which strobed our steps and confused my already jumbled mind. Because why would she bother with a warning? She had been the one to tell Zeus how to find me, if that had indeed been him, and if it wasn't it should have been.

If I had ever seen a better representation of a golden god, I didn't know where.

It didn't make sense, but it did mean trouble; I had no doubt of that. I had thought Ray and I to be safe here where the sands veiled us, lost with a group of dark fey somewhere in Faerie. But it seemed not.

We needed to leave.

But I needed answers before we did so, and my father was still the best person to provide them. And that meant navigating the maze that was the queen's capitol, which was harder than it looked. Especially when the bridge suddenly shook, hard enough to throw the ogre against a column at the end.

And it wasn't only happening to us. I saw the waterfall judder off course for a moment and douse a passing pixie, causing her to fly wildly in a circle and chitter furiously. And the ravens abruptly took flight, most of them, maybe all of them, I didn't know. Just that the air was suddenly thick with feathers, a furious cloud of winged darkness, and then they were gone.

And my last chance went with them, because the ogre had had enough. He sat down, unplugged his stolen cask and took a hefty swig. And then another and another, until he'd drained half of the barrel and slumped over, allowing the remaining liquid to trickle into the dust.

There was a great deal of that now, with the great thud having caused all the soil that had been lying on the slumbering city to rise up and billow into the air. I assumed that a certain amount must have sifted in through the portal as we traveled, along with the sharp, earthy smell of its desert. But I doubted that any more was to follow.

We had finally stopped.

I tried to rouse my ride, I tried hard, but he was snoring now and I had no success. But a troll guard came by a moment later, his bootheels ringing on the steps. And in desperation, I leapt from one mind to another.

That was tricky in this guise, but I managed it, only to discover that the troll I'd found was going the wrong way. So, I jumped to a passing duergar instead, but was immediately detected and cast out, with harsh curses ringing in my ears. Leaving me flying over the city and floundering in space, just a disembodied mental echo tumbling through the void and about to lose any connection I had to—

I slammed into someone, several streets over, and grabbed hold thankfully. Until I realized: I'd slammed into some*thing*, a large, shaggy something that I couldn't control, having found no mind to speak of. At least, none that I could understand.

It also did not have eyes or a nose, and was basically deaf as it could only hear through vibrations. It *could* feel however. I detected the smoothness of the stone path under whatever was passing for its feet, which seemed to have a great quantity of long, scrawling toes that allowed us to shuffle along fairly quickly.

But with no sense of smell, I could not follow Mircea's scent, if it even existed anymore. It had become increasingly thin the farther we went from the palace, but not because we were going in the wrong direction. But because there were so many other scents now to compete with it, and no hallways to keep it contained.

Instead, I had been bombarded with the smells of people cooking their evening meals, full of strange and odorous spices; others sweating as they hurried back to their homes after the end of a long work day; and others heading off to indulge, with music, laughter and the sharp reek of alcohol emanating from cookshops and taverns seemingly everywhere.

I had been having enough trouble holding onto that thread of scent before this newest problem, and now it was literally impossible! I had to come up with something, and not just for that. But because the epic strangeness of my new ride was starting to make my absent skin crawl, my grip to wither up, and my mind attempt to release its grasp, shuddering away in revulsion, confusion and dismay.

I did not know what this was, only that it was far too alien for me to grasp for long. Instead of a lifeline, I'd found—God, I didn't know what I'd found! Just that I wanted *off, off, off!*

But the creature I was riding was being given a wide berth by others, and no one came close enough to identify with such limited senses. Finally, I took a leap of faith and threw myself back into the void although that could have spelled disaster. But instead, I landed on another troll, which I latched onto as strongly as I dared, my mind reeling, and my mental fingers feeling bruised and far too unsteady for my liking.

But they held; somehow, they held! And the troll's blissfully simple mind was like a balm to my jittery nerves, making the feeling of that other slowly recede as I clung to him. He was also going back in my original direction, but I managed to get him to look over his shoulder for a moment.

And saw what appeared to be a lumbering tree, complete with cascading moss that looked like shaggy gray hair, long, limb-like arms—at least half a dozen of them that ended in fingers so distended that they almost touched the floor—and tentacle-like roots on which it was skittering down the hallway.

I stared after it until it disappeared around a bend, my absent heart pounding. And then mentally shook my head and told myself to focus! We were running out of time!

I needed information, and a moment later, I caught the faintest trace of the scent that might give it to me.

Mircea had come this way, but it had been a while ago now, and worse, many streets converged at this point, dumping the late-night traffic into a central plaza. There was a profusion of interesting smells from all sides as a result, especially from a large central fountain perhaps four stories high that grounded the plaza. Or had done so at one point, before a profusion of ramshackle shops and food stalls had been built on top of it.

It was currently serving as the anchor to a thriving group of businesses providing the street traffic with whatever they wanted in the form of food, drink, shoe repair, toiletries for the needs of a dozen races, woolen outerwear and attractive leather goods. It was like the faire, if all the vendors had piled their shops on top of each other, with rickety ladders and heaps of overstock forming a path in between.

Most of the shops appeared to be closed for the night, although the troll spotted a goblin-like face with long, tufted ears waving something from halfway up the pile. It turned out to be a sausage on a stick, which had my ride pricking up his small ears. And tossing up a coin, after which the vendor threw down the proffered item.

It was a large sausage, but the troll ate it in a single gulp and carried on, past pretty girls of a dozen races lounging in doorways and trying to entice him over to their houses, where laughter and music were emanating from within. Some were taverns, some I suspected had other purposes, but to my surprise, he ignored them all. And headed where I needed to go, exiting the plaza on the other side and striding down an empty alleyway where Mircea's scent was fresher with fewer ones competing with it.

In fact, everything smelled fresh here, and green and dewy and bright, cutting through the dusty haze swirling in the air everywhere else. That only became more the case when we ducked through a door, down a hallway, and out into a cavernous room, half of which was made up of large, greenhouse-like panels of clear glass. Oh, I thought, staring upward as they curved far overhead to cover half the ceiling, and to let in light under the right conditions for the vast area underneath, which was packed with plants and trees.

I supposed such a thing made sense for people who moved as often as the dark fey court. They had many mouths to feed and having orchards and cultivated ground on board, so to speak, would make things easier. But the gardens, as lovely as they were, were not what held my attention.

That would be what was visible outside of the glass, which for once was not blowing sand. Instead of glittering golden bands, there was the biggest cavern I had ever seen, so large in fact that the massive stalactites and stalagmites edging the great space looked miniscule by comparison. There was water there, too, glimmering in the distance, but I couldn't tell in the darkness whether it was a lake or river.

Either way, it gave me an uneasy feeling, as Ray and I had almost died in a cave system similar to this one recently. I did not know if the two were connected, and in fact assumed that they were not as this one looked far colder. Icicles hung off the ends of the stalactites and some snow appeared to have followed us in through the cave mouth, dusting the rocky floor ahead.

Gooseflesh broke out on the troll, courtesy of my memories, causing him to absently rub his arms as he crossed the room, taking up what appeared to be a guard station by the windows.

He turned around to face inward instead of out, and the spear that had been on his back was now over his shoulder. It won him a cursory glance from a man sitting under a nearby flower draped arbor alongside the Pythia.

Mircea, I thought, my pulse quickening, as the unmistakable form came into focus.

Chapter Thirty-Six

I tried to focus my scattered thoughts, and hoped that Mircea couldn't see me looking at him out of the troll's small eyes. Or that the Pythia couldn't, I thought, remembering her reputation. But she didn't spare us so much as a glance with the two immersed in conversation.

"I don't care. It's creepy," she was saying, looking upward. I followed her gaze and noticed a ledge, high up on one of the walls not composed of glass, which was supporting a shaggy raven's nest.

"They are everywhere here, save for the palace," Mircea said, giving it a disinterested glance. "The boarding house I stayed in while trying to gain admission to see the queen had one on the roof. Chicks had recently hatched and they squawked all night, loudly enough to shake the walls."

"Why are they allowed here?" She looked angry. "Caedmon said that Zeus can see through their eyes, hear through their ears. It's like he's bugged the whole of Faerie and nobody does anything about it!"

"Yes," Mircea agreed, leaning back and rubbing the bridge of his nose. He hadn't changed from dinner, and the rich velvet nap of the royal blue doublet and trousers he wore under his robes caught the light as he moved. "But they also spy on Zeus for everyone else, something that he does not appear to have yet figured out."

"Or maybe it's us who hasn't figured it out," the Pythia said. "How do you know we can trust them?"

"We don't, not entirely. But they've been giving us more information than they have him, and of more import. I do not know if they can ignore his commands, but they seem to be selective about what they share."

"In other words, they have an agenda, like everyone else," she said sourly.

"You sound like this surprises you."

She got up, looking agitated. "No, I just hate politics—"

"Unfortunately part of your position."

"—especially fey politics!" She whirled on him, causing the tiny jewels sewn into the silver tissue of her dress to sparkle in the low light. "How do you do it? Just smile and smile—"

"And be a villain?" he asked, quoting Shakespeare.

"You're not a villain, Mircea."

"Tell that to my daughter—either of them."

Her expression softened, and she sat back down beside him. "I take it things didn't go well tonight?"

"If by well you mean being mocked by my subordinate and screamed at by Dorina, then yes, it went well."

"I'm sorry. I know how much she means to you."

That caused him to huff out a brief laugh. "Do you? Well, that makes one of you."

She frowned. "Things didn't get this way overnight. They won't be solved so quickly, either. You have to give her time."

"Yes, the very thing we are running out of!"

He abruptly got up and started walking around, not quite pacing, but close enough that it made me blink the troll's tiny eyes. Mircea did not pace. Mircea was decisive, focused and determined. Pacing was . . . the opposite of those things.

I had never seen him like this, and it seemed that the Pythia had not, either, because her pale eyes grew troubled. "You're nervous."

"Ridiculous!"

"You are, though. Why?" She got up and went to him, where he had paused by a flower that he had no interest in but was examining anyway. She put a hand on his shoulder. "If Radella says it's here, then it's here. She knows these lands like no other, and she promised—"

"Yes, she promises a great many things!" His hand crushed the delicate blossom, causing the petals to cascade through his fingers redly. "One of which is likely to get my daughter killed!"

"I think . . . that might be difficult," the Pythia said, smiling slightly.

"Difficult is not impossible," Mircea snapped, "particularly not here. And that damned pixie has clouded her mind with thoughts of a child. It's all she can see, all she can think about, and she won't listen—"

"You both seem to have a problem with that," she agreed, wryly.

But that just seemed to enrage Mircea more. "I am glad this amuses you!"

"It doesn't. I'm sorry."

She did look it, her smile fading and her brow wrinkling. Mircea didn't see it, however, being lost in his own concerns. "I wish we'd never come here," he said, low and fervent. "I wish I hadn't called you when the 'queen' wouldn't give me an audience, that you didn't know her—"

"Then Dorina would have faced the arena alone."

"And done quite well, it would seem! Which has made her overconfident, made her believe—" he whirled on her suddenly, something that would have sent most vampires, even most senior ones, scrambling back a few paces. But the Pythia never even flinched. But her look of compassion grew at the struggle on his face, one that confused me to the point that I didn't know what to believe.

Was it genuine? Did he really care, after all? Had I misjudged him?

Or had he spotted me inside my latest guise, and was busy trying to recruit a new power into his hands?

And did it even matter at this stage?

The answer to that leapt in my chest, infuriating and undeniable. Yes, it mattered, he mattered, and probably always would. But I was starting to doubt that there was any way for me to truly know if he felt the same about me.

"—Dolgrveginn," Mircea was snarling. "You know damned well that's where the old king is, despite what Dorina may have been told. The queen will suddenly discover it and make much of her surprise, and beg Dorina not to even think about going into such danger—I know how the game is played!

"But she'll go nonetheless, with her fondest wish on the line and thinking herself invincible, and how well do you think she'll do there? Against Aeslinn's whole army, and whatever surprises he's set up for us? Not to mention a god at his side!

"And even if I find a way to get through to her and end this madness, that doesn't even touch on—"

He stopped abruptly.

"Doesn't touch on what?" the Pythia asked.

He turned away from her again, but I saw his expression before that, and it was another thing I had never before witnessed. Whatever he might say, he truly did not know what to do, he who was never at a loss. I stared at him, shocked, and then became even more so when he spoke.

"What the devil am I going to tell her mother?"

The troll and I went completely still, barely even breathing, as a thousand thoughts tumbled through my mind. Marlowe had said that Mircea was looking for my mother when Ray and I first met up with him, and had repeated that story several times since. He'd said that father had communicated with the consul mentally to explain his absence and cited that as his reason.

But that was all he'd said.

I'd pressed the chief spy, wanting details, but coming from Faerie, the message had been garbled and indistinct. To the point that they hadn't been sure what father had actually said, only what it had sounded like. And when they tried to tell him to return, that they needed him for the war and that personal issues would have to wait, the communication had cut out.

Upon reflection, I had dismissed the story as Marlowe's way of distracting me from whatever he was really doing here. It hadn't worked, as I had never known my mother and rarely even thought about her. Why should I?

After all, she was long dead.

Wasn't she?

The Pythia also frowned in puzzlement, although apparently for a different reason. "Tell her what?"

Mircea looked back at her, and his dark eyes were tortured. "That we didn't have one child but two. A hidden twin who I locked away for most of her life and have completely alienated as a result. And who, because of that alienation, and a desperate wish for a family that isn't me, is about to risk her life on a damned fool errand for a coldhearted bitch and get herself killed! How do I explain *that*?"

The Pythia shook her head, her pale eyes somber. "Honestly? I don't know. But assuming that we find her, how can your wife judge you? She also left the girls—"

"One of whom she didn't know about, and the other who she thought would be better off in my care. The Svarestri were after her, and thus anyone with her was also under threat. I cannot blame her for wanting to get as far away from all of us as possible, but she *can* blame me. And she would have every right—"

He broke off and walked away, pacing in truth now, as if he could no longer hold himself still. And when he turned to face her again, what he said made no sense. Except to make me question if I knew anything about my life at all.

"I worked five hundred years for this," he said, his voice low and savage. "Changed myself out of all recognition, remade my life with one thing in mind: finding her. Bringing her back. Making my family whole again and undoing the sins of my past, insofar as that was possible.

"Everyone said that I was mad to even try. Let the past lie, they told me, but how could I? When it was her that was lying—stiff and cold in the ground or so I thought, and it was my fault. It was all my fault and I couldn't get around that, couldn't live with it, couldn't even die with it! I had to make it right—

"And in pursuit of that, I sacrificed everything else. I sacrificed *you*. Not intentionally, but in fact. Our relationship was never going to work no matter how much love was there, because it was poisoned from the beginning."

"By your love for her," the Pythia said quietly.

"By my obsession with proving myself! That I wasn't a man who had lost everything, that I hadn't lost at all! That there were simply problems that had to be worked out, obstacles to be overcome. I focused on that, on the next stumbling block and the one after that and the one after that.

"It was why I didn't try harder with Dorina. She was just another obstacle to me. She could do things, could possess people, which wasn't a dhampir trait. Or even a vampire one, for that matter. I thought she was a demon tormenting my girl, or the evil dhampir nature rearing its ugly head. So, I dealt with it, put it behind me, and never bothered to ask myself if there was any chance that I could be wrong."

"No one else knew, either," Cassie said, looking unhappy. As if she partially agreed with his harsh assessment, and yet wanted to comfort him. "No one knew anything about dhampirs—"

"The Pythias might, had I asked them," Mircea said, refusing to take the shelter her words offered. "But when I went to see them, what did I ask? It wasn't about Dorina—"

He broke off again, shaking his head. "They thought at court that I was fearless, that nothing phased me, that I was almost preternaturally composed no matter the circumstances, when in truth I simply didn't care about their politics, except insofar as they brought me closer to my goal. Everything I did, every negotiation, every back door deal, every risk—all of it was to climb that mountain a little higher, to put me into a better position, to give me power—"

"To talk a Pythia into taking you back in time?" Cassie said wryly.

She did not look upset by all this; it was as if she already knew. Perhaps she did by way of her power; she was the Earth's greatest seer, after all. There was no way to know how much it told her.

But I didn't think so. It sounded more as if they'd spoken about this before, some of it, maybe all of it. And that made me both sad and angry. I could have helped him, I would have helped him, had I thought there was any way to see my mother again, much less to save her.

Yet he had told me nothing, not even when we spoke today.

But of course, he hadn't. He wanted me out of Faerie, not given another reason to stay, and it sounded like he had somehow located her. I didn't understand that, but he had said it; I knew he had: "What the devil am I going to tell her mother?"

Not what would she have said about any of this, but "what *am* I going to tell her?" He used the present tense, as if she was still alive, as if he was close to obtaining his goal. Only now that he had, he did not seem to know what to do anymore.

"Tell her the truth," the Pythia was saying, for their conversation had continued while my head spun. "The senate runs on lies, but relationships don't. It is poison, so if we're lucky enough to find her—" she shook her head and got up, going to him and grasping his hands. "*Tell her the truth.* All of it, not to try to salvage your relationship, but because she deserves to know. And because she can help you. The girls are her children, too; she may be able to get through to them in ways that you can't."

"If she even wants anything to do with us, after so long," Mircea rasped. "If we even have anything to say to each other." He put a hand behind her head, his face anguished as he looked at her, and if this was an act, it was the best I'd ever seen. "I lost you for a woman I barely remember anymore, and never really knew. What if she was just using me, all along? What if my whole life has been a lie, not some grand romantic journey but a *lie*, one that I never had any chance to undo? Will the truth help with *that?*"

"Yes." The answer was stark. "You're right; this whole situation has been poison, and has now become your obsession. Most vampires don't live any longer than you already have, because they can't get past that final test. You have to finish this, for your sake, for Dorina's, for Dory's. Even if the answer isn't what you seek or anything like what you planned, it's better to *know.*

"It's the only way to heal and move forward."

Mircea looked down at her, and his expression, so tortured a moment ago, was suddenly different: softer, sweeter, gently amazed. "And when did you become so wise, *dulceață?*"

She smiled back, somewhat ruefully. "I've always been that way; you just never listened. But Faerie . . ." she looked around and shivered slightly. "It teaches lessons to us all."

And if that wasn't the truth, I had never heard it, I thought dizzily. The troll was shifting his feet restlessly, almost marching in place as my agitation and hope and fear and anger all made their way into a mind that wasn't set up for complex emotions. Any more than I was, it seemed.

I managed to calm him down, but it was difficult with my own mind whirling. They were still talking and I tried to listen, but found it almost impossible. It was too much; I could not take it in, not after everything else that today had brought me.

I felt like a mental punching bag, one with the stuffing coming out and scattering everywhere, or like someone caught in a crowd with every voice shouting something different that needed to be dealt with.

Ray, and the drastic change in our relationship—would it work, and was it fair to him to try and make it work? Faerie was dangerous, and his status as a master vampire didn't impress much here. I could be leading him to his death.

Dory, how to tell her that I wasn't coming back, that I wouldn't be there for her as I had in the past? I had recently made her a promise, that two souls in one body could work, that I would make it work. That we could both have a life, and yet that had been a lie. I hadn't known it at the time, but I did now.

How could I tell her?

Zeus, or Odin, or whatever name the vile creature was calling himself—what did he want with me, and how close was he to getting it? And could I even remain in Faerie at all if I was being constantly hunted? And by the king of the gods at that?

Mircea, the father I loved and distrusted in equal measure—could he be sincere this time, or was this just another game? And toward an end I couldn't even begin to guess at, because I couldn't trust anything he said? And now my supposedly long dead mother was in the mix, as well . . .

The troll had already recovered and was picking the remains of the sausage out of his teeth, while wishing that he'd bought two. And I viciously envied him that, would have loved something mundane and easy to focus on, because I couldn't do this. I had the best chance of my life to uncover some of my family's secrets, right here, right now, and yet I couldn't do any of it.

It was getting hard enough just to breathe.

And, as it happened, I didn't have time, anyway. For we were interrupted by an honor guard of massive troll hybrids who were headed this way. They dwarfed mine, with their huge, ogre-like tusks hitting well above his head, yet they looked to be part of the same group. They all wore deep red tunics with the gold and white blossom on the front, which seemed to be the queen's symbol.

And as if on cue, there was the queen.

"All right," she said briskly, flying in ahead of her guards. "Let's get this show on the road."

Chapter Thirty-Seven

The trolls lined up all the way down a set of steps leading to a door in the wall of glass. The queen and an entourage of her pixie bodyguards came next, the latter dressed in tiny sets of armor instead of their usual leathers, including helmets, greaves and pauldrons. And we brought up the rear: Mircea, the Pythia, and me, along with a few of the other trolls serving as a rearguard.

The door in the glass wall swung open and we passed through, and began traversing a set of colossal steps carved into the blue-black rock of the cave. They were as oversized as the cavern itself, far more so than any I'd encountered yet, as the ones inside the palace had been based on light fey height. That made them difficult to traverse for someone barley over five feet tall, but these would have given me real trouble had I been in my own body.

The troll navigated them well enough, however, jumping heavily down from one to another, causing all the armor he wore under his tabard to chime. I did wonder how easy it would be for him to get back up again, however. Mircea also had no issue, although the stairs were almost as tall as he was, and the Pythia simply flashed out and then reappeared at the bottom of the steps, waiting for us.

"You shifted," Mircea called out to her. "Does that mean—"

"There's another portal near here," the queen said, before Cassie could answer. "Up in the mountains. Some smugglers used it until it was blocked off on Caedmon's orders—as if he has a right to order anything here!"

"Blocked but not closed," the Cassie added. "I can pull some power through it, but I wouldn't be able to with the other, assuming it still works. It doesn't go to Earth."

"Yes, of course," Mircea said, joining her.

He didn't look embarrassed for what appeared to have been a mistake, because Mircea never looked embarrassed about anything. But I didn't think he would have in this case anyway, as his whole attention was focused on the void ahead. To the point that his body had stiffened like a dog on a scent.

Or maybe a wolf would be more accurate, as his eyes were gleaming golden bright in the darkness, and there was something distinctly feral about his expression suddenly. I felt the same, as if I could sense danger, although I could not have said why. The troll shifted under me, his muscles flexing and his hand adjusting his grip on the spear.

Only to get knocked out of the way by Marlowe, coming out of nowhere and leaping down the too-high steps behind us. Several trolls growled, although nobody attacked him, probably because he was known to be the queen's guest. The chief spy ignored them with the insouciance that kept getting him into trouble, and in a moment, we were all at the bottom of the stairs, clustered in a group.

It looked like an expeditionary force, and felt like one, too.

"All right." The queen said. "Listen up. This area is known to be safe as there's nothing here worth stealing. But that can change in a moment as we're all aware. So, we don't clump up like this and give anyone a target. We fan out, keep our wits about us, and make this a quick, silent trip. All right?"

She looked around sternly.

"And if we do run into an ambush?" Marlowe demanded, which appeared to annoy her.

"Who invited you?" she asked pointedly, her eyes going to the Pythia.

"Don't look at me," Cassie said. "I thought he was asleep."

"So did I," Mircea shot his fellow senator a look.

"Sorry to disappoint," Marlowe said. He did not look sorry. "Where are we going again? And what happens if an ambush finds us?"

"We throw you to them first," the queen said dryly, and my troll grunted in agreement. "Protect the Pythia if she needs it," she added to her troops. "She is fey friend. The others," she shrugged. "Good luck."

Then we were off.

The hike was long and difficult, for the only semi-level part of the cave was near the entrance. And since most of the rocks surrounding us were black, it was increasingly hard to see anything the further we went in. The lights of the city gave out quickly, lost in the murky air behind us and blocked by rockfalls of shattered stalactites everywhere.

I eyed them unhappily; this cave system did not appear to be entirely stable. And the darkness felt oppressive after a while, despite the ceiling soaring high overhead. It didn't feel lofty, however, and the usual cool air I would have expected to be circulating had a weight to it that I'd only ever encountered in close, tight-fitting tunnels.

I was not claustrophobic, but this place made sure that everyone was, including my troll, who was of a species known to like being underground. But he didn't like this, and his poor eyesight made it worse. I was soon missing my own body and envying the vampires' easy strides.

The hybrids seemed to feel the same, most of whom had not gotten improved eyesight in the genetic lottery and were floundering about much as I was. Instead of quick and quiet, therefore, our hike was slow, stumbling and full of muffled curses. And the pixies didn't help, waiting with barely concealed impatience for us ground-based types to catch up.

I wanted to point out that the tiny lights they'd brought were making things worse, as every time they shone in my eyes, I went completely blind. But of course, I said nothing. I was not going to be discovered and ordered back.

Not this time.

But Marlowe had no such reservations, and talked constantly. Unlike with Ray, I did not find his conversation to be soothing. It was enlightening, however.

"Alright," he said, as soon as we got underway. "As I understand it—"

"You do not need to understand anything," Mircea informed him. "You do not need to be here."

"Then send me back."

"If I thought it would do any good, I would."

Marlowe smiled slightly, probably because, as a first level master, Mircea's mental tricks did not work on him. Or at least, not well enough. "Then we understand each other," the spy said. "And what I want to know is—"

"Oh, give it a rest, Kit!" Cassie said. "We've told you what we're comfortable with."

"Yes, but not what I am comfortable with—"

"And your comfort is of paramount importance," she muttered, scrambling over some rocks and snagging the hem of her lovely silver gown in the process. "I should have changed after dinner," she grumbled, as Mircea helped her to free it. "But I didn't expect it to be this dark, and I thought I could shift—"

"Can't you?" Mircea asked, looking back in the direction of the stairs, although we couldn't see them anymore.

"Not if I can't see where I'm going—"

"And not by way of the portal we are headed toward," Marlowe broke in. "As it 'doesn't go to Earth.' So, where does it go?"

The Pythia shot him an irritated glance. I could just make it out in the light from a passing pixie, whose lantern lit up her face for an instant. A group of the creatures had taken their queen's command literally, and were buzzing about her head, creating a blur of fire that almost looked like a crown in the troll's terrible vision.

"Don't look at me like that," Marlowe said. "I think we can all agree that I have a right to know—"

"You have no rights," Mircea snapped, but it seemed that father's nerves weren't the only ones a bit frayed of late. Because the consul's chief spy turned on him with what was almost a snarl.

"I have *every* right! When I thought this was just a wife hunt, it was one thing. Stupid, ill-advised, even moronic to do it now, knowing what we're up against, but I understood. I lost someone once, too. I know how it feels, how it guts you at unexpected times—a scent, a smile, a glance from a pair of pure green eyes— I *know*. But this isn't just about your wife, is it? This is about the war and don't try to deny it!"

"I don't recall denying anything," Mircea said grimly. "But I will tell you this: you won't find anything ahead that you are going to like. Go home, Kit. Tell the consul that you couldn't find me—"

"As if she'd believe that—"

"You *didn't* find us," Cassie pointed out.

"No, I found Dorina, who you didn't even know was here." He glanced at Mircea. "You're getting sloppy."

"I'm also getting tired of this!"

"Then tell me the truth. This isn't about saving the dark fey king. That may be what Radella wants—"

"Queen Radella," a passing pixie said, and shocked him lightly with her tiny spear. It was a testament to how focused Marlowe was that he didn't retaliate or even break stride.

"—but that isn't why you're here, or Cassie, either. She didn't remove herself from Earth in the middle of a war, call in favors from powerful friends, and derail a whole city full of dark fey for that. Not when the bastard has already been replaced!"

"There are things he knows," Cassie began, but Marlowe ignored this. He clearly did not think that Radella's problems were big enough to explain the presence of two of the heaviest of heavy hitters and neither did I.

"And before you evade again, let me point out that this isn't merely your war," he added. "This is the Senate's war, the Circle's war, *Earth's* war—and Faerie's, too. We're all in this together, so stop dodging my goddamned questions and tell me what is going on!"

"He has a point, Mircea," Cassie said quietly, after a moment. "This does concern him."

"Finally! Listen to the oracle!"

"I did," Mircea said dryly, something that did not mean much to me, but the Pythia seemed to take it as permission to explain a few things. Things that had Marlowe's eyes widening in disbelief as she spoke, and mine probably following suit, although the troll's were so small that likely nobody noticed.

"You're both mad," Marlowe whispered, when she finished.

"Then go home and let us handle this!" Mircea said angrily.

"Go home? Go home? And do what?" Marlowe exploded, his voice echoing around the cave until a pixie zapped him again.

He brushed her away, his eyes never leaving Mircea, but his voice did drop to a harsh whisper. "And do what? Tell the consul that you're on a damned fool errand to another world because the *spirit of Faerie* told you to?"

"Told Cassie to," Mircea corrected. "And thank you for proving, yet again, that I cannot trust you with anything that requires the slightest bit of—"

"She helped us," Cassie broke in. "Any number of times. If she was on Zeus's side, she would have no reason—"

"She doesn't have to be on his side!" Marlowe whisper shouted. "The gods hate each other more than they do us! There's not one side in this conflict—there's dozens, maybe hundreds! Everyone is out for themselves and that includes her—assuming she even exists, and it wasn't another god fucking with you—"

"She *is* a god. But if she hates Zeus, too, I'll take it."

"Then you're a fool!" It had a hard edge I had never heard from him before. Marlowe played the fool when he thought it would get him anywhere, or the annoying, whiny guest, or whatever guise, I was starting to suspect, he thought would best serve the moment.

But that had not been a guise. I stared at him, wondering if I was seeing the real man for the first time, and had a hybrid step heavily on my heel as a result.

I hurried along, getting out of the creature's way, and Marlowe gave a speech.

"We've been seeing signs that Aeslinn and his godly backer may be falling out. I get reports, just whispers so far, but indicators that perhaps the King of the Svarestri is regretting the deal he made. And if you don't think he's clever enough to realize that he'll need help someday, if he wants to shed his terrible master—"

"I didn't speak . . . to Aeslinn!" Cassie huffed, because she was on her way up yet another incline and not enjoying it. "He almost died in battle . . . when on Faerie's advice . . . I took on him and his master. He wouldn't send me . . . after himself!"

"He might have had a plan and things got out of control—"

"Oh, they got . . . out of control, all right," Cassie said, laughing, only it did not sound amused. "Way out. The furthest out . . . they've ever been, and he was . . . right in the middle of it. It wasn't him."

That last was said as flatly as I'd ever heard it, and was a clear dismissal. She had learned to use her voice well since coming to her position, it seemed. Only things like that rarely worked on Marlowe.

I was starting to wonder what *would* work on Marlowe, and had the impression that beating him repeatedly in the head might be the only one.

Perhaps that was why father's fist kept flexing.

"That doesn't mean it wasn't somebody else with their own agenda," the chief spy pointed out. "Or let's give you that much, and say that you really have been communing with the soul of a damned *planet*. Do you really think she's on our side? The enemy of my enemy isn't always a friend, as people have been finding out for centuries once the battle is over and their 'friend' turns on them!"

"I'll take my chances with her . . . over that bastard Zeus . . . any day," Cassie panted, finally reaching the top of the latest mountain of rubble.

Only to curse, because it was evidently not the last one.

"I can't believe you," Marlowe said, looking between the two of them and sounding genuinely bewildered. "I thought you were smarter than this."

"Smart won't win this war," Mircea told him, helping Cassie down the other side of the heap. "Smart merely leaves us dying a little later. There are times for prudence and careful planning, and there are times for taking risks, Kit. Had you ever been a battlefield commander, you would know that."

"A risk, yes, maybe, but this isn't one! It's . . . it's . . ." Words finally seemed to fail him, and he just floundered for a moment.

"Kit," Cassie said, reaching over and taking his hand until he snatched it away. She sighed. "We need help. So does Faerie. She's tired of seeing her creation destroyed, or warped out of all recognition. All she wants is the gods gone and some peace for a change. And, sure, she could be lying, but right now, she's also *helping*. And she has information that we don't and could never get—"

"Like Mircea's wife jumping into a lake leading to another world?" Marlowe said sourly.

"To try to find us allies, yes. She was made by the gods; she knew them better than we ever will. She understood what we were facing long before the rest of us, and went to seek help. Maybe she found it—"

"Five hundred years. She's been missing for *five hundred years*. If she found anyone, you know damned well—"

"Careful," Mircea rasped.

"—they killed her ages ago! And no, I won't be careful! You're talking about following your dead wife off a cliff and *I* should be careful?"

"Faerie told us to find her," Cassie said, getting in between the two men, and likely just in time. "She said it was urgent, along with two other tasks that might decide the outcome of the war. But if you want to sit this one out, Kit, please feel free—"

"Two other tasks? What two?"

"None of your business!" Mircea snapped.

But the consul's chief spy was like a bloodhound on a scent, now that he had one to follow, and was not about to drop it. "Stymying Zeus's plans in Romania was job one, I presume?" he said, referencing a trip Cassie had taken recently, along with her entire court, that had thwarted some scheme that the head of the gods had had, back in time.

I had heard about it during a meeting of the World Senate, the body handling the war for the world's vampires, which Dory had slept through. She didn't like politics, and normally, neither did I, but this story had been . . . Well, if even part of it was true, I understood why the Pythian Court was often seen as an equal power in the supernatural world to the Senate or the Circle.

They had foiled Zeus's plans and sent him back to the present, where he had run off into Faerie with his proverbial tail between his legs. I had wondered, however: what happens to a god who has been humiliated by a dainty woman who was now hopping about, cursing softly, because she had a rock in her shoe? She had made the war personal, and that did not bode well for her or for us if he got his way.

Marlowe must have been thinking along the same lines, as his dark eyes were intense on the ground as he followed them down the hill, working it out as he went. "That *would* take a Pythia to do, wouldn't it," he asked, "as it was in the past. Like this requires Mircea, since his wife would be unlikely to trust anyone else. So, the third mission must also require something that only a specific person could do . . ." He looked up sharply. "Where is Mage Pritkin? No one has seen him for a while. Is he working on the third task?"

I said nothing, but for the first time, I gained a measure of respect for Marlowe, and understood why the consul valued him so highly. He might have certain unfortunate qualities, but he was sharp. Sharp enough to have Mircea scowling again.

But before anyone could answer, there was a sudden shout from ahead, where a group of pixies had been sent as scouts. I didn't understand what they said, but Radella did. She turned back to us and waved her small sword.

"Stop arguing and hurry up. They found it!"

Chapter Thirty-Eight
Dory

"What the hell is *that*?" I yelled, peering into the night. The yelling was necessary as we were still on dragon back, or should I say again, after a brief stop. Louis-Cesare was ahead of me, holding onto Regin's gigantic mane and shielding me from some of the wind with his body. But talking was like being on the back of a motorcycle doing eighty, only without the engine noise.

That didn't appear to bother the dragons, whose deep voices rumbled through the air like thunder, and seemed to have a permanence that ours lacked. Meanwhile, we had our words blown away as soon as we spoke them, along with the bonuses of chapped faces, frozen fingers, and tear-filled eyes, the latter of which was making me think that I might be seeing things. But no.

Louis-Cesare was also squinting and blinking and looking like he doubted vision that was considerably sharper than mine. "It... appears to be... a city..." he trailed off, because he knew what it looked like as well as I did and it was stupid.

Even for Faerie.

"Ah, it's wedged itself into the cave's mouth right and proper," Regin said, from beneath us. "Good luck to them getting it back out again."

I took a moment to absorb that.

It didn't help.

"*What?*"

"Hrafnavirki, the queen's capitol," he gestured with a gigantic claw. "It moves about. But the pixies only just assumed control and haven't yet learned to park properly."

I waited for the rest of that sentence, and for something that made even a slight amount of sense.

I didn't get it.

"What?"

"The city moves?" Louis-Cesare said, somewhat more eloquently.

"Yes, indeed," Regin said proudly. "It is the main reason the dark fey managed to avoid what happened to Nimue for so long. The green fey have been thrown into disarray due to the recent assassination of their queen, and Caedmon has dodged I don't know how many attempts on his life and that of his heir. The Svarestri have been trying to decapitate all of the leadership of their rivals, but it is difficult to kill someone if you cannot find them.

"Of course, they did manage to get Kaliphranges in the end, but the wily old thing avoided them for some time—"

"But . . . the city *moves?*" I reiterated, because I was fairly certain I had heard wrong.

"They stash it in a pocket dimension for easy portability," he explained not at all, because that was not how pocket dimensions worked. I should know. "But they have to re-emerge at their destination, and well . . . they sometimes misjudge the distance. Still, I'm sure they'll get the hang of it eventually, should it survive long enough."

I didn't comment. I was still trying to wrap my brain around the concept of a bunch of pixies tear-assing across the countryside in a floating city, which they were driving like a bunch of drunk teens with their first car.

That wasn't working so well, but the city was getting closer, and damned if it didn't look like someone had rammed it smack into the cavern's mouth. But it didn't entirely fit, leaving worrying cracks radiating deep into the mountain on either side, crumbled bits of former buildings scattered around the bottom, and a group of tiny people prowling about the rocks, gesticulating and looking pissed, even at this distance. I rubbed my streaming eyes, but the view didn't change.

"There goes their insurance," Louis-Cesare murmured, as Antem came up alongside.

He was doing better despite a beat down from his father, which had looked fairly savage to me. But it seemed to have been the dragon equivalent of a cuff upside the head and it had knocked some sense into him. It had also caused him to spill what he knew, not that I understood half of it.

Neither did he, as he'd gleaned it by hanging around Steen's court and overhearing things, not by anybody explicitly telling him anything. You don't clue in the stooge, I'd thought but hadn't said, because I was grateful for whatever I could get. Even if it was a confusing jumble about an ancient gateway, another world, and my sister, who was supposedly the key to both.

Antem didn't know why she was believed to have this power, but Regin thought that it might be because our mother had been designed as a godly assassin, and would need to be able to stalk her prey wherever they went. And where they went was apparently more extensive than just Earth. There were nine worlds that the so-called gods had explored and partly colonized, all linked by the ley line system that bound our two universes together.

While on Earth, their usual hunting ground, they were ever watchful, for the demon lords that were their favorite prey sometimes returned the favor and set traps for them. But on worlds that they held more tightly in their grip, they dropped their guard a bit. Giving an assassin a better chance—if she could reach them.

Regin thought that Dorina's mother must have been designed to follow the gods on their travels, even through portals locked to everyone else. Of course, that shouldn't have mattered once Artemis's spell blocked them all anyway, cutting off Faerie and Earth from the gods' highway system. And resulting in the situation we had now, with them on one side of a cosmic door and us on the other.

And we really, really wanted it to stay that way.

But Zeus did not, because this war wasn't turning out to be as much of a slam dunk as he had hoped, and he likely wanted the reinforcements that waited on the other side. Why Aeslinn did not also want that Antem didn't know. Or why either of them thought that Dorina could get around a spell that had held back godly armies for thousands of years.

But that had been their conclusion, after learning of her existence from a survivor of the band who had kidnapped her on the orders of Efridis, Aeslinn's queen, who had wanted to use her as a weapon against her hated husband.

She had figured out who Dorina was before anyone else, having met the two of us on Earth, but most of the fey she'd sent after her had quickly done what enemies tended to do when they encountered my sister. And the lone survivor probably wished he had, having been picked up and tortured by the king until he spilled his guts.

To recap, then, Zeus wanted to use Dorina, Aeslinn and his puppet Steen wanted to kill her, and if she got to the portal before either of those things happened, whatever was on the other side might be even worse.

I wasn't having a good day as a result, and it was not improved by the sight of what had just come over the mountain range to our left.

Louis-Cesare said a very bad word in French, which was echoed by some roaring from the two dragonkind, which the translation spell interpreted merely as outraged squawking. I didn't know if that was because the spell tended to avoid profanity, or if the sounds were an approximation of their feelings. But either way, it hurt my ears.

Like the thunderous boom that had me jumping out of my skin a moment later. It was so loud that I looked up, thinking that it must be about to rain. But the skies were clear, with nothing to see but a field of stars and some vague flickers of aurora borealis limning the mountains.

And the body of a burning dragon plunging through the air like a winged comet, screaming all the way down.

I started and looked back at the city, following a trail of smoke from where the dragon had just fallen, and saw—

"What are *those*?" I yelled, causing Regin to glance at me over his shoulder, probably because he didn't know human voices could get that high.

"They've brought out the big guns," he answered, and that . . . Was undeniable.

Those were big guns.

"What the hell?" Louis-Cesare said, because he was staring at barrels the size of lighthouses, with a few that were two or three times that big, that had just poked out all over the city. Leaving it looking like a hedgehog wedged into a mountain with its butt hanging out.

Its very well protected butt.

But considering that it was facing what looked like every dragon in Faerie, I did not give much for its chances. While Lord Rathen gathered his allies, Steen must have been doing the same. And his were all here, peppering the sky in force, a magnificent sight that was as unreal as it was deadly.

And the dragons weren't the only problem, because two Svarestri warriors jumped us the next moment, despite the fact that we were nowhere near the ground. But then, they hadn't come from the ground, had they? They'd come from the weird, small, roughly pyramid-shaped, wooden craft that was hovering silently in the air over top of us.

I tried to make sense of it, but it didn't have a propeller or wings or anything to help me out. And I didn't have time anyway, as the damned thing was like a clown car vomiting up four more silver-haired bastards. All of whom jumped down onto Regin's back like it was no big thing while I was still grappling with the first.

Or with one of the first, because Louis-Cesare had just grabbed the other and popped his head off one handed, like thumbing a cork out of a wine bottle.

The others paused at that, having apparently never met a furious, first level master before. And he was furious, crouching on the dragon's back with his color high, his nostrils flaring and that glorious auburn mane blowing around his head. But there was a smile tugging at his lips, because he hadn't had a chance to defend me before, and now he did.

I saw him give into the sentiment and full-on grin at the fey, showing a lot of fang; I saw them look at each other with far less concern than the moment warranted; and then I didn't see much else, except for a blur and a bunch of flying bodies.

And another weird little pyramid zooming up to help the first.

In fact, there was way more than one suddenly, with Regin and his son being buzzed like they'd accidentally stepped onto a hornet's nest. The small vessels were zipping about, spiraling over and under and everywhere I looked, although most were keeping their distance due to the thrashing of great tails and the snapping of teeth filled maws. Although I wasn't sure what they thought they were going to do even if they got closer against creatures the size of a freaking Airbus.

And then they kindly demonstrated, with a mass of lightning scrawling all over Regin's hoary hide.

He let out a bellow that I felt in my *bones*, just about the time that the lightning, which was coming from the base of one of the little vessels, reached the area that my attacker and I were on. And dropped us. We hit the deck, juddering and helpless, and unable to do anything but watch as one of the vessels attacking Antem was annihilated by a vicious swing of that massive tail.

The entire top half of the ship was destroyed, sending the base bouncing over top of us like a lightning-edged band saw, spitting fire. It somehow missed our bodies, just showering us with sparks, but the debris didn't. Including a shard that tore through my jacket and ricocheted off a rib, and another that stuck in my shoe and felt like it severed a toe.

But I barely noticed because I was currently being electrocuted.

What felt like fifty thousand volts had just torn through me, which would have likely incinerated Louis-Cesare, but he had jumped at the last second. And grabbed hold of the doorway of one of the little crafts strafing us, causing it to sling wildly around and dump out another contingent of surprised looking fey. They had not seemed to know how high a master can jump, or how hard I could kick, until I demonstrated by sending one of them flying.

Although not because I had planned it that way.

But because that jolt had done something to my nervous system that made me spasm and kick uncontrollably, including my Hubby. Who was trying to grab me while being dragged around by the crazy little craft he'd caught and wasn't letting go of, despite the fey he'd shaken loose attacking him all at once. Some of them trampled me and my fellow sufferer in the process when Louis-Cesare slung around this way again, and they followed him like a bunch of lemmings.

Deadly lemmings with bows and spears and machete-length knives, but he still wasn't letting go, I didn't know why.

Oh, that's why, I thought, when Antem spilled a wash of fire across his father's back. It carved a swath through the fey, sending four puffing into clouds of black ash and the rest diving out of the way. And one of the latter was tripped up by the remains of the first group of warriors, causing him to barrel off into the air with a vanishing scream.

That would have been great except that I'd almost gone up alongside them, since the blast barely missed me and the heat alone had set my jacket on fire.

"C-come the f-fuck on!" I yelled, my teeth still chattering from electricity as I tore off the burning leather before it melted to my skin. The motion jerked out the stake in my side, causing me to gasp and heave, so I ripped the one out of my foot as well, since I was already at maximum pain.

Or maybe not.

"Son of a bitch!" I screamed, attracting Antem's attention.

"Sorry!" he yelled. "Didn't see you just lying around there!"

I assumed that was dragon speak for "get off your ass and help us" so I did, although mainly because the fey who'd eluded the dragon fire had just snatched me up. So, I fed him a fist, and then decided that he still looked hungry and fed him a few more, while Louis-Cesare zoomed about, trying to keep the other little vessels from spewing out reinforcements. That didn't work, the fey having realized that we weren't as soft a target as they'd initially thought, maybe because we'd just run through two ships' worth of their warriors in about a minute.

So, they sent three this time, which meant eighteen guys, which meant fuck, I thought, staring at them blankly.

Or make that sixteen, since Louis-Cesare managed to skewer two with a spear that he'd found somewhere as they were jumping down. Or make that fourteen, I thought, getting off a couple of shots from my favorite gun before my attacker knocked it away. And then there were eight, because Louis-Cesare must have figured out the firing mechanism of the small craft he'd commandeered.

And the third little vessel got zapped all to hell as it was bringing up the rear.

But two of its falling, burning fey managed to grab hold of Regin's back, clinging onto the sides with crazed looks and burning hair, and then heaving themselves up and rolling to put out the flames. That was easy as our ride had started to shake and shimmy, slinging us all over the place in an attempt to avoid the electric blasts targeting him on multiple sides. He largely succeeded, but the two fey stubbornly clung on through the tumult, making the number of our assailants ten again.

The only saving grace was that Regin's back was ridged and scarred and vaguely mossy, providing at least a few footholds, although not enough. And that the fey I was fighting was a lot taller and sturdier than I was. So, I leapt up, wrapped my legs around him, and continued trying to punch a hole through that hateful expression to remove one problem before I was swamped by the others.

And to keep my mind off the fact that I was basically surfing a giant dragon across Faerie!

Stuff like that tended to freak me out, even when my hair wasn't crackling from residual electricity, my teeth weren't chattering uncontrollably, and my side wasn't bleeding like a stuck pig. Not to mention the wind trying to blow me off my very tenuous perch, who went down the next second, looking shocked that I could hit that hard. And probably suffering from a concussion, only his friends didn't know that.

They'd stayed focused on Louis-Cesare, expecting the little woman to be no problem for a fey warrior. And now they were enraged that I'd just killed him even though I hadn't. So, they did it for me, riddling his slumped back with arrows while trying to get one into me, while I cowered behind the now corpse because I am not stupid.

Although considering the shit that I get into, I might need to reevaluate that.

The only good news was that I found my gun, which had ended up tangled in the great mane. And although fey armor managed to stop even a .44 Magnum slug, fey brains did not. I got off a satisfying headshot, sending blood and bone flying and almost slapping me in the face because of the wind and the way that Regin was undulating. I ducked, and when I looked again, the remaining warriors had shielded.

Because yeah.

They had magic, didn't they?

But magic has its downsides, and so does forgetting about the master vamp circling overhead. Louis-Cesare's craft had somehow kept pace with us, despite being mostly burnt out from some attack I'd been too busy to see. But it must have been impressive, because he was dangling one handed off the little contraption, putting out flames that had caught on his thigh by slamming the face of a fey into them a couple dozen times.

Until he realized that a bunch of bowling pins had been essentially lined up for him.

He bowled a strike, or threw one, or threw the fey . . . my analogies were suffering at this point, but the basic idea was sound. And the shielded warriors didn't handle having their buddy chucked at them with vampire strength any better than a bunch of pins. Like, really didn't.

They scattered, with a few getting knocked off of Regin's back, the wind stirred up by the two dragon's wings immediately catching and whipping them away. The rest hit the deck and I got off three more shots in the confusion, and missed both heads I aimed at, because nothing was staying still, damn it! But I hit a knee, dropping a fey who had been about to put an arrow into Louis-Cesare.

Because nobody was shielded anymore, as that required concentration, didn't it? Something becoming difficult for all of us, including me, as I tried to reload with shaking hands while keeping an eye on electric blasts and burning crafts and leaping fey. And when I finally managed it, I didn't even get a shot off before four more crazed little vessels joined the fight, breaking off from the attack on Regin to ambush Louis-Cesare.

"Goddamnit!"

Chapter Thirty-Nine

When things go south for me in battle, it's rarely the threats I see coming that does it, and this proved to be no exception. Because Louis-Cesare spotted the oncoming vessels, too, and snared one of the fey below him with his legs for leverage. Then used it to pull himself down to dragon back, dragging the remains of the small craft along with him, before spinning a few times and sending the wicked little thing flying—

Straight at the closest two vessels, at least one of which must have been carrying explosives. Because they detonated in a fireball that enveloped Antem, who was flying nearby, in a mass of secondary explosions and burning shards. None of which appeared to have done any harm, except to his temper.

"Sorry!" Louis-Cesare called, as he turned on us with a snarl. "I didn't see you just flying around there!"

Antem did a double take, something that looks extremely weird on a dragon's face, having not expected his own words to be thrown back at him. Or maybe it was for another reason. Because the remaining two oncoming vessels suddenly sped up and kamikazed Regin, the fey inside pouring out of them as soon as they crashed with wild expressions that I didn't understand—

Until their ships blew up, too. They detonated in twin fireballs that sent a mass of flames shooting skyward, catching one of their allied ships as it sped by overhead. And riddling the dead body I was using as a shield with burning debris, including gobs of flesh, because some of the fey hadn't shielded in time.

But that was all secondary stuff, because none of us had been the target. Regin had. And he gave a scream that let me know some damage had been done.

They had probably targeted him because, unlike his son's sleek covering of scales, he had numerous areas where his protection was less than perfect. And some of them were now on fire. I saw flames leaping from cracks in his hide on the side they'd hit, and if I'd thought he was thrashing before, it was nothing to this.

My fleshy shield went flying and it was everything I could do not to follow him, clinging for all I was worth to the huge mane and feeling like my fingers were about to tear off. Even worse, the fey jumped onto Louis-Cesare en masse, and before I could help him, the bastard who had been electrocuted at my side in the initial attack suddenly decided to get back into the game. And punched me.

Only no, he *punched me*, hard enough to send me skidding on my back down the great spine. I can take a hit or three, but that one shook me. Enough that while I noticed him running at me full tilt, I couldn't do much about it.

Except to catch his fist with my face a half dozen more times, each landing before I had a chance to recover from the last.

And it looked like the shock we'd sustained had rattled his brains, because he was freaking suicidal, acting like he'd forgotten that we were half a mile up. The wind was threatening to send us flying at any moment, his long hair was blowing everywhere and intermittently blinding us, and our bodies were slipping and sliding on the large, slick scales right above the thrashing tail, where there was no mane to catch us.

Yet all he could seem to see was me.

Looked like one of the guys I'd killed had been his friend, assuming these bastards had such a thing. And he was furious about it, knocking away my favorite gun before I'd gotten off a shot, not that it would have hit him. I couldn't aim; I could barely see; and my punches weren't landing with anything like their usual force.

So, I bit him instead, sinking tiny fangs into his neck and hoping for the jugular.

I missed because I was dizzy and not a vamp, and gnawing somebody to death isn't nearly as easy as it sounds. But it sure as hell does panic them. He screamed, an inhuman sound that echoed like all the demons in hell had decided to form a chorus, and was so completely unexpected that it flustered me.

Enough that I drew back and stared at him out of a bloody face, only he wasn't looking at me. He was looking past me, with an expression that said he had something else to worry about. And then that horrible sound came again, but it wasn't coming from him; it was a dragon's scream, although not one I knew.

It was higher pitched than any I'd heard, enough to be a weapon all on its own, slicing through the air like a blade straight to my eardrum. And it was getting closer. It was getting a lot closer, but I couldn't tell the direction, I couldn't tell anything, and I wouldn't have been able to even if I could see straight.

Because in the few seconds while I was being beaten to death, things had gone completely fubar.

Fire was everywhere, although whether from Antem or someone else, I didn't know. But it was probably more than one source, because slashes of flame crisscrossed above us, shedding hellish light onto the scene. It didn't help with visibility, as the smoke from the remains of the burning vessels was spreading everywhere, since our forward momentum had stopped while Regin fought it out mid-air with somebody or something.

Something with claws that scraped across the great back a second later and almost raked us right off, leaving my assailant and I rolling out of the way and looking up—

And finally seeing the new problem, a massive purple dragon, although that was as much as I could tell with the smoke and the fire and the wildly bucking surface underneath me, as Regin finally decided that the threat was too great to worry about providing us with a stable platform.

I felt him start to roll, felt my body start to slide, and grabbed the fey a split second before we flipped upside down. He'd been doing his best to kill me a moment ago, but he was now my savior, only not by choice. But by virtue of the knife that he'd just plunged into Regin's back in a desperate attempt to hang on.

He'd found a chink in the armor, and driven the blade in sideways, all the way to the hilt. That allowed him to hit the still whole scales below the knife as we rotated, preventing it from slipping out again and us from plunging to our deaths. It probably wasn't enough to seriously damage such a huge creature but did not make him happy.

It did me.

I held onto the fey as the great body rolled over, spilling some of his comrades off the side while he clutched the knife for all he was worth. His feet scrabbled for purchase on the smoother hide down here, and somehow found it, like mine found some around him. And he didn't even try to throw me off, as he was clearly too terrified.

Guess Svarestri boot camp didn't cover this one, huh? I thought, and stabbed him.

He looked back at me in shock more than anything else, because he must have thought that he was safe as long as we were upside down. But I didn't need him, I needed his knife; the same one he was going to stab me with as soon as we rolled back over. Which we did as I grabbed his blade, as I twisted my own, as I saw the light die in his eyes and pushed him off.

And stood up again, bloody, beaten, and holding two knives now, as I tore the fey's free of Regin's back.

Because they *do* cover shit like this in dhampir boot camp. The lesson was the first I'd ever learned: survive. And make sure that your partner does, too, only Louis-Cesare didn't need the help.

He raised a bloody face to me with fangs fully extended, and then threw away the empty he had just finished draining. It looked like the group who'd jumped him hadn't had a good time, including those who had somehow managed to hold on for the ride. Maybe especially those, I thought, seeing drained, withered fey with hands and feet still tucked under scales or tangled in that great mane, and all but fluttering in the breeze as they were now basically husks.

And the dragon who had been menacing us wasn't doing any better, as he or she was currently getting eaten by Antem.

Lord Rathen had been right when he said the guy liked to show off. Because he'd wrapped his body all the way around his father's attacker while he feasted, and now he let his prey go with half of the creature's face missing and a long stream of blood spurting over the crazy, smoke riddled scene. And roared his defiance at the skies.

I stared at him for a moment, my heart threatening to beat out of my chest, because that was one of those images that stayed with you. Years from now, centuries even, I would remember that. Assuming I survived, which was debatable as our orientation had just shifted.

We were diving, so suddenly that I ran down the length of the spine helplessly, and practically airborne. Until Louis-Cesare grabbed me and pulled me back from the abyss, and I clung to him, both of us crouching and grabbing onto the great mane, while I stared around, looking for the next attack. But there didn't seem to be one.

Amazingly, the fey were gone now and we were moving so fast that I defied any more to catch us, so fast that the only reason I wasn't blown off was the strong arms around me.

And then the lights went out.

It happened between one blink and the next, to the point that, for a moment, I thought my brain was on the fritz again. But I wasn't unconscious, and I could hear Louis-Cesare reassuring me. Not what he said, but the rumble in his chest against mine.

After a moment, I began to be able to see intermittently, as there were cracks in the enveloping darkness, cracks that I finally recognized as gaps in an overhanging tunnel of rock. One that we were flying through at mind numbing speeds, to the point that the dim moonlight did nothing but strobe the scene, showing me little. Until a city emerged from the enveloping rock, so fast that it basically slapped us in the face.

It was the capitol, as the *crack-boom* of one of the great guns made clear, at almost the second we appeared. The sound was so deafening in the enclosed cavern that I thought my head was going to explode, and what I could see wasn't any more reassuring. The city had already sustained damage, and more was coming.

We had exited whatever shortcut through the mountains Regin had found and flown right into a crowded street filled with running, screaming pedestrians of all species, many sheltering children in their arms, and most with bags of possessions thrown over their backs.

But there was no refuge here, with buildings shattering and coming down as huge fireballs boiled through the city. One hit a nearby tower, strewing massive blocks of stone across the street; another tore by overhead, sending the huge amount of dust that was in the air for some reason curling up behind it, lashing our faces and burning our eyes; and a third hit Antem a glancing blow, causing him to whip about with a snarl on his bloody maw. Not surprisingly, fires had broken out in numerous places, adding black smoke to the mix that made it hard to breathe, much less to see.

But people could see us, and the appearance of two of the creatures currently attacking the city brought pandemonium to the fleeing civilians. Regin shouted something, but for once, the great voice didn't manage to reach far enough to reassure them, or even to hit my own ears. But it must have his son's, because we swooped up and landed on the same rooftop a moment later.

It was higher than most of the street, to the point that I was surprised that the dragons had been able to get there at all, as I could have reached out and touched the end of the nearest stalactite. There were masses of them hanging down from the cavern's ceiling, sparkling in the reflected flames like uncut diamonds, and quivering menacingly every time one of those cannons went off. Which was pretty much constantly, to the point that the limestone forest overhead was chiming almost as loudly as the guns.

I didn't see much of the cavern that didn't have them, meaning that flying above street level was basically out. Columns of rock also speared down in places, far enough to block whole avenues, forcing people to go around. Only where they were going, I didn't know, as outside was—

Not good, I thought, as an explosion rocked us, almost causing me to be thrown off my feet. A fireball had caught something flammable in a nearby building, which went up like a bomb. And caused the screaming in the surrounding streets to ramp up to a decibel level I hadn't thought possible.

"Why are there no shields?" Louis-Cesare was yelling.

"Good question," Antem rumbled and transformed, because he'd clearly made the same assessment on the chances of flying anywhere that I had.

Louis-Cesare and I slid down Regin's back, dropping onto the roof. And allowing him to transform a second later, causing a bunch of fluttery, drained fey to fall to the rooftop beside us, their desiccated, staring faces looking up accusingly. I looked back at them and then all around, at the exploding, chiming, burning city, and had another of those dizzying, you-are-in-over-your-head moments I had been experiencing ever since I got here.

I mentally slapped myself, because I *was* here and I had better get a goddamned *grip*.

The building moved under our feet, causing me to stumble. It was in the area nearest the cavern walls, so had probably been weakened by the parking job the pixies had done. At least, I truly hoped it wasn't like this everywhere, as I had to get across the city to the portal that Antem claimed Dorina was likely headed to, which . . .

Wasn't looking fun, I thought, as several stalactites cleaved off the ceiling and fell like massive icicles, one shattering in the street below and one spearing down onto a nearby building, which fortunately had a stone roof.

Not all of them did, and there were a lot of icicles. Or to be more accurate, there were a lot of limestone daggers poised to fall on whatever was left of the city once the dragons finished with it, not that they were in here yet. One of the reasons I couldn't concentrate was the relentless boom-boom-boom of the mega cannons that the fey were firing non-stop at the attacking army.

I wondered how much ammo they had. I wondered what happened when it ran out. I wondered why I was wondering, because the answer was freaking obvious, Dory!

And then Louis-Cesare was shaking me. "All right?" he all but screamed in my face.

I nodded, and then shook my head. I had no idea what they'd been saying, and not just because of the distraction of being in a city coming down around my head. I'd been there before, but the *cannons*—

They need to reach the controls for the shields, echoed through my mind. *If they don't, everyone will die. I told them we would take it from here, all right?*

I looked at him like he was crazy, because I'd just been calculating the odds of making it across this place *with them*. And they hadn't been good! Going without wasn't just insane; it was futile.

And I hadn't come this far to die without getting out of the goddamned city!

No, I thought as hard as I could. *We'll go with them.*

I didn't explain any further. I couldn't think well enough, and wasn't even sure that my answer got through. But I guessed so, because Louis-Cesare turned and shouted something at the dragons, and then a very tactile tail was wrapping around me, was throwing me onto a spreading mass of scales, was—

"What is he *doing?*" I screamed, because Antem had been the one to grab us this time, throwing us on his back less than gently, although that wasn't the problem. The problem was—*goddamn!*

My head jerked back, my hands scrambled to find purchase on the great mane, and my legs flexed uselessly as there was nothing to hold onto. And if I thought that Regin had been insane in the air, I now understood that he had been doing everything possible to give us a smooth, controlled ride. Because his son . . . did not.

Antem took off like a bat out of hell, ignoring the fact that flying was all but impossible in here, and made it happen anyway. He dodged the masses of stalactites with the liquid speed of a snake swimming through water, with them coming at us so thick and fast that I could do nothing except hang on, getting whiplash. And wondering what would happen if we plowed into some of the ones as big as houses that must have been growing for hundreds of years.

I decided not to think about that, right before we brushed one too closely, scattering chunks across the great back and sending cold, limestone dust flying into my face. And had another break free just after we slid underneath, and fall, crashing to the ground somewhere very far below because this city wasn't level. Wasn't close to level, I realized, staring down at chasms and then almost slamming face first into a cliffside springing up out of nowhere because we were breaking every speed record known to man.

Nor was it looking like a single city. From what little I could grasp in between the obstacle course from hell, it looked like maybe a dozen smaller ones that had been squashed together and built on top of each other and—and it was a mess, an utter jumbled mess, and it was getting worse. Because, in the short amount of time we'd had, Steen's creatures had started to make it past the cannons.

I twisted my neck around and saw three behemoths bulldozing their way into the city, strafing it with fire and causing an avalanche of falling limestone spears, and knew we were too late. The *boom-boom-boom* still shivered the air around us, but the dragons were now behind the guns, which probably had minutes left, if that. And once they were gone...

So was everything else.

Regin, who I hadn't even noticed following us, broke off to grab an iridescent green monster of a creature almost his own size, and they fell writhing onto a nearby building, crushing the upper floors in the process. But there was only one of him and there were more of them, and I wasn't even sure that he was winning. Neither was his son, who screamed and banked and shot back to help, only to have his father roar something at him.

It was likely "get to the shield" but I couldn't tell. I couldn't hear even the translation spell crackling in my ear, couldn't hear anything. Because the dragons were flooding in now, with several working together to melt the biggest cannon, sending three streams of brilliant crimson fire down on it that didn't stop it from getting another shot off, and plucking a black specimen out of the sky, sending him shooting backwards out of the cave's mouth.

But that was its last gasp, after which it fell silent.

And that created a breech in the city's armor. One that was taken advantage of by dozens of sleek, firelit forms that were suddenly spilling in on what looked like a wave of flame near the cavern's mouth, one that was about to roll over the whole damned place. And there was absolutely nothing we could do to stop it.

I saw the truth on Louis-Cesare's face, his hair flame red in the reflected light. He had seen first hand what Steen's people had done at the faire, knew what was coming. And so did I, my gut knotting as I fought to hold on, as Antem ignored his father's orders and joined the fight to save him, because it was already too late for anyone else.

And then a new sound came to my suffering ears. One that cut through the din like a sword through flesh, cleaving it until it receded into the background, until it left only that one, pure note singing above the rest. It echoed around the cavern, vibrated through my bones, and caused me to look around wildly because I knew that sound.

I shouldn't have, but I did, because I'd heard something like it a hundred times before, and so had Louis-Cesare. A note from another time, but one that, once you heard it, you never forgot. A trumpet's cry, rallying troops to battle.

And to battle they came, a mass of dragons streaming in the cavern's mouth and screeching a challenge, so many and so loud that it ran together into a mad chorus in my head, deafening and indistinguishable from each other. But I didn't need to hear them to understand: Lord Rathen had arrived. And he'd brought friends.

I guess he won the argument, I thought dizzily, as the army he'd been gathering in the forest flowed into the breech, chased down the enemies who had already gotten past, and tackled fire-breathing behemoths in mid-air. It wasn't an overwhelming force; the odds looked even to me, because Steen had supporters, too. But it was enough.

Instead of a slaughter, we suddenly had a battle, and a reason for Regin to turn on his son, his maw bloody and dripping from savaging his enemy. "Go! Get the damned shield up! We'll take care of the rest."

Chapter Forty
Dorina

The "it" Radella had mentioned turned out to be a fissure in the back wall of the cavern, although that description didn't do it justice. It was maybe fourteen stories high and blazing with light, although the weird air of the cave gobbled it up at any distance, ensuring that it did not help much with the gloom. But it was easily visible as we moved forward, if hazy at the edges.

We made for it as fast as we could considering that the debris field was becoming thicker, with some of the fallen stalactites the size of redwoods, requiring us to go around. Or to find a path through the thousands of splintered fragments standing higher than our heads in places. Mircea and the Pythia suddenly vanished, probably shifting to avoid the extra effort, and the queen flew ahead with her bodyguard.

That left the me, the trolls and Marlowe to flounder around in the dark, but he floundered fast. To the point that I could not keep up with him in this guise, despite the fact that trolls could move quicker than you'd expect when motivated. They were also perfectly suited for this sort of work, with skin that didn't tear on jagged edges and with instincts honed from years of living underground, almost negating the need for eyes.

As a result, we caught up with the chief spy again at the fissure, where he had stopped to examine it before going in. He was gazing up at the great scar, where the rock of the cavern's back wall had been cleaved in two. It was strangely sharp-edged and shiny, completely unlike the fractured forest we'd left behind, possibly because this wasn't limestone.

It reminded me of the hard, obsidian-like stairs we'd used to descend into the cave, with the same dusty black color. Only those had been hewn by axes and then smoothed out by the wind that blew in the cave's mouth over who knew how many years. While this looked more like glass that had been cut by a laser and then fractured in places than anything naturally occurring.

When Marlowe had examined it sufficiently, he turned around and looked behind us, still staring upward, so I did the same.

And realized what had given him pause.

The stalactites that had made up the rocky hills we'd been laboring across had been sheared off the ceiling in a rough cone shape, radiating outward from the fissure. It looked almost as if something had burst through the massive wall, then slashed a wedge through the thick field of hanging limestone deposits, causing them to hit the ground and smash into rubble. It looked almost exactly like that.

That gave us all pause, and I didn't know about the others, but my troll was growing increasingly unhappy. He did not like unstable caves; too many of his people had been lost in them, and that was when the cause of the instability was naturally occurring. He definitely didn't like unstable caves that contained something that could do that!

He didn't like it at all, and judging by the shifting of the other trolls, they didn't, either.

But after a moment, we turned back to the fissure itself, because their queen and my father were in there. It could have easily accommodated a giant's height, but not his build as it was not even as wide as a regular door until perhaps three stories up. It was more of a crack at our level than an entrance, yet Marlowe squeezed inside anyway and we followed.

Of course, by "we" I mean my troll and I, although he had to turn sideways and suck in his gut to sidle along the twenty-foot-long crevasse. The rest of the guards were left behind, their hybrid size simply too big to fit. They called out encouragement behind us, and that they were going to find another way in, but my troll didn't answer.

That was just as well, as it would have been profane if he had. He was breathing a little quickly, as if he didn't enjoy the too tight space, being forced to be the hero, or much of anything else. With the light coming from within, I could see his reflection in the side of the crevasse, which was almost mirror-like in places, and it wasn't happy.

It contrasted with my own growing excitement, for if anything seemed likely to hold a portal to another world, this was it.

But a portal wasn't what we found on the other side. The crevasse let out into a sizeable, mostly empty, roughly round cave that did not contain Mircea, the Pythia or the pixies. And what it did contain I didn't understand, even when I squinted, bringing the troll's best eyesight to bear.

That was actually pretty good for once, as there was plenty of light to help him out. The source of the illumination was a large egg-like structure in the center of the cave suspended by nothing that I could see, yet its bottom didn't quite touch the floor. It was roughly twice the size of a human in height, three or four times as wide, white in color and . . . well, looked almost exactly like a large, glowing egg.

On the floor beside it was another of the things, this one not floating, or at least not anymore. It reminded me of Humpty-Dumpty after his fall, as it was on its side and shattered into pieces. Inside was a hollow area and some dried up . . . stuff . . . clinging to the "shell".

It was no longer glowing.

Marlowe knelt down and gingerly poked at a piece of the dried stuff. When it failed to melt his skin or do anything else except lie there, he broke some off and brought it up to his face to sniff it. I doubted that that was going to tell him much, however, as troll noses were also quite good and I couldn't smell anything. Except for the black, coal-like substance that coated everything here other than for the sloping side of the egg, the remnants of the fissure's creation, I supposed.

We sent the black dust swirling upward every time we took a step, and its strangely fine texture caused it to stay suspended in the air for a time, making it hard to breathe. While little avalanches in the remaining ankle-deep stuff on the floor filled in our footsteps almost as soon as we'd made them. As if the cavern was erasing any evidence of us being here even before we left.

It was eerie and I didn't like it, and I wasn't the only one.

I had been watching Marlowe, not concentrating on controlling my ride, and he was becoming skittish. He didn't like this place; he didn't like it at all. And while I wasn't paying attention, he had been slowly moving toward the crevasse again.

But he'd been doing it backwards, one step at a time, and had gotten a little off course. So, instead of hitting the exit, he had stumbled across something else. Something weird.

Our foot broke through what I guessed was a ward, and the air around us lit up like a searchlight had just gone off. Or like a video had started to play, I realized, as someone walked right through us, making my troll jump and swing his weapon. But the ax cleaved only dusty air, as whatever this was, it wasn't real.

At least, not anymore.

"What is that? What did you find?" Marlowe demanded, coming over.

Neither my troll nor I answered, as neither of us knew. But I moved him further into the room and turned us around so that I could see what was going on. And there it was: a 3-D image that reminded me of Zeus in my crow-vision, shining and oversized, only this one was maybe fifteen feet tall, blue-tinged and ghostly.

She was also female.

Her dark hair was the first thing I noticed, being elaborately braided and piled up on top of her head, although the beautiful mass was leaning to the side somewhat precariously, as if she hadn't bothered to secure it properly. She was dark skinned and pretty, with African features, yet was wearing a silvery gown in the Grecian style, although not as I would have expected a possible goddess to do. The material had been bunched up under a plain leather belt to keep the hem from tripping her up; she wore no adornment other than a brooch to hold the gown together; and had a fussy, no-nonsense air about her that I hadn't expected from one of her kind.

I didn't recognize her, but Marlowe, surprisingly, did. "Fortuna," he muttered, those sharp dark eyes taking her in.

"What?" I asked, before I could stop myself. But he barely seemed to notice that he was talking to a curious troll.

"The brooch, you see here?" he tried to indicate the lone item of jewelry, but his hand broke the light, causing that part of the image to disappear. So, he settled for gesturing at it instead. "Carved like a cornucopia. That was one of her symbols. The Romans regarded her as the personification of luck, but to the Etruscans who came before them, she was a fertility deity who ruled over the bounty of the soil and the fruitfulness of women."

I didn't say anything, still trying to take that in, but my troll did. He had been staring at the ghostly figure, who had begun speaking although I did not know the tongue. But he did; I felt the recognition in his mind and heard it in his sudden, high pitched, piercing wail.

The one he made right before diving for the exit.

Marlowe caught him halfway there and pulled him back. "You know what she's saying, don't you?" he demanded.

The troll looked down at the spymaster's hand, which appeared tiny and almost childlike next to his massive bicep. Yet when he tried to break away, it didn't work. He tried some more, putting muscle behind it, and still went nowhere.

This did not help his panic.

"Answer me!" Marlowe said, shaking him slightly. "I'm working with your queen. She will want to know about this!"

That seemed to get through, and the troll finally stopped fighting and licked his lips. But his eyes flickered nervously around the room, as if expecting an attack at any moment. "Old tongue. Gods' tongue," he finally said, his voice hoarse.

"Can you translate it?"

The troll listened for a moment, then nodded unhappily. He spoke English, so I assumed he was one of those who had been to Earth at some point. But like most trolls, he was not loquacious.

"She say . . . he number five."

Marlowe waited, for the goddess was still talking, but that was it. "Five what?" he finally asked.

"Five . . ." the troll searched for the English word, but it wouldn't come. "Like that," he said, threading his fingers together and then waggling them at Marlowe.

Marlowe looked from the fingers to the troll. "*What?*"

My ride was surprised that the strange Earth creature wanted more, as from his perspective they had had a good chat. But he obliged. "She say he too violent. Not good."

"Not good for what?" Marlowe snapped, losing patience, which was never his strong suit. Something he demonstrated again by not giving the troll a chance to answer. "I need a translation—word for word—not a damned summary! Especially not one like that! What the hell does 'not good' mean?"

The troll looked offended, probably because he thought he had been clear. Even in their own language, his people tended to speak in short sentences that conveyed simple concepts. They could go for hours without saying much at all, preferring to communicate through deeds instead of words.

But the spy was not likely to accept that, and I needed to find Mircea, not be here all day. And the more I listened to the language, the more sense it made. I found myself able to decode words and then whole sentences, as if I was remembering a language that I hadn't used in years.

Of course, I hadn't used it at all, but the troll had. It wasn't that different from the tongue his people still spoke in religious rituals. Our mental link must be allowing me to borrow his linguistic abilities, something I had not been able to do on Earth.

But it seemed that I could here, and after listening a bit more, I decided to help out.

"—fifth crossing appears viable both in water and on land," I said slowly, concentrating on the goddess's words. "Although in the case of the latter, its speed is outside of acceptable parameters. But its mental state is the most . . ." I searched for the right word. "Undesirable trait, as it does not take orders nor understand them well, or possibly its . . . aggressive tendencies are overriding its intelligence. Recommended fail with possible crossing with a more . . . even-tempered subject with better mobility."

Marlowe blinked when my partner and I had finished speaking. "Er, thank you."

The troll inclined his head with dignity.

But then the image faded out, with the goddess's silvery gown reminding me a little of the Pythia's as it fluttered into nothingness, which did not seem to please Marlowe.

"Start over," he said. "Go on, show me all of it!"

But the troll just stood there, not understanding what the human wanted now, as he didn't realize that he had caused this. Resulting in Marlowe saying a bad word and pushing him to the side, before feeling around on the floor with his foot, looking for whatever had triggered the recording. And succeeding only in stirring up a lot more dust.

I was looking at something else, namely the sides of the chamber, which I hadn't paid much attention to before. But which I now noticed were covered in indentations of varying heights and widths, with some almost as tall as the fissure, while others were tiny, and so shallow that I wasn't sure they weren't mere ripples in the stone. But all were empty, with just the rough, black rock of the wall visible inside them.

All but one.

It was the one the goddess had been projected in front of, and was only about three feet high. But it had the sheen of a ward over top of it, pale blue and almost invisible, especially when her blue-tinged recording had been playing. But now that she was gone, I could just make it out when I moved right, and I didn't have to ask why it was there.

This alcove was occupied.

I just didn't know by what.

And I didn't care, when the troll got a little too close while trying to sidle his way back to the door, and the bumpy, yellowish blob inside suddenly opened one bleary orange eye and lunged for us. We jumped back, just as something mucous-y and tube-like hit the ward where our face had just been. Another dozen of the tube things quickly followed, scrabbling hard against the ward, which was flickering and then burning, with an acrid stench that filled the troll's nostrils and had him stumbling back.

And hitting down on his behind while still scrambling away, panting and making small, panicked noises that I had never heard one of his kind utter.

Things got a little confused after that, as the troll inadvertently triggered the recording again, causing the goddess to return. And she soon had friends, because Marlowe had noted the place on the floor which had activated the image. And immediately started running around the room, setting off recordings in front of the other alcoves, although we couldn't understand what they were saying when they were all talking at once!

Even worse, there wasn't a single recording for each. Ours had only triggered the one, perhaps because the latest occupant was still in place, so there hadn't been any question of what to show first. But others had a life-sized, merry-go-round of images flash into being in front of them, and not all showed the same person.

Fortuna was prominent among them, but there were others, both men and women, although I could not see all of them very well. The ones in front of the circles were more than life-sized, but those on the sides were smaller and more indistinct, like a necklace with graduated beads. Or they were until Marlowe started scrolling through them, pushing them aside like someone swiping right on an app.

And he was swiping fast, as if searching for something, causing the images to blur together as he sped about the room, and hundreds of voices to echo off the walls. It was a sizable cave, but not sizeable enough with a crowd of oversized, ancient gods suddenly jostling us for space! Or with their voices deafening me as I wrestled with my troll, who had had enough of this weird, scary place.

I finally glimpsed the reason for his panic in his mind, and it was a good one. His kind were taught from the cradle to avoid areas where the old gods had been, as they often were protected by traps that could be deadly, causing curious little troll boys to never be heard from again. And the conditioning had stuck.

He wanted out of here; he wanted out now!

But I wanted to stay despite the chaos, my attention having been caught by the fact that not all of the gods were staying still.

Some of the merry-go-rounds were still spinning even after Marlowe moved on, showing flickers of dozens of people and their cut-off greetings as they flew by. But elsewhere had settled on a single spokesperson, who was pacing back and forth in front of their alcoves and gesturing at the things inside, none of which I would like to meet in a dark alley. Still others were panning their cameras, or whatever had been recording them, to the center of the room, where the eggs stood whole and unbroken in the past.

The glowing structures were linked via various tubes to other, smaller versions of themselves hanging in the space above. Sometimes, there were two or three glowing orbs attached; at other times, as many as twelve were visible. And one flickering blue image across the room showed the end result of all this.

Something was emerging from one of the large eggs it depicted and tentatively stepping down to the ground. Something I would never have expected in this cavalcade of horrors. Something... familiar.

It was a woman, naked except for a transparent sheen that clung to her, glistening in the bright light, which evaporated as soon as the air touched her. I was having to view her out of the corner of one of the troll's eyes, as he was still fighting me, but she was nonetheless beautiful. So much so that, after a moment, even he paused and then just lay there, staring.

At long dark hair, still wet with the shimmering substance and falling halfway down her back; at huge dark eyes flicking with confusion over the group of people around the egg; at the heavy breasts, trim waist and shapely hips of a woman grown, which is what she was although she didn't act like it.

She didn't seem to know this place or these people. She didn't seem to know anything at all, because when she spoke, a wordless sort of keening was all that came out of her mouth. Her eyes darted about in confusion and growing fear, and then began to glow, bright, bright, so unearthly bright, that I wanted to shield my face yet I couldn't look away.

Something was about to happen, with even the troll rolling over onto his stomach, like a kid on a living room floor watching a show on TV. One that had almost gotten to the good part. Only the good part never came, because the people in the recording were crowding around her now, were draping her with a robe, and were talking to her softly.

I couldn't hear what they were saying, but it looked like they were making soothing noises as you would to a child. Perhaps because she was one, I thought, staring from her very familiar features to the egg she'd just walked out of. Or been birthed from, I realized, my eyes moving to the rows of alcoves while a strange white noise buzzed in my ears.

It was like the roaring of the ocean, which I couldn't seem to hear over, causing even the cacophony of the room to fade away. My brain was suddenly full of it, with no room for anything else. Except for a single word.

"Mother," I whispered, and lurched to my feet.

Chapter Forty-One

It had to be her; it simply had to be. She looked like Dory as she had as a young woman—sweet, vulnerable, dangerous. I had seen that look a thousand times, that glance, those eyes; I simply couldn't be wrong.

I had crossed the room unthinking and stood in front of her, my hand unconsciously lifting to touch her hair, her cheek, expecting . . . I didn't know what. That she would look at me? That she would somehow see me over the centuries?

But my hand went right through her, as Marlowe's had done with the goddess's image. Vaguely blue light silvered the troll's fingers for a moment, before I dropped our hand, beaten. And had to content myself with staring at her.

Only I wasn't content; it wasn't enough. People kept getting in the way, and even when I could see her, it was hazy, with the picture quality on the gods' video feed less than ideal. I backed up, almost to where I'd been before, and it helped somewhat, but it still wasn't clear.

I wanted to drink her in, to examine every pore, every micro expression. But instead, she looked like she had in my dreams sometimes, fuzzy and indistinct. Like a memory of a memory, looked at too often and worn almost to nothing, with just a few frayed threads remaining that I wasn't even sure were real anymore.

But that was the only time I thought of her, when waking from one of those dreams, her voice still ringing in my ears and a yearning squeezing my heart. I did not think about her when awake, for she was dead. Dead and gone; I had been told that all my life.

Why think about a corpse you never knew? Why torture yourself with someone who wasn't there and wasn't going to be, just another ache in a life filled with them? No, I had thought very little about my mother.

But now . . . I could think of nothing else.

Was this where she had been made? Tinkered with by the gods from any number of creatures, hewn from the flesh of a thousand crossings, until they found one that they liked. Until she found it?

She was there now, standing to the side—Fortuna, goddess of fertility, which made a strange kind of sense in the circumstances. Had she run this place, bringing about life in a different way? She seemed to show up in more of the images than anyone else, and appeared very pleased with her latest creation.

But she was watchful, too, standing back from the others, trying to assess her handiwork with my mother barely out of the womb. And looking for what? I thought, my anger rising. And what happened to those who failed her tests? To all the things that had once been in those alcoves, and were now... where were they now?

Discarded, having exhausted their usefulness, like the dark fey had been? Or put down as failed experiments too dangerous to keep alive, like the dragons? Or left behind and forgotten about, like the wretched thing in that first alcove?

From what Dory and I had seen, it was all of the above.

And to those who passed her rigorous standards, what had happened to them? From what we'd heard, it wasn't any better. Just cannon fodder in the gods' perpetual wars, easily disposable soldiers, casualties that no one cared about.

Like the green fey had made out of the hybrids they created from the human slaves they bought, so that their own soldiers wouldn't be lost on the battlefield. We'd been told about them in council meetings on the war, yet never paused to wonder where they had learned such behavior. Straight from their godly overlords, it seemed.

Let the mutts handle it, I thought. Let the crossbreeds, the mistakes, the unwanted bleed out while we play our games, while we rake in the rewards, while we toy with their lives and those of others. While we remake their worlds in our image, toddle off and die for us, won't you?

"What did you do to my mother?"

The furious question echoed around the room, but I received no answer from Fortuna. She winked out of sight as the "video" finished, as most of the others had already done. I didn't know how long I had stood there, staring mindlessly at my mother's recording, just that the noisy images had flickered out and the changing light shadows they'd thrown over the room had all but receded.

Until it was just us again, me and my troll, as even Marlowe had gone off somewhere. And the last remaining creature, the only real one behind the ward, finally lost interest. It had been shrieking bloody murder this whole time, adding to the discord, but now it quieted down.

The eye—and there was still only one—looked back and forth for another moment, as if it could no longer see us. Then the scrabbling stopped and it settled back into its alcove, merging with the shadows. Leaving us with the acrid smell of burning flesh in our nose, watery, stinging eyes, and no answers, no answers at all.

But I wasn't sure that the troll wanted any. My control had slipped to basically nothing at this point, and he was taking advantage. He was heading back to the fissure, gripping his ax hard enough to threaten to break it, and not wasting any time.

Until I came back to myself and turned him around, and we had a little struggle in front of the wall. Back and forth, back and forth, he kept turning toward it and I kept turning him back, whispering reassurances that he couldn't care less about, especially when the sounds of an altercation came to our ears from further into the cavern. It was so far away that I couldn't make out words, only that the voices were those of our party.

They had probably been lured back from wherever they'd gone by all the noise, but I suddenly didn't care about them, any more than the troll did. I wanted to go back across the room. I wanted to play that one particular recording again. I wanted to see if there were any more of her, any with *answers*, but my ride wasn't having it.

The best I could do resulted in a stalemate, while I fervently wished that my body was with me. I needed my own limbs, I thought, struggling with the troll's. And my own senses . . . including my sense of . . . adventure . . . because don't you want to know . . . what's going on?

No. No, he did not. And the answer was clearly going to remain no, with him planting his feet and crossing his arms and simply standing there, impervious to any and all persuasion as if he didn't even hear it.

And then making a break for the fissure again, as soon as I was distracted trying to hear what was out of range. Damn it! I finally gave up and let him go, throwing myself back into the void again, hoping that I could find another mind to latch hold of before I lost my connection to this place.

And to my relief, I did.

I found Marlowe's.

The realization shocked me, as invading a first-level master's mind should not have been possible even for an instant, which was why I hadn't tried it. I had been attempting to snare a pixie, although I wasn't sure that that would work, either, as it hadn't with the duergar. And pixies were at least as strong minded and magical as the dwarves.

But I'd had no choice, as Mircea or the Pythia were my only other options, and neither of them was a remote possibility. I had placed Marlowe into that group as well, but it seemed I had been wrong. Because instead of immediately throwing me out, he barely flinched as I grasped hold of his mind.

Maybe because he was busy doing something else.

I did not know what that was, having come in a little late, but it involved running about, ignoring the others who were trying to talk to him, and tightly grasping something in his hand. I could see it in flashes whenever his eyes turned that way, especially when it suddenly jerked, causing him to hold it out in front of his body. It appeared to be some kind of staff, although it did not look sturdy enough to be a weapon.

But maybe it wasn't that kind of staff. Because there were runes etched into the side of it in a crude sort of way, as if whoever had done them had been in a hurry. Instead of stylized, well-made markings, they were mere scratches. And so shallow that I probably wouldn't have noticed them at all except that they were glowing.

I saw them again in his mind, saw my father coming toward him down the corridor a moment ago, saw Mircea holding the item in his hand, which was dark and uninteresting until Marlowe came close. And then it lit up like a beacon in the gloom, shedding a bright glow onto the surrounding stone. And the spy darted forward and snatched it out of a very surprised looking Mircea's hand.

He had been about to tell father what we'd found in the other room, even had mother's name trembling on his lips. But that fled his mind as soon as he saw the staff. And once he grasped it—

Everything changed.

It didn't feel like touching wood, but like taking someone's hand, someone with soft skin and a strong grip, someone who I saw in his mind for a moment, standing on a grassy hilltop with her bright red hair blowing in the wind.

I didn't get a name, but I didn't need one. She was important to him and she was powerful. I could feel her magic running through the wood, coursing through the fibers like blood. Could sense when it leapt onto our flesh, flowing up our hand and onto our body. The staff was imbued with it and it knew Marlowe, knew him immediately and instinctively, as she did.

We have been waiting.

The words came out of nowhere, echoing in our shared mental landscape, and then were gone, so fast that I thought one of us might have imagined them. But no. The woman's voice hadn't been mine, and the taste of it . . . like her lips . . . lips like honey and nectar and fine spring days, all combined . . .

Marlowe could taste it, could taste *her*, and for a moment, so could I. And then he was off, tearing down the hallway like a man possessed. So, it was a wizard's staff, I thought dizzily, trying to pull back from his mind without entirely letting go.

I wanted to give him privacy, for he was remembering things that were none of my business. But I also wanted to be sure that the magic didn't snare me, too. Because there was magic at work here, old magic, powerful magic, sparking off the walls and sinking into our pores, magic that approved of me for some reason that I didn't understand.

But it had a distinctly self-satisfied air when it enveloped me, which frightened me more than anything that had happened in a long time. Because it knew I was here, knew I wasn't Marlowe, and didn't care, which meant that it had a need for me. But what that need was, I had no idea.

Suddenly, I was wondering if perhaps the troll hadn't been the smart one.

I should go, I thought, but the idea no sooner flitted across my mind than I had a new sensation: cuffs twining around my mental wrists, cuffs of roses and sweet honeysuckle, perfuming the air around me.

They were gentle and light, so much so that I could hardly feel them—until I tried to pull away. At which point they tightened, enough for me to sense the edge of thorns hidden in all that lovely profusion, and the strength of them, which I fought against but couldn't break.

They left me a prisoner, being carried along by a madman, who was running hell-bent-for-leather through a maze of stone, and how did I get here?

I didn't know, only that I wasn't alone, and I didn't just mean Marlowe.

There were indentations down both sides of the hallway that we currently found ourselves in, and these were mostly inhabited, although the things in them were long since dead. I could see them in flashes in the light that the staff was shedding, and in the vague, ambient lighting their wards gave off. The latter wasn't very good, however, and the former was slinging around as we ran, giving me only glimpses.

But they were enough.

Skeletons, some with the delicate scaffolding of wings still attached, stared out at us, held in place by dried up ligaments and old restraints. There were many versions of them, some as small as my hand, being barely pixie size, tiny and delicate and strangely beautiful. While others were twice as big as a man, with one so large that it had been housed in a long indentation in the ceiling, as nothing else would fit.

I stared into their dead eyes and felt a hard shiver go up my spine.

Or perhaps that was my father. He brushed Marlowe's mind, trying to calm him, but was shoved aside. The spy hadn't been lying about being resistant to that sort of thing. And then the Pythia stepped out of nothing, using her unique powers to get in front of us.

"Kit!" she called. "Talk to me! What are you *doing?*"

"I knew we should have left him behind," the queen said, flying just above us.

"Grab him, Cassie!" Mircea called, from somewhere behind us. "Get him out!"

And I guessed she tried, because a nearby chunk of rock suddenly vanished, causing us to slip on the rubble that cascaded off the damaged wall.

But Marlowe recovered quickly, leaping up to the stone above her head and pushing off to the other side, before hitting the ground, rolling, and pelting headlong down the hall, only to get jerked abruptly through a door to the left by the staff.

The doorway led to a series of interlocking caves. Some were small, barely larger than an average house; some were medium sized, like the one where we'd come in; and several were huge and echoing, with stone eruptions form the floor in uniform rows that reminded me of library shelving. But instead of books they held more specimens, as did the towering walls where they were packed in alcoves five and six high depending on their size, which . . . ranged big.

Overhead in one room were great dinosaur-like creatures in the process of rotting away in the shadows. The stasis fields they were behind seemed to have some sort of preservative nature, but there was apparently a limit, and these had exceeded it. In another of the great rooms we pelted along an enormous wall with what looked like the remains of dogs or wolves, with many of them now only piles of bones and half rotted pelts, which quickly became crosses between humans and canines as we went on.

Huge crosses, I thought, seeing things that did not look much like the Weres I knew, but something far larger and more terrifying. I glimpsed elongated arms giving perhaps a twelve-foot reach; strange, hunched backs, as if the bodies couldn't contain all the musculature of the shoulders and had piled it up there like a camel's hump; and elongated jaws filled with teeth, more than even any wolf would ever have. And realized that I was seeing the evolution of the werewolf.

But I didn't see it well, because Marlowe had sped up, although I didn't think that was his idea. The staff was all but dragging him along now, and so quickly that even a master vampire was having trouble keeping up. Or a Pythia, I thought, as Cassie flashed in and grabbed for him, but he swerved around her and carried on.

He did not elude Mircea, however, who tackled him just as we hit the next cavern in line.

Just by sound alone I could tell that this one was larger even than the others. Possibly a lot larger, but it was hard to get a visual with Mircea wrestling with a positively crazed Marlowe. Who belted him upside the jaw with a crack that echoed around the huge space, and then tore loose—

Only to be tackled again before he'd gotten six yards, and sent face first against the unyielding stone.

"Get off me, you maniac!" Marlowe snarled.

"Then listen to me," Mircea replied urgently, flipping him over and getting in his face. "You're being controlled. The staff is doing something to you—"

"It's doing nothing! It's *her* staff, it's taking me to *her!*"

"Who is 'her'?"

But Mircea didn't get an answer. Unless you counted a blow to the ribs followed by a sharp uppercut, and a hit well below the belt that made father curse and bought us a few seconds of freedom. And Kit used them, scrambling back to his feet and taking off, and if I thought he'd been fast before, it was nothing to this.

He almost flew across the room, giving me my first look at what was ahead in the process, and it was even more impressive than I'd expected. The huge cavern seemed to go on forever, with parts of it vanishing into adjacent caverns under forests of stalactites, and others fading into darkness but with echoes that seemingly went on forever. It didn't help that it was part lava rock, black as pitch, and part pearly limestone, with the two meeting and washing up together on the floor where an old volcano had spewed its last.

And it must have been a very old one, because some of the overhanging stalactites were so immense that they had met and fused with the stalagmites growing up from the cave floor. And formed massive limestone columns scattered around the space that were reflected in myriad little pools of water. And in one big lake at the center, too large to be called by any other name, the black surface of which had started to bubble like a cauldron.

I could see it clearly, although this cave didn't have any alcoves in it, or the ambient light they gave off from their wards. But it was illuminated. Only in this case, the light came from the water, beams of which were spearing upward and moving about, sending flashes radiating outward as we approached.

It was almost as if it sensed our presence, because it started to churn faster as we came closer, like someone was stirring it. Or something, I realized, as the portal underneath the water abruptly swallowed the lake that had hid it for who knew how many centuries and began spiraling outward, with clouds of whitish gasses like spectral hands. And I finally started doing what I should have before, and attempted to slow Marlowe down.

Father didn't need much help; just a little lag and he would catch him—

"Like hell," Marlowe hissed, sloughing off my feeble attempts at control.

"You knew I was here?" I said, and heard him laugh.

"Of course. You were in the troll before, and then jumped to me. Do you think me a fool, girl?"

No, his intelligence wasn't in question; just his sanity, I thought, and tried throwing myself back into the void, only to be dragged back again by him and the damned handcuffs.

"Not a chance! I need you to get through the portal."

"What? Why?"

"No idea. But the staff only started reacting when you came on board. Like you were the missing piece. So, we go together."

"Go where?" I screamed, fighting in earnest now.

"Let's find out." And then we were jumping, across the limestone deposits around the lake and into the chasm it had left, straight into the center of all that light.

Chapter Forty-Two
Dory

The shield was in the palace, which would have been great except that the massive structure was currently teetering over an even more massive chasm. Or part of it was. A huge statue of a bearded man cracked and splintered and fell into the void as we approached, causing Antem to have to pull back to avoid being swept along with it.

He halted in the air near a decorative fountain of a type I'd never seen before, which had a stream of water leaping between pretty, flower covered islands on top of a bunch of descending pillars. Or at least, it had in the past. The delicate little thing had already lost two towers and a third was looking questionable.

As a result, the water was now flying off and hitting Antem in the face, who was too busy dodging falling stalactites to notice.

And then apparently deciding that inside the crumbling edifice was safer than out here, where there was no cover of any kind. Because he darted through the main doorway, even as the statue guarding the other side of the entrance cracked down the middle with a sound that would have been deafening, except that everything was!

Louis-Cesare was yelling something as we hit a hallway large enough to fly through, but I couldn't hear it. I couldn't hear him in my head, either, if he was trying that, because the chaos was drowning out everything, including my thoughts. The only things that registered were crashes, screams and explosions, the latter mostly from outside, although whether because more limestone teeth were clamping down on the city or because of the fireballs the dragons were spitting, I couldn't tell.

And I didn't care, as my body suddenly hit the ground when my former ride transformed in an eyeblink, rolled to his feet and went sprinting down a hall.

Louis-Cesare and I sprinted after him, through a maze of oversized corridors which Antem must have known well, as he was navigating them despite the fact that they were currently collapsing onto our heads. And there was a lot to collapse, with ceilings so high that darkness swallowed them, giving us no way of telling what was coming until a chunk was already falling. But I could see ominous cracks everywhere, and—

And there was another one, I thought, as Louis-Cesare took a hit, jumping in between me and a shattering wall, allowing the half ton stones to break on top of him instead of crushing me into a puddle of blood and bone. Then he swept me up and put me on his back, because we were going to lose Antem otherwise, who was not waiting for us.

Normally, I was almost as fast as Louis-Cesare, but with the dust billowing everywhere I couldn't see basically anything, and doubted that he could, either. He was following the dragonkind by nose, although how he could in all this, I didn't know. But that's what being a first-level master gets you, I thought, right before he had to pull his final trick out of the bag, despite the fact that we'd been in here for less than a minute.

But there was no other choice when a dragon burst through a wall practically on top of us, and we burst into the vague, hazy world of the Veil, where the creature's human form was hunched and waiting. And then unconscious and falling, as Louis-Cesare punched him with the force of a dozen men. I didn't know if he recognized him as one of the enemy or was just being cautious, but I saw the dragon's human form collapse, and his dragon side abruptly reappear in the Veil to protect him.

And then we were haring back out into real space just ahead of a burst of fire, and sliding down a collapsing staircase on our butts before catching up with Antem by skidding into him.

He paid us no more mind than the hundreds of screaming, pelting civilians clogging this artery, trying to get anywhere else. And then skewing and falling, like a fleshly waterfall, as the corridor abruptly tilted twenty degrees. People were screaming and scrambling, packs of belongings were spilling and rolling, and I was tripping and being thrown into a wall hard enough to wind me.

Louis-Cesare grasped my arm a second later, as we'd gotten separated by the jolt, and we stayed pressed flat against the wall for a moment, breathing hard. Until I spotted a smaller, mostly empty corridor down the hall a little way, and we made for that. I looked around for Antem, who had disappeared, thinking that he might have dodged in here, too, but didn't see him.

"Damn it!" I yelled. "Where is he?"

Louis-Cesare just shook his head; he didn't know, either. And I doubted that even a master's nose was up to following a single line of scent through so many scared, sweating, people. I watched them stream by, half running, half falling, and wondered what the hell we did now.

And then my sister tore out of a room near the end of the hall, wild eyed and as naked as the day she was born, followed closely by—

"Ray!" I screamed, loudly enough that he actually heard me and turned his head. And fell over because he was trying to put some trousers on and run at the same time and it wasn't working.

He hit the carpet, his butt in the air, and Dorina sprinted away, although she sprinted poorly. The floor was no more level in here, although that shouldn't have bothered someone of her abilities. But it was bothering her, with her hitting the wall, clawing her way off of it, trying to run again, and then sliding back down.

It looked like she was blindfolded or drunk or something— I didn't know, and didn't know what to do first.

But Louis-Cesare did. "Help him; I'll get her!" he yelled, and ran after my sister.

Leaving me with Ray, who had fought his way free of his trousers and was sitting down, trying to pull them back on when he looked up and—

"The *fuck?*"

We stared at each other for a startled second, before I grabbed him and shook him and hugged him and—

"*Why aren't you dead?*"

"Why do you look like you are?" he demanded, finally getting the damned trousers on and standing up. "What happened to your face? Or your hair?" He grasped my chin, turning it to get a better look at the swelling and the colors and the partly-shorn head, which was only now starting to fill in some gaps from a previous disaster. "I leave you alone for a few weeks and this is what happens?"

"Why. Aren't. You. Dead?" I screamed, and then hugged him again, hanging on tight because I was afraid if I let go, he'd disappear.

That was fair since he'd already done it once, getting ripped to pieces by a bunch of Svarestri in the service of their queen, and then being swept away into Faerie with Dorina when she was initially kidnapped. I hadn't seen him since, and had obviously assumed the worst. Because there was no way in hell he had survived something like that!

"You should stop underestimating me," Ray said, as if he'd heard me, and then Louis-Cesare was back with Dorina, who he was trying to put his shirt onto but she wasn't cooperating.

"Why is she naked?" I asked Ray, and then a thought occurred. "Wait. Why were you naked?"

"It's not what it looks like," he said, seeing my expression change. Because my sister, who was now fighting Louis-Cesare, looked drugged, and he looked—

I didn't know, because Dorina took that moment to clock me upside the head.

"What is wrong with her?" I heard Louis-Cesare snarl, and when I stood back up with my cheek burning once again, I had to grab her, because he only had her by one arm and it wasn't enough.

He had Ray in the other, by the hair of his head, which he looked like he was about to pull out of his scalp. Which . . . I wasn't necessarily against, depending on how this went. I stared at Ray, who I honestly didn't feel like I knew anymore, because this... I would never have expected this.

"What?" he asked me, not even bothering to try and fight Louis-Cesare. "What the hell, Dory? It's not what it fucking looks like!"

"Then what is it?"

"Like I know? I was asleep. I woke up. She was going crazy, all dead eyed and violent—"

"And how did you know that if you were in your own room?"

"I was in *our* room and—"

An explosion rumbled through the building, the tilt in the hall became more like forty degrees, and Dorina got away from me. Louis-Cesare let Ray go to grab her and I grabbed my so-called Second, slamming him against the incline harder than I'd planned because I basically fell onto him. He was talking but I couldn't hear him, couldn't hear anything over the noise, until something echoed in my head.

—listen to me! Things have changed since we saw each other last, okay? Your sister and I are together, it's consensual, we're all just gonna have to get used to that, and—

How are you in my head? I snarled.

I dunno. Maybe 'cause I'm Dorina's Second now, same as yours? I could always read some stuff from you, but it's easier now. I think I'm leeching off her abilities—

I stared at him. *You're* together? *What the hell does* together *mean? And why are you still alive?*

Ray gave me one of those looks, the ones he saved for when I was acting stupid only I wasn't acting stupid. I shook him again, banging his head against the tilted wall a couple times, hard enough to make him wince. And was about to give him a lot more reasons for that if I didn't get a goddamned answer right goddamned now!

I'm alive 'cause she saved me! Ray yelled in my head. *We've saved each other more times than I can count and then it turned into this thing. It was her idea, but I love her, okay? I'm sorry, but I do, and nothing's gonna change that. I wouldn't have broken it to you this way, but—*

"What have you done?" Louis-Cesare demanded, coming back and grabbing him around the neck.

"Urp," Ray said, and considering that I had recently seen Louis-Cesare literally pop a guy's head off one handed, I decided to slow things down. Or maybe speed them up, because this place was not going to last.

"Let's get out of here and—no, don't do that!" I said, because Ray's eyes were starting to boggle. "Let's go somewhere I can think!"

"That would be nice, but your sister is fighting me!" Louis-Cesare snapped. "I cannot get through to her!"

Let me try, Ray pleaded, and I glared at him, not knowing what to do. But the Ray I knew had saved my bacon a few times, too, and I trusted him. It remained to see if I could trust this one.

"Let him try," I told Louis-Cesare, who looked at me like I was crazy, but released his hold.

And Ray grabbed Dorina's face, looked her in the eyes, and kissed her. Something that would have won him a dual attack, both from me and an enraged Louis-Cesare, who hated rapists and had already decided for himself what this was. But that didn't happen because . . .

It worked.

The wildcat I had barely been holding onto suddenly calmed down and stopped fighting. And smiled absently at Ray, before offering him her hand. I stared at the two of them, not knowing what the hell, and Ray led her back up the corridor, walking in the ditch the tilt had created out of the corner of the hall until they reached their room.

While Louis-Cesare and I just watched, our mouths hanging open.

And then followed them as fast as I could, because they didn't need to be going in there. We needed to be getting out of here, all of us, before this whole place went up in flames or dropped into the void or just plain collapsed. Or all three, which was getting to be more likely by the second.

Louis-Cesare seemed to have figured out the same thing, because he scrambled down the hall alongside me, bursting into a large room with a rumpled bed, a balcony, and—

"Holy *shit*," I said, with feeling, because the balcony was showing the mother of all battles outside.

For a moment, I forgot about everything else, holding onto the door to stay upright and watching what had to be hundreds of dragons, storms of blowing sparks and masses of crumbling buildings. Balls of fire the size of city blocks tore downward from massed groups of dragons working together. And blasted everything below them before the ricochet headed back upward in smaller, but still deadly explosions that looked like miniature atom bombs going off.

Fire tornadoes caused by all the heat and burning wooden buildings swirled across the ruins, which was all the city was going to be if this kept up for much longer, before running into small lakes, ponds or fountains and sending pillars of steam shooting skyward. Despite the need to hurry, I just stayed there for a second, having never seen anything like it in my life, and I'd seen a lot. I couldn't even tell who was winning as I didn't know Rathen's people well enough to differentiate them from Steen's.

And didn't know what good it would have done if I had, since there was nothing that I could do about any of it.

The same feeling of utter uselessness that had plagued me this whole trip came back with a vengeance. I wasn't used to standing by and just watching carnage happen. And Louis-Cesare clearly felt the same.

I saw his jaw clench, and his hand reflexively reach for a sword that wasn't there because he'd lost it in the battle to get here. Not that it mattered, as this was beyond even a master's abilities. We didn't lead armies; that was father's job. We were a surgical strike team and we needed a job we knew how to do.

And Ray provided it.

He grabbed my arm, but when I turned toward him, he spoke mentally, because there was no way else to be heard. *We gotta go!*

Go where? I gestured at the apocalypse outside. *Steen's people are all over the place—*

Well, we're gonna hafta figure it out! Dorina's not all here—

I know, you said—

No, listen. I mean she's not all here. Her body is, but her mind, the conscious part anyway, went on walkabout—

What? Louis-Cesare interjected. *Make some sense!*

I'm trying! She can do that here. It's a new thing. It's like she throws her consciousness outward and hitches a ride with someone else—

With who? I demanded.

Don't hate me, but I think it's Marlowe—

Kit Marlowe? Louis-Cesare said. *What the devil is he doing here?*

Looking for Mircea. He said—

Mircea's here, too? In the city? That was me, trying and mostly failing to keep up.

Will you two stop asking questions? Ray screamed, probably because a huge black dragon had lost a fight and been whipped this way, its limp, burning body speeding at us across the fiery city.

We hit the ground, even though it was too late—and it would have been, except that another couple of brawling beasts fell in front of us at the last second, taking the hit. Which resulted in all three slamming into the side of the building, only at a much-reduced rate. That still left the two who remained alive brawling half in and half out of our room, having obliterated the balcony with tearing claws and snapping jaws, and a tail that whipped across the small space and only missed us because we were flat on the ground.

Then they were gone, taking a third of the room with them, because this battle was measured in split-seconds with no time to breathe in between. Or to think about anything but getting the hell out. But Ray wasn't finished yet, and he grabbed me by the collar of my shirt.

"We have to reunite her with her body!" he screamed, practically in my ear, since none of us had enough concentration left for mind speak. "Marlowe just went through some kind of portal with her still attached!"

"What?" Louis-Cesare said.

"I can see flickers of what she's up to if I concentrate," Ray said, obviously trying to do just that as his eyes went vague and almost crossed. "I can't see everything, but I know enough to know that! And it's not good on the other side! It's not good at all!"

I could see that from the expression on his face, but Louis-Cesare was having a little trouble keeping up.

"Portal?" he said harshly, and then I realized that I was one not keeping up, as I recalled what Antem had said. But there were bigger problems right now, like trying to save her body—and ours.

"We'll worry about it later!" I told Ray, but he wasn't having it.

"We'll worry about it now!" he screamed, pointing at Dorina. Who had collapsed beside the bed and was no longer moving.

Shit! Shit! Shit!

"Where is this portal?"

"Back of the cavern, but it's a long way! Damned thing goes halfway through the mountain!"

"At least we have a job now," Louis-Cesare said grimly, staring out the window at the battle, which . . . yeah. We weren't getting through that.

"We're getting through," he told me, reading my mind or maybe just my expression.

"*How?*"

He winced slightly, while the blue eyes reflected flames. "You aren't going to like it."

Chapter Forty-Three
Dorina

We hit the ground on a rocky slant and went rolling. Only we'd been moving so fast that it was more like flying, out of the portal's mouth and down a steep hillside, before tumbling headlong into a huge snowbank. One littered with more stones, as if this was where avalanches often ended up, along with whatever debris they'd swept down the mountain along with them.

Marlowe cracked his chin on a rock, hard enough to leave even a master rattled, but then he was up again, looking around wildly. There was a lot to see. There was a damned lot to see, I thought, alarmed—

"Auggghhhhh!" he screamed, and moved with a speed that even most masters would have envied. Although they wouldn't have envied the cause—a boulder the size of a house that obliterated the area where we'd been crouching, leaving a divot that looked like a major asteroid had hit the Earth.

Only this wasn't Earth. I didn't know where this was. But I doubted that it was Faerie, either, as they . . . weren't fey, I thought, staring farther down the slope after the bouncing boulder, to where it ended at a cliff. One towering above a valley filled with a battle such as I had never seen.

On this side were huge, hulking, crystalline giants, ones that made the fey variety look small by comparison. Some were so large that their heads almost reached the top of the cliff, allowing me to see the ice spikes they wore instead of hair flashing in the sun like diamonds. Others were smaller, or perhaps merely farther away, as the battlefield was as huge as its occupants, taking up the entire valley between mountain ranges.

The giants had spears, swords and shields made of the same brilliant matter as their bodies, while on the other side . . .

I squinted, for the sun was blazing and the frozen landscape it ruled over acted as a reflector, increasing the glare. It made it difficult to see clearly even with Marlowe's eyes, as the light was behind the advancing army. But the other side appeared to be composed of two distinct groups.

The one in front looked like the stories I had heard of yetis, massive, lumbering, shaggy, off-white creatures with primitive leather shields and stone tipped spears, as well as a few bows and arrows. Their clothing, in so far as they had any, was leather, too, only so worn that no self-respecting troll would have had it, and so minimal in the cold that it must have been mainly their fur keeping them warm. And behind them . . .

I squinted again, as the crystalline giants kept getting in the way. Their extremities were as clear as glass, showing me a distorted view of pale blue skies, black stone mountains, and a great deal of snow. But their trunks and heads looked like the cloudy center of an ice cube, white and opaque, obscuring the view.

"Not crystalline," Marlowe rasped.

"What?" I pulled back slightly and refocused on him, because his voice had sounded . . . odd.

He looked it, too, with his face flushed, his eyes staring and his hair everywhere. "Not crystalline," he rasped again. "Frost. Those are frost giants."

I remembered something from mythology about such creatures, who inhabited a world very different from ours—or that of the fey.

Theirs was Jotunheim, one of the nine realms that the gods had explored before they reached Faerie and then Earth, only I did not know much about it. And from what I could see of Marlowe's expression, I did not think I wanted to.

"How do you know?" I asked.

"They are famous for resisting the gods," was all he said. And all he needed to, because behind the ranks of the yeti-creatures was a second wave, which had been too distant for me to see clearly a moment before, but which was moving this way fast. And at the forefront—

"Who is *that?*" I asked, my own voice sounding hoarse in my head, despite the fact that I did not currently have vocal cords.

There were a number of strange creatures in that second wave, but the one that Marlowe's telescoping vision had brought instantly closer was enough to cause anyone's mind to stumble, or to shut down entirely. I would have said that it looked like a god, had I been talking merely about its height, which was staggering, being easily as tall as the bigger frost giants. Or its aura, which was shining as brightly as some of the previous specimens I had seen of its race.

But that description would have given a very wrong idea of the whole. For here was none of the health and vigor and, for lack of a better term, humanness of the other gods I had seen. Instead, a death's mask met my eyes, not made out of bone but of skin so sallow, so yellowed, and stretched so tightly over the skeleton beneath that it may as well have been.

Thin, brittle hair, gray as steel, hung limply around it. Eyes that might have been brown once, but which were so faded that I could no longer say their true color, shone out of it. And then its teeth, cracked and blackened and in some cases missing altogether, bared themselves in a grimace of such hideous proportions that it felt like a hammer blow straight to my spine.

"Some don't have the power to shed their physical forms anymore," Marlowe said hoarsely, as if repeating something he'd heard. "Or else they wouldn't be strong enough to take another. Yet they cannot die as we do. They are therefore forced to experience what decaying flesh feels like from the inside."

But that was not the worst of it, for he was noticing things that, in my shock, I had overlooked: a helmet on the head, golden bright and of ancient Greek design; tattered robes that might once have been beautiful, and still showed glimmers of gold embroidery on the edges; a shield—

I held breath I didn't have when his eyes landed on the big round shield on one skeletally thin arm, which was unadorned except for a single, small figure in the middle. Had anyone else bore it, I would have called it cute, being that of a tiny, large-eyed, gray owl with a few bits of the underlying bronze showing through its paint. As it was, I felt a chill creeping up my spine, as that symbol could only mean—

"Athena," we whispered together, and I wasn't certain which of us sounded more horrified.

Or which of us had initiated the order to start scrambling back up the cliffside, away from the chief strategist of the gods, one whose beauty had once been thought to rival Aphrodite's. The daughter of Zeus was now something else entirely, something with a keen intelligence staring out of those narrowed, corpse-like eyes. Who didn't even flinch when one of the huge boulders that had almost hit us tore past her head.

They were being thrown down the slope by frost giants on the mountain above us, I realized, to be used as projectiles by those below. Huge slings were being filled and their contents, in some cases the size of buses, sent screaming across the battlefield. But Athena did not waste energy ducking when she had already calculated the trajectory.

Like she never entered a battle without already knowing the outcome, or so the old legends said. Everything was planned out ahead of time with her, including her victory. Which did not bode well for anyone on this side of the divide, no matter how strong they appeared.

I wasn't sure if that last thought was mine or Marlowe's, or if it mattered anymore. For once, the chief spy and I were in perfect agreement. Which was why our fingers were digging into the loose, rocky soil so fast, trying to get away, that we didn't see Mircea being blasted out of the portal's mouth until he crashed into us.

We went rolling back downhill, and farther this time as he was almost immediately beating on us and yelling, and smacking our face into the dirt whenever we rolled that way again, which was constantly as we were picking up speed. And only caught ourselves on the very edge of the precipice, near enough to one of the frost giants that I might have almost reached out and touched it. But I didn't, because something was happening.

"Athena!" a voice rang out over the battlefield, and it must have been magically enhanced, because it was as clear as a bell in the cold air. "Great warrior of the gods, why do you cower behind your men? You let these paltry creatures do your fighting for you, these days? I had thought you better."

The words were not English, but I understood them perfectly, and not because the spell that Marlowe wore had translated them for me. It had, but I didn't need the tinny overlay in our ear. I knew this language; it was the same one that Fortuna had spoken.

My link with the troll was long gone, yet it sang in my veins nonetheless. But the goddess seemed to be having a different reaction. The terrible face jerked up, and the strange, colorless eyes searched the field.

"And who do you cower behind, reject?" The voice was low and hissing, but cut through the air like a knife. "Fortune's Folly, traitorous girl who always runs?"

"No one. I'm through running."

And true to her word, a woman walked out onto a jutting finger of the cliff, perhaps half a mile away, her long dark hair flowing on the breeze.

The sight of her rang through me like a struck tuning fork, many times harder than the oddly familiar language had done. She was the one I'd seen on the old recording from the cave with the eggs, but I didn't need that. I knew her instinctively, as did

Mircea, who went completely still at our side, while the goddess's searching eyes finally locked onto her.

And she smiled.

"Come then, and meet your destiny, as your maker did before you."

My mother didn't hesitate, pelting headlong down the spear of land while a scream built in my throat, then jumping straight into the abyss with nothing below her but air—

And a wild looking redhead on a swift flying broomstick, who came out of nowhere before I'd even had time to utter a sound. Instead, Marlowe yelled something unintelligible as they whooshed by overhead, before swinging outward in a wide arc and tearing straight for the goddess. And straight for death.

Because she might be strangely emaciated and tattered, and barely recognizable save for her shield. But she was fast—unbelievable so. The broomstick was clipped by the edge of her sword, swung so swiftly that I hadn't seen it move until the duo tumbled out of the sky, flipping end over end before disappearing into the ranks of the yeti creatures below.

I felt my breath catch in fear as Marlowe jumped to his feet, looking for a way down the cliffside when there wasn't one. Wasn't a normal one, that is, but he jumped onto one of the frost giants, who barely seemed to notice our presence. Perhaps because we were the size of a bug to them, or because the abbreviated fight . . . wasn't so abbreviated.

For my mother was rising again from the valley floor, although not on a broomstick this time.

She was growing to many times the size of a human, although not even coming up to the goddess's waist. I did not know what this was, whether one of her skills or some kind of spell, but suspected the latter as the redhead was helping her. She had landed on a rocky outcropping in the center of the field, wand out and pointing at the battle, something I could see clearly as Marlowe never took his eyes off her.

And that was despite the fact that we needed to pay attention to make it down to the ground in one piece! I found myself having to do most of the navigating, finding rougher patches of cold "skin" to help us keep a grip while he was distracted, and thus missed much of the action. But what I did see was not encouraging.

My mother had a liquid speed worthy of a master vampire and what appeared to be matching strength, as she parried the blows of the goddess several times. She also had considerable skill with her weapons of choice, a set of short swords that were the only thing allowing my eyes to track her as they flashed under the sun. Yet it was not going to be enough.

Not even with the goddess fighting fairly, albeit with a slightly contemptuous lift to her lips, and allowing no others into the duel. She clearly did not think she needed them and I tended to agree. My mother's skill would have overcome most foes in our world or in Faerie, but she looked like a rank amateur in comparison to Athena.

I had never seen anyone fight like she did, to the point that, despite everything, I paused for an instant in wonder. It was as easy for her as breathing, as natural as the sun or wind or tides. She wasn't performing war, she *was* war, the personification of it, and when she moved, she was still beautiful.

This would not take long.

Or it would not have, but one of the yeti creatures either did not see the goddess's "hold" gesture or did not care. He let an arrow fly that missed my mother but hit a frost giant on the other side of the field and exploded, as if he'd sent a bomb. Followed by a crack that echoed off the surrounding cliffs as the massive creature's chest splintered and cleaved.

Half of his body fell away like a calving glacier while the field paused in shocked silence for one heartbeat, two, three . . .

Then the roar of two oceans slamming together rent the skies, and almost split my head, as both sides charged simultaneously. The ranged fight was suddenly over and the hand to hand commenced, flooding the battlefield with combatants and causing me to lose sight of my mother. The only way I could still track her were the bloody swathes the goddess's weapon were carving through her own people as she hunted for her.

We have to get to them! Mircea yelled in my head, shaking Marlowe one handed while clinging to an icy shin with the other. A shin that was not moving toward the battle like the rest, for a line of the largest giants had stayed in place, to guard the portal presumably. Although how they thought they could possibly hope to succeed I did not know.

The gods might be starving, but they were numerous, and their followers even more so. I saw strange things in the crowd, things I did not understand. Perhaps the successes from that chamber of horrors behind us, or the denizens of other worlds.

I did not know which and, right then, did not care. Like father, I cared about only one thing, and I could not see her anymore through the running, fighting, screaming throng. Even great Athena had had to break off the attack, in order to parry the flurry of huge stones being slung across the field, all of which seemed to be targeting her.

But that meant that I had no idea where my mother was or even if she was still alive.

Where is she? Mircea screamed, echoing my thoughts, and Marlowe cursed in several languages and held out the staff he had picked up back in the caves.

How badly do you want to find out?

Badly enough, I guessed. Because the next moment both men were slinging their legs over the staff and pushing off from our icy perch. And plummeting straight for the ground since this was not a broom, much less an enchanted one!

Or perhaps I was wrong. Because the magic caught just as we were scant feet above the ground, which had rushed up to meet us like a swung fist. Then we were curving upward, dragging our boots through the snow and sending it spraying outward on both sides for a moment, before pelting for the skies in a headlong, but very wobbly and uncontrolled way.

Because I did not think that Marlowe knew how to fly this thing!

"Do you even know how to fly?" Mircea yelled.

It was a testament to how grave things were that Marlowe didn't give one of his usual scathing replies. He was too busy wrestling the staff into line, levelling it out, and scanning the ground. Which even with vampire vision was almost impossible as it was just a churning sea of ice and fur and blood, with even the outcropping that the redhead had been using having been swallowed by the roiling masses.

But Marlowe had good spatial memory and pointed us in the direction of the rocks, nonetheless, and a second later I glimpsed her—that flaming hair was hard to miss. And then we were landing, or rather crashing with style as Marlowe somehow kept to his feet and started running, although the rocky outcropping was nowhere near level. And swept her up and kissed her—

Until she slapped the hell out of us, a bright, stinging pain that Marlowe didn't seem to mind but that I did, because she was about to spell us for a chaser. But he caught her wrist before she could, and slapped the staff into her open palm, and as soon as he did, she gasped. And looked from it to him, her eyes getting huge for a second before she flung herself back into our arms.

"What are you doing here?" she screamed, when she finally let go of his lips. "*How* are you here?"

"I could ask you the same! You're supposed to be dead!"

"I am supposed to be a great many things," she said cryptically, and then said no more. This was no time nor place for conversation, as we were in danger of being crushed to death by our own forces at any moment. We sought shelter under the rocky overhang, as frost giants spilled by us on both sides.

"What do you need?" Marlowe screamed.

"They're trying to break through the portal. They're going to retake Faerie and Earth besides! We have to stop them!"

"Any ideas?"

"Yes! Kill Athena! She's their leader; they'll scatter if she falls!"

Yes, very likely, as that was the habit on ancient battlefields, and despite their tendency to shatter like ice, the frost giants and their slings were taking a heavy toll on the yeti creatures. The long, white fur of those still on their feet was dripping red, with much of the earlier waves already having been ground underfoot. Or sent flying through the air courtesy of the giants' clubs, which many wielded with devastating force.

The giants also regenerated shattered limbs, as if drawing power from their element all around. I saw one reach down to the snow with a splintered arm, and have all the nearby crystals flow into him, rebuilding what he had lost. But there must be a limit to that, as some of them had fallen and were not getting up again.

Yet on the whole, the yetis were starting to look like a group that might break and run, given the excuse. But the gods wouldn't. They were hanging back, were letting their servants bleed for them, were watching them take as much of a pounding as the enemy wished to deal out.

They were saving their own strength while they tested ours.

And we did not have an army of gods waiting in the wings.

We didn't have a champion anymore, either, I suddenly realized. Mircea, who had climbed back on top of the outcropping to see into the crowd now that the main rush had ended, made a sound that I had never expected to hear from him. And while the echo of my father's scream was still ringing in my ears, I saw my mother fall.

Or fly might be more accurate, as she was sent sailing backward by a blow from her opponent, her neck at an unusual angle, and blood blooming on her face and torso. I couldn't tell the extent of the wounds; didn't have time before she disappeared amidst the churning sea. But they were bad, and she was trampled as soon as she landed.

Father leapt off of the rocks to go after her, disappearing into the mass of combatants almost immediately, but Marlowe wouldn't let me follow. "We'll get killed out there! We can't help him!" he yelled at me, as I fought and scratched and felt like I was bleeding, too. My mental landscape was nothing but red.

"No, but I can," the redhead said, knocking us aside. And extending her staff, which for a brief second, I didn't see as wood. But as a hugely elongated forearm stretching out from her body, with slender fingers longer than a man's leg that looked more like tree limbs covered in flesh than anything human. Then the glimpse was gone and she was normal again, except in one regard.

Because her hair had started to lift around her head, and her eyes had started to glow, and all the hairs on my borrowed body raised as Marlowe and I stared at her. Then the end of her staff erupted in green fire, carving a path for Mircea through a hundred furry bodies. They went flying, he raced ahead, and the witch, for witch she absolutely was, turned her fire on Athena.

"Burn, bitch," she whispered, yet somehow, I heard. And Athena must have as well, as she suddenly looked our way, just before the bolt hit her and almost knocked her off her feet. But with that uncanny fluidity, she had already sent one of her own back at us, so fast that it passed the witch's in mid-air and struck almost simultaneously.

It was powerful enough to have fused stone and bone together, leaving us as nothing more than a fossil record on an alien world. And would have done, but another witch was suddenly there, blonde and panting, with half of her silver gown burnt away. Yet holding some kind of shield spell in front of us thick enough to eat away at the goddess's bolt until there was nothing left.

"Time spell," the Pythia panted, seeing our stunned faces. "Ages it . . . out of existence—"

"Where the hell have you been?" Marlowe yelled, as if she hadn't just saved our lives.

"Dragons—"

"What?" he repeated, grabbing her arm.

"Dragons, in the cave . . . caught them in a slow time spell . . . stopped 'em for now." She gazed around, and despite the glittery eyeshadow and the bright pink lipstick that she was somehow still wearing, the pale blue eyes were assessing. "I have limited ability here, as I'm having to pull power through two separate portals. But is there anything I can do?"

This time, it was me who grabbed her. "Yes."

CHAPTER FORTY-FOUR
DORY

"You want to do *what?*" I yelled, when Louis-Cesare explained the plan. "I said you wouldn't like it," he reminded me from over by the missing balcony, where he was clinging to the shattered stone and waiting for another dragon to fly by. Preferably a big one, because he intended for us to catch a ride. Which would have been insane enough, since half of the dragons out there were our enemies and all of them were crazed with blood lust, but the way he planned to do it—

"*You want to do what?*"

"Do you have a better idea?"

"Don't even start that with me!" I snarled, because that was how our worst ideas ended up getting green-lit, and this was not getting green-lit!

"I'm kinda voting with Dory on this one," Ray said, while dressing Dorina.

"Why are you wasting time with that?" I asked, because he was putting her into a set of elaborate black leather armor with a cape of raven's feathers across the shoulders.

"'Cause it's all I got. The queen's people delivered it this afternoon. Her stuff was destroyed in the arena—"

"What arena?"

"—when she changed a little too fast and—"

"Why was she changing clothes in an arena?"

"More like changing skins—"

"What?"

"—and the queen's people felt bad about it, or so they said. I think she's planning to make Dorina her new champion, or something worse, and wants her to look the part—"

"What's worse?" I demanded, not understanding anything.

"You don't wanna know," Ray said darkly, which made me think that I very definitely did want to know, about all of it, right the hell now.

But then a tiny man flew by my face.

I stumbled back, because he had zoomed past my nose so closely that his wings grazed me, and so quickly that I hadn't even noticed he was there before it was too late. Or it would have been, had he been planning to shiv me with the miniature sword he clasped in one hand, despite the fact that it was mostly melted. But one look at his unfocused green eyes and I didn't think he could tell that anymore.

I didn't think he could tell much of anything, since he almost looked like he was melting, too. A quarter of his body was all but burnt away, and what was left . . . wasn't doing well.

Something he demonstrated by flying straight into Ray, who caught him when he bounced off.

He would have fallen to the ground otherwise, as there wasn't much life left there. But there was enough for him to whisper something when Ray brought him up to his ear. Something that caused my Second's look of shock and concern to change to one closer to dismay.

"What is it?" I yelled, to be heard over the sound of a dragon screeching outside.

Ray looked up. "The heir to the throne! Steen's targeting him!"

"I thought he was after the portal!"

"What portal?"

"The one inside the mountain—"

"The one Dorina just went through?"

"The one her *mind* went through; we have her body here—"

"And that *helps*? How are we supposed to get through an army of *dragons*?"

"The army is here," Louis-Cesare said, "Attacking the city despite having orders to the contrary. And having already taken out the guns that were impeding their progress. Why?"

And I suddenly realized that I was no longer hearing those deafening booms. Just intermittent dragon screeches, explosions, and distant screams. It was why we were able to talk at all.

"Steen's after the queen's son," Ray said, listening to something the tiny man was saying. "She won out in the contest over who would replace the absent king, and he lost. He's never forgiven her—"

"Sounds like him," I said.

"—and the pixies are making a last stand in the nursery. They want Dorina to help—"

An explosion interrupted the conversation, close enough to shake the entire building and to rain dust down over my sister's face. "She's busy!"

But Ray was looking between her and the little man, his expression changing from worried to confused to resolute, and I got a bad feeling in my gut.

"I will do my best," he told the creature, who nodded, a look of pure relief overtaking his features for an instant. Before the small wings fluttered as a shudder shook him, and he lay still. "Change of plan," Ray croaked at me.

"What?" I didn't get an answer, so I grabbed his arm as he strode past, but he shrugged it off.

"No time. Get out of here. I'll handle this."

"Handle—wait! What are you doing?" I demanded, catching him again as he headed back into the hallway.

A hallway which was now a precarious slide down to an empty main corridor, because yeah. Everybody with sense had already left!

"What I must," Ray said, turning to me with eyes blazing. "What Dorina would want me to do!"

"She'd want to live!" I said, putting both arms on his and bracing with my legs in the doorframe.

"Which is where you come in. Get her to safety. And tell her . . . tell her I love her."

And then he was gone.

Motherfucker!

"If we're going, we have to go now!" Louis-Cesare said, watching an approaching dragon.

It was huge and black and I didn't think it was one of ours. But it looked like it was going to crash straight into us. I watched it come with horror dripping down my spine, chilling me to the bone, but not because of the approaching fury.

But because of the choice.

I just wanted to get my family out of here; that was it, my sole wish in the whole damned world. It was all I'd wanted since I came into Faerie, and faced the biggest challenges of my life. I'd fought hard to create a little group of my own out of nothing, to surround myself with people that actually cared about me, to build a life.

And yet, after five hundred years of sharpening my skills, I'd been slapped in the face by the fact that I wasn't good enough. And that one of them, maybe all of them, were going to die because I couldn't protect them. Leaving me forced to choose between two terrible options and right freaking now.

"*Dory!*"

"With Ray!" I yelled, right before Louis-Cesare jumped, causing him to break off with a curse and almost fall out of the window. The dragon curved right before hitting the building and a second later was gone, leaving a very unhappy Louis-Cesare behind. But unhappy was better than dead, and I didn't think that his idea had a chance in hell.

He'd planned to enter the Veil to assault the human form of a passing dragon and hold it at knife point, in order to make us a taxi straight out of here, avoiding the hellscape below. That sounded great, only I'd tried something similar with Steen and had not enjoyed the result. Dragons didn't take well to coercion.

As far as I could tell, they didn't take to anything except beat downs from other dragons, and that was questionable. They were the stubbornest, craziest, most completely infuriating people I had ever met, save one. The one I slid into a moment later, hard enough to knock him off his feet.

"What the fuck?" Ray said, looking up at me wildly.

He had already run into a problem, being hip deep in debris—only most of it wasn't fallen stone or splintered timber. Instead, packs of hastily assembled clothing were everywhere, which had been discarded when the going got rough. Along with casks of jewels, fancy rugs, silk hangings and actual furniture, much of which had been busted up as people slid into it, leaving us with what amounted to a garbage heap at the bottom of the hall.

One which Ray started determinedly floundering through until I grabbed him again.

"We don't know this city!" I snarled, my fingernails eating into his flesh. "We need you—"

"My boys are coming to help—"

"What boys?"

"I got two of the family here. They're on the way; I just called 'em, and they know this place better than I do. They've been here a while—"

I shook him. "*Your* family? They're nightclub workers, not soldiers! What the hell do you think they're going to do?"

"What do you think I will?" he looked at me wildly. "If you and Louis-Cesare can't get her out, do you think I can? I'm useless against what's happening out there. But I can *do this*—"

"What you can do is stop being an asshole!"

"Listen! Steen don't know me from Adam! I can get the kid out 'cause nobody'll be targeting me. I'll just be another refugee—"

"And you can die alongside them!"

But Ray wasn't listening. I didn't know what was wrong with him. I left him for a month and he got delusions of grandeur!

"Dorina will never forgive me if I don't help! I know she won't!"

"And I'll never forgive you if you—"

"Auuugghhhh!" he screamed, loudly enough to have me jerking back, before he shoved me into the garbage pile as an enormous fireball tore over our heads.

It burnt a swath down both sides of the corridor before exploding against a wall at the far end. And sent a hail of sharp-edged bits flying, along with a wash of flames that threatened to incinerate me for a second time. And along with those it had already shed while passing overhead, quickly turned the garbage pile into an inferno.

Dragon fire burns fast, but it didn't burn us because we were suddenly in the Veil. Louis-Cesare, with Dorina flung over his shoulder, had joined the party and rescued us from getting flash fried with a split second to spare. And then from being trampled, as the dragon who had sent the fireball came crashing down the corridor, its vague, ghostly form trashing the hall while looking for us, as if knowing we'd survived.

Which we had by pushing through a wall, since walls don't matter in the Veil.

Nothing matters in the Veil except time, which was ticking down fast. Very fast, as there were four of us in here, and Louis-Cesare could only hold this state for a couple of minutes with just himself. That time lessened considerably for each extra person he brought along, and once it ran out, that was it for at least a day. Not to mention the fact that we'd used up precious seconds when we first came into this freaking death maze!

Which was probably why he and Ray weren't wasting any time. They took off, plowing through several cantilevered walls, intangible things that I barely noticed, even as a tug against my skin; then through a deserted kitchen, where the staff had long since fled, leaving behind a mass of dirty trenches now scattered across the floor; then through what appeared to be a burning forest despite the fact that we were still inside the palace, with a group of battling figures spewing flame ahead of us, one of which looked like Antem. And finally, into another small corridor leading to—

I wasn't sure.

All of that had lasted barely a moment, leaving me confused and out of breath and staring around at a room I couldn't half see, with the Veil making everything hazy and washed out. It was small, the size of a storage closet, and there were magical murals on the walls. I could see a spell flitting across them like the sparks outside only paler and blue-tinged, for the Veil revealed things as well as concealed them.

Although I didn't need its help to see a double row of pixies here, hovering in the air with swords out and game faces on, I didn't know why.

Until I spied something in the crook of one small arm, belonging to a pixie behind all the rest. He was large for one of his kind, and looked frankly deadly, with a battle-scarred face, well-used armor, and a scowl twisting his lips. He appeared to be ready to kill, yet was clutching the tiny bundle in his arm as gently as if it was made out of spun glass.

"What is that?" Louis-Cesare demanded, catching sight of it at the same time I did.

"The heir to the throne," Ray said, as a tiny face peered out of the blankets.

And I found myself staring at something so small, so unbelievably adorable, so . . . so . . . so . . .

"Precious?" Ray asked sardonically, reading my mind again.

"Yes," I whispered, wanting to touch it but not daring to in case I hurt it. No, not even like this. It was so sweet and so vulnerable, not even the size of my *thumb* . . .

"Grab it and let's go," Louis-Cesare instructed harshly, while Ray stared at him.

"Grab it? Those pixies are a lot more dangerous than they look, and they're guarding the queen's son. They're going to go bat shit—"

"I don't care what they're going to do! We are going to *die* if we don't get out of here and I cannot hold the Veil much longer!"

"Then what do you suggest? I have to talk to 'em, make 'em understand—"

"They sent someone after you! They'll understand!"

"They sent someone after *Dorina*, who's basically the queen's new champion! They don't know much about me, and probably care less. I'm gonna need a minute—"

"*We don't have a minute!*"

And Louis-Cesare was right on the money there.

Because the door behind us suddenly blew off its hinges, the pixies gave a battle yell and charged, and I saw someone I knew standing in the ruined frame.

Steen had come himself, it seemed, to get his revenge, to destroy the royal line and to dissolve the remaining dark fey resistance to his master, all at one go. I didn't know if he'd already found the queen and dealt with her; didn't know if that was Antem's blood dripping from the maw of the hulking beast I could see like a shadow over his human form; didn't know anything except that he wanted the baby, he wanted Dorina, and he was getting neither of them.

Because he had to get through me first.

I grabbed a knife off of Louis-Cesare's belt. It was broken, with the remaining blade less than an inch long, another casualty of the day we'd had. But if you use it right, that's enough.

I used it right.

Steen's human form staggered back, blood gushing from a severed artery; we stumbled into real space, because Louis-Cesare hadn't been wrong about that, either; and Steen's dragon form popped into the Veil at basically the same time we left, to find out what the hell was going on.

It never had that chance, but not because of me.

But because the queen, whoever she was, had chosen her guard well. They fell on the wounded man like a swarm of locusts, if locusts had magic, genuine hate for the people attacking their city, and every weapon in the medieval arsenal. Not that most of said weapons touched him, because he was hit by a couple dozen spells before they could, which had him covered in a rainbow of snapping, snarling, hissing pain.

He screamed and fell to the floor, thrashing, and a second later his dragon self attempted to emerge back into our world to save him. It managed to heal the wound I'd made in his neck, but then abruptly disappeared again. Only to re-surface a second later and have the same thing happen all over again.

Steen was glitzing like a T.V. on the fritz, with his two forms repeatedly replacing each other and making it hard for the pixies to approach. One moment, his massive dragon body took up the entire hallway and half of the room besides, and the next, an old, screaming man lay on the floor outside, wrestling with nothing we could see. It was as if his dragon form kept trying to claw its way back into our world, but something kept pulling it back in.

And then I noticed: Louis-Cesare was missing.

"No!" I screamed, staring around at nothing and startling a pixie.

He slashed a sword at me before stopping and looking confused, but I barely reacted to the two-inch gash on my arm. Because my husband was battling Steen in another world, having not dropped out of the Veil along with the rest of us. And I couldn't reach him.

But I could damned well reach something else.

"Fuck!" Ray grabbed for me as I launched myself at Steen. I had no weapons worth mentioning, having lost everything I'd brought with me at one point or another, but that was okay. I had myself.

Or I would have, if Ray would get. The hell. Off!

"Louis-Cesare . . . in the Veil . . . we have to help him!" I panted, and saw his eyes get big.

And then two of us were beating the ever-loving crap out of Steen, alongside two of Ray's boys, who burst in at the last minute and clearly had no idea what the hell was going on. But the boss was shit kicking somebody, and that was all they needed to know. They leapt on, and while neither was exactly powerful, they were decent enough street fighters.

And we needed them, because despite the pixie's spells, and despite whatever was going on in that other realm, Steen was a goddamned *beast*. He sent one of Ray's guys, a popinjay in turquoise silk, flying through a door with a ward that caught him like a spider's web and minused one from our team almost immediately. And then broke the neck of the other guy, but not before he'd gotten a knife into the shoulder joint of Steen's right arm.

It didn't actually separate from his body, but it didn't seem to be working so well, either. That was a major help, as the armor the bastard kept manifesting had destroyed my knife and the pixies' weapons weren't doing any better. But it was moving armor, sprouting up in places where he was being threatened, then fading away to pop up somewhere else. Maybe because he was having to fight in two realms and didn't have enough to go around.

Which was how I got in a couple of good blows, by waiting for it to fade and then hitting the unprotected spots hard. But he returned the favor, and even with his injured right arm, the blows were stunning. But he couldn't use his left because Ray had wrapped his body around it and appeared to be trying to gnaw it off.

That was how my Second lost a fang and got pulverized between the floor and the wall of the hallway, with Steen slamming him back and forth repeatedly. But Ray hung on, immobilizing one of Steen's pile drivers, because he was nothing if not tenacious. And I guessed that was a trait he shared with his boys, who leapt back into the fight a moment later, Turquoise having wrestled his way free of the ward at the cost of his snazzy outfit, and the scrawny little bastard with the impressive knife skills lurching back into the fray despite his lolling neck.

They tipped the balance, because while they weren't all that dangerous as far as vamps went, Steen didn't know that. And with four of us now on the attack, he didn't have enough armor to go around. Not without removing the heavy gorget around his neck, which had never budged until now.

I paused in surprise as the gorget was sacrificed to protect his chest, leaving his throat unprotected. Only he knew that, too, because his dragon face emerged a second later, and sent a torrent of flame at the ceiling of the hall, evaporating it in one go. Just as he would anyone who got too close.

The scaley version faded after a moment, having made its point, leaving me staring at the man's furious features. But all I could see was Louis-Cesare, dead in another world whose rules I didn't fully understand. I didn't even know if I'd get him back if he died in there, or if we'd be forever parted, his body left in that hazy place with no way home to me.

I wouldn't even be able to bury him, and that thought was so enraging that I went for Steen's throat irregardless, tearing into him like I had the fey on Antem's back.

Only this time, it worked.

I felt the pixie's magic rip into me from all sides from the spells still snapping over Steen, felt Steen himself pounding away at my ribs with a fist like a sledge hammer, felt my bones break when they never did.

But I also felt his skin rip, his artery snap, and his blood, so much blood, fill my mouth and gush everywhere: over my chin, across my face, and down my throat. The latter would have disgusted me at any other time, but now I gulped it down to make room for more, trying to drain him dry, to take him with me. Because I was pretty sure I was dead, with bones snapping everywhere now.

But I wasn't going alone, I wasn't if all the demons in hell came to carry me off!

Because my teeth were so far into his flesh that they'd have to take him, too.

And it felt like they were trying. I could feel them vaguely tugging at me, pulling me away. Little demons with tiny hands but surprising strength. But I fought them and I fought them hard.

Because he wasn't dead yet.

He should have been a hundred times over by now, but dragons don't go down easy. I could feel his heartbeat in my throat with every gush of red, could sense him struggling weakly beneath me. Could smell his fear on the air and dead men don't feel fear.

Dead men don't feel anything, and neither do dead women, so I must be alive, I must still have a chance. And I took it, tearing at him some more with everything I had left, even as the world pulsed and darkened around me. Ripping the already severed artery part way out of his neck and seeing it spew everywhere, in bright droplets that seemed to glow in the darkened hallway, like fiery rubies on the air.

And across Louis-Cesare's face when he picked me up, when he pulled me back, when he cradled me in his arms, while weeping and screaming and stomping a boot into Steen's face repeatedly, until there was nothing left but mush.

I smiled at that, with blood dripping from my mouth, and spat out a piece of the bastard's flesh into what remained of his face.

Ha.

Dhampir.

You bitch, I thought.

And then I passed out.

CHAPTER FORTY-FIVE
DORINA

"If you're going to do it," Marlowe hissed. "Do it now!"

"I'm trying." The Pythia had wedged herself into the limited space under the outcropping with us at her side, and was muttering something I couldn't hear beneath her breath. I assumed it was an enchantment of some sort, but it was not one I knew. Her magic was strange to me, and based on Marlowe's expression, it was to him as well.

"Well, try harder! We're getting annihilated out there!"

This was undeniably true. Our troops had done well against the yeti creatures, but the gods had now entered the fray, and they were quickly winding this up. The Pythia had placed a silence spell around our little bolt hole, cutting down on the din, but I could still hear the constant sound of ice splintering as shards were blown off the frost giants, leeching away their strength before they could replace it.

Not that there was much material for them to work with anymore. The snow and ice, which had once been knee deep on the vast plain, had mostly been absorbed, showing the dark colored sand underneath in great swaths. Even the mountains were shedding their pale cloaks, as the frost giants nearer to their heights pulled strength off them before running to the forefront, to take the place of their faltering brothers.

Yet it wasn't enough. The gods were relentless, and despite their withered appearance, were far stronger than us. This was a last stand, but it wasn't likely to be a victory.

But it also wasn't over yet. Because the redheaded witch had climbed back on top of the rocks, and as she raised her hands to the heavens the staff shot something skyward. I didn't understand what she was doing for a moment, as there was nothing up there but crows, hundreds of them, waiting for the feast that followed every battle.

But then, out of nowhere, soft flakes started sprinkling down. Just a few at first, delicate and ephemeral, like the one that landed on Marlowe's lashes. And melted before our hand could raise up to touch it.

Yet it was not alone. More fell and then more, not as individual flakes anymore but in clumps, faster and faster. Until a snow storm swept across the valley, with winds howling and waves of white lashing our enemies and blowing across our army, allowing them to heal.

Several of those nearby who I had thought finished must have had a spark left in them still. As the snow blanketed them, I saw the cracks in their bodies begin to fill in; shattered and missing limbs regrow; and the ice spikes on their heads, which they seemed to use to store additional strength and which had withered away to nearly nothing, begin to swell. After a mere moment, they were on their feet again.

They were tough, this army, but they were still losing. I kept hearing the great *craaaaacks* as more energy bolts calved soldiers in two. And the resounding thuds as giant bodies crashed to the ground, sending blasts of ice and hail everywhere. One colossus hit down only a few yards in front of our refuge, shattering into chunks and showing me the battlefield through a haze of ice.

If the Pythia was going to do anything, it had to be soon.

"Almost there," she muttered, and her left arm disappeared up to the shoulder.

I jerked slightly in surprise, because there was no wound. No blood or torn flesh, no sign of damage at all. Her arm simply stopped and the sleeve along with it, as if part of her had been erased from this world.

"What the hell are you doing?" Marlowe demanded.

"What you asked for. Shut up."

And to my surprise, he did, perhaps because those pale eyes had gone distant, as if she was seeing something other than the carnage all around us, and was no longer listening. She was still talking, however, although it didn't make a lot of sense. "Gotta be here some—there! No, that's the other one. God, she looks like shit."

"Who does?" I asked worriedly, glancing around, but saw no one. Not even the redhead, who was still on the rocks above us, calling the storm. But the Pythia didn't reply.

"Okay, Louis-Cesare is carrying her, so that must mean—no, damn it. That's a pixie."

"Oh for—let me see," Marlowe snarled. And the next thing I knew, he was in her head. And he must have taken me along for the ride, because I was suddenly seeing a familiar party pelting down a shaking corridor that seemed weirdly lopsided, dodging bursts of flame from the duergars' forges, and having a ceiling partly collapse on top of them.

"Dragons," the Pythia said, before we could ask. "Attacking the capitol. Radella went back to—look, there she is!"

The queen appeared at the end of the hall, where the duergars' area gave way to that of the trolls, and she had a group of her tiny guards with her. She looked terrified, furious and lethal, all at the same time, to the point that our party paused for a second as she raced up to us. I thought she was going to barrel straight through, but then a scarred, male pixie flew up, holding out something that stopped the queen in her tracks.

She just hovered in the air for a second, her small wings whirring, before diving at him and snatching a small bundle out of his arms, which she frantically checked over. "It's okay," someone said. "He's fine. We got there in time."

That was Ray's voice—I'd know it anywhere—and it caused a wash of pure relief to go through me. He was alive! He had survived!

I wished I could see him, but the angle was off. He was out of my field of vision, mostly hidden behind a tall man with bulging muscles and a short brown hair cut. And then obscured even further by a swarm of pixies, who came from behind us and started talking all at once.

The queen waved them off. There were tears in those huge eyes of hers as she finally finished her inspection and hugged her son hard against her. Enough that he protested with a tiny squeak.

"You saved him," she whispered, staring in Ray's direction. "You saved my son."

"Dory saved him," he said, "and almost died as a result. She killed Steen—"

"That bastard!" Rage suffused the miniature features. "I would have liked the chance myself!"

"—but his people are still going wild and we can't get the shield up—"

"It was damaged in the crash," the muscle man said. He was unarmed and had his palms facing upward to show that fact, something that did not stop every pixie in the queen's party from abruptly drawing swords on him.

"Everybody calm down!" Ray said. "He's a dragon, but he's with us."

"Antem-Rael, son of Regin-Lar," the man said. This meant nothing to me, but it must have to the queen, who called her people off. "I was sent by my father to restore the shield, but ran into some of Lord Steen's men—"

"Just Steen," the queen spat. "He deserves no title."

"—but the mechanism cannot be easily repaired, and worst of all, your duergars tell me that the well that powers this city was cracked in the attack—"

"Well?" Ray repeated, sounding worried, probably because of the look on the queen's face. "What well?"

"The city is powered by a well of energy from a ley line sink," the queen answered, hugging her child.

"The various communities that live here came together, siphoned it off, and created wards to contain it some years ago. It's what allows us to move about and hide as we do."

"It is a marvel of magical engineering," someone else put in, but Ray wasn't listening. Ray was flushing puce.

"Siphoned? What do you mean 'siphoned'? Like gas?"

"I beg your pardon?"

But Ray was on a roll and wasn't stopping. I had seen this before. "You're telling me you siphoned *ley line energy* like you would gas from a pump, then just . . . drive around with it? Is that what you're freaking telling me?"

"It is the closest thing to a portable ley line sink that exists," that same small voice said, sounding offended.

But not as much as Ray was. "Portable my—we've been sitting on a nuclear bomb this whole time!"

Everyone looked at him.

"I do not think they know what a nuclear bomb is," Louis-Cesare volunteered.

"I don't give a damn what they know! They know boom, right? You know big fucking boom—"

"Which is why it can power a city," the queen said, shutting him down. She might be small, but she had a presence, there was no denying that.

"*Could* power," Antem said. "Before Steen and his people interrupted us, a group of your best magic workers were trying to contain the breech. But the fight intervened and now it has gone on for too long. We have to get out!"

"Go, then. My guards are seeing to the evacuation, with the help of Lord Rathen's people." Her eyes narrowed and her lips suddenly curved into a vicious smile. "I have something else to do."

"But the portal—"

"The Pythia has it handled."

"Cassie is here?" Louis-Cesare interrupted, sounding hopeful for the first time.

"And?" Ray said. "What can one person do against half the dragons in Faerie?"

Radella only laughed. And then a new image rose in front of my eyes, whether from the Pythia's mind or the queen's I didn't know, but it showed the mouth of the portal from head on and above, as I had briefly seen it when it caught us in the cave. Only . . . things looked a little different now.

The ghostly spiral was surrounded by what had to be a hundred dragons. Enough that their enormous size and wingspan almost filled the great cave. They looked as ferocious as they had in the arena, but strangely beautiful, too. Their savagery was its own sort of beauty, with talons outstretched and shining in the portal's light, maws gaping, fire-lit eyes glowing, and scales of every hue and configuration gleaming—

But not moving. The portal was still churning beneath them, but they looked like a fixed tableau, except for a few tiny exceptions. I saw a piece of wing, tattered from the battle for the city, fluttering as if in slow motion; a few coronas seeming to expand in the growing light; and a handful of dust mites spiraling gently toward the portal's heart.

But all of it was slowed to the point that it might have been a static painting on a wall.

Caught 'em in a slow-time spell, I remembered the Pythia saying. And immediately revised my estimate of the small woman with the questionable makeup skills. But Ray was less impressed.

"And what happens when the spell ends and they blow the fuck outta that portal? And strand everybody on the other side? Dorina went through that thing!"

"They can't blow it up," the queen said. "This isn't a normal portal with a talisman to destroy. It's sitting on top of a ley line sink—the same one we use as our 'gas pump'. That's how I knew about this place when Lord Mircea asked. We come back here often to—"

She broke off as the picture skewed even more heavily to the side, throwing them all into a wall. It looked as if the whole place was coming down around their ears. The queen flew off without another word, still hugging her child, and our party pounded in the other direction, I assumed looking for a space big enough for the dragonkind to change and carry them away.

And then to one side, I suddenly glimpsed—

"There she is!" the Pythia said, spotting my body at the same time I did, in Ray's arms. And the next second I spotted something else—her missing limb, which appeared in the air above them and took a swipe.

She grabbed for my hair, Ray yelped and jerked back, and she reoriented herself and tried again. But he had spotted the danger now and a master vampire is fast. Faster than her it seemed.

"Tell him . . . to stay still," she gasped at Marlowe.

"Like he'll listen to me!"

"He better." It was grim. "I'm running on empty here. I opened a small portal to save power, piggybacking off the big one, but I can't hold it forever. And if I have to go get her, I may not have enough power to shift back. So, call him off!"

"I can't call him off. He isn't one of my family. He doesn't answer to—"

"Ray!" I yelled, and his head jerked up. His eyes scanned the space, and then narrowed in fury.

"Marlowe? You son of a bitch! What are you doing?"

"It isn't Marlowe," I said. "It's me, Dorina. And I need my body."

"Dorina?" He stared around some more, still clutching me tight. "What are you talking about? What's happening?"

"Look," I said, and showed him, sending the images from in front of the small cave directly into his mind. "They're losing, and if they do, so do we. I need my body."

"Your body? *Your body?* It's bad enough that your mind is trapped in there! I'm not sending your body, too! You need to get out—"

"Ray. I am the weapon a goddess gave her life to create. Not my mother, but me. They need *me*."

"Bullshit! *I* need you. And Dory needs you! She almost died to save you—"

"And I would honor that. I would honor her—"

"Stop talking crazy shit and get back here! If the portal works one way, it works the other. I've got your body right here, and we finally got a ride out—"

"And what good will that do if the gods return on my heels? The battle is here; I cannot run from it. You have to let me go."

He stared at nothing for a second, his eyes huge. I don't know what he would have decided, but the Pythia made a mistake and grabbed for me again, and it spooked him. "No! No, fuck that! Fuck that!" And he took off running.

Antem partly transformed, snaring him with an evil-looking talon. And dragging him back despite everything that Ray could do. And he did a lot, considering that he had only one hand to work with and was battling something far larger than himself.

He might even have fought his way loose, but he wasn't fighting just one, but two.

Because the Pythia learned quickly. She managed to grasp hold of my left shoulder from behind when Ray was busy fending off the dragonkind. And started to pull me away, but he refused to let go.

But she had help. Because there was a portal there; I could not see it, but I could feel it, tugging at me with a strength greater than his. And I assumed that he could, too, because this time, his face was tragic as he realized he couldn't stop me. But he was holding on nonetheless, was feeling around in the purse that hung from his belt, was pressing something into my hand.

"Give 'em hell," he whispered and kissed me.

And then I lost him as darkness descended, lost the feel of his arms around me, lost the taste of his kiss. But not for long. Light broke over me again, brilliant and shocking as I blinked my eyes open on another world.

And they *were* my eyes, and my limbs, although they didn't feel that way. I did not know if it was the shock of being back inside my own flesh after hours beyond it, or the transition through the Pythia's strange portal. But for a moment, the world spun crazily around me.

And then solidified abruptly, as I saw what was heading for us.

Great Athena was coming, having finally spotted the witch who was delaying her army's progress with a blizzard. And she was coming fast, eating up the battlefield at a run and slashing her own men with her sword to get them out of the way. She was trying to get to the witch before she absconded, but the redhead took off on her makeshift broom just before she arrived, ducking and dodging the vicious swipes the goddess was making at her.

The storm immediately began to calm without the witch's magic fueling it, but there were still snow flurries partially obscuring the vision. It wouldn't last, however, so I had to be quick. And for that, I needed some help.

The ravens were still circling the field, riding air currents far above this sordid business. I stared up at them, wondering if this was where they came from, for they looked the same as those in the city. The ones who had warned me about the gods. The ones I should have listened to.

I listened to them now, opening myself up, filling my ears with their calls. They were chatty, probably talking to each other about the folly of anyone thinking they could defeat the divine, while secretly hoping we would. *Did he enslave your brothers?* I thought, concentrating on them as I once had some bats who had come to rescue Ray and I in a desperate situation. Not because they'd had to, but because they'd wanted to.

I had found common ground with them.

Could I do it again?

Did he take them away, to unknown lands? I wondered. *Did he make them his slaves, force them to spy for him, to help him in his conquests? Is he forcing you to show him what is happening here, all the way in another world?*

Did he steal your eyes and make them his?

Would you like to do something about it?

I couldn't tell if they were listening. It was hard to see them, as the witch was at it again, circling the field, calling the storm in fits and starts and slapping Athena with the results. But it looked like the small black specks might be getting closer.

Or maybe that was a mirage; between the sun and the sand and the snow, I couldn't tell. But I could hear. And a goddess's scream echoed over the landscape a second later, causing the whole battlefield to pause.

And me to stick my head out long enough to see a mass of birds flocking around the great head, as if attempting to peck out her eyes. Along with a sole, gigantic specimen who landed by me, sliding a little on the frozen ground, and tilting his head curiously. As if wondering who this strange creature was who called to them from the ground.

One who would ask a favor, I replied, and carefully reached out a hand.

The bird's feathers ruffled, and it shed a single, dark quill, black as night and iridescent as dragon scales under the sunlight. It looked like the ones on my shoulders, but much larger. I carefully picked it up.

"Thank you," I murmured, and he ducked his head. And then flew off to help his nest mates, for they were all one big, extended family. And as it turned out, they did mind, very much, the gods' intrusion.

"So do I," I thought, as Marlowe grabbed my arm. He had a bad habit of that.

"What are you doing?" he demanded.

"What I was made for," I said, and changed.

CHAPTER FORTY-SIX

The taste of the candy that Ray had pressed into my hand was sweet on my lips, until I suddenly didn't have lips. It was sticky on my fingers until I abruptly didn't have those, either. It was lost in the tastes and sensations of this new form, this wild, unfettered, dark sleekness that washed over me as easily as the tide.

It was the only thing that was easy, as I quickly discovered that I did not know how to fly. I had the body for it but not the know-how, leaving me floundering in the snow, all wings and taloned feet and newborn awkwardness for a moment. And I wasn't the only one.

Birds were falling all around me, their black bodies leaving splatters of red wherever they hit down, or flinging droplets about as they tried to fly away with broken wings and missing limbs. Athena was taking out her ire over not finding the witch on them, creatures which she probably thought the redhead had conjured up to torture her. But she had not.

I had seen them when I came in, and received confirmation from the thousand minds I had touched in our brief communication. This was *their* world, their home, and the fact that she didn't even know that seemed another defilement. It told me, if I'd had any doubt, how we would be treated should the gods win through.

So, they didn't get through. But that meant that I had to get past her guard. And that... would not be easy.

I finally managed to get my body and wings sorted out, mostly by stopping trying. My new form knew what to do, and once I got out of its way, it figured things out quickly. That was good, since the witch appeared to have been driven from the field.

The storm, once fierce and frenetic, was barely discernable now. Just a soft, cold mist slapping my face as I began to run and then to fly, soaring up and over the battlefield while feeling as light as a feather, despite being far larger than any bird on Earth. But the cold air bore me up like a helping hand, exhilarating even now, ruffling my wings and streaming by my face, and leaving me feeling strangely at home.

I banked, slicing through the air with split second precision, which was needed as the goddess's rage was still white hot and her flashing blade was deadly. I had a perfect view of the battlefield from up here but couldn't use it, as I had to dodge a sword that was moving so fast that it was virtually invisible, save for the corpses it was raining down in pieces all around me.

But the birds were not retreating, and not because I had done anything to force their hand. They were furious and frenzied, attacking the goddess right in the face, dive bombing her from all sides, still going for the eyes. They didn't succeed, but I saw blood on that skeletal face, on the bare shoulders above her golden cuirass, on the arms around her gauntlets.

They were actually giving her a fight, but they were paying a price for it. One tumbled out of the sky, sliced straight in two by that terrible blade, and part of it hit me, causing me to almost crash. Another sent a bleeding arc to splatter me across in the face on its way to the ground, temporarily blinding me, and I had no hands to wipe it away.

And once I shook my head enough to finally clear my vision, it was to see a flash of light headed straight for me.

I dodged, but the edge of that terrible blade clipped my left wing, throwing my body off balance and causing me to tumble uncontrollably for an instant. But I tumbled into something instead of hitting the ground, and had just enough awareness to grab hold. Which was how I found myself hanging off the tattered skirts of a goddess as the battlefield slung all around me.

To your left! To your left!

Crazily, I could still hear Ray's voice in my head. I didn't know how, but it was there and it steadied me, allowing me to sort myself out. And to crawl awkwardly to the left, where I found—

Yes! *Thank you, Ray*, I breathed, because there was a rent in the goddess's skirts, showing the thigh guards she wore underneath. They protected the legs until the greaves began below the knee, and like the cuirass, were bronze covered in a thin layer of gold that was starting to flake off. It wasn't something my beak was likely to penetrate, but there was a gap in the back where they were held in place by leather straps, and in between, bare flesh peeked out.

It was an awkward angle, as I was still swinging off the front of her skirt, wildly in some cases as she slung her body around in combat. It made me dizzy, but I had to attempt it. She could notice me at any moment, and as soon as she did—

I had a sudden, vivid flashback to the bird's skull I'd seen on the troll witch's necklace, dead eyes staring, and that was enough. That was more than enough, I thought, as the ravens made a sudden, screeching assault, perhaps fifty of them all at once, and I took my moment. The skirt slung around as Athena whirled to face them, and I pecked wildly for flesh, any flesh.

I do not know what I found, or where it lay, as the tattered mess of a skirt was in my face. The fabric was overlaid with leather strips to help deter sword slashes at the hips, but they were slinging about all over the place and did not succeed in deterring my beak. Somewhere, it found an opening, and I struck.

The next moment was confused, and composed primarily of sensation: blood on my beak, in my mouth, just a smear of it, but that was enough; fire swelling in me, burning, boiling, flooding outward from my center down all my of limbs, and they were not the ones I'd had a moment before; the slush of sand and blood beneath my feet, squelching up between my toes; the cracks of tiny bones from the corpses littered around as I stumbled back, as I found my footing, as I looked up—

But not very far. Because I was as tall as the goddess as I stood up, my shining new form born of my power and her blood still encased in the leather armor that I vaguely recalled Ray dressing me in, which must have been enchanted. For it had stayed with me through everything.

But the body underneath . . . was very different.

The body underneath looked a lot like a goddess.

And finally, I had Athena's attention.

The remaining birds wheeled away, black spots on a pale blue sky, and the sounds of battle seemed to diminish. Or perhaps I simply couldn't focus on it anymore, as holding a goddess's eyes is not an easy thing. But hold them I did, remembering all the pain these creatures had wrought, all the arrogance they had shown, all the blood they had spilled.

I would not give her the satisfaction of showing fear, although I did feel it, no one could have done otherwise in her presence. But I felt something else, too. Because she wasn't the only one who battle loved, whose blood sang with it, who had been born specifically for it.

I was terrified, but I was excited, too, so much so that I forgot one small matter, but Ray did not.

A sword! A sword! Get to a goddamned sword!

Ray's distant, distorted voice echoed through my mind, and I dove, just under the slashing blow the startled goddess aimed for me. I hit the ground hard, on my left shoulder, and it felt injured, probably from one of the blows I'd taken in the skies. But right now, it felt good, too, like the lip I'd just bitten through. I smiled a bloody smile, and grabbed one of the fallen colossi's abandoned weapons.

It was huge and bitterly cold, but the unbroken edge gleamed in the sunlight, and although my mind was busy telling me that I couldn't lift that thing, that it was the length of a railway car, that it would break my arm to even try, lift it I did.

And found it surprisingly light in my grip, as if it had been made for it, so much so that I snatched up another after dodging several more blows. And stood up with both of them in my grasp, mirroring my mother's former stance with her short swords. And causing great Athena to pause again.

"Who are you?" the harsh voice rasped. "*What* are you?"

It was the same strange language that I had instinctively known before, and which now tumbled off my tongue as if I had been born to it. "Destiny," I whispered, and struck.

The battle that followed wasn't one that can easily be described. I had fallen into crazed fury in combat many times; it was practically my default. But this was different.

This was art and poetry and music: the rich red blood splattering the pale blue of the sky; the sighs and grunts and pants of exertion, each telling their own individual story; the ringing together of swords in a staccato, brutal rhythm. This was pure adrenaline pounding through my veins, a strange, overwhelming, savage joy because this was what I was meant for. If I had ever doubted it, I did so no longer.

Fortuna had done her job well, and designed a creature who lived for war, breathed it, reveled in it. But so did Athena. And for every blow I landed, she struck two. Most of them I parried, but not all, and while I bled her, she bled me back, and she bled me more.

The odds were supposed to be even I thought, as a brutal blow struck one of my swords from my hand, sending it flying. I was built to match my opponents, to counter them one on one! It was why I had wanted her blood, to take her form, to be her equal—

And maybe I was physically. But five hundred years of practice paled beside five thousand, or five million, for all I knew. Her skill was simply unparalleled, and I was outmatched.

This wasn't going to work.

I'd no sooner had the thought than she laughed, loud and echoing, perhaps having glimpsed it in my mind, for I did not know what her powers were. Or perhaps simply seeing it on my face, in my faltering steps, in my rapid breathing. Hers had not changed, had never quickened even the slightest, as far as I could tell. Indeed, she seemed to draw strength and vigor from combat, as if her love of it overrode any toll it took of her.

She must weaken eventually, but I doubted I would be here to see it.

I doubted I would be here to see anything for much longer.

And she agreed.

"Destiny," she mocked, with a wicked twist to her lips. "Yes, one of us will taste it soon, I think, just as Fortuna did. And her spawn, your . . . mother?"

I didn't answer, but I didn't have to. That keen intellect had already seen the truth. And had no problem exploiting it.

"Yes, your mother. Sad, to give birth to a child just to watch her die. Do you hear me, wretch?" she called out, her voice echoing over the battlefield. "I am about to slay your child! Are you watching? I hope I left you enough life for this, for you to see the final blow after all the trouble you've caused me!"

A shield hit me in the face that she hadn't had a second ago, and her foot tripped me up, both happening so quickly that I had no chance to dodge. My feet were swept out from under me and I hit the ground, rolling even as I saw her sword flashing down, despite knowing that I wouldn't be fast enough. I could only hope that Athena was wrong, and that my mother would not see this, wherever she was.

And if she was close, I did not see her. But I saw something else, something . . . unexpected. For another sword parried the killing blow, and the clash was so loud that it cracked across the battlefield like a lightning strike, echoing off the mountains and ripping apart the skies, sending the ravens flying again, this time in startlement.

They tore through the air in a scattering of black, and I looked up to see something that my brain could not fully take in. It was my father, but not as I knew him. But as a literal giant of a man, taller than Athena, and looking at the goddess with such all-encompassing rage that I barely recognized him.

And then the ice sword he held scraped all the way down her blade, a rusty, ringing sound that felt like it deafened me before it reached the hilt and he shoved her away. "My child, too," he hissed, through fully extended fangs.

Right before a fight started that made mine look slapdash by comparison.

Not because my father was better with a sword, although he had practically been born with one in his hand, learning to fight almost before he learned to walk. But because of sheer, animalistic, all-encompassing fury. It was the blood rage of a master, and a first-level one at that, fighting for family, honor, and perhaps, just perhaps, for love.

I stared at him in wonder, because I couldn't quite believe it. But it must be true. I didn't know if it was for my mother or for me, but no one fought like that for any other reason, not caring if they hurt, not caring if they bled.

He was struck a hundred times as he pressed her, with both of them moving so quickly that I could barely see the fight, and could only track it by the way the rest of the field's combatants surged out of the way. He was injured so many times that even his prodigious healing abilities weren't enough anymore, and he was soon covered with blood. But this time, so was she.

And he never faltered.

But I had, I realized, lying there in shock and awe, instead of getting up and helping him! I surged back to my feet, slightly dizzy from the blood loss, for she had bled me well. But my hand was steady as I picked up my weapon and leapt back into the fight.

Athena grabbed up a second sword, and used it to parry us both. But she was going to need a third arm, because the redheaded witch was back, seeing her chance and taking it, throwing bolt after bolt of blazing power at the beleaguered goddess. Or a fourth, because my mother appeared, herself bloody and battered, and dragging one leg behind her before one of her creatures picked her up.

And together, they led a charge of the frost giants across the field from her perch on one icy shoulder.

The remaining yeti creatures broke and ran, crashing into the gods behind them, who had not come to their leader's defense. They weren't leaving, but they were backing off, were giving us room, were staring at something behind us, I didn't know what. And then I did, when I turned my head and saw that Athena had lived up to her reputation for being the cunning side of war, the thinker, the planner.

And she had planned this well. For, while she was keeping our attention elsewhere, a group of gods had flanked us and made it to the portal, which they were now streaming through. We were fighting a battle that didn't matter except as a distraction, while the real war was about to begin on the other side!

But then three things happened at once, almost too fast for me to follow: Athena laughed, her eyes sparkling, knowing that she'd won; Mircea took the moment of her distraction to strike, plunging his sword deep into her neck while a smile still curved her lips; and the Pythia, who I had almost forgotten about, emerged from under the outcropping of rock, and made a gesture in the air while facing the portal.

A gesture which, I assumed, must have released the slow-time spell she had cast on the dragons on the other side. Because they suddenly burst forth, spewing fire and seeming half crazed, and fell on the first creatures they found on the other side: the gods. And the ensuing battle was almost as fierce as ours.

But I didn't get to see how it progressed; I didn't see much at all as I was too busy stabbing great Athena in the side, in the back of the knee where the greaves left her unprotected, in the stomach. And looking up to see my father gnawing on the neck wound he'd made, so that she couldn't close it, draining her of power even as I helped to punch her full of holes. All while trying to stay out of the way of the redheaded witch, who was still circling, and firing blast after blast into the massive body, shaking it to the point that I missed several strikes as it twitched out of the way.

But I had help, because Marlowe, tiny Marlowe, suddenly appeared, and what he lacked in size, he made up for in fierceness. Crawling up the body unnoticed by anyone but me, with one of the yeti's spears in hand, he reached the screaming face of the goddess. And plunged the weapon straight into one of her eyes, before being flung what looked like half a mile away as she thrashed in pain, as she arched up, as she gave Mircea the perfect opportunity.

Not my destiny, after all, I thought dizzily, as he jerked back, as he grabbed his sword, as he brought the massive weapon down. And screamed his defiance as the head of great Athena went bouncing across the dirt. And as the gods, menaced on all sides, did something that I had never expected.

They broke and ran.

Chapter Forty-Seven
Dory

"Then what happened?" I croaked, trying to sit up in bed. I had woken up back in the beautiful bedroom at Lord Rathen's court half an hour ago, feeling like death and probably looking worse. Someone had taken the mirror away, I noticed, so I couldn't be sure, but the very fact that it was missing was ominous. But I had quickly forgotten to care, because I was so enthralled by the story Ray had been telling.

And was suddenly not telling as Louis-Cesare pressed me back against the pillows, and made me drink some more of the vile stuff Claire had concocted. It was the grossest thing ever, and I could swear I felt it moving on its own as it slithered down my throat. But I swallowed it anyway while watching my shifty looking Second.

Who wasn't meeting my eyes.

"What?" I demanded.

"You must tell her," Lord Rathen said gravely, causing me to look between the two of them in confusion and mounting alarm.

"Tell me what?"

Nobody said anything, which was a first. I'd been out for two days, apparently, during which my dhampir resilience and Claire's brew had somehow pulled me back from the brink. And had finally woken up to find my bed ringed by people with a story to tell, since Ray had kept his mental link to Dorina even after she was pulled away from him.

He had seen most of what happened in that other world, and had been getting me up to speed with occasional input from the others. Not only with what had occurred while I was unconscious, but about their whole mad journey across Faerie. And I thought I had been having adventures!

Dorina and Ray had left me standing.

"Could we have a moment?" Louis-Cesare asked, and everyone took that as permission to go. It concerned me that people like Tanet, Claire's brother with a temper as fiery as his hair; Lord Regin, with his arm in a sling and half of his torso bandaged, because he had been injured so badly that even dragon healing abilities were taking their time; and Antem, who had gotten us out of hell despite having to fight his way through the Steen's forces to do it, were suddenly scrambling to get out the door.

"What the hell?" I croaked as Lord Rathen, with apparently more fortitude than the rest, bent over my hand.

"My gratitude, my lady," he told me. "And . . . my regrets."

He left and closed the door behind him, leaving me alone with Louis-Cesare, Ray and Claire, the latter of whom was fussing about, winding some bandages and deliberately not looking at me. Which would have troubled me more, but a coughing fit took me, and hurt enough to leave me gasping. Collapsed lung from one of my own broken ribs stabbing me, or so I'd been told.

I only knew that it hurt like a bitch.

"Here, take some of this," Louis-Cesare said, and held a glass of water to my lips. It was better than Claire's foul brew, but it made me angry that that seemed like a herculean task to drink it, to the point that I was panting again afterward. But I did it, because I was damned if a cup of water was going to defeat me!

"I have yet to find anything that can," he said softly and kissed me.

That was very nice, and would have been nicer if his lips hadn't been so tentative, almost as if he was afraid I'd break.

"You already did that," he murmured. "No, don't move."

"Why not?" I lifted an arm, trying to cup his face.

"You need to heal."

Yeah, it felt like it.

I relaxed back against the bed, trying not to notice how weak I was. Claire had said that it would be weeks before I was back on my feet, which was ridiculous. I had never been down for that long in my life.

"You never tangled with an enraged dragon lord, either," Ray said, bringing my attention back to him.

"Are you going to finish the story or what?" I asked.

"You're not gonna like it."

"Yeah. I already got that part."

He nodded. "Well, after Athena bought it, courtesy of the Basarab clan, the plan was for everybody to book it back through the portal. The Pythia thought she could shut it behind them—

her mother was Artemis, who had power over the paths between worlds—but not destroy it, because it was feeding from a ley line sink and had practically unlimited power—"

"Wait. Weren't the dragons there to do that? To destroy it?"

"Yeah, but they were busy taking on the gods, even before the big boom—"

He broke off abruptly, and started looking sketchy again. And then at Louis-Cesare, with an expression that said he'd done enough, and now it was my Hubby's turn. Only he didn't seem to want the job, either.

"Would somebody please tell me what the hell is going on?" I said. "And where is Mircea? And Dorina? And my moth—" This time it was me breaking off, because I'd just had a sudden, terrible idea. "No."

"Dory—"

"Tell me you got them out. Tell me that right now. Tell me, Ray!"

He didn't tell me.

"Louis-Cesare—" He looked at me, and everything I didn't want to know was written on his face. "*What the hell?*"

"You need to stay calm," Claire said, putting a slender arm across me as I struggled to get up again. "You're going to tear your stitches—"

"I'm going to tear a lot more than that if—"

"They're alive," Louis-Cesare said. "That is, we assume so—"

"You assume? What the—"

"It was the goddamned pixies, all right?" Ray said. "Specifically, that queen of theirs. It was her fault!"

"What?" I frowned at him. "What does she have to do with anything?"

"A lot, as it turns out. She was furious at Steen for trying to kill her baby, but couldn't take him on 'cause you already had. So, she decided to kill the rest of his dragons instead. But Lord Rathen was already cleaning up the ones in the city, and helping the dark fey to evacuate, not that they needed it much. If there's one thing they're experts on, it's getting the hell out of—"

"Ray!"

"So she targeted the rest of 'em, the ones who went for the portal. And, uh . . ."

"And, uh, what? Spit it out, man!"

He swallowed, threw his shoulders back, and finally manned up. "She threw a city at 'em."

"What?"

"Her city," Louis-Cesare added. "The containment spell on its power source had ruptured and she needed to get it as far away from her people as possible. But instead of sending it off into the air—"

"She threw it at the dragons," I finished for him.

Because of course, she had.

"Yes, I'm afraid so."

"The dragons who were right at the portal."

"Who were still going through it, in fact. The explosion took place on both sides of the opening, as a result. And apparently, that is one of the few ways of destroying a portal linked to a ley line sink."

"It acted like a fuse in a bomb," Ray clarified. "Causing an eruption from the sink like a hundred nuclear weapons going off, most of which was sucked down through the portal and out into non-space, or none of us would be here. But there was enough left for a hell of a—"

"Boom," I said, and he nodded.

"We think they're all right, given how far away they were from the portal when the images cut out, and how far the destruction went on this side," Louis-Cesare said. "But . . ."

"But they're trapped in another world."

I said the words, but didn't believe them. We'd come so far, only to end up right back where we started. Only this was worse, since we'd lost Mircea, too. And my mother. And the Pythia—

"Not the Pythia," Louis-Cesare said, reading my thoughts. "Cassie shifted out at the last second. She tried to take your father with her, but he jerked away."

"He wouldn't leave them." It didn't surprise me. He'd gone through so much to have his family back together again, and had come so close. Yet it still wasn't.

I wasn't there.

It hit me then that I might never see any of them again, and I didn't know what to do with that; I just didn't. I'd lost everyone, hadn't I? And if I'd panicked at the thought of losing Dorina, it was nothing to this.

I was completely alone.

"You're not alone," Louis-Cesare told me, blue eyes blazing. "You have me!"

"And me," Claire said, leaning down to gently hug me.

Ray didn't say anything, but he took my hand, almost the only thing on my body that didn't hurt, and squeezed it.

"And us," someone said from the doorway, causing me to look up. And to see a motley crew of the various groups we'd left behind on this crazy journey: Claire's light fey bodyguards, armed to the teeth and looking jumpy, here in a bastion of dark fey power; the vampires we'd last seen getting drunk in a fey village, as we and our nag headed for the mountains; my personal group of mercenaries led by a guy named Tomas and his girlfriend, Sarah, who hadn't found Dorina because I had beaten them to it.

And behind them, bringing up the rear, the Pythia herself.

She was looking harried as usual, with her blonde hair in flyaway curls that all seemed to be going in different directions and her blue eyes smeared with truly unfortunate glittery, powder blue eyeshadow. If she'd had a jumpsuit to match, she could have come straight off the dance floor at Studio 54 in its heyday, complete with smeared pink lipstick.

I guessed the Pythian sense of style was still evolving.

"I can't stay," she told me, trying to squeeze past the others, then giving up and shifting to my side, close enough to make Ray jump. "There's another disaster waiting to happen in the Alorestri lands and—anyway. I just wanted to see how you were doing and, uh. Have a word. If I could?"

It took a while, because everyone wanted a word, until Claire noticed me flagging and shooed them all out. All except the Pythia, because you didn't tell the chief seer of the supernatural world that she'd overstayed her welcome. No, not even Claire.

"It's not your fault," I said, when the door had closed again. "If what Ray said was true—"

"It was." The blonde hair bobbed, causing a little tinsel earring to dance. She appeared to have only one. "Your father wouldn't leave your mother, and your sister—"

"Wouldn't go without our parents." Our parents. That was an extremely strange phrase on the tongue, I thought dizzily.

"There may be a way you can see them again," she said, almost idly, but it focused my attention as nothing else had.

"What? How?"

She glanced around the room, despite the fact that everyone had left. "It's what I came to tell you. Mircea would kill me, if he knew, but . . ."

"But Mircea is gone."

She nodded, biting her lip. And then came out with it. "I need him for the war. I know how that sounds, especially to you, especially now. You almost died and lost practically your whole family, and here I am, worried about politics. But I am; I have to! And your father and I and another man, a mage, are in a triumvirate of power and without Mircea it doesn't work. Without him it's all screwed up!"

She got up before I could comment, if I'd had one, because little of that had made sense. And paced slightly away from the bed before whirling around again. "Do you know where I'm going when I leave here? To help our third, a mage named Pritkin, in a fight for the Green Fey throne and possibly his life. I was feeling pretty good about his chances, but now, with Mircea gone—"

"Triumvirate?" I croaked, because I was still trying to catch up.

She paused, as if realizing that not everybody was up on whatever weirdness the Pythias thought normal.

"A spell in which we share power and abilities," she explained. "It magnifies what we would have alone, many times over, and is how your father was able to do what he did in the battle. Pritkin is part incubi, and their royal house has a talent for taking on the form of any being whose soul energy they consume. And your mother had been splattered with Athena's blood in their fight—"

"And my father is a master vampire." The clever son of a bitch.

She nodded. "He ingested the goddess's blood, then took on a body with her attributes using Pritkin's power. That sort of thing is one reason, maybe even the main one, why we aren't losing this war. But we aren't winning it yet, either, and with him gone—"

She bit her lip again and came back over, kneeling on the tile beside the bed. "You did an amazing thing. You and Dorina and everyone—just amazing. You stopped an invasion, killed a senior goddess, and sent her allies running. But they'll be back; they have no choice. You saw Athena. They've outgrown their energy sources back home and need this universe to feed on."

"And you need father to stop them."

She nodded. "But I can't feel him anymore, his power, his strength. And Ray . . . he lost the link to Dorina when the portal blew out. I think it's too far, this world, too different—" she shook her head. "I don't think I have my triumvirate to lean on anymore, just when I need it the most. I am going to help Pritkin, but I don't know any more that we'll win. We'll do our best, but we *need* your father. The war is in jeopardy if Mircea isn't found."

I regarded her steadily. "What do you want me to do?"

She swallowed, looking miserable. "I'm so sorry. You've done so much already. I hate to ask—"

"You're not asking. I'm telling you—if there is a way to find my father, my whole family, I want it. And you're going to give it to me."

She smiled at me through watery eyes. "You remind me so much of him—"

"Then tell her what to do, already," Ray said, emerging from the corner where he'd wrapped shadows around himself to hide from us, and to spy more easily.

"It would be helpful," Louis-Cesare said, from a crack in the door, where he'd been doing the same. Not that he'd needed it, since even good, stout oak doesn't stop vampire hearing.

Or magic, I thought, as Louis-Cesare pushed the door wider, allowing me to see my team stumbling out of a cloaking spell that Ranbir, their resident dark mage, had erected for them. "Um," Sarah, the pretty brunette leader of the group, said. "We were just, uh, we were . . . we were about to . . . um."

"Oh, please," Ranbir said. "You've been a mercenary for how long and you haven't learned to lie better than that?"

"Well, at least I'm trying!"

"Why bother? No one else is."

Point to Ranbir, I thought, and cleared my throat.

"Come on out, Claire," I called, because I knew she was there somewhere.

"I wasn't eavesdropping," she said, as she and the bodyguards she didn't need appeared a little farther down the hall. And she managed to do it with dignity, although whatever spell her light fey guards had used to hide them had left her hair looking a little frazzled. "I just wanted to make sure that your guest didn't tire you out."

"Damn. I should have thought of that," Sarah muttered.

"Are the vamps under the bed?" I asked dryly.

"No, they went to get a drink," one of the fey said. "They aren't doing so well in a place with this much fire."

Typical. "Tell me," I said to the Pythia, in tones she probably wasn't used to hearing. But to her credit, she didn't even seem to notice my *lèse-majesté*.

"There's a portal in my basement," she said simply. "It . . . doesn't exactly go to Jotunheim . . ."

"Then where does it go?"

She bit her lip at me. At this rate, she wasn't going to have any left. "The, uh, the arch—the portal is through an old stone archway in the basement of my court—is one the gods were said to have used to visit the Pythias, back when we were their servants. It doesn't work since my mother's spell went into effect, but you had a pass key to another supposedly closed portal, so maybe it will for you."

"Dorina was the key," I reminded her, my head spinning. "I'm . . . I'm nothing—"

"You're her sister, and closer than a sister. You can probably open it, too," Ray said, and then turned on the Pythia, his blue eyes snapping. "Are you trying to say that you expect her to sneak into the realm of the gods, the people currently trying to *kill* us, find another portal from there to Jotunheim, and then what? Retrace her steps with a bunch of the gods' most wanted in tow? Is that what you're saying?"

More lip chewing commenced. "Kinda?"

"Well, okay then. I'm down."

"What?" I said, staring at him. Because that plan was insane, even for me. And Ray was usually the voice of reason.

"Oh, like you're not gonna go."

"Of course, I'm going to go! I don't have a choice! My family is there!"

He looked at me soberly. "So is mine."

I blinked at him, and belatedly realized that I might not have a Second anymore. I might have a brother-in-law. It was a bit of an adjustment, or it would have been at any other time.

Now, it just sort of washed away on all the crazy.

I glanced at Louis-Cesare, and he shrugged. "If you are going, so am I."

"And us," Sarah said, looking around at her men. "I mean, that was the deal, right? We find Dorina. And we haven't found her yet."

"Can I talk to you privately?" Tomas hissed.

"Around here? Probably not."

But they went off to mutter at each other in a corner.

"They'll come," Ranbir said, drifting back inside with Ev, their muscle man, and Sarah's brother Jason. "Professional pride on her part and the other sort on his. First team to ever assault the stronghold of the gods. . ." His smile turned almost beatific. "The ads practically write themselves."

"You're really going to do this?" Claire asked me, after the Pythia took the opportunity to say her goodbyes and flee.

"Don't have a choice. How fast can you get me functional?"

"I already told you. Three weeks, perhaps more." She slapped my hand as I tried to sit up, to evaluate my progress for myself. "And that's assuming you don't reinjure yourself by being stupid!"

"She won't reinjure herself," Louis-Cesare promised.

"Well, then. We have three weeks to prepare."

"We?" I repeated. "You're going, too?"

"Of course, she isn't," one of her guards said, from beside the door. "The very idea is absurd!"

"Eske," Claire told me. "He's new."

Obviously.

"Okay, okay," Ray said. "You guys heard what you wanted. There's no more juicy stuff, all right? Let's let her get some shut eye."

They left again, and this time Ray went after them, I supposed to usher them down the hall and make sure they really did leave.

"I'll check on you in a little while," Claire said, and followed them out, her troubled looking guards, most of whom were not new, trailing after her.

Leaving just Louis-Cesare and me.

He decided to join me in bed, spooning up at my side, careful not to jostle me. He kissed my hair, which was about the only option right now. "This is a lot," he whispered.

"Yeah."

We just lay there and breathed for a while.

It was nice.

"You know," he said, after a few moments, "You're rather a legend among the dragonborn."

"I am?"

"Hmm. The soft little human who took on Steen twice and finally ended him, all by herself."

I shot him a look. "I wasn't all by myself. You and I doubled teamed him or I would be a cinder right now. Not to mention Ray and his boys."

"Hmm. It was more fun to tell it the other way, though."

I would have punched his arm, but didn't have the strength. "You did that deliberately."

He chuckled. "In concert with Lord Rathen. It did help to get the rest of the houses on board. I think he shamed them into it."

I sighed and managed to throw an arm over my face. "I hate politics."

"And yet, in the short time you've been here, you have achieved more than anyone could have hoped. Killed Aeslinn's chief operative in Faerie. Helped to stop an invasion. Succeeded in bringing the dragonkind together into a firm alliance which, as far as I understand it, has never been done before."

"And lost my sister. Again."

My voice roughened; I couldn't help it. Because the rest of that . . . yeah, it was important. But the part that mattered to me personally, I had failed.

Damn it! I missed her so much!

"We'll find her," Louis-Cesare promised. "I gave you my word, remember?"

I dropped my arm to look at him. "But you can't know that. You can't even know for sure that they're still alive."

"No, not through reason," he agreed, his eyes going distant. "But I feel it. Don't you?"

I concentrated, my mind searching for them, for any trace at all. I didn't find it, but there was something there . . . something warm. Or perhaps that was simply Louis-Cesare's arm around me.

"And while I don't know what awaits us," he added. "I do know you. And your sister. And your parents. I know what you can do."

Parents, I thought. There was that word again. Along with sister, husband, brother-in-law.

Family.

The words felt strange to even think, like something that applied to other people, not to me. But they were mine, all of them. I just had to go and get them.

And I would.

Louis-Cesare laughed, whether reading my mind again or my face, I didn't know. But his arms tightened as much as possible right now. And I felt his lips on the top of my head.

"Frankly, the gods should tremble."

Other Works by this Author

Dorina Basarab Series

Midnight's Daughter
Death's Mistress
Fury's Kiss
Shadow's Bane
Queen's Gambit
Time's Fool
Fortune's Blade

Cassandra Palmer Series

Touch the Dark
Claimed by Shadow
Embrace the Night
Curse the Dawn
Hunt the Moon
Tempt the Stars
Reap the Wind
Ride the Storm
Brave the Tempest
Shatter the Earth
Ignite the Fire: Incendiary
Ignite the Fire: Inferno

Author's Website

KarenChance.com

Milton Keynes UK
Ingram Content Group UK Ltd.
UKHW010138110424
440894UK00003B/80